"Make no mistake, Mr. Drake.

"I will accept this *temporary* marriage. But you and I will continue on a formal basis, let tongues wag as they may."

"Are you a gambling woman, Lyris?"

She eyed him cautiously. "Why?"

"I'm willing to wager that within a few weeks' time, you will lose interest in the formal relationship you propose. I trust I won't be forced to remind you of our vow of celibacy."

"Your conceit is rivaled only by your insolence."

"Here are your parents," Nick warned. "Smile, sweetheart. You are not to be a spinster after all." He raised her hands to his lips, his eyes mocking.

"Spinster? You, sir, may soon wish that I were."

Dear Reader,

Welcome to Harlequin Historicals and to a world of adventure and romance where almost anything can happen.

This month we bring you Barbara Bretton's debut novel for Harlequin Historicals. *The Reluctant Bride* is the delightful tale of the battle over a dilapidated hotel between a stubborn American woman and a cynical Englishman.

Rose Among Thorns is Catherine Archer's first published work. This talented newcomer is sure to delight with her story of a conquering knight and the proud Saxon woman who meets his every challenge.

In *The Naked Huntress* by Shirley Parenteau, a society columnist finds herself at the mercy of a notorious saloon keeper when she unwittingly poses for a scandalous portrait.

Kit Gardner's *Arabesque* was one of our 1991 March Madness promotions. In her second novel, *The Dream,* straitlaced schoolteacher Elizabeth Burbridge must match wits with the dashing Lord Alec Sinclair. Those of you who recall the author's fast-paced, lighthearted writing will not be disappointed.

Next month look for new titles by June Lund Shiplett, Isabel Whitfield, Suzanne Barclay and Mary Daheim.

Sincerely,

Tracy Farrell
Senior Editor

The Naked Huntress

Shirley Parenteau

Harlequin Books

TORONTO • NEW YORK • LONDON
AMSTERDAM • PARIS • SYDNEY • HAMBURG
STOCKHOLM • ATHENS • TOKYO • MILAN
MADRID • WARSAW • BUDAPEST • AUCKLAND

Harlequin Historicals first edition August 1992

ISBN 0-373-28737-2

THE NAKED HUNTRESS

Books by Shirley Parenteau

Harlequin Historicals

Hemlock Feathers #34
Golden Prospect #88
The Naked Huntress #137

SHIRLEY PARENTEAU

is a contemporary romance author who has now moved into the exciting field of historical romance. Shirley grew up in small logging towns along the Oregon coast, and presently lives in an eighty-year-old farmhouse in northern California that she and her husband restored themselves.

In memory of Olive Stanbrough Brunson,
journalist, international doll artist, beloved mother;
And for Bill, David, Scott and Cherie,
adventurers all

Chapter One

Seattle, February, 1889

Dear Heaven, this was horrible. She had never even seen her unclothed body in a mirror. Did she look like that... creamy and curved like a peach?

Only her fierce grip on the carved back of a chair kept Lyris Lowell upright. Rain streaked nearby windows of the Seattle artist's loft, but she no longer heard its rhythmic drumming. Blood pounded in her ears until the room roared. The bite of turpentine and the greasy smell of oil paints threatened her stomach, but not as severely as the larger-than-life canvas set on an easel before her.

The artist, Samuel Castor, stood just beyond, fussily cleaning his brushes. She knew he watched her, but she was unable to drag her horrified gaze from the painting. This couldn't be her portrait. She hadn't posed for this! Yet there was her face—and the painted hand wore the deep amber agate she had once discovered on a trip to the ocean and had fashioned into a ring.

For a moment, the rich colors blurred, then with stunned disbelief she forced herself to take in the details of a sun-kissed sea, a quiver of arrows leaning carelessly against an ivory pillar—and herself in a shocking depiction of the goddess Diana. The huntress had turned her naked back to the viewer while smiling provocatively over one bare shoulder.

Curved lips and sparkling eyes expressed an invitation Lyris knew she had never offered. Below the delicate frame of her upraised arm, one high breast was fully revealed.

She remembered the uncomfortable pressure of her breasts against her linen shirtwaist while she had held the pose. Her muscles still ached from lifting unbound black hair from her neck while smiling back through the arch of her arm. The weight of her heavy skirt had threatened to drag her to her knees.

She had remained fully clothed, only setting aside the jacket of her corduroy outing costume. Yet in the portrait, light glowed along the smooth length of her bare arm and down the graceful curve of her back as it narrowed to a tiny waist, then flared over sensuously rounded buttocks.

No doubt the work was masterfully done. It was also quite obscene. Except for the gauziest of veils draped about her hips, the goddess was nude.

Lyris's imagination flooded with whispers and sly laughter. She had no need to picture Papa's fury should this painting be exhibited. He might well succumb to apoplexy. Mama would be unable to face friends for months, perhaps years, maybe never!

When she found her voice, it came out with a quaver. "I did not pose for this."

The artist was a small wiry man with quick furtive movements. Earlier, she had thought he resembled a chicken. Now his small sharp eyes and beaked nose took on the aspect of a buzzard as he said unpleasantly, "Sue me, my dear. Seattle will enjoy the scandal."

Scandal—or the prospect of it—had brought her here, hoping for a story to win a journalist's post. She had expected flirtations, attempted kisses, perhaps indecent suggestions. All were to be rejected, then discussed in print.

But this... Lyris's thoughts whirled. Now she understood why Castor had refused to let her see the work before it was finished. Anyone viewing the portrait would believe she had posed without wearing a stitch of clothing.

The portrait must never be seen. She lurched toward the easel, her still-unbound hair swirling around her. Castor was quick, and stronger than she expected. Before she could scrape her fingers through the wet oils, his arms whipped around her. He dragged her, shrieking and kicking, toward the door.

Although scarcely larger than she, Castor forced her from the studio and hurled her cape after her. The lock slammed home.

Snatching her cape from the floor, Lyris wrapped it around her shoulders. Helpless tremors made the brush bindings of her heavy skirt dust the stairway landing. Below, a woman scolded a butcher. Other voices sounded from an adjoining barber shop. To Lyris's frantic mind, they were no more than the sharp cries of gulls.

She heard a familiar rumble of carriage wheels on rain-washed streets and a shrill blast from steam whistles at the lumber mills. Salt wind swirled up the staircase from the bay. All seemed lost to her.

The boy sent from the newspaper had obviously slipped away—again—to a pool hall. His instructions were to linger nearby and come at her call. It no longer mattered.

Every nerve urged her to find a public carriage and rush toward the safe haven of her home. But such safety would be temporary, at best. She was bringing unspeakable shame to her family name, a name at the very height of Seattle society. How *could* she have been such a fool?

Gilt lettering on the frosted glass of the studio doorway mocked her. The letters all but smoked in her sight as she remembered her self-assurance on the day she'd thought of writing a gossipy story of an artist's atelier from the model's point of view.

Why hadn't she given up after applying to a succession of lofts where artists treated her as if she were little more than a stick of furniture? Instead she had followed rumor to

Samuel Castor, who was creating a series of classical goddesses. He had displayed a completed canvas, one showing Persephone draped in concealing veils. Lyris remembered her delight on recognizing an avid note in the artist's voice.

He'd circled her while listing her attributes aloud. "Seal black hair as rich and curling as deep surf. Long-lashed eyes as green as the underside of a wave, with a directness and candor that I find most interesting."

He tilted her chin with proprietary fingers. "You possess a complexion as fresh as our coastal mists, Miss Lowell, and the bonus of a rosy bloom as natural as sunrise."

The flowery words embarrassed her and she pulled away, then saw she had offended him. With thinning lips, he added, "Your form could use rounding, my dear. You are far too slender for Aphrodite."

Did he mean to reject her? She regretted having stepped away and barely breathed while he continued his appraisal.

"I have it!" he exclaimed. "You are Diana, Mistress of the Hunt."

She concealed inner elation, certain of her story. During the two weeks following, the artist chatted while he worked, complaining often of a snub from a gallery that attracted wealthy patrons. "Never mind," he said only a few days after they began, an oddly smug tone in his voice. "Those highly placed gentlemen who rejected me will soon appreciate my talent."

He hadn't named his client—or for that matter, the offending gallery. Lyris began to wonder where her portrait would hang. Suppose it had been commissioned by someone who patronized her father's bank? Papa would be livid to learn that she had posed as a common model.

Yet it was he who'd arranged for her to work at the *Seattle Tribune,* declaring that if she would not marry, she must support herself. "You are too headstrong for a governess and too impulsive to succeed as a lady's companion," he had thundered. "Let us see if you can manage to keep from tangling your fingers in the keys of a typewriter."

She knew he expected editor Jonathan Brunswich to keep an eye on her. He also believed typewriting would be so dull she would be driven to consider marriage as an alternative. His sour warning burned in her memory, "You have nearly set yourself on the shelf through being choosy, miss. Why, you have already reached a spinsterish twenty-fifth year."

Spinsterhood was her goal, but she couldn't tell him that. As far as she was concerned, the dullest occupation was preferable to binding her life to some autocratic male who would expect to possess her material possessions, her body, and worst of all, her mind. She had the example of her mother, and for that matter, her godmother, as a woman whose once-lively spirit had been crushed beneath the strictures of matrimony.

With an eager heart, she went into the workplace. The smells of fresh ink and new paper, the racket of the press and clatter of typewriters, the shouts and bustle heralded an exciting new world. Soon, though, she found herself envying the journalists who breezed by her desk, fresh from challenging assignments.

Chance gossip about an artist sent her to the *Tribune's* editor with a daring proposal for a story. While dubious, Brunswich agreed, only insisting that a boy wait outside as an unseen chaperon. Modeling proved even duller than typewriting, but just this morning, Castor at last had offered an improper suggestion that would give spice to her story. "Perhaps, my dear, you will remove your shirtwaist? I find your costume constricting to the imagination."

She concealed her secret triumph. "I certainly will not."

He waved away her indignation. "A passing thought. Let us complete the work." His voice gave no hint of treachery.

She knew now with sickened understanding that the artist had mocked her because of her place in society. She knew his bitterness over having work excluded from a favored gallery. Why hadn't she paid more attention? Papa sat on many boards, but until this moment she had forgotten they included an art gallery.

Castor had hired her because of her name. He must have planned his revenge on the day she applied for a job. Despair swept her. She forced it back, telling herself to *think!* Somehow, she must get into the studio and destroy that painting. Anger overcame caution and again she slammed a gloved fist against the glass. "Samuel Castor! Open the door!"

Steps on the stairs made her swing about. A powerfully built man ascended from the street. He was dressed like one of her father's associates, in a dark wool suit. Jeweled studs gleamed in the front of his stiff white shirt below a silky black cravat.

With her heart in her throat, Lyris watched him approach. It was not his size that held her rigid as he stepped into the wavery reach of a rain-blurred skylight, but shocked recognition.

Nicholas Drake was not only devilishly handsome, but according to rumor, he was a rake who hoped to marry his way into society. She knew from personal experience that the rumor was true.

A derby hat slanted carelessly over unruly hair as black as her own, but it was Drake's eyes that held her like a bird enthralled by a snake—eyes the same piercing amber color as her agate ring. He surveyed her with bold speculation.

Four months ago, she had summarily rejected this man's attempt to court her. He was a tradesman, the owner of a saloon on the wharf, with a rogue's luck in shipping, as well. Having gained wealth, he now craved social position.

Whatever else he might be, Drake was all that she had vowed to resist, a forceful, arrogant man who would expect his wife to submerge her personality in his. When she learned that her father actually considered allowing the man to court her, she had panicked, then made her feelings against the match brutally clear.

Now Drake studied her tumbled hair and exposed throat as if she were on public display. Lyris pulled her cape closer and lifted her chin, struggling to put forward the manners of a lady while aware that she must look like a hoyden off the street.

Drake greeted her in the hard tones of a dock worker, his words underlined by sarcasm. "The lofty Miss Lowell. A pleasant surprise."

Her rejection may have bruised his pride, but that had been months ago. A man as self-assured as Nicholas Drake should have forgotten the disappointment by now. Yet the air between them felt as if a storm were about to break.

Lyris stared at a jeweled keg suspended from his watch chain while she tried to steady her thoughts. What was he doing here? A chill ran through her. He must not see that portrait.

"I've commissioned a painting for my place of business, Miss Lowell," he said, lifting the words from her mind while her horror deepened. "A depiction of the Greek mistress of the hunt. I'd invite you to examine the work, but since it's meant for a saloon, it might offend your sense of modesty."

Dizziness slid over her and she groped for support against the nearest wall. To her dismay, Drake slipped one arm beneath her cape and around her waist. "You aren't going to faint, are you? I haven't much patience for swooning females."

She wouldn't give him the satisfaction, she told herself furiously. The pressure of his hand violated her skin through her layers of clothing, feeling large and masculine and unaccountably intimate. She tried to struggle free, only to learn an unsettling lesson on the hard planes of his body. As she twisted in his grip, the lower curve of her breast thrust against his palm.

She felt his swift intake of breath, but he neither freed her nor adjusted his grip. Contorting instinctively, she sank her teeth into the offending hand.

He jerked free and she flattened herself against Castor's door. Her glance flashed to the stairs, but Drake blocked them. He scowled at the welling blood, then pulled a crisp linen handkerchief from a pocket and wrapped it about the wound. "I thought you had class, Miss Lowell. Couldn't you see I was trying to help?" Turning, he rapped sharply on the door.

The sound struck Lyris more painfully than his insult. She couldn't believe she had actually drawn blood. What on earth had she been thinking? She *wasn't* thinking. Sane thought had vanished at her first sight of the odious portrait.

Pressing her palms against the gritty wall, she dragged words from a stiff throat. "If you have any kindly regard for me, Mr. Drake, you will leave at once."

The amber eyes glittered. "Kindness is rarely credited to me, and I can't see that it's owed to you."

She felt her flush deepen and gestured uncomfortably toward his hand. "I apologize for... for that."

Without answering, he rapped again.

"The artist is not in," she said, offering a silent prayer that Castor would think it was she who demanded entrance.

Before the prayer was complete, footsteps approached the door. Satisfaction glittered in Drake's remarkable eyes. "Of course he's in, Miss Lowell. He's expecting me."

The door eased open. Lyris grasped her skirts in both hands, preparing to charge the easel. Castor foiled her adroitly while admitting his guest. Drake stepped inside without looking back. At the last possible moment, Lyris whipped the hem of her cape forward. The heavy wool caught between the latch and the closing door.

Had they noticed? She waited, breath held. From beyond the panel, Castor said, "The portrait was completed just minutes ago. I believe you will be pleased."

Their footsteps moved deeper into the studio. It cost Lyris all her self-control to remain on the landing while the insufferable Nicholas Drake prepared to survey *The Naked Huntress*.

Wait, she warned herself. *Let them become engrossed in their business. Then rush inside and destroy that abomination.*

Chapter Two

Nick stared at the canvas, feeling as if he had been punched in the stomach. The huntress held him mesmerized. It was impossible to look away from the brilliant welcome in those sea-green eyes.

While his eyes feasted, his thoughts reeled. He had commissioned a tasteful nude for the Golden Harbor, expecting the usual anonymous, voluptuous model. This was unbelievable. Lyris Lowell had posed as a naked Diana. She held a wealth of black curls away from the silky column of her throat, while offering a look of abandon and invitation that his entire body answered.

There was no mistaking the lovely Miss Lowell. She glowed, golden and lifelike, curved and inviting. No man could study the portrait without imagining his lips on her bare throat—or of taking greater liberties, especially if he'd experienced her supple body against his own just minutes before.

To control his fierce physical response to the unexpected vision of Lyris Lowell's creamy skin, he cast himself back several weeks to the searing memory of her rejection. The studio seemed to shift and change until he stood again in the midst of a late-October garden party held to raise funds for charity.

The languid sensuality of the last roses of the fall enfolded him with their sweet scent. A breeze sent petals skittering over the grass. The affair provided an opportunity to brush shoulders with the city's upper echelon and he allowed himself a moment of satisfaction.

It had taken thirty-one years to fight his way up from a poor childhood on the Seattle waterfront. Now he owned several pieces of city property, including the Golden Harbor, a prosperous saloon near the bay. Soon he would own the elegant home he had coveted since childhood.

He needed only a wellborn wife to run his household and ease his way among the blue bloods. Women were attracted to him. Most of the time, he had driven himself too hard to care, but now he was ready to consider marriage.

He counted less on personal appeal than on his hard-won wealth, for he was looking among the well-bred daughters of the city's elite. A woman possessed of an elegant social background could ease him into the high position he had craved all his life.

Miss Lowell, daughter of a prominent Seattle banker, had attracted him at once. He liked her laughter and the way her eyes danced as she talked with her friends. She was beautiful, but he had learned that beauty could be misleading.

While he considered the bright-eyed Miss Lowell, a small ragged boy sneaked in from the street and edged through shadows toward a linen-draped table laden with sweets. His wary gaze flicked from left to right before settling on a tray of iced cakes. As his hand darted out, one of the serving men hauled him backward. "Here! What do you think you're about?"

The boy's shriek brought every eye around. Nick stepped forward, but stopped as Miss Lowell's clear voice dismissed the servant. She knelt in the grass and held the sobbing child against the apricot silk of her dress. With soothing words, she quieted his sobs. Ignoring the disapproving click of nearby tongues, she tucked cakes and cookies into the boy's pockets, then rumpled his hair and led him to the street.

Nick stood transfixed, while his thoughts flew to an earlier garden, where he'd been the intruding child and the outcome had been far different.

As a boy, he had often lingered outside a magnificent home that belonged to his grandparents. Every time he stopped, it seemed to have grown an added turret, gable or wing. He knew that his grandparents had moved to Seattle because his parents were there. Yet they never visited his home. He was not allowed to approach them.

The hard-hearted pair had disowned their only daughter for marrying a common fisherman. While his father was at sea, his mother told wonderful stories of her childhood in San Francisco. Nick gazed up at leaded windows and imagined remarkable toys within, and tables heaped with trays and bowls of wonderful food, enough to satisfy any hunger.

One day, the sound of violins reached through high garden shrubbery, drawing him closer. After slipping between the prickly shrubs, he saw elegantly gowned women and handsome men talking and laughing together. He knew his grandmother, Amelia Chambers. He had often watched her enter or leave her carriage, always hoping she would recognize him and invite him to join her.

On that day, she looked as beautiful as a queen. When she smiled with her friends, he believed he saw kindness in her eyes. On impulse, he stepped from hiding and called out, "Grandmother! I'm Nick."

He would never forget the horror on her face and in her voice. "How dare you speak to me? What a terrible, rude boy!"

Red blotches marked her face. In a sharp, angry voice, she ordered the nearest servant to throw him into the street. More than twenty years later, the memory still scalded, so much so that Miss Lowell's compassion touched his heart.

He located Spencer Lowell at once and requested permission to court his daughter. Class consciousness gleamed in

Lowell's considering gaze, but wealth earned its own class and the banker knew Nick's worth.

"I fear she has been overindulged," Lowell warned. "My daughter expects to have a say in matters of the heart, but I will speak with her."

Miss Lowell's kindness had awakened old pain. Nick felt consumed with longing for her tender glance, her gentle voice. When Lowell went in search of her, he followed, impatient to begin his suit.

He heard her voice from beyond a screen, but her words were far from musical. The not-so-compassionate Miss Lowell roundly berated her father for even daring to suggest the courtship of an ignominious barkeep, a man whose handsome appearance could not disguise his lowborn past. She was obviously just warming up, but Nick had heard enough and stalked away from the party.

Miss Lowell's rejection reinforced every hurtful memory ever inflicted by his unfeeling grandparents. As days passed, resentment smoldered. He buried it in hard work until three months later, when their paths crossed again at a lecture given by a visiting statesman.

Nick had rushed from his carriage through pounding rain into the lecture hall. As he paused in the entrance to shake off his coat, a ripple of laughter drew his attention to Miss Lowell.

She stood below a high window, talking with another young woman. The watery light fell over her like a sunbeam, sparkling in her radiant black hair and bringing a glow of summer to her fair skin. Her entire appearance was animated and vivacious.

Then her eyes met his and the light left her. She withdrew a step, looking as if a crab had scuttled up from the harbor and might soil her hem. Deliberately, she took her friend's arm and moved into the hall.

Furious, he stalked into the meeting room. Other young women smiled and flirted with their fans. He scarcely noticed. Taking a vacant chair next to Brunswich from the *Tribune,* he fought his dark mood.

Brunswich offered a few good-humored comments in an obvious effort to lighten the atmosphere. He succeeded in catching Nick's attention when he mentioned that Miss Lowell was now working for his newspaper.

"Her father suggested I hire her as a typist," Brunswich said with amusement, "but the young lady is far too adventurous to be satisfied with that. She considers herself journalist material."

Could that have something to do with why she had posed for Samuel Castor? The question brought him back to the painting and the artist's studio. Nick thought of Miss Lowell's panicked state outside. Could Castor have painted his own vision? The man had the nature of a wharf rat, for all his talent. He had made comments suggesting a grudge against the banker, Lowell.

Had he tricked his model? She seemed half out of her mind with dread. The painting must go into her hands at once.

And yet, a second thought came slowly. What a comedown for the prideful beauty. She was too haughty to accept a saloon keeper's courtship. Now her nude likeness was slated to hang over his bar.

The irony pleased him. The lady's own arrogance had probably brought her into this situation. Why not allow Miss High-and-Mighty Lowell a few weeks of mortification before delivering the portrait to her?

It would never be exhibited, of course. But what sweet satisfaction there would be in presenting her with the crated canvas. In the future, she might think before making someone the object of her sharp tongue.

He studied Castor's work, trying to resent the model while being fascinated by her beauty. His fingers curved, remembering the supple strength of Miss Lowell's waist and the soft, unexpected fullness of her breast. His hand still throbbed from her reaction to that mischance.

Yet the canvas offered a naked breast revealed with careless pride. The tight raspberry nipple begged for a man's lips. Nick swallowed, shaken by the depth of his response.

Castor spoke smoothly. ''The model is less voluptuous than customary. Still, you must agree she expresses a feline elegance well suited to the huntress. No doubt, your customers will enjoy the contrast with your other canvases.''

His customers would never see it. *The Naked Huntress* was not for the hot eyes of men in their cups. The studio suddenly looked tawdry. Nick became newly aware of dust in the corners and of cheap satin cushions piled on a stained couch at the back. The stink of turpentine made the painting seem vulnerable.

Resenting even Castor's eyes on the portrait, he reached for his pocketbook.

Lyris had waited as long as she could. The silence in the studio was excruciating. Was Drake disappointed? Good. Let him reject the work.

Carefully, she eased open the studio door. Her entire being focused on the painting. It should take only seconds to dash across the studio, topple the easel and canvas and smear the oils with her body. She was long past caring about her clothing, yet felt herself grow hot with embarrassment at the prospect of rolling about on the naked portrait in front of Nicholas Drake.

Then think of this painting placed on view in a waterfront saloon, she told herself without mercy. *Think of what the shame would do to Mama and Papa.* Any embarrassment she might suffer now was nothing compared to the unspeakable humiliation in store for her parents.

Warily, she studied the broad shoulders turned toward her as Drake talked with the artist. While his dress was impeccable, there was a ruthlessness in his stance that spoke of a lifetime on the waterfront. If he were to approach her home, Mama would instinctively refer him to the trade entrance.

Lyris knew her only hope was to catch both men off guard. When Drake took out his pocketbook, she decided the two were as preoccupied as they were likely to be. Whispering a small prayer for courage, she burst into the studio.

Even Castor was taken by surprise. She flew past him, her fingertips stretching hungrily toward fresh paint.

Strong arms snatched her back. A hard embrace crushed out her breath. She struggled blindly toward the easel, but was lifted and turned aside. Drake's voice rasped in her ear. "Calm yourself. The portrait belongs to me."

He set her down, still holding her by the shoulders. His amber eyes pierced her soul. Desperate with frustration, she exclaimed, "The clothing of a gentleman does not make one of you, Mr. Drake."

The only reaction Nick allowed was a tightening of the muscle in his jaw. "Perhaps not, Miss Lowell. Just as an accident of birth has not made a lady of you."

A hot flush rose to her face. He saw misery beyond the anger in her eyes and was almost sorry for her. Still, she had brought her humiliation on herself.

"I suggest you learn from this," he told her shortly. "But the painting belongs to me."

Lyris clenched both hands in her skirt, despising her need to plead with the lout. "That portrait is a lie."

He studied the canvas's details with such an insolent eye that she felt she would burst into flame. She started to speak but he waved her to silence. "I'm trying to decide. Don't distract me."

"You are insufferable."

There was no warmth in his eyes when he turned to her. "And you are not only the model, you are also becoming tiresome."

With a gasp, she whipped off her cape and swung it toward the wet oils. Drake moved quickly to block her. The heavy cape slapped across his face.

While a red mark bloomed from his temple to his jaw, he wrenched the cape from her hand. Lifting her by the waist, he strode through the doorway and deposited her on the landing. The cape dropped beside her as he said coldly, "Consider the matter closed."

As the door snapped shut, Lyris kicked the panel with her boot. Pain lanced through her foot. That was nothing compared to the anguish in her heart. The oils would take days to dry, she consoled herself. She would find a chance to destroy the painting when Drake was not around.

As she limped down the stairs, her spine stiffened with resolve. Outside, gulls wheeled overhead, declaring stormy weather at sea, but Lyris was lost in a memory of the October garden where she had first seen Nicholas Drake.

Her close friends had pointed him out, Reba giggling as she pretended to swoon over Drake's dark good looks. Widowed two years before, Reba was actively interested in attracting a second spouse. While she considered Drake unsuitable, he made an interesting subject for gossip. "They say he keeps a mistress at the Golden Harbor," she reported avidly, "and another at a fishing camp to the south."

Evelyn laughed above the lace of her fan. Like Reba, she had married young, but not as happily. Bitterness often sprang to Evelyn's tongue, but today the garden party had put her in good spirits. Her voice lilted as she discussed the handsome Mr. Drake. "I have heard that if a female should dare to look directly into his golden eyes, her virginity will be lost."

Laughing, Lyris said, "I believe that dire fate requires more than a glance, however attractive a man's eyes."

She didn't feel as lighthearted as her friends, however. She sensed danger in Drake. He was not a man who would sit patiently through a musical recital or indulge a wife's interest in pursuits of her own. He was exactly the kind of man she most dreaded, and she made a mental note to avoid him.

Reba reported rumors that Drake was interested in marrying. Certainly, he had acquired age and wealth enough to turn his thoughts in that direction. Lyris decided the rumors were true when she saw him study the marriageable females attending the charity party as if choosing among a litter of pups.

It amused her to see his expression change. Clearly, the litter disappointed. That one was too frisky, this one too quiet. And the pretty one there complained far too much and would likely keep her master awake all night.

Humor faded when his glance reached her and lingered. Apprehension clutched her. Although she looked away at once, she felt his continued study.

Fortunately, an urchin provided a distraction by slipping in from the street to filch a sweet. He was a dear child, if a bit grubby. She would have gone to his rescue at any rate, but with genuine gratitude, she had seized the chance to walk with him to a gate well away from Drake's riveting amber eyes.

She was twenty-five and on her way to the blessed single state that was her life's goal. Lately, however, Papa had become adamant that she accept a suitor. Just minutes after she used the boy to escape Drake's notice, her father called her aside to say that the wealthy Mr. Drake wished to court her.

In desperation, she drew on her father's weakness, the pride he took in his elevated position in society. That pride had amused her in the past. Now it became her only hope to avoid a man who would attempt to crush her into a dutiful wife.

She had railed against women's treatment by society at such length that her friends no longer listened. Six years ago, when the territorial legislature had given women suffrage, Papa had forbade her to join torchlight parades meant to encourage women to use their new opportunity.

She'd joined anyway, along with her widowed and willful grandmother, thus discouraging several potential suitors, according to her enraged father. He took smug pleasure in the fact that after only four years, voting rights were taken away again. He said women had brought it on themselves by voting in a reform ticket that closed down gambling halls and revoked liquor licenses.

Just six months ago, the United States Supreme Court had upheld the lower court's decision. Papa agreed loudly with the newspapers' claim that women's suffrage had brought nothing in the way of public good, but only caused dissension and trouble.

It was useless to argue. Still Lyris seethed that even the legislature believed women to be lesser creatures. Once she avoided the threat of marriage, she meant to live as freely as possible from the domination of men.

Nicholas Drake threatened those plans. Her best hope to avoid him was in convincing Papa that the saloon keeper was dreadfully beneath their class. Perhaps she'd overstated her case. She was somewhat embarrassed now to remember her haughty words. But she heard no more from the wretched Mr. Drake.

It was then that Papa demanded she accept work if she would not marry. The position at the newspaper opened a door into a self-sufficient future. Lyris accepted gladly.

There had been an unsettling moment before a lecture in January when Drake came into a hall where she was talking with Reba. When she saw him looking at her as if he might renew his suit, Lyris felt her spirits plummet. She escaped into the hall, praying he would forget her.

Clearly, he had not. The man's pride must be as fragile as his social position. He had exacted a horrible revenge. She couldn't imagine the train of circumstances that had led to the odious portrait, but there was not a shred of doubt in her mind that Drake had conspired with the artist to ruin her.

She splashed across the wet street, taking bitter comfort from the pain in her bruised toes. It helped focus her anger. While the monstrous painting existed, she had no future.

Chapter Three

The rain lifted as Lyris approached her father's home on Denny Hill. For a moment she stood outside the two-story gabled house, which rose from a glossy embrace of rhododendrons. Tears blurred her eyes. She had once run carelessly through the white picket fence and up the walk. Now she felt barred from the door.

That was ridiculous. Nothing could have changed yet. Still, she felt almost a stranger as she followed the path to the rear of the house. Inside the kitchen, a kettle boiled as always on the black iron range. Lace curtains in the window framed a vase of early narcissi she had placed there this morning—a lifetime ago.

A tang of chopped onions came to her, along with a rich aroma of roasting venison. There was a clatter of pots and plates and the busy swish of skirts and aprons as the staff rushed about their duties. Despite the sheltering familiarity of it all, Lyris continued to feel as if she no longer belonged.

Nor would she, if the portrait were displayed. Her father might deny he ever had a daughter. Lyris swayed against the window. The vase tottered. She caught at it, scattering water and flowers over the floor.

A maid darted forward. Waving her away, Lyris thumped the vase onto the nearest table and grabbed a towel. Enough, she told herself as she mopped up the spill. There is a solution. Find it!

Castor was greedy. If she offered more than Drake, surely the artist would sell the portrait to her. Where was she to get the money? She could hardly ask Papa. Lyris sat back on her heels as a possibility struck her. Castor had betrayed her out of bitterness toward her father. Suppose she promised to intervene in the matter of the gallery? That should be worth more to the artist than his agreement with Drake.

For the first time in hours, the painful tension left her shoulders. She still had a problem, but a resolvable one, although it would not be easy to convince Papa to sponsor Samuel Castor with the gallery. Once Papa's mind was set, he rarely changed it. And he was still annoyed with her.

His voice proved it, rising sharply from the parlor. Shouted phrases roared above the friendly bubbling of the kettle and the sizzle of coals in the stove. "Charity affair…expected to attend… Madam, you will speak to your daughter."

Lyris's groan drew a sympathetic glance from the housekeeper and an envious one from the nearest maid. The mayor's charity ball was an annual affair, one she had openly scorned. She despised being drawn about on Papa's arm as bait to attract a suitor.

Jonathan Brunswich had invited her to write a description of the ball for his paper. "Who better than a young woman of quality to gather details of costume, decoration and menu?" he'd proposed amiably. Social news, when she longed to gather stories of importance. She had answered that she did not plan to attend. Now she felt her shoulders droop. She needed to be in her father's good graces more than ever before.

Putting the vase aside, she followed his voice down the hall and between the velvet hangings of the parlor doorway. Beyond, her mother cowered on a chaise longue.

Papa waved a sheaf of papers above her. His voice rose a full octave and Lyris realized he had moved on to the sub-

ject of expenses. "By gad, woman, you and your daughter
will have me in the poorhouse. The two of you must think
gold eagles drop with the rain."

Mama visibly trembled. If she had ever had spirit, marriage had defeated her. Lyris had no intention of ever wilt-
ing so before a man.

Still, she could hardly blame Mama for her tremors.
When Papa's brows lowered, the entire house seemed to
draw into itself. Even the gas lights appeared to dim in their
prism-hung sconces, while the carved wainscoting took on
the sullen glow of coals in the open hearth.

Forcing a cheerful note into her voice, Lyris intervened.
"Papa, you have convinced me. I am now looking forward
to the affair."

His assessing glance made her squirm inside. "Can it be
possible you have had enough of the work world? Are you
now prepared to launch yourself in search of a husband?"

Lyris choked back the answer she wanted to make. If she
could charm Papa out of money for a new gown, then make
do with an older one, she might have enough to buy the
portrait. She managed a smile. "Husband hunting can be
expensive, dear Papa. I will need quite a large sum to put
myself on the market, considering my advanced age."

His scowl implied that he recognized her sarcasm. "You
both have closets filled with gowns. Between the two of you,
my finances have been transferred from my bank to the
dressmaker's vaults."

"Think of your daughter," his wife said carefully. "Lyris
must dress in fashion to attract a man of your caliber."

"Maybe. Maybe." He strode back and forth across the
Persian carpet, a heavily built man whose waistcoat
stretched to accommodate him. Pausing, he examined a
statuette as if considering its worth.

He set the piece back with a thud. "You will wear one of
your present gowns." His wife's soft protest made his scowl
deepen. "No one will notice if it is not tomorrow's fash-

ion, for Lyris will be wearing her grandmother's sapphires."

Lyris clutched the velvet hanging. The sapphires had been Gram's dowry. One day they were to be hers, but they were kept in a vault. She had only seen them twice in her entire life.

"They were to go to you at your marriage," he said gruffly. "I believe your grandmother would have no objection to their being used to attract a spouse. Join me at my bank in the morning and I will place them in your hands."

Stunned, she could only breathe, "Papa, the sapphires!"

He studied her dispassionately. "You are pleasant enough to look upon, although most gentlemen prefer a more malleable age. Still, the sapphires would overcome such objections. Take care to select a bodice that will display them at their best."

She had never felt more like an object, an unwanted one at that, a daughter he hoped to pawn off on the first eligible man. In her distress, one word repeated itself: *pawn*.

She forced it away. She had loved her grandmother and missed her every day since her death two years ago. The sapphires were a link. Of course she would not pawn them. *Only a loan.* The words burned through her. The jewels could be retrieved later. First, they would bring money to buy the painting.

Again she rejected the idea. There was no need for money. Papa's influence with the gallery would be enough. Trying to sound lighthearted, she said, "I've meant to talk with you, Papa, about an artist named Samuel Castor. I believe he's quite talented."

Her father cut in brusquely. "Have nothing to do with him."

"But talent should be encouraged."

Her father's tone was as unrelenting as Drake's. "If I know men's natures, and I believe I do, that fellow Castor is untrustworthy. Someone has made a mistake in recommending him."

"Yet I'm told his work is much admired."

Her persistence brought a suspicious glint to her father's eyes. Quickly, she added, "I was hoping to surprise you. You mustn't spoil it with questions."

He would be more than surprised by the truth. But she had turned away his doubts and he actually smiled. "It's well that you spoke with me, my pet. If you're considering a portrait, I will provide you with worthier names."

Hopes dashed, she murmured only, "Yes, Papa." But she couldn't pawn the sapphires. That was out of the question.

All night, her sleep was troubled by dreams. In the worst of them, she saw herself handing her beloved grandmother's jewels to Nicholas Drake. As he accepted necklace and eardrops, each dazzling stone became a tiny black pool of blood.

She sat upright with a jolt. For one horrified moment, she thought the man was actually inside her bedroom. The pale light of dawn told her she was alone. She sank back on the pillow, heart racing, and tried to find comfort in the steady beat of the rain.

Before going to the bank, Lyris walked to the hillside cemetery and her grandmother's grave. The fresh-washed day made colors vibrate as she climbed. The lot held a clear prospect of Elliott Bay and the tree-covered islands below the snow-topped Olympic Range, which kept the worst of the Pacific storms from Seattle. She felt threatened by a different storm, one that could forever shatter her life.

Turning briskly to the graves, she saw that a rosebush wrapped tendrils as if in loving memory about the joined headstones. It was a relief to confront a problem she could control. First, she cleared the clutch of thorns from the grave of her grandfather, an abstracted man who had died while she was still very young.

When she tugged at the roses wreathed about her grandmother's marble monument, Lyris felt overcome with sadness. She pulled aside the insistent vines while picturing a vibrant, pretty woman with laughing eyes. Many times, Gram had protected her rebellious granddaughter from the results of her own mischief.

"I need you," Lyris murmured. "Now more than ever. I wonder if you would be disappointed in me."

A breeze swirled up from the bay, tangling her hair. With it, she felt a return of rebelliousness. She had done nothing shameful. There was no comfort in the thought. At fault or not, her problem remained. "It's about your sapphires," she whispered. "Oh, Gram. If only I could talk to you."

Even in her Gram's last years, the lively sparkle had never faded from her eyes. Nor had she lost her joy in teasing Papa, who was her son. Wistfully, Lyris said, "I need you, Gram. What am I to do?"

The wind swirled again, catching a rose tendril and raking its thorns across Lyris's outstretched hand. She jerked back, instinctively sucking the wound. She almost believed Gram stood behind her, tapping one shapely foot while waiting for her granddaughter to end her sulking.

Only graves stretched out against the hillside. Yet the sense of her grandmother's presence remained strong. And Lyris knew without question that if she were present, Gram would be first to pawn the sapphires.

That certainty remained until she entered the bank vault with her father. The jewels were laid out on a square of velvet and her heart caught at their beauty. When she held them in her hands, she felt sick with longing. The jewels were a link to a grandmother she had dearly loved. How could she let them out of her possession, even for a few days?

As if in answer, an image of *The Naked Huntress* rose in her mind. Lyris returned the jewels to their silk-lined case.

Not trusting her voice, she leaned forward to kiss her father's cheek.

When she returned to the carriage, she came close to asking the driver to take her home. For a painful moment, she pictured the stones against her skin. She even decided which gown would best display them.

Resisting, she sat back against the cushions, then called to the driver in a voice steadier than she had dared to expect. "Stop here and wait. I have business to conduct. Then I'll want you to drive me to a studio belonging to the artist, Samuel Castor."

An hour later, when she entered Castor's studio, she saw at once that the easel stood empty. None of the canvases stacked around the walls were as large as *The Naked Huntress*. Her hands curled as she turned. "Where is it?"

He feigned boredom, although she noticed he moved backward a step. "Are we to have another tiresome argument about this?"

He hadn't stepped far enough. Taking power from despair, she grabbed the front of his smock. "Where?"

With a grimace of distaste, he picked her hands loose. "Nicholas Drake was quite taken with *The Naked Huntress*. He insisted she be delivered at once."

Denial rushed through Lyris. She had believed he would wait for the oils to dry before taking possession. Now she felt as if Drake once again had shut a door in her face.

At this very moment, drunken men might be leering at her portrait. Through a wave of humiliation, Lyris demanded, "Where has he taken it?"

Castor's voice reminded her of the way his oil paints smelled. That oily scent would haunt her the rest of her life. "Drake owns a place near the waterfront, my dear. Not the sort of establishment a well-bred young lady should frequent."

With thickening dread, she pictured the exquisite gold keg Drake wore on his watch chain, a symbol of his profession. As Castor continued, she saw that his hatred for her family ran even deeper than she had first believed. "The Golden Harbor is located near Front Street. Even as we speak, my dear, your naked likeness is titillating rough sailors."

With desperate effort, she kept her voice steady. "I had intended to purchase the work. You have missed a large profit. As you have lost my intended intervention in the matter of the gallery."

She was pleased with his frown of disappointment, but the pleasure was empty. Castor had already done his worst. Gathering her skirts, she started toward the door. "I will buy the painting from Mr. Drake."

"Don't raise your hopes," Castor snapped. "Nicholas Drake dislikes high-nosed blue bloods even more than I do."

Her hand shook when she reached for the latch. She hid the tremor by settling her cape more securely about her throat. Castor chuckled nastily. "That's right. Hide yourself. Remember, every man who crosses your path may have already enjoyed your likeness."

"You are beyond contempt."

"I would think twice about entering the Golden Harbor," he called as she hurried down the stairs. "The patrons may expect you to provide entertainment."

The warning was unnecessary. It would be impossible for her to enter a saloon under any circumstances. She would send a message stating that she wished to discuss a business matter. Drake was a tradesman. He would surely respond.

Chapter Four

With the heaviest veil she owned cascading from her hat brim and over her face, Lyris picked her way across un-planked streets, trying to avoid muddy chuckholes. The rain of the past few days had washed a great deal of the hillside down to the bay, leaving behind a mass of dirt and debris. Horse-drawn trolleys splashed along, spattering passersby while their bells clanged in careless disregard.

The sun was already dropping toward the Pacific. Lyris moved quickly along a wooden sidewalk, passing commercial establishments—a barber shop, a Greek restaurant and a Chinese laundry. Every imaginable business was jammed together in the downtown blocks.

The mixture of languages and boisterous laughter made her uneasy. She clutched her brown velvet reticule, heavy with the pawnbroker's gold coins, and looked straight ahead as she hurried on. She rarely came down to this area, certainly never on foot, but she couldn't risk having the driver confide to Papa that she had visited a saloon.

The air reeked of the overworked sewers. Papa often complained that in downtown businesses such as his bank, the plumbing facilities had to be placed on the second floor. Otherwise, every incoming tide flushed the commodes in reverse.

Lyris forced her mind to concentrate on the message she would send in to Drake, then came to an abrupt stop at a corner. The Golden Harbor Saloon loomed directly across the street.

The lively piano music and bursts of rollicking laughter from behind the doors made her cringe. With one gloved hand shielding her nostrils, she looked about for a likely messenger.

None was needed. She recognized Drake's voice from a hotel doorway behind her and spun about to see him taking leave of the owner, Alex Shore. He had almost stepped past her into the street when she raised one hand. "Mr. Drake. I must speak with you."

His brows rose as he recognized her beneath the veil. "If this is about the canvas, Miss Lowell, you're wasting your time."

Mud splashed beneath his boots as he strode toward the saloon. The abrupt dismissal left her staring after him, but only for a moment. She darted into the street. "You don't understand. I wish to buy the portrait."

Her foot skidded and she slid wildly, her arms flailing. Drake turned instinctively to catch her, his grip inflexible. "Go home, Miss Lowell."

Again, he walked away. Furious that a tradesman would turn his back on her, she rushed after him. "Mr. Drake! I am speaking to you!"

They had reached the opposite sidewalk. Men grinned, stopping to watch. She saw Drake's mouth thin as he turned. Stepping onto the walk, he grasped her around the waist and lifted her up beside him. "All right, talk."

She moved hastily aside and gestured across the street. "We will return to the hotel lobby."

"No, Miss Lowell. We'll go into my office." He swung open the door of the saloon.

Appalled by the noise and the smells of strong liquor, unwashed men and fresh sawdust, Lyris exclaimed, "I can't go in there!"

"Sure you can. Just put one foot after the other and you'll sashay right inside."

She looked at him icily. "I beg your pardon."

Someone snickered. Drake's eyes flashed. "Do as you will. I've better use for my time than arguing with a female." He strode into the saloon, letting the doors swing after him.

"Mr. Drake!" She hesitated, her cheeks burning as she became conscious of rude laughter. She couldn't simply stand there. Neither could she turn away. Jerking her veil closer about her face and raising her chin high, she marched into the Golden Harbor.

She lifted her veil for a furtive inspection of the nude paintings behind the bar. All were of fat, rosy women smiling through unbound hair or silk ribbons while looking inordinately pleased with themselves.

The Naked Huntress was not among them. With a gulp of relief, Lyris dropped the veil, but not before noticing that men crowded the tables and stood two or three deep along the bar. Several called amused comments, few of which she understood.

Drake waited at the rear of the room. When her glance found him, he inclined his head with a look of satisfaction that sent fury boiling through her.

Stiff with indignation, she followed him through a hall and into a richly paneled office. Inwardly, she writhed. Mama would swoon dead away to know she was inside a saloon, not to mention alone with Nicholas Drake.

The room suited him, she saw in a fleeting glance. A massive but sparely ornamented desk was set before a shuttered window. A library table piled with leather-backed volumes stood at one side, opposite a large oak wardrobe flanked by straight-backed chairs.

Her gaze flashed around the paneled walls, but found only steel engravings of ships. Where had he put her portrait? The threat it posed overwhelmed even her need to escape.

Drake tossed his hat aside and shoved rough fingers through his hair. "Miss Lowell, you may be the most annoying female I have ever had the misfortune to meet."

Once she got through this humiliating experience, Lyris vowed she would obey every rule society and her father could set. Resolutely, she said, "I have come to buy that portrait."

"The portrait is not for sale."

She dropped her reticule on the desk with a solid clank. "There is enough here to pay for three canvases." Authority rang in her voice. "All of it is yours for *The Huntress*."

Nick surveyed her sourly. An hour ago, he might have given her the portrait. Not now. Not while she treated him like last week's fish. And he sure as hell couldn't be bought. He answered coldly, "Have you raided your father's till?"

"I would expect that from you," she shot back. "As if a woman hasn't the right to pawn her own jewels."

He thought she regretted the revelation the moment she made it, but her chin stayed high. He used a hard tone to settle the matter. "*The Huntress* belongs to me."

She moistened her lips, betraying nervousness. Did she think he meant to attack her? Maybe he looked as if he would. The flick of her tongue over the moist surface of her lips went straight to his blood.

He blamed the tussle in the street. When he'd lifted her onto the raised sidewalk, he couldn't help comparing her supple warmth to the sweet curves of the painted goddess. Yet every word she spoke dripped with disdain. He moved closer, trapping her against the desk, reminding her that high birth meant little in a saloon.

Lyris pressed backward, dismayed by Drake's insolence. How dare he treat her so! Her hands brushed the polished oak, fingertips searching for a weapon.

He guessed her intent and slid his hands down her arms, capturing her wrists while she shivered with apprehension. He was far too close and looking at her in an odd way, as if he wasn't sure what to do with her.

Then he lowered his mouth to hers, startling her into momentary stillness. His lips were firm and warm. A rush of forbidden pleasure spun through her. She knew she should twist away, but her body would not obey her mind.

His unexpected gentleness was distracting. When he moved his mouth tenderly over hers, she felt spreading excitement. Reason brought an equal flood of shame. This man had treated her abominably. Why was she kissing him? With a strangled gasp, she dragged her mouth away.

He straightened, looking bemused. "Poor mouse. Has Diana's bright confidence deserted you?"

Lyris drew breath for a sharp reply, but a loud knock startled her into falling backward against the desk. Drake tugged her upright, while calling toward the door, "What is it, Sam?"

A slender young man edged into the room. Curiosity glittered in his animated face, deepening Lyris's sense of disgrace. "There's a messenger out front with a telegram, boss. Says you have to sign."

"In a moment." Drake dismissed him, then strolled to the wardrobe and pulled it open. The hated canvas stood inside.

With a mortified cry, Lyris snatched a brass letter opener from the desk and lunged forward. Drake's hand shot around her wrist. He yanked her against him, trapping her within his arms. She twisted impotently. "Only a lowborn barkeep would treat a lady this way."

"Lady?" he exclaimed. "You can't mean yourself." Prying the blade from her hand, he tossed it onto the desk. "Until you learn better manners, Miss Lowell, the painting will stay with me."

He shoved the wardrobe closed, locked it and dropped the key into his vest pocket. "After I see about that telegram, I'll have a carriage drive you home."

The moment the door shut behind him, she seized the letter opener and pried at the wardrobe lock, which proved hopeless. Time was short. And her mind was distracted by the memory of his hard body pinning her against the desk. How dare he kiss her, and in so intimate a manner?

Her face became heated when she remembered her shameless response. It was insane to remain here. Nor could she return home in Drake's carriage. She shuddered to think of the questions that would raise.

Darting behind the desk, she swung wide the shutters. They opened onto an alley. She felt a swift stab of relief. After retrieving her reticule, she climbed over the sill.

This horrible experience hadn't been a complete failure. She knew where *The Huntress* was kept. Now she simply had to think of a way to get to it. Dropping to the ground, she hurried toward home. Her thoughts raced, but to her considerable dismay, they turned more often to Nicholas Drake than to the portrait.

Nick wasn't surprised to discover that the innovative Miss Lowell had departed by way of a window. But the revenge that had once seemed sweet now made him feel petty.

The telegram presented a greater problem. In three months, his younger sister would be set into his care. How in hell was he going to raise a little girl in a saloon?

By then, the solicitor would have completed the purchase of his widowed grandmother's house. Nick decided to authorize the fellow to give Amelia Chambers whatever she wanted to rush the sale, but she was to leave the furnishings. She wouldn't be taking them back East, where she meant to live with her late husband's sister. They belonged where they were.

Amelia didn't know he was the buyer. She would probably burn the place rather than have him take possession. There would be satisfaction in sitting at last at his grandfather's table. More important, he would have a respectable home for the sister his father's parents were no longer able to control.

He tried to remember how long it had been since he'd last seen the girl, but could only draw up a memory of a skinny little waif skipping stones at the waterfront.

Fanny's birth, sixteen years after his own, had surprised both parents and further weakened his mother, who had never been strong. When their father's trawler went down in a storm a few years later, Ida Drake stopped fighting her difficult health and simply faded away.

Fanny deserved better than life had given her. In the back of his mind, Nick had always meant to send for her when he got his own life in order. What would she need? A governess? Nanny?

There was a hell of a lot he didn't know, but that didn't mean he couldn't learn. Swinging onto the chair behind his desk, he dipped a pen into ink and began a list. He would order some dolls. And laces and frilly hats. A parasol. She was probably as tan as beach sand. He frowned. Ladies of quality never exposed their faces to the sun. He vaguely remembered a female acquaintance who used lemon juice to lighten her skin.

Leaning back, he let the pen fall. Frills and dolls weren't enough. If Fanny was to grow into a proper lady, she must have the daily example of someone whose own upbringing had provided a natural instinct for correct speech and walk and a thousand other things.

He could have the solicitor hire a companion, but he rejected the idea as quickly as it arose. The telegram called his sister rebellious. Whatever the case, she would need considerable refinement before entering society.

He didn't want to hire a companion. He wanted to grace his new home with a wife whose social position could open doors for both him and his sister. His gaze rested on the wardrobe. Rising impatiently, he fished out the key.

For long minutes he studied the portrait. Castor was scum, but he knew his work. The woman in the painting was so vibrant he could all but feel her silken body in his arms. He still smelled her fragrance.

The bright anticipation in the painted face reached a lonely place deep inside him, leaving him confused. That must be why he'd reacted like an overeager schoolboy the moment he'd tasted Miss Lowell's lips.

No wonder she had fled. With a curse, he circled back to the desk. The sooner he had the canvas delivered to the maddening creature, the sooner he would have her off his mind. With swift dark strokes, he wrote her address on a sheet of paper, then just as abruptly crumpled it.

Who was he kidding? He didn't want to rid himself of Miss Lowell. Last October, her impulsive act of kindness had made him want her for his wife. Her superior attitude was infuriating, but she certainly had mettle enough to take on the training of his imp of a sister. And there had been unexpected sweetness in that kiss.

He smiled grimly. Miss Lowell might scorn his courtship, but he had the upper hand as long as he possessed the painting. She was sure to attend the upcoming mayor's ball. He would approach her there.

Chapter Five

Lyris succeeded in slipping into the house unquestioned, but suffered all night with the need to reclaim the sapphires before Papa learned they were gone. She had a bad time during dinner when asked about them. Fortunately, both parents accepted her murmured assurance that they were safely put away.

A new storm gathered during the night and pounded the city all the next day. Lightning flickered through the heavy sky, while sheets of rain blew along the street. Trees bent under the force of the wind.

"The newspaper can spare you today," Papa said severely at breakfast. "It wouldn't do for you to take a chill just before the ball."

Lyris looked unhappily at the streaming window. The sapphires were safe. Another day would scarcely matter, as long as she could keep Papa from asking to see them.

She spent the morning with her mother, going through the gowns in their closets and discussing how a seamstress might make them appear new. There was some truth in Papa's complaint of money already spent. Gowns of satin, taffeta, faille, silk and brocade crowded together, most with heavy bustles. Trying them on one after another became fatiguing.

While her mother rested, Lyris went down to the kitchen for tea. A maid was forcing the door closed against blustery wind. "Oh, miss," she exclaimed. "A package just came for you. I was about to bring it upstairs."

A narrow box lay on the table. Lyris felt her heart leap. The dimensions were startlingly similar to the case she had left with the pawnbroker. After asking the maid to take tea to her mother, Lyris carried the package into the privacy of the solarium. She jerked loose the strings and tore into wrapping paper, revealing a jeweler's case.

With trembling hands, she raised the lid. The rich blue gleam of Gram's sapphires dazzled her. A sob of relief caught in her throat. But how was this possible? Except for the broker, only one other person knew she had pawned the jewels.

A folded paper lay beneath the necklace. With misgivings, she drew it out. Drake's script looked as forceful and spare as his office furnishings, giving Lyris the impression that he was capable of forming graceful swirls with his pen, but chose not to do so.

The words were as brusque as the writing.

A lady should not do business with a pawnbroker. I've spared you the need to go back. In return, I'll expect a dance at the mayor's ball. We have an urgent matter to discuss.

He must mean the portrait, Lyris thought. He had reconsidered. He must have. And yet, if he meant to give her the painting, he could simply have done so. She forced her mind over the humiliating episode in his office. In no uncertain terms, he had refused to sell the painting to her.

He also had spoken of teaching her manners. As if she could learn from a tradesman! With a grimace, Lyris faced the truth. Where Drake was concerned, she had behaved badly. But for the life of her she couldn't imagine how she could have done otherwise.

Unhappily, she gazed at the black initials slashed at the end of his note and knew she would have to dance with Nicholas Drake.

On Saturday, Lyris's father fastened the sapphires about her throat, unaware of their brief stay in a pawnshop or their unexpected return. His voice warmed with pride. "Exquisite, my pet."

She raised her fingertips to the blaze of jewels, cherishing their link with Gram, yet deeply troubled. Nearly a week had passed since her attempt to buy the portrait. Each day she had racked her mind for a way to destroy it.

Frame buildings were forever burning. Why not Drake's wretched saloon? Seattle had an efficient fire department, however, with at least four million gallons of water held in a reservoir. She had quickly put arson out of her mind.

With a deep sigh, Lyris considered her appearance. She had first pulled her hair into a bun so severe that it stretched her skin over her cheekbones. Papa, however, had sent her back to her room with a maid to create a more appealing effect.

Now her reflection in the mirror revealed curling tendrils framing her face. The weight of her hair was caught into a swirl of black curls that began at the crown of her head and spilled down the back of her neck. The sapphires glowed like blue fire against her flushed skin. Papa beamed with satisfaction, and she knew he saw her as suitable bait for any eligible man who might be flushed from the pack.

Why worry? she asked herself cruelly. Once the portrait is put on display, men may offer many things, but marriage will not be among them.

"You're shivering, pet," her father said. "Dancing will warm you." He patted her bare shoulder above the satin bodice that tightly enclosed her bust and waist. Her draped skirt, of matching dark blue taffeta, was patterned with ostrich feathers in gold.

Lyris pictured herself dancing with the arrogant Mr. Drake and shivered again.

The mayor's mansion shimmered with light, and music drifted from the third-floor ballroom. Lyris recognized a song by the Messrs. Gilbert and Sullivan, introduced in London last year. Despite her earlier misgivings, she stepped eagerly from Papa's carriage. The storm had finally subsided and the evening sparkled with promise.

In a room set aside for the ladies, attendants took her cloak and offered to touch up her hair and toilette. Reba had arrived already. Eyes shining, she clutched Lyris's arm. "We must locate Evelyn. She has promised delicious gossip about the handsome Mr. Drake."

Lyris's breath caught, and her mother frowned at them both. "I do wish you young ladies would set your minds on a higher level."

"We'll discuss Mr. Twain's latest novel, Mrs. Lowell, I promise." Giggling, Reba drew Lyris with her toward the ballroom.

Lyris bit back a smile. Reba knew her mother disapproved of the acerbic author as much as she did casual gossip. "What is it?" she demanded the moment they were away. "What has Evelyn heard?"

She trembled to think that Evelyn might have learned of the painting.

Nick stood at one side of the ballroom, beneath hundreds of candles gleaming from chandeliers suspended from the high-coffered ceiling. A hundred guests mingled, the ladies taking chairs along the walls or accepting invitations to dance. He watched for Miss Lowell while listening to a group of town council members debate the need to improve the streets. There had been no answer to the note he'd sent with the sapphires, but he was sure the lady would be here.

His attention swung back to the conversation as one of the council members, Richard Thompson, spouted another of his self-serving opinions. Thompson was a young dandy who fancied himself a boxer. He made challenges of every statement and, between outbursts, fondly stroked his heavy mustache.

The group parted to include Spencer Lowell. Nick greeted the banker with caution, but saw no sign that Miss Lowell had taken her problem to her father. He was certain the haughty firebrand would be forced to accept the proposition he meant to offer, but she would not do so gladly.

Lowell was not likely to object. A few careful questions had revealed that while the banker adored his daughter, he despaired of coaxing her into the care of a good husband.

Thompson broke into Nick's musing with a loud argument for planking the remaining streets in the muddy business district. Lowell mentioned the need for businessmen to assess themselves to pay the cost. Thompson replied that the sin taxes on gambling, whores and saloons were doing the job so far.

Thompson was a self-righteous fool. Nick threw in his own opinion, which matched Lowell's. Thompson scowled. Rumor had it that the fellow had been rejected by the banker's daughter. For once, Lyris had shown good taste. The mayor's wife interrupted, chiding gently, "Gentlemen, the ladies are waiting to dance."

As the men separated like well-trained schoolboys, Lowell offered his hand. "If you ever think of running for a seat on the council, Drake, you will have my support."

"I'm hoping for a greater prize," Nick said quietly. "Your daughter's hand in marriage."

Lowell let out an embarrassed cough. "I've warned you before that she is headstrong."

Nick cut off an apology before it could be voiced, nodding across the crowded ballroom toward the stunning Miss Lowell. "I think we'll find she's changed her mind."

She was radiant. The sapphires glittered against her creamy skin. The ladies with her faded in comparison. Nick smiled to himself. Headstrong she certainly was. Haughty, as well. But she was also a rare beauty, with a spark of independence that set her apart. She would make a fine hostess for his new home.

Women in taffeta and brocade appeared like a garden of flowers among men made elegant by black frock coats and dazzling white shirts. Lyris took mental notes for the *Tribune* while waiting impatiently for Evelyn to share her news.

Lyris had been terrified that it concerned the portrait, but was reassured by the expression on her gossipy friend's face. If Evelyn knew about *The Naked Huntress,* she would not have been able to conceal the fact.

"Do get on with it," Reba urged.

Evelyn tapped her with a lacy fan. "You both realize that our servants know more about us than we know about ourselves."

"If you don't tell us something new," Reba protested, "I may pinch you."

Evelyn giggled. "My maid has developed a romantic interest in Mr. Drake's man, Sam."

Reba turned laughing eyes to Lyris. "I apologize for dragging you over here. I thought she had learned something interesting."

"I have," Evelyn protested. "According to his man, the handsome Mr. Drake is buying one of the city's grandest estates. He hopes to elevate himself in Seattle society."

As one of her neighbors? Lyris frowned and Evelyn turned toward her. "Sam says that Nicholas Drake had hoped to ride into society on the skirts of a lady and just months ago was roundly set down."

"After all," Reba exclaimed, "he is a tradesman."

"A wealthy one," Lyris murmured, feeling a need to say something.

"As if wealth would induce a lady to lower her sights." Evelyn spread the fan and spoke behind it. "Sam told my maid, Rosy, that Mr. Drake came back to the saloon in a thunderous state. He had offered for a lady and she'd responded that his good looks could not disguise his low birth."

Reba gasped, while Lyris remembered with shock the garden party where Papa had suggested that she consider Drake as a suitor. She had responded with horror. Could Drake have overheard? That would explain his insulting behavior.

He meant to dance with her tonight. She dreaded the prospect. Perhaps he would be willing to sit out the dance. After all, his note had suggested a talk. She would ask for a lemonade. Maybe she could explain. Experience warned that Drake wasn't very good at listening.

Richard Thompson approached, stroking a finger across his mustache. She had once told him the habit made him look as if he wore a kitten above his mouth. As a result, he'd ceased his unwanted romantic pursuit.

Reba blushed as his gaze settled on her. When he offered his arm, she let him draw her onto the dance floor. Evelyn murmured, "We'll soon be hearing wedding bells for those two."

"I think Reba has better sense," Lyris answered tartly. "Mr. Thompson's brains are all in his mustache." She had nearly told him that, as well.

Evelyn laughed. "Who do you suppose insulted Mr. Drake?"

More sharply than she intended, Lyris said, "You should discourage your maid from gossip."

Her friend sniffed. "I believe you feel a tenderness for the handsome tradesman."

Lyris's look of disdain caused a rapid flicker of her friend's lace fan. "I intend never to marry, Evelyn. But if I should, it would be for love, not social standing."

"You are rather old to believe in fairy tales."

Lyris didn't bother to answer. How badly had she hurt Drake's considerable pride? He knew she would be destroyed socially if the portrait were displayed. Obviously, he enjoyed his advantage. With a sinking heart, she watched him stroll toward her over the gleaming parquet floor.

Female eyes followed him over a flurry of fans. He looked striking in black broadcloth and a dazzling white shirt. Unlike most of the other men, who wore white bow ties for the ball, he had chosen black, with a black sash at his waist. As before, he wore a jeweled gold keg on his watch chain, a symbol of his saloon. Lyris couldn't help staring at the keg as Drake offered his arm.

The need to resist a dance made her blurt out her words. "I was about to inspect the buffet, Mr. Drake. For the newspaper. I have been assigned the story. As a journalist."

His warm fingers brushed the sapphires at the curve of her throat. "We'll inspect the buffet together."

His touch was as possessive as his tone. In a sense, the wretched man did possess her while he held the painting. With regal poise, she allowed him to escort her into an adjoining room, where lavishly decorated tables held a shimmering array of jellies, creams and sweet dishes. She tried to note them in her memory, but her mind wouldn't focus on nougat almond cake or towering blancmange while Drake toyed with her composure.

"As a writer, Miss Lowell, you no doubt possess a clever turn of phrase. Tell me, how will you describe in print this bowl of crystallized fruit?"

The only analogies that sprang to her mind were of fangs and silver tongues. "I'm afraid you will have to wait for the printed copy."

She moved along the table. He followed. "You're looking flushed. Will you have a lemonade? Or don't journalists drink on the job?"

She glared at him. "Mr. Drake, your life must be dull for you to find amusement in taunting me."

He lifted a curl from the back of her neck and let it slip slowly between his fingers. "You're mistaken, Miss Lowell. Life is anything but dull."

She stared at a shimmering triple-tiered dish of grape jelly. By tomorrow, the story would be all over town that Nicholas Drake had paid her unwanted attention. She burned to introduce the subject of the portrait, but too many people were within hearing.

"Let me guess at your creative efforts, Miss Lowell," he said in a mocking tone that made her inwardly brace herself. "Will you compare the sweets of the buffet to the charms of a lovely woman, say, as an artist might fancy her?"

She shot him a fierce, warning glance, but he studied the table with feigned innocence. Taking an iced orange from a silver bowl, he turned the golden fruit in supple fingers. "Consider these," he murmured. "Peeled and deliciously juicy."

As she stiffened at the insinuation—peeled and juicy, indeed—he broke a shining segment free and offered it to her. She shook her head. He shrugged and bit into the fruit with strong, white teeth. She could see his throat move behind his stiff collar. Deliberately, he added, "Begging to be tasted."

Lyris had held her tongue for as long as possible. "I hardly think that oranges care what becomes of them," she said as she moved toward a particularly creamy concoction at the far end of the table. "I have, however, heard that chocolate mousse can offer a grand answer to a mocking tongue, when served with the proper enthusiasm."

His laughter drew questioning glances. Clasping her elbow, he urged her toward the door. "I still bear the marks of your earlier enthusiasms, Miss Lowell. I believe it's best to leave these weapons behind."

An orchestra on the stage at one end of the room had just struck up a waltz. Before Lyris could refuse, Drake swept her into the midst of the dancers. He moved with easy grace, swirling her on the curve of his arm as if he were born to the ballroom.

"You look surprised, Miss Lowell," he said after a few turns. "Did you expect me to tread on your dainty toes?"

"I had heard that your earliest years were spent in hard work on the docks," she said. "And your later years in saloons."

His brows lifted, but he chose not to respond to her insult. "A man learns grace while he avoids uncoiling ropes and falling cargo, or soon wishes he had." He spoke lightly, but she saw that his expression had become guarded.

Nick took care to hold the delectable Miss Lowell at a proper distance while they circled the floor. She felt warm and supple despite the unneeded corset that armored her trim waist. He thought of holding her trapped against his oak desk, her heart fluttering with excitement.

He turned his mind to a safer subject, the steps his mother had taught him long ago. She had loved to dance. As a boy, he had danced with her, feeling awkward at first, then learning to enjoy the music that sang from his father's violin and into his blood.

It was a skill that served him well enough in later years, although as a child, it had been just one more way in which his mother set him apart from the working class she secretly scorned. Had his sister learned the graceful steps of the ballroom? If not, he would find an instructor.

He felt briefly defeated by the number of skills Fanny must need, things he might not yet know himself. That was where Miss Lowell came in.

The music was ending. Adroitly, Nick whirled his partner to the side of the ballroom and through open doors onto a balcony. She looked up at him in breathless surprise, still leaning against his arm.

"You are beautiful tonight," he said, adding with a wry tone that might have been a shield, "Much like the creations of the buffet."

"All artifice?" she asked. "Molded and decorated to spark a man's appetite?" She moved away from his arm. "Believe me, Mr. Drake, that's not by choice."

"Are you offended?"

She studied him with a level look that seemed to combine regret with resolve. "Apparently, I unwittingly offended you some months ago."

He captured her hand, lightly caressing the delicate veins of her inner wrist with his thumb. "An apology? You put me in an uncomfortable position, Miss Lowell. To accept, I'd have to admit to listening in on your conversation with your father."

"So you continue to make my life miserable without saying why." It occurred to Lyris that she had trembled more in the past week than in her entire life. Still, she meant to get through this. "I do apologize, Mr. Drake. My words were not intended to embarrass you."

"Do you think I embarrass easily?"

She looked into his eyes. "I think we should speak honestly. I will never marry, whatever Papa hopes. It was to discourage him that I used harsh words on that day."

"Again, we're at cross-purposes," Nick said quietly. "You may be the one woman in Seattle whose heart is not set on matrimony. But you see, my lovely Miss Lowell, I intend to insist."

Chapter Six

The lovely Miss Lowell drew in a shocked breath. Nick tightened his hold on her hand. "Shall I attempt poetry?" he asked softly. "A song, perhaps, comparing your charms with your lyrical name. I might go down on one knee. The balcony is still damp from the rain, but if that's what you want..."

Lyris snatched her hand free. "I just told you I will never marry. You will have to look elsewhere."

"The choice is not yours." Nick smarted inwardly. His pride lay exposed, while the maddening woman took jabs at it. "You have something I want—high social position. I have something you want. I propose a trade."

"A trade." Her voice sizzled with understanding. "Are we not speaking of blackmail?"

He felt almost as low as she saw him, but continued grimly. "We're speaking of a temporary marriage. You will have your own bedchamber. I'm not interested in forcing myself on a woman who has probably been told to lie back and endure."

Her breath hissed. "You are plainspoken, Mr. Drake."

"Why don't you try calling me Nick? After all, we are to be married."

"We are not!"

He ignored her exclamation, giving her time to think the situation through, but she curled her hands in fury. "You would not be comfortable with me, I assure you, Mr. Drake. Look elsewhere.''

''I have a young sister who will soon come into my care,'' Nick said, holding his temper with an effort. ''I'm determined to give her a better life than she has led so far, including the company of a gently bred woman who will know how to train her.''

''Hire a companion.''

''You say you will never marry, yet your father is set on it. I'm offering you the freedom you crave. Launch Fanny into society and you may have a divorce, and wealth enough to live however you wish. As well as the portrait.''

Lyris paced the short length of the balcony, rubbing her hands against her bare arms. She felt chilled, although the evening was unseasonably warm. ''If I refuse?''

Nick thought of Fanny. He remembered his own childhood and the sense of never belonging. It was within his power to give her the comfort their mother had lost. He put steel in his voice. ''Refuse and *The Naked Huntress* will be donated to a public gallery.''

''Blackmail!''

''If necessary.'' He drew a harsh breath through his tight chest. ''I'm a businessman, Miss Lowell. As you know.''

''You are a—''

''We are to be married,'' he cut in quickly. ''Let's not have ugly words between us.''

Lyris felt as trapped as the swallow that once had blundered into her mother's solarium. Clearly, Drake meant to carry through his ridiculous scheme.

That abominable painting! She forced herself to think of it. What was the worst that could happen if he donated the work to a public gallery? She would be shunned by most of her friends. She could bear that. No man would consider her for a wife. Fine.

As a journalist, she would develop a certain notoriety. Jon Brunswich of the *Tribune* might even take the matter in a positive light. If the painting proved her to be fearless, surely he would assign her to more interesting stories.

She reached the far end of the balcony and turned to tell Drake to do as he would with the miserable painting. A burst of music from the ballroom drew her glance. Men and women swirled around the floor, the very picture of propriety.

She wanted to escape into them, to resume her place in the society she had taken for granted and had even resented at times. Regret cut bitterly. She might do without all of that, if she must. Mama could not. Her parents would suffer horribly if the portrait were shown.

She forced her gaze from the dancers back to Drake. Light from the ballroom glittered on his white shirt and in his eyes. His face was shadowed and dangerously attractive.

She sensed his impatience. How could she answer? To deny him would be to deny her mother, not to mention Papa. To accept was to commit herself to living under Drake's roof—for how long? "How old is Fanny?"

"How old?"

He looked unsure. Drake was obviously a man who liked to have all the answers. She had caught him off guard and took a small pleasure in it. "Yes, Mr. Drake. How old?"

"She was seven or eight when I last saw her. That was a few years ago."

Lyris gladly deepened his discomfort. "You are so fond of her that you wish to shackle yourself in an unwilling marriage. Yet you don't even know her age?"

"She lives with our father's parents in San Francisco. I've taken little time away from business in several years." He stopped abruptly and ran a hand through his hair. "I won't apologize for hard work."

She let silence accuse him.

"She's twelve or thirteen," he said with irritation. "Can you spare a few short years for her, Miss Lowell, given the advantages you will receive in the bargain?"

Her voice was as hard as his. "Let us have the terms understood. Separate bedchambers?"

He nodded.

"Who would stand up with you?" she demanded. "Your goals won't be served by having a bartender as attendant."

He flinched. "Will Jon Brunswich satisfy you? He's the closest friend I have at your rarified level of society."

Drake no more wanted a wife than she wanted a husband, Lyris told herself. He felt a need to protect his sister as she wanted to protect her mother. They would both be making a sacrifice.

"It would have to be a home wedding," she mused. "It's dreadful enough to make pledges we don't intend to keep without doing so in church."

"We might elope."

"Would you have society think even less of us?" She shuddered at what her friends would say, as it was. They would think her desperate for a husband, after all her brave words against marrying.

When it was over, however, and the sister had made her debut, Drake meant to have his freedom. And she would have hers. Along with fresh gossip. "Divorce invites scandal."

His eyes glittered as he saw that she was beginning to consider the possibility. "I will happily bear the blame for our broken union, my sweet. Your friends will congratulate you on your escape. You will have the sympathy of all Seattle."

"I would have more sympathy as a widow," she said tartly. "I suppose you would object to that."

Nick grinned. For several minutes, she had looked like a trapped kitten, worrying her predicament like a ball of yarn while prowling the balcony. He was glad to see her spirit return, even at his expense. Whatever else their marriage might be, he did not expect to find it dull.

Women were drawn to him. That was a matter of fact, not vanity. In time—a short time, he hoped—the delectable and high-spirited Miss Lowell would see that she had married a man she could respect and perhaps learn to care for.

In the meantime, she wished him dead. He answered lazily, "Shall we pledge our betrothal with a kiss?"

"The relationship will be platonic, Mr. Drake," she said, emphasizing the formal use of his name. "I have your word."

"As a gentleman."

Her eyes flickered at the sarcasm. Then she said with savage warning, "It is not only your sister whom I intend to refine. You *will* be a gentleman, Mr. Drake, when I have finished with you."

He felt a moment of foreboding, then inwardly scoffed. She was only a woman, however sharp-tongued. If she expected to make changes in him, she would soon find she was mistaken. He inclined his head toward the ballroom.

Feeling chilled to her soul, Lyris accepted his arm. A grand march was in progress, her parents near the head. Neither must know the sacrifice she was making for them.

Drake placed his free hand over hers. He had an uncanny way of sensing her thoughts. Not that they could be hard to fathom at the moment. How on earth was she to convince her parents that she wanted to marry this man?

"They will think I have lost my wits," she muttered.

"On the contrary," he said blithely. "Considering that you are somewhat long in the tooth, they will believe that your scattered wits have finally returned."

She pulled her hand free as the march came to an end and rubbed her fingers to erase his touch.

"Come, my sweet," Drake said softly. "Let us begin." Amusement warmed his eyes. "If you will not cling to my arm, at least try to smile."

"To show my joy in having captured such a prize? I would rather snarl."

"Continue as you are then. No doubt our friends will take your state of high excitement as anticipation for our marriage bed."

"You are—"

"Softly." His hard grip on her elbow stopped her from finishing. "Smile."

She looked into his eyes. The amusement had faded. On that miserable day when she collided with him outside Castor's studio, she had seen his background in his stance. Now she saw it in his face, a look of hard-won dominance in a world where decisions were made with fists instead of words.

She let him see that she had fire to match his—and no intention of having her spirit crushed. "Make no mistake, Mr. Drake. I will accept this *temporary* marriage. And I will do my best for your sister. But you and I will continue on a formal basis, let tongues wag as they may."

"Are you a gambling woman?"

She eyed him cautiously. "Why?"

"I'm willing to wager that within a few weeks' time, you will lose interest in the formal relationship you propose. I trust I won't be forced to remind you of our vow of celibacy."

"Your conceit is rivaled only by your insolence."

"Here are your parents," he warned. "Smile, sweetheart. You are not to be a spinster, after all." He raised her hand to his lips, his eyes mocking.

She hissed in answer, "Spinster? You may soon wish that I were."

Her father greeted them with puzzled heartiness, while in her mother's eyes, Lyris saw a wrenching vulnerability. Papa spoke for his wife in nearly all things. Mama's only recourse against his will was to point out where society, not she, disagreed. In the face of scandal, she might crumble completely.

Gently, Lyris took her hand. "May we have your blessing? Mr. Drake and I have decided to marry."

"Each other?" Her mother covered appalled disbelief with a tearful hug. "Oh, my dear! Is this really what you wish?"

"Of course it is," Papa exclaimed, again sounding much too hearty. "I saw from the first that the two would make an excellent match."

Lyris could not lie to her mother, but sidestepped the question. "You must share your housekeeping secrets, Mama. Mr. Drake is purchasing a fine new home."

"Indeed," Papa said warmly. "It is my understanding that he has been buying a sizable portion of Seattle."

Drake answered with mock gallantry. "For so sweet natured a bride, I would gladly surrender it all." Lyris saw Papa wisely choke back a comment, while Mama clasped her hands in nervous dismay.

The rest of the evening went by in a blur. When Papa stopped the band to announce to the crowd that he had accepted Nicholas Drake's offer for his daughter, Lyris felt as if she were stepping onto a stage. For the next few years, she would act a role, while waiting for her real life to resume.

She avoided Evelyn and accepted Reba's stunned compliments. "But we were just speaking of him," her friend whispered, her fascinated gaze on Drake while he accepted the handshake of a well-wisher. "Lyris, why didn't you tell me?"

"We meant to surprise everyone," Lyris said, and felt as if her face would crack from her forced smile.

Chapter Seven

Nick was surprised to find Lyris nearly inaccessible in the following weeks. Apparently, marriage took a great deal of a female's time. Whenever he called, it was invariably to find that she had visitors, or was studying fabrics and dress patterns with her mother and a seamstress, or discussing floral arrangements or teas or the engraving of invitations, at-home cards and calling cards.

A courtship was not necessary, he told himself. Why go out of his way, by ordering his carriage to pass her house? To please her? She was not pleased. To satisfy her friends that the marriage was desired?

That was closer to the truth, but with ruthless self-searching, he realized his own pride drove him to call on her. Each time, he hoped to spark at least a sign of interest. He had not dreamed the sweetness in her response to his kiss that day in his office, although, as he drove once more to her door, he was beginning to question the memory.

Lyris glanced from the window of the sewing room when Drake's carriage stopped outside. For six weeks, she had successfully avoided him. Wasn't it enough that she had committed herself to the marriage? He might allow her to enjoy her final weeks of freedom.

As she watched her fiancé spring from his carriage and stride up the walk, she cast through her mind for a way to avoid him. Excuses leapt like hungry trout. She had been a little surprised to learn how much effort a wedding required.

There weren't enough hours for all that must be done, and Drake had given them less than three months to prepare. He meant to be married by the time his sister arrived.

Today, she had to decide on the music. Lyris clutched that excuse as a servant admitted Drake into the room. His forceful presence made the space seem far smaller than before. Lyris felt momentarily breathless as his expressive gaze took in her close-fitting afternoon dress. He was strikingly handsome, a fact that hit with new force each time she saw him. He was also unutterably ruthless.

He greeted her mother, then stopped Lyris before she could begin to explain why she had no time for him. "Whatever it is, it can wait. I need your company."

She tried to ignore a breathless quickening. "So do a host of others, Mr. Drake. You are the one who is rushing the process. You can scarcely complain."

"Get your cloak. It may rain again."

"The more reason to stay inside."

Her mother looked warily from one to the other, then surprised Lyris by intervening with a firmness that was unlike her. "Darling, you have paced this room until I've become dizzy. At least walk in the garden for a few minutes. The fresh air will be good for you."

She threw her mother a baleful glance. Considering the sacrifice she was making, however secretly, Mama might support her. Drake had raised his brows on hearing that she had been pacing. Pacing!

"If I have dizzied you, I am sorry, Mama," Lyris murmured. "But there is so much to do that it is hard to remain still. And more reason not to fritter away this busy afternoon."

Drake called to a passing maid. "Bring Miss Lowell's cloak." As she darted away, he added to Lyris, "We're going for a drive. You may wish to change your footgear."

Lyris glanced down at her velvet slippers. "We are expecting Mr. Simmons shortly."

Again her mother interrupted. "I will confer with Mr. Simmons, dear, and relay his musical suggestions to you." She seemed not to notice an exasperated glance from Lyris.

The maid returned with surprising speed. Drake took Lyris's velvet cape, wrapped it about her and lifted her into his arms. She struggled to free herself. "Put me down at once!"

Her mother's amusement incensed Lyris as much as Drake's casual handling. He carted her toward the door. She braced both hands against the jambs. "You bloody bully! Let me go!"

He stepped back into the room so that her hands came free of the doorway. "You're making a spectacle of yourself. And using language I don't expect to hear from my wife. Behave, or you'll wish that you had."

She told herself he was bluffing, but was afraid to test him. She was far too conscious of his strength. He held her as if she were weightless, when she knew very well she was not.

He took advantage of her hesitation to carry her into the hall. A servant rushed to open the front door.

"Have you cast a spell over my staff?" Lyris demanded, trying to regain dignity through a haughty tone.

"If I knew any spells," he said, "they would not be wasted on servants."

He deposited her inside the carriage and climbed in beside her. She whisked her skirts out of the way moments before he might have crushed them. "This abduction is far from proper."

"Is it proper to avoid the man you have promised to marry?"

"Since it is my position that interests you, rather than my aging charms, I don't know why you should care."

"Aging charms?" Leaning back, he surveyed her thoughtfully. "Do you mean the curls that are so vibrantly glossy that I can nearly see my reflection? Or the dark eyes that could bewitch a man if they weren't so often snapping with sparks? You can't mean the supple form that earned me a bitten hand for trying to support what I took to be a fainting female.''

"I see you are set on turning my head. I wonder why?''

"There is no reason we can't be pleasant.''

"When you force your way into my home like a . . . a savage to carry me off?'' She heard him sigh and sank into her corner of the carriage, feeling graceless. After an uncomfortable silence, she asked quietly, "Where are you taking me?''

"We've arrived.''

They were short blocks from her own home, traveling down a familiar drive. When she peered through the carriage window, Lyris recognized the splendid Queen Anne mansion with tall narrow windows in a half turret in front and a full turret at the back, each topped with a pink-shingled dome that looked like a stocking cap.

The steeply pitched roof embraced an attic where, as a child, she had spent many happy hours. She turned to Nicholas in wonder while the carriage rolled toward the porte cochere. "It's the Chambers House! Why are we here?''

The answer struck her with disbelief. The house had been sold. In rising delight, she asked, "Are you the buyer?'' She looked again at the porches and turrets and gingerbread, at the walks and landscaping and the peaked attic. She had always loved this house and felt her heart catch at the thought of living here.

She forgave him instantly for carrying her away. Had he bought this house especially for her? Could he know what it meant to her? "What a lovely surprise!''

Instead of sharing her pleasure, he regarded her with a frown. "You know this place?''

"Of course. Seattle is not yet so crowded that those with similar interests fail to find each other." She realized too late that she had excluded him once again from polite society.

As the carriage rolled to a stop, his voice became brusque. "The house has been closed for several months. I'll want your suggestions on ordering supplies and staff."

She accepted his hand and stepped onto the paved carriageway. In her mind, she was a child running carelessly through the halls. As a woman, she pictured the mistress's bedchamber, where she had on occasion been allowed to visit, and an adjoining door into the master suite. She had never dared venture in there.

Amelia and Edwin had enjoyed separate bedchambers, as would she and Drake, but the thought of his sleeping so near made her uneasy. Could she trust him to keep his word? With a wary glance toward him, she decided to have the servants move a wardrobe in front of that adjoining door.

He pulled an ornate key from a coat pocket. "We'll go inside."

"Together?"

He looked at her with irritation. "Yes, together."

"We are not yet married," she said, and mentally winced at her prim tone.

"I hope you don't think I plan to ravish you." He frowned. "If you thought that, you would never have approached the Golden Harbor."

She glanced swiftly at the driver, mindful of Evelyn's warning about gossiping servants. "Here is your first lesson as a gentleman," she said, trying to sound lighthearted. "A lady does not go into an empty house with a man who is neither kin nor husband."

"All right. We'll take the driver."

"The driver!" Her voice rose a full octave. "Two men are even less acceptable than one."

Nick felt like a fool and disliked the feeling. The blue bloods lived by rigid rules. If he meant to join their level, he would have to live like them.

It galled him more to know that he didn't want to go into that house for the first time alone. His reluctant bride would be mistress here. He wanted to set her stamp on the place as well as his own.

He was counting on her tart presence to exorcise ghosts, but would never tell her so. It was more than pride that kept the old wounds hidden. They held power over him that he was not willing to place in her hands.

"Will you enter marriage with a poorly staffed home and no food in the cupboard?" he asked, bluffing past her objection. "Or will you take a few minutes to discover what is needed?"

Lyris placed one hand lightly over his arm, surprising herself. Where had a feeling of tenderness come from? Perhaps from his uncharacteristic look of indecision. She had expected him to stride gladly into his grand new home. He looked at it as if suspecting a trap. Did he think the house would collapse on his head before accepting a commoner?

Gently, she said, "I have already spoken to Mama of our need for a housekeeper. She is seeking recommendations from all of our friends as well as of her tradespeople."

Again he stiffened. She had unthinkingly separated friend from tradesman. How was she to guard against insulting him? "We will find a suitable woman, Mr. Drake. One who will manage the household as if she were at the head of her own family."

She had very nearly called him by his given name. His brilliant gaze stopped her. Hesitating, she said, "I have been meaning to speak to you about your man, Sam. He is romantically involved with my friend Evelyn's maid."

Drake scowled in disapproval of gossip. As well he might, considering how often he was the subject. Lyris hurried to explain. "I would rather not have him in our home. Servants inevitably know too much and they talk amongst each other."

"And ladies don't visit saloons." He smiled at her discomfort. "Don't worry, sweet. He won't embarrass you."

"How can you know?"

"I trust Sam."

"I don't."

They glared at each other, standing on the paved carriageway outside the magnificent house while the sky steadily darkened. A raindrop struck Lyris's upturned cheek.

Drake glanced upward. "We'll go inside until the cloud passes."

Lyris turned toward the carriage. "We will return to my father's house."

The sky exploded. Lightning struck without warning, so near that Lyris squeaked with shock. The horses whinnied and leapt. As the driver fought them, Drake swept Lyris onto the shelter of the porch. Thunder deafened any response she might have had breath to make. While he shoved his key into the lock, rain drummed upon the street.

He pulled her inside and slammed the door on the storm. "At last!"

The words were spoken with startling intensity. She braced, then saw that he wasn't referring to being alone with her, but to being inside the house. Despite the shuttered dimness, his eyes looked very bright.

He glanced about the hall, taking in the great staircase at its end. He touched the stained glass of the door while rain streamed behind the panes, looking as pleased as if the sun made jewels of them, as she knew it could. He stroked a porcelain vase on a nearby side table. She watched him turn slowly, eyeing tile and carpet, wainscoting and furniture with a look of burning possession.

Leaving his hat on the table, he walked ahead of her into a front parlor and stood with hands on his hips, feet spread apart, taking everything in with fierce intensity. As she realized how much this meant to him, she tried to see it all through eyes accustomed to humbler surroundings.

She knew her friends gossiped behind her back. Evelyn had even mocked aloud that despite her vow never to marry,

Lyris had grasped swiftly and below her station once the opportunity offered—but of course, mere minutes before, she had sworn to marry only for love. Lyris couldn't tell them the marriage would be temporary, with her freedom promised at the end and love no part of it. Her bargain with Drake was that no one should know of their arrangement.

She ran a fingertip over the dusty molding, uncomfortable with the silence. "Are you pleased?"

Pleased. The word couldn't come close to expressing how he felt. Nick tried to see into himself, then backed away, afraid he might reveal the rawness inside. He had expected to feel triumph when he stepped into this house, but it eluded him.

He watched Lyris run a gloved fingertip critically along a molding, as if preparing to call the housekeeper to account, and he couldn't quite keep resentment from his voice. "You look as if you belong here."

She understood. "So will you. When you have had time to grow used to it."

"When you have made a gentleman of me?" He said it to mock her, but suddenly, unexpectedly, her confidence caused a rush of pleasure.

She moved to examine a large ugly bronze lamp in the shape of a naked woman wreathed in dulled grape leaves. The arms were stretched upward with snakes coiling about them, the hands clasping a dark globe.

"What in blazes is that?"

"Don't you like her, Mr. Drake?" Lyris tilted her head. "You appear to have a natural eye for the finer things in life."

"I don't see anything 'fine' about that monstrosity."

"Edwin inherited it from some ancestor with a sad lack of taste." Merriment lit her eyes. "Now it's yours."

I hope you're watching, Grandfather, he said silently as he took the lamp in both hands. "Where shall we dump it?"

Lyris offered a leather wastebasket. "No doubt one of the maids will carry it away to beautify her own home."

Nick dropped the lamp into the basket with pleasure. Although rain still drummed outside, Lyris was like a living sunbeam bringing light to the dark, overfurnished rooms. On sudden impulse, he caught her about the waist, lifted her high and whirled her into the hall.

Gasping, she braced her hands on his shoulders. "Civilizing you may be an even greater chore than I thought."

He lowered her onto the bottom step of his grandfather's staircase. She stood on a level with him, laughter dancing in her eyes. "We aren't married yet, sir. Restrain yourself."

"I swore not to bed you. I didn't promise to resist a kiss."

Ducking beneath his arm, she darted deeper into the house. He tossed off his heavy coat and followed. As in a child's game she led him on, seeming to have forgotten the impropriety of being alone with him.

He startled her from hiding, but failed to catch her. Laughter rippled as she darted away. His own laughter surprised him.

He watched Lyris duck into a passage. Beyond her, a farther door opened into the room beside him. He ran silently over thick carpets. She burst through the second door and with a breathless shriek found herself caught in his arms.

He looked into her laughing eyes and felt his heart stir in a way he would never have believed possible. Teasing her to watch the rose deepen in her delicate skin, he asked, "Are these the games the great folk play?"

Her lips twitched. "Only those with careless dignity."

He claimed the kiss she had made him earn. Her lips were softer than he remembered, her skin warm and fragrant. Beneath her thin tea dress, her heart beat against his.

The women he knew were never so elusive or so happily trapped. He chuckled and lifted his head.

She demanded an explanation. "You kiss me, then laugh?"

"Because of our bargain, my hot-headed prize. If this is the formal relationship you mean for us to have, I look forward to it."

She straightened. "It's the storm…or this house. They've made me giddy."

He watched her gather haughtiness like a well-worn cloak, but didn't mind. That habit, like any other, could be altered. He was patient when it suited him. He could wait.

Smiling inwardly, he stepped across the hall and into a second room, larger than the others, with a marble fireplace and overstuffed furniture. Hunting prints graced the walls. He should probably learn the names of the artists, and with his wife's help, he would.

She moved down the length of the room, her taffeta petticoat flirting, as she now refused to do, in whispers and rustles. He moved toward her, then saw that she was studying a large oil painting.

His grandmother glared from the canvas. He wasn't prepared to come suddenly on her likeness. Shock raked him. Amelia Chambers wore the same gown, the same jewelry— the same expression—as she had on the day she'd ordered him thrown from her garden. Her voice echoed in his memory, stirring the pain he would never forget. *What a terrible, rude boy. How dare you speak to me.*

Through a haze, he heard Lyris say, "I promised her that I would never marry."

"Promised! Her! Why?"

She didn't seem to notice his shock, but continued to look with longing at the woman in the painting. "She was Gram's closest friend and my godmother."

Godmother! "Bloody hell!"

Lyris couldn't have missed that. Or the anger that turned his shock into a cauldron of rage. His ears roared with the hot rush of blood.

He wanted to rip the portrait from the wall and grind it under his heel. That cold-hearted bitch had denied her own daughter, her own grandchildren, then opened her heart to one of society's spoiled elite.

He heard Lyris ask, "What is it?"

Her words were drowned by a voice in his memory, amplified, shrieking. *How dare you speak to me! Terrible! Rude! Boy! Terrible! Rude!*

He strode blindly from the room, then slammed a fist into the nearest wall. The crash reverberated. Nearly mindless, he caught up a vase. Behind him, Lyris cried, "Don't!"

His voice rapsed. "Who owns this?"

"You do."

He hurled the vase into the wall. Shards flew. The explosion did not produce the satisfaction that he needed. Seeing his bride-to-be's horrified expression, however, he continued down the passage, trying to tamp down his rage.

Lyris stood stunned, realizing how little she knew him. Men like Drake lived by emotion, not reason. What was she getting into?

Common sense told her to run out to the carriage, order it home and call off the wedding. And yet minutes ago he had been playful and romantic. There had to be a reason for so frightening a change. She followed cautiously and located him in a doorway, hands braced at either side. "What is it?" she ventured. "Why are you so angry? Please tell me."

"Come here." Turning, he caught her in his arms and buried his face in her hair.

She resisted briefly, then became aware of such raw pain that she ached in response. Wrapping her arms tightly around him to offer comfort, she kneaded her fingers over the corded muscles of his back. "Please," she murmured. "Tell me."

She felt the effort it cost him to regain control. His arms eased slightly. His tension lessened. When he raised his head, he looked away, guarding his eyes.

"I apologize," he said stiffly.

He moved away from her, then leaned one arm against a doorjamb while he stared into another room. The skin was drawn tight over his cheekbones. A muscle beat in his jaw. She hesitated, then placed a hand over his arm and realized he was as rigid as before. "Is it because the portrait shows the previous owner? We'll take it down. We'll take all the portraits down."

"No."

"They upset you!"

"I want them there. I want them to see me take possession." He stopped, looked away. "Understand one thing, Lyris. That woman is never to set foot in this house."

Shocked and confused, she blurted, "She is my godmother."

His gaze chilled her. "If Amelia Chambers should come back to Seattle, she'll find no welcome here. I will not be made to feel an intruder in my own home."

She understood that he felt like an outsider in her world. He meant to force that world to take him in. She wasn't as sure as he that it could be done. The former owner of his house must seem to represent all those who had ever shunned him.

Lyris had first thought that he'd bought the house especially to please her. Obviously, that was not the case. She wondered uneasily if he now felt that with Amelia's goddaughter as mistress, he would remain on the outside.

There could be more to his fury. Edwin Chambers had been a hard man. As a child, Lyris had learned to fade into the woodwork whenever he stalked past. While she didn't know Drake well, she knew his pride. He may have had a run-in with Edwin.

This was not the time to question him, but one day she meant to learn the truth. His pleasure in the house was obviously ruined. Bitterness edged his voice. "I'll take you home."

In silence, they walked back through the hall. Drake reclaimed his hat and coat, crunching over broken porcelain. Lyris stepped carefully, conscious of her thin soles.

He placed her in the carriage, then stood hatless in the rain. Fists clenched at his sides, he stared at the house. He owned it, but the house did not welcome him.

Lyris realized her own hands were knotted together in her lap. She forced them to relax. But she couldn't take her gaze from the man she was committed to marry. She had believed he wanted social position to advance his business and his sister.

Now she saw that his need went far deeper. Beneath the mocking arrogance he presented to the world, he burned for acceptance. The need was so painful that she felt flooded with sympathy.

And with alarm.

Chapter Eight

When Drake returned to the carriage, he sprawled in his corner, looking unreachable. They were approaching her home before he turned toward her at last, taking her hand with apology. His expression was guarded, his voice stiff. "I'm glad to see I'm marrying a female who doesn't feel a constant need to rattle her tongue."

"I know when to be silent."

A grim smile flickered briefly, without changing the dark look in his eyes. He may not have even heard her, for he mused as if to himself, "I wasn't thinking clearly. Too much hit me too soon. Now I see I've won a greater victory than I thought. I not only possess her home, I'll soon possess her precious goddaughter."

His eyes burned and his grip tightened painfully. Lyris did not care to be an instrument used against her godmother. And she didn't like having her fingers crushed. She used her free hand to pry at his. "There is still time to cry off, embarrassing as that might be."

"Cry off and you will be more than embarrassed," he said shortly, then visibly forced himself to relax. "I've frightened you. I apologize."

His outburst had frightened her. There were depths to him she had not expected and that made her uneasy. She was accustomed to men who veiled their deepest feelings behind curtains of words.

He continued with obvious discomfort. "You have nothing to fear from me. I hope you'll forget this day."

His pride was raw. She suspected that she would rarely find him willing to discuss his feelings and probed carefully. "Why won't you tell me what is behind all this?"

As she expected, he pulled back. "The marriage will be short. There's no need for you to snoop into my heart or my past."

Lyris felt as if she had been slapped. "I have already seen into your heart. And you hate that. You're embarrassed."

"Be silent!"

The carriage rolled into her driveway—not, she told herself, a moment too soon. Drake escorted her to the door, his manner as rigid as his expression.

Lyris felt equally strained. "Considering the nature of our arrangement, there is no need to call on me again. I'm sure you have a press of business to occupy your time."

He lifted her hand and brushed his lips across her wrist. "It may be a charade, but we will play it to the end. Invite me in. Your mother will expect it."

Leaning past her, he opened the door, then motioned her forward. She moved past him with her sweetest smile. "Dear Mr. Drake, won't you have a cup of hot chocolate to warm you on this dreary day? Only give me a moment to locate my arsenic."

He pulled her backward against him and kissed the top of her head. She spun around, surprised and reluctantly pleased to see the tension gone from his face. "Never mind the arsenic, Miss Lowell. Your tongue holds poison enough." For a moment he looked bemused. "I seem to find it addictive."

"I expect you'll soon feel cursed by the addiction," she warned, and sent a maid to bring a pot of chocolate to the parlor.

Her mother sat at her desk while a portly man with a thin beard bent over her. Lyris recognized the florist, who had already visited twice. They were studying an array of cards illustrating floral arrangements.

Both looked up eagerly. "Lyris, darling," Mama exclaimed. "Mr. Williams strongly advises orange blossoms."

The florist bowed over Lyris's hand and was introduced to Drake. "In the sunny state of California," he explained, "these remarkable trees bear blossoms and fruit together. Innocence and fertility, don't you see?"

Drake handed his hat and coat to a maid. He looked as if he might be having trouble keeping his opinion to himself as the florist concluded grandly, "I visualize a forest of orange trees, their evergreen leaves symbolizing lasting love."

"Absolutely not." Lyris swept the cards together and handed them to the startled man. "Try again, please, Mr. Williams, with an eye to roses."

Disappointed, he bade them all good-day and took his leave. With a wry smile, Drake said, "I see there is more to this undertaking than I realized." Restored humor lightened his expression. "You're sure we won't have orange trees?"

Lyris ignored him to speak to her mother. "Has Mr. Simmons stopped in?"

"We had a very satisfying discussion," Mama reported with pleasure. "Did you manage to enjoy your drive, darling, despite the storm?"

"The storm was...interesting." Lyris settled onto one end of a damask-covered couch, daring Drake to play the smitten suitor and join her.

He chose a chair nearby, choosing to charm her mother instead. "I hope you've forgiven me for stealing your daughter away. Has the music been settled?"

"Very nearly." She launched happily into a description of each piece. Lyris watched Drake try to conceal his boredom and silently told him that it served him right.

Her mother brightened with sudden memory. "Lyris, I nearly forgot. A package has arrived from Amelia." She rose quickly, missing the change in Drake's expression.

Lyris felt herself grow tense as his eyes questioned her and saw the answer. There might be more than one Amelia among her acquaintances, but they both knew of this one.

Why in the world couldn't Mama have continued her discourse on music? Instead, she hurried to a side table, collected a large package and carried it to Lyris. "I've been burning to see what she sent for your wedding."

Drake spoke quietly, but his words were as shocking as if they had been shouted. "It's going back."

Lyris looked helplessly across the package. Her fingers itched toward the knots in the string. Whatever the gift, it would be exquisite and chosen especially for her. "You can't mean that."

Nick closed his mind against the dismay in Lyris's face and the shocked confusion in her mother's. When he first learned that his grandmother had chosen Lyris over her own blood, hot anger had nearly driven him out of his senses. Lyris would soon belong to him, not to her godmother. He had won a sweet revenge, but the bond between them must be broken.

"Mr. Drake," Lyris protested. "You are too hard."

"Send it back," he said. "Unopened."

Her mother fluttered her hands as if she might snatch the package to safety. A distraction arrived in the guise of a maid with the chocolate service. Lyris set the package aside, clearly hoping he would forget it.

Quietly, he said, "Give me your promise."

Her mother spoke for her. "You don't understand, Mr. Drake. The gift is from her godmother."

"I do understand."

Lyris felt her temper snap. "You are muleheaded as well as barbaric."

"Pretty words for a lady," he countered.

She was tempted to serve the hot beverage by flinging it at him, but knew she wouldn't like his reaction. "You already possess Amelia's home, furnishings and even her portrait. Why balk at one more item?"

"It's not the item, my love. You are to have no contact with her."

She glanced toward the package, wondering what he would do if she began to open it, then decided she didn't want to find out. She was by no means his love.

"Jenny," she said as the maid finished arranging the tray, "take this package to the kitchen. Have one of the boys see that it goes back to the sender."

"Lyris, you can't mean that!" her mother exclaimed.

The horror in her mother's face was not just for the gift. Mama knew only too well how it felt to have her spirits quenched by a domineering man. "If I might just speak with you," she pleaded. "I'm sure Mr. Drake will excuse us."

Lyris had no desire to argue with her mother, who had clearly remembered all her earlier doubts about the suitability of this marriage. Suppose she were to share with Mama her reason for going through with it? The thought tempted her.

Nick drew out his pocket watch and flicked open the cover. "As a matter of fact, I find I'm called by the press of business that so concerned Miss Lowell earlier. I had better be on my way."

"Oh, but..." Her mother twisted her hands together, clearly debating whether to argue that he stay longer or thankfully see him out.

Lyris accompanied him to the door. Once there, she spoke in a taut low voice that would not carry to the parlor. "You have your reasons for this marriage. I have mine. But make no mistake, Mr. Drake. This is a business agreement. There will be no flirtations. No kisses. No friendship."

"And no connection with Amelia Chambers," he answered. As Jenny sidled past them with the package, Drake took it from her. "I'll save the boy a trip, since I'm passing by the post office."

"I believe in honor, too, Mr. Drake," Lyris said sharply. "I had no plan to keep the gift."

"Of course not." He smiled without humor. "Good afternoon, Miss Lowell."

In the days following, Lyris's resolve wavered with her courage. She felt trapped by the countless wedding details being woven together.

Freedom at the end of a few years beckoned. But those intervening years were like the roiling depths of the sea. Every day her doubts multiplied. She felt as if she were preparing to leap overboard from a reasonably safe vessel with no assurance she would be able to swim.

The portrait was a sword at her back, forcing her to jump. It consumed her every thought. Without it, there would be no need to marry. A broken engagement to a commoner would produce her desired single state as well as a divorce. What man of her class would want her after that?

She thought again of destroying *The Naked Huntress*. Shortly after Drake's visit, Lyris talked Evelyn into accompanying her to a. meeting of the Women's Temperance Union. Rising to speak, she passionately urged the ladies to make an example of dealers of spirits by marching on the Golden Harbor.

While they distracted Drake, she would slip into his office and take a hatchet to the wardrobe and the wretched portrait. Excitement swept through her when the others fell in with the idea, but her hopes sank when they decided to march on a place called the Happy Sailor instead. And they would merely hand out tracts, not risk arrest.

One of the ladies took her aside to explain. "Evelyn told us the Golden Harbor belongs to your intended, dear. We wouldn't wish you to begin marriage on an uncertain footing, however ill-gotten your groom's fortune may be."

Lyris protested to Evelyn. "I thought we were friends."

Evelyn looked blank. "But we are. Haven't I just prevented a nasty scene with your Mr. Drake?"

The wedding drew nearer. Lyris suffered successive nightmares, which she could never remember, except that she woke with a wildly racing heart.

Chapter Nine

"Lyris! You looked in the mirror! You *must* not look once you are fully dressed."

Women crowded Lyris's bedroom, each chiming in with advice while they prepared her for the wedding. There were five cousins, two aunts and Mama, as well as Reba and Evelyn, who were to be her closest attendants. Her aunts' pinched lips announced their disapproval of marriage vows taken in a garden rather than a church, but to Lyris's relief, they had given up stating their reservations aloud.

After her cry of dismay, Reba darted forward to pin an extra bow at the end of a graceful train that flowed from the creamy white satin and lace of Lyris's wedding gown and over the carpet. "There. Now promise you will not look in a mirror again until the preacher has pronounced the happy words. Otherwise your marriage will turn out badly!"

"Goodness knows," Evelyn added, "it has more than enough against it already."

Someone hushed her, but it didn't matter. Lyris felt as excited as if the marriage were real. She wanted to sing—or to cry. Her nerves felt as tightly wound as the spring in her ormolu clock. A quick glance at the timepiece showed the hour was swiftly approaching. She wished the ceremony were over. She wished it would never begin.

"Your hair looks gorgeous," Evelyn said, making amends for her previous comment. "Such a wealth of curls for Mr. Drake to take down! Who arranged them so nicely?"

"Fortunately, not you," Reba answered tartly. "Her hair was dressed and her veil set in place by a happily married woman, to insure Lyris's similar happiness."

Lyris smiled to herself. She would be happy. On the day her divorce was granted.

For weeks she had urged her friends to pass on to her every wedding charm they could learn. She, who usually laughed at superstition, felt a need to guard herself in every possible way. She listened especially to advice for gaining influence over her husband. Men would surely be surprised to learn the number of those! They ranged from advising the bride to put her right foot ahead of the groom's while at the altar to setting her thumb above his when their hands were joined.

With all that to remember, it was little wonder she forgot about looking in the mirror. Not that it mattered. This marriage was meant to turn out badly.

And if that caused her a twinge of regret, she chose to ignore it.

Her gown was an exquisite confection of antiqued ivory satin enriched with a high lace bodice and puffy gigot sleeves that tapered from the shoulders to fit closely over elbow and wrist and onto her hand. A circlet of moonstones and ivy anchored her grandmother's whisper-sheer wedding veil.

The belief that wearing her grandmother's veil would bring good fortune was a custom Lyris gladly observed. The gossamer creation had been recovered from a trunk in the attic and tenderly restored. She fingered the gold-threaded edges, feeling that her own dear Gram clasped her in a loving embrace.

There were no pearls on her costume. Lyris refused to ignore a warning that each pearl on a wedding dress represented tears the husband would cause his new wife.

Her mother clasped her hands and looked at her through misty eyes. "I have never seen a lovelier bride. Nicholas will be enchanted with you, darling."

"He will, as long as she doesn't serve him any more rose petals," Evelyn said, causing a ripple of giggles from several of the others.

Lyris smiled. She would never forget his expression when he'd been served a sandwich of thin brown bread, cream cheese and rose petals. Drake had come once more to the house—to make sure she hadn't changed her mind, or so he said. Apology in his eyes made her believe he regretted having returned Amelia's gift.

Lyris had experienced regrets of her own. After all, they were not pledging their entire lives to each other. His order against contacting her godmother was outrageous, but apparently sprang from personal anguish. Certain that some horrible mistake lay at the bottom of that anguish, Lyris renewed her vow to learn the truth.

She had written to her godmother, thanking her for the gift and explaining that there had been a misunderstanding with her fiancé, one she meant to resolve. She hoped Amelia would understand and would hold the gift for her.

There was no reason to tell Drake about her letter. She had had very little contact with him, at any rate. When he did come by, his unannounced visit coincided with a tea she was holding for her attendants. They urged him to stay. Looking rather like an eagle among a flock of gulls, he'd allowed himself to be persuaded.

After the first startled bite of bread and roses, however, he'd pulled the sandwich apart and looked with disbelief at the filling. "What in blazes is this?"

His answer was a peal of musical laughter and good-hearted teasing. Evelyn's eyes sparkled as she warned, "It is a taste of your future, Mr. Drake. Surely you approve?"

They waited with amusement to hear him flatter his fiancée's kitchen skills, but his expression remained one of dismay. Lyris then served him a glass of white wine with pink rose petals steeping within, followed by a slice of whipped cream cake filled with rose-petal jam. He made the excuse of a forgotten appointment and fled to the tune of female laughter.

Now with the wedding about to begin, Lyris glanced across her crowded bedchamber to Reba. "We may reach the garden only to learn he has changed his mind."

Reba dashed that hope. "Nonsense. He's set on the marriage. One can see that whenever he looks at you."

What did he see? Lyris wondered. She hadn't forgotten the paintings above the bar in his Golden Harbor saloon. They were all of voluptuous women. Was that what he preferred?

She chided herself for wondering. She knew very well what he saw in her. He saw a lofty birth and a lifetime of training in the social arts.

With romance in her eyes, Reba asked, "Where will you be honeymooning? You haven't told us."

"There won't be a honeymoon." Breaths were drawn throughout the room. Hastily, she covered the damage. "Not just yet, I mean. Mr, uh, *Nicholas's* young sister will come into his care within a few days. Naturally, we mean to give the poor motherless child as much attention as possible. So the honeymoon will be delayed."

And never taken, she added silently, while around her the women clucked admiringly at her selflessness. She began to feel guilty, but there was nothing to be done for it. Honeymoon? Heaven forbid! The thought of spending weeks alone with Nicholas Drake made her shiver with apprehension.

"Then you will spend your first night here?" Evelyn asked, with a speculative glance at the bed.

Where Mama might expect to find proof of consummation and virginity? Lyris felt hot blood flood her cheeks. Nerves, she told herself. Of course, she was easily agitated. All brides were nervous; especially one whose entrance into the married state was secretly a sham. "We will spend our first night and those following in our own home."

"But Lyris, that isn't done," one of her aunts said, shocked, while the other shook her head, clearly swallowing disapproval at still another violated tradition.

"You're inviting bad luck," Reba warned.

Evelyn added, "You are the one who asked for charms to insure a happy marriage. Heaven knows you'll need them."

"At least," Reba said with a sigh, "do not let him see you undress. According to folktale, that always causes trouble and maybe a divorce."

Fate was ironic, Lyris told herself. One of the few superstitions she might use was one she could never evoke. She had absolutely no intention of removing her clothes where Nicholas Drake might see her.

Nick studied himself critically in the mirror of his new bedroom. He had moved into the Chambers House weeks before. A newly hired staff had the place shining, yet it felt as uncomfortable as a wrong-size coat.

That couldn't be said of his present apparel. He prided himself that he wore the gear of a swallow-tailed dandy without quite looking as if he should be stuck on top of the cake. "I wish to hell this was finished."

Jon Brunswich clapped him on the shoulder. "Wedding nerves? A word of advice, Nick. Never let your bride forget that 'husband' means 'master of the house.'"

Nick grimaced. "Are we speaking of the same female?"

"I suspect you are in for an interesting time," Brunswich admitted with a grin. During the past weeks, he had undertaken Nick's education in the matter of a proper courtship. It was Brunswich who chose flowers with appropriate meanings to be sent often to Lyris, beginning with forget-me-nots for true love and working up to dark red blooms to symbolize ardent impatience. He also dictated syrupy messages to accompany each.

Nick doubted that Miss Lowell swooned over the sentiments. From what he knew of her, she was more likely to laugh. Brunswich insisted that a courtship must be heavily sugared to please modern young ladies. If Lyris's friends were to believe there *was* a courtship, Nick knew he would have to follow tradition.

"You should know, my friend," Brunswich said now with amusement, "the ladies observe all manner of superstitions meant to assure them of having their own way in the marriage." He chuckled. "It doesn't hurt to let her see you are on to the game and mean to come out ahead."

Nick thought back to the tea he had interrupted. Lyris had looked like a ray of sunlight in a gown of white lace over lemon-colored silk, all of it set with clear beads. After their previous parting, he'd expected to find her nourishing a healthy resentment. Her lovely green eyes held sparks, true enough. He suspected they always would. He *hoped* they always would. Yet they appeared to hold welcome, as well.

Her parlor was crowded with chattering females, but he let her settle him in their midst. He felt like a damned fool while they glanced over their fans and whispered behind them. He might as well have been a breeding stallion brought in for their inspection.

Then he'd accepted a sandwich and bit into rose petals. Rose petals! He would have believed her to be deliberately baiting him, except that she hadn't known he would stop by. If she had known, she would have included the thorns.

"Jon, did you know the ladies eat flowers at their teas?"

Brunswich grinned, looking more youthful than his fortysome years. "I'd say you had better begin with a firm hand on the menu. And speaking of that, one of their beliefs is that the first of a newly married couple to drink a glass of water after the ceremony will be the one to rule."

"She may have the water," Nick declared. "I'm looking forward to champagne."

Chuckling, Brunswich arranged a corsage of white rosebuds in Nick's lapel. "Then be sure to watch closely when we reach her home. It's also said the first to see the other will acquire the greater influence."

"I'll see her first," Nick assured him. "And make certain she knows it." He glanced at his watch for what might have been the twentieth time in the past half hour. "Shall we go? It's nearing four o'clock."

He saw her first. Lyris knew it the moment she started down a white carpet that stretched from the house to the rose-decked trellis where Drake waited. How could he fail to see her, with the orchestra loudly announcing the bride's arrival?

Lyris moved serenely forward on her father's unsteady arm. He had asked her this morning if she truly wanted to go through with this. Imagine! Papa, who cared so much about public opinion, had been willing to endure the embarrassment of a wedding called off in the final hour.

As she felt her eyes mist, she focused ahead. Reba, Evelyn and her other attendants preceded her, along with a tiny girl in lace who flung rose petals haphazardly, some on the carpet, most over the laps of the guests.

Drake was incredibly handsome. Lyris peered through her veil, frankly admiring, then with a sigh of disappointment that he had seen her first, modestly lowered her eyes.

Nick watched his bride approach, feeling an unexpected tightening in his chest. She was breathtakingly beautiful, a vision in ivory satin and lace.

Memory swept him back to a garden where she'd comforted a crying child. He thought of kissing her on his grandparents' staircase, tasting lips that yielded with unexpected sweetness. He heard her laughter and saw the bold sparkle of her eyes as she led him on a chase through the rooms.

He remembered that she had held him while he struggled to overcome the desolate fact that it was not all children his grandparents loathed, only him. He thought of laughter in her lovely green eyes while she'd served rose petals for tea.

The memories slipped away when she reached him and her father relinquished her. Dazed, Nick reached for her hand. At the last moment, she turned it so that her thumb rested above his. Beneath her veil, she smiled.

That small victorious smile brought him abruptly to earth. He rearranged their hands, setting his thumb above hers.

The minister's words became a backdrop to a discreet test of wills as she attempted to reverse the clasp and Nick retained control. He glimpsed one satin-clad foot emerging from her ivory hem and stretching ahead. He blocked it with his own while gazing tenderly into her veiled face.

Lyris told herself the words she repeated were not supposed to matter. Yet her voice sounded tremulous. Drake's eyes glowed more brilliantly than she had yet seen them.

He repeated the vows in a firm if husky voice. His black frock coat flattered his dark good looks and emphasized his remarkable eyes. His foot intercepted hers as once again she edged forward. The minister subtly stepped back.

As Lyris repeated vows she didn't intend to keep, she felt she was falling like the storied Alice, with no idea where she would land. Hoping to catch Nicholas off guard, she shifted her hand to bring her thumb above his, dared him with her eyes, and at the same time scooted her foot ahead.

Again, he blocked her. The flower girl giggled. Lyris became aware of the fascinated attention of their attendants. The minister's brows arched in obvious confusion. Feeling her face heat, she brought an end to her not-so-subtle manipulation. Brunswich handed a gold band to the groom.

As Nick relinquished his bride's hand to accept the ring, he recognized her embarrassment over a tussle that should have been kept private. Tenderness swelled through him as he held the gold wedding band above her delicate fingers. God, she was beautiful. He wanted to take her away from all these people, to get her alone where he could cover her with kisses—and with savage pride, he reminded himself that he would not touch her until she invited his caress.

Touching the ring to each of her fingertips, he repeated the minister's words. "With this ring, I thee wed, and this gold I thee give, and with my body I thee worship."

With his body. He had to stop to swallow. The image was too intense. He thought of struggling with her outside Castor's studio and, later, holding her in his office. Ahead lay greater promise.

Her eyes became unfathomable beneath the veil. He forced himself to finish. "With all my worldly chattels I thee endow."

He placed the ring over her third finger and heard the minister's heartfelt, "Amen."

"You may kiss the bride." The minister's words sent panic flaring through Lyris. Nicholas Drake had just, however unwillingly, pledged his life and fortune to her. She scarcely noticed Reba lift the veil. She was having trouble enough focusing on her new husband—*husband!*—to notice anything else.

Drake bent toward her. His lips brushed hers, then pressed harder, claiming control as surely as he had when his foot thwarted her own. Lyris reacted instinctively, kissing him back with as much force as she could manage. He wrapped his arms about her. She pressed closer.

A murmur of voices and the minister's cleared throat brought her to earth. What was she doing? There wasn't even a superstition about gaining influence through the force of the kiss, so far as she knew. She felt her cheeks heat as she pulled away. Drake looked amused.

Music swelled. Her friends surged forward to wish her happiness. Many of the women shed sentimental tears, Mama especially, but Lyris saw that many also questioned the marriage. Evelyn was not the only one who thought she had grasped at what might be her last opportunity to take a husband.

Lyris knew that Nicholas was aware of those unflattering thoughts. He kept one hand possessively at her waist. After a head-spinning flurry of good wishes and kisses, they were led to a linen-draped table where banks of roses surrounded a many-tiered cake lavished with sugar bells and birds.

Drake steadied Lyris's hand while she cut the first slice, then offered him the traditional first bite. He looked wary, but she was not about to entertain their guests by making a public display of their private combat. They had done more than enough of that with their kiss.

The flower girl wandered by, carefully balancing a glass of water. "May I have a sip?" Lyris asked, snatching the glass from the startled child.

Drake took it from her. "Water, my sweet? The occasion calls for champagne." Placing a crystal flute in her hand, he returned the glass to the girl.

Toasts were offered, the first by Jon Brunswich, his words florid and more than slightly ribald. Reba nearly overran the younger women waiting to catch the bouquet and succeeded in filling her arms with flying white roses and lace.

As the afternoon wove into early evening, the reception swirled around them. Friends offered more toasts and kisses. Everyone had advice. A wedding supper was served. Lyris had eaten little all day. Her head spun from the steady attention and the champagne.

She reached with relief and not a little triumph for a crystal water glass near her plate. After the first startled swallow, she nearly spit it out. Champagne! Her husband's amused expression told her he was ahead of her.

While she glared, he deliberately picked up his own crystal tumbler, offered a silent salute and drank.

As the night garden became a candlelit fairyland, her mother drew Lyris aside to speak in private. Despite her troubled expression, Lyris wasn't prepared for her words. "Darling, I haven't had a chance to tell you. We've received a letter from Amelia."

Lyris looked swiftly toward her husband, who stood in the garden talking with Brunswich and a few other men, one of whom clapped him soundly on the shoulder. Even so, she lowered her voice almost to a whisper. "Was Amelia very hurt that her gift was returned?"

"Not hurt, but concerned. Edwin was a difficult man. I believe she fears you have begun just such a marriage for yourself."

Of course she would think that. "I'll write at once to reassure her."

Her mother looked as if she thought any reassurance would be self-delusion on Lyris's part. "You may have the opportunity to tell her in person, dear. Her letter states that she is not getting along with Edwin's sister and misses her friends. She is thinking of returning to Seattle."

Lyris felt the ground sway beneath her. She braced one hand against the nearest table. Her glance flashed to Drake, then back to her mother. "Return! When?"

"I have no idea, but you know your godmother. When Amelia decides on a plan, she carries it through." Her mother looked more closely into Lyris's face. "You've become exceedingly pale, darling. Had you better sit down?"

Lyris reached for her mother's hand. "Promise me you will say nothing to Nicholas. He...feels the house still bears her presence and is uncomfortable with it. I must find the right time to tell him that she may return."

She was already playing the role of protective wife, she thought with some amazement. Yet whatever wrong Amelia had done to Drake, it was rooted deeply and Lyris would not expose his private pain.

If Amelia returned to Seattle, she would expect to be welcomed. Again, Lyris felt the ground reel. Perhaps it was fortunate that Drake had sent back the wedding gift. Her godmother would surely be discreet before making any contact.

Chapter Ten

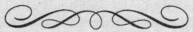

Drake rejoined her, looking concerned. "Your radiance has dimmed. Tired, love?"

Tired, no. Stunned, worried, tumbling once more down Alice's rabbit hole—all that, yes. But she wasn't his love. She answered with a low-voiced warning, "Living a lie does wear one down."

His brows lifted, but he said only, "I'll order the carriage."

The gold band on her finger felt like a millstone. Soon they would be alone to begin their sham of a marriage. Could she trust him? She had to believe so, but felt shaken with the realization that she had on this day placed herself legally under his control.

The moment the carriage was ordered, silver bowls filled with uncooked rice passed from hand to hand. Lyris and Drake rushed through a shower of grains.

A thud on the carriage roof announced that her father had thrown one of her shoes, symbolically relinquishing authority for her to Drake. And ultimately, Lyris vowed, into her own hands.

Her skirt billowed about the enclosed carriage and over Drake's knees. He smoothed a fold between his fingers, then looked at her cryptically. "Well, Lyris. We begin."

She answered with caution. "It was a lovely ceremony. So many guests!"

"All of them curious to see the commoner whose name you were desperate enough to accept."

She decided to ignore that. It was true, after all. "I missed Gram." She fingered the gold-edged veil. "This belonged to her. How I wish she could have been here."

He touched her hand, his fingers surprisingly gentle. "She was. Didn't you feel her presence?"

More moved than she wanted to admit, Lyris put up a barrier. "Then only my godmother missed seeing me wed."

The momentary truce ended. Quietly, he said, "I'm not an unreasonable man, but I insist you accept my restrictions against that woman."

What on earth could Amelia have done to him? He must have seen the question in her eyes. As if in answer to her thoughts, he said flatly, "The matter is settled. The subject is closed."

The subject was not closed at all, she thought rebelliously while the carriage rumbled through the darkness.

Drake insisted on carrying her over the threshold. "Since you're uncommonly obedient to custom." She resisted an urge to cling. It would be comforting to nestle against him, to stop feeling as if at every minute she must keep her guard up and her thoughts ranging ahead like scouts anticipating the next skirmish.

The housekeeper was a large woman with a no-nonsense air until she smiled. Then she radiated warmth like one of the porcelain stoves. Mrs. Ramsey had been recommended by one of Mama's closest friends. If she was surprised they had chosen to spend the first night of their marriage in their own home, she succeeded in hiding it. With a broad smile, she said, "Jenny has your things all unpacked for you, ma'am."

Lyris thanked her, trying to sound authoritative while being set on her feet in billowing satin and lace. Mrs. Ramsey beamed before adding, "Two of your friends stopped by earlier, Mrs. Drake. They left a gift in your bedchamber."

Evelyn and Reba had mysteriously disappeared for a time. Feeling apprehensive, Lyris turned to Drake. "I believe I'll go on upstairs."

Gallantly, he raised one of her hands and kissed her palm. "Of course, love. I'll check the fires and dismiss the staff."

With her train billowing behind, Lyris hurried up to the room that had been her godmother's. At once, childhood memories crowded.

She glanced through an open door into a moonlit room that overlooked the back garden. This had been hers when she stayed overnight here. Now it held ruffles and lace and a profusion of china dolls in preparation for another young girl.

Fanny was to arrive any day. As, perhaps, would Amelia. Lyris felt her world closing in as she hurried to the chamber that would be hers—one that adjoined the room occupied by her husband. Her eyes flew to their mutual door, mercifully closed.

Cautiously, she tried the knob. Unlocked. Her heart skipped a beat. Cracking the door open, she peered into a large room with massive furniture, mostly in shadow. The only light was from a stove at one side.

One of Edwin's additions had been a turret in a corner of this room, with stairs leading to the street. He preferred to come and go without passing through what he termed "the nuisance of the household."

Backing into her own room, Lyris pulled the door tight. Here she felt more at home. A coal fire burned cheerfully behind the windows of a delicate porcelain stove. Her gown spread an ivory glow above the pale blue Oriental carpet as she gazed from the half-tester bed to an enormous oak armoire, and near it, an oval mirror suspended in a rosewood frame.

Lace curtains embraced a bay window. Lyris perched there for a moment, remembering the many times Amelia had settled nearby, reading from books of fairy tales.

Her glance kept returning to that unlocked door. She clenched her fingers in the curtains, trying to quiet jumpy nerves. An exquisitely wrapped box on the dressing table drew her eyes. Thankful for the distraction, she slipped a card from the small envelope on top. Reba and Evelyn wished her "a romantic wedding night."

How little they knew. Parting the folds of tissue paper, she discovered a delicate nightdress of the sheerest possible crepe de chine, trimmed with lace and satin roses.

She held it before her, marveling over the exquisite stitching—surely, French work—then became breathlessly aware of the door opening from the adjoining room. Drake said approvingly, "I hope that's for my benefit."

Lyris crumpled the gown into the box. "You know it is not."

"Too bad." He leaned against the doorjamb, coatless, his dazzling white shirt contrasting with the bronze tan of his skin. He looked dashing. He looked dangerous. He sounded dangerous. "You were a beautiful bride, Mrs. Drake."

She caught her breath sharply. "You claim to be a man of honor. Our arrangement..."

His smile became rueful. "Don't look so frightened, sweet. I'm on my way out. I'll use the tower stairs, so the servants won't have cause for gossip."

Out? Where? To a mistress? She refused to ask. Proudly, she asked, "Is there a key to this door?"

"I'm ahead of you." He held an ornamental brass key on his palm. "And no more eager than you to have my rest disturbed." Stepping inside, he closed and locked the door.

"You are on the wrong side," Lyris said.

He gazed at her somberly. "Sweet wife, I have not yet sunk so low as to force myself on an unwilling woman."

She felt a hot blush spread upward through her throat and face. For hours, she had braced herself to reject him. She had not anticipated his rejecting her. When he offered the key, she took it with stiff dignity.

In the same moment, a tap sounded at the hallway door. Nicholas admitted Jenny, then said to Lyris, "You apparently have everything you need."

His pained expression lent a deeper meaning to his words. Lyris answered in a level tone, "Not quite. You may bring the portrait when you return."

His smile showed a flash of white teeth. "Not yet, sweetheart." After a glance toward the crumpled gown in its box, he sauntered into the hall.

Lyris concealed the key in her palm to avoid her maid's curiosity. She would sleep more comfortably with that door locked. She believed Drake to be a man of his word. But he was a man. And legally, her husband.

With Jenny's help, Lyris was out of the wedding finery much more quickly than she had been put into it. The maid lifted the sheer nightgown from its box, murmuring approval. Lyris nearly told her to repack it, but remembered again the gossiping grapevine.

Drake was not only an honorable man, he had tremendous pride. She would not humble him by having it known all over town that his new bride refused to dress appropriately on the first night of their marriage.

The gown fit as if made for her. Her skin glowed through the sheer fabric. How disappointed Evelyn and Reba would be to know that no one other than herself and Jenny would ever see her in it.

After dismissing the maid, Lyris brushed her hair, began to braid it, then realized that might raise questions in Jenny's mind tomorrow. She knew, too, that she was postponing the moment when she would climb into Amelia Chambers's bed. It was hers now. She was mistress of the household and must behave as such.

After setting the brush firmly on the dressing table, she crossed the carpet to the elegant half tester. The polished rosewood frame cradled a lavish down-filled comforter between heavily carved head- and footboards. Pillars at the upper end supported the half tester, a rosette of white silk.

"I suppose you're expecting Amelia," she murmured to the bed, then claimed ownership by dropping firmly onto the middle. A jangling crash of cowbells sent her flying to her feet. Her heart jangled an echo.

Behind her, the door banged open. "Lyris? What...?"

"Bells." The absurdity of it brought laughter bubbling. She tried to choke it back. "Reba. And Evelyn. They brought more than..."

She broke off, abruptly aware that she was wearing her friends' other gift, a remarkably sheer one; realizing also that Drake had retained a key to the door. With a gasp, she leapt into bed and pulled the comforter around herself. The cowbells jangled merrily from under the springs.

Drake had stopped just inside her room. Ambling to the bed, he looked lazily into her widened eyes. "You may have trouble sleeping through all that, my sweet. Not to mention raising the lusty speculation of your staff whenever you move."

Nervously she twisted her ring. "I don't suppose you would..."

"Crawl under your bed and remove the bells?"

"Please?"

He reached out one hand to stroke her bare shoulder. She had never in her life guessed that her skin could respond in so intense a fashion. Swallowing against a sunburst of unwanted sensation, she clutched the comforter. The bells clattered. Nicholas's hand felt very warm as he stroked the curve of her throat. Beneath it, her skin seemed to vibrate. She gulped again and he stepped back. "I'll do what I can."

She edged to the far side of the bed, dragging the comforter with her, pretending she didn't miss his touch while he stretched out on his back and eased beneath the bed. The bells jangled and he said, "Stop moving around, will you?"

"Sorry." Laughter bubbled up and she pressed her face into her hands while her body shook and the cowbells clanged.

"What in blazes are you doing?"

"I'm sorry." She gasped for breath. "I just remembered a spinster aunt who is always worrying she will someday find a man beneath her bed."

"Very funny."

She heard a bell drop to the floor and leaned over the side as he tossed it out onto the carpet. "How many are there?"

"Five. You have ribald friends." Another bell rolled out. "With excellent taste in nightwear."

She felt her face heat. Why hadn't she put out the lamp before climbing into bed? "I thought you had gone."

"I was about to when a herd of cows began stomping around in here." He tossed a third bell noisily against the first.

"Is there an insult in your remark?"

"Are you angling for a compliment in *yours?*"

"Certainly not!" She sat straighter. "You didn't mention a second key."

"For use in emergencies. Such as this." He eased from under the bed with the last two bells in his hands and tossed them with the others. "You deserve compliments, sweetheart. You were exquisite in your bridal gown. You are even more exquisite out of it."

Pointedly, she asked, "Are those the last of the bells?"

"I'm not sure." Amusement flickered in his eyes. "Bounce a bit to see if I have them all."

He was probably making fun of her, but she jiggled the mattress just the same. "I don't hear anything."

"Maybe it takes more weight." He pulled off his shoes and stretched out beside her.

"Mr. Drake," she said carefully.

"Nick," he corrected, adding, "Comfortable bed. The old lady pampered herself. Do you suppose they ever used that mutual door?"

"I have no idea!" Lyris felt shocked to even think of an intimate side to her friends' lives. She wanted to discuss Amelia with him, but not in that way.

"They must have, once at least," he mused. "Since they managed to produce a daughter."

She stared at him. "You're mistaken. The Chambers had no children."

His entire body stiffened. Then he sat up in a single lithe movement. His eyes glowed as if suddenly realizing that he himself had introduced the forbidden subject. "Why are we talking about them?" he demanded roughly. "Let's talk about us."

"There is nothing to say about us, except that we have an agreement and will follow it to the letter."

"My sweet," Nick warned, "if you clutch that coverlet any tighter, feathers will fly all over the room." He leaned toward her. She tried to scoot backward, but he put one hand on her nearest shoulder and pressed her onto the pillow.

She struggled to sit up. He held her trapped beneath his arm and, lying close beside her with the comforter between them, blew softly against her throat. "Will you write the details of our wedding for the *Tribune?*"

"Of course," she said, trying to deny sensations that skittered along her nerves with his breath. "I write of all the society weddings for Mr. Brunswich."

Drake's fingers played across her skin, making her both heated and shivery. "How will you describe this particular embattled couple?"

She wished he were not quite so close and yet, perversely, wanted him to stay at least a little longer. "Surely you mean loving couple, Mr. Drake. All wedding stories describe loving couples."

He laughed softly, his breath again brushing her throat. "So loving that this pair nearly crushed one another's hands?"

"Bridal nerves," she murmured, trying to order her thoughts enough to compose a sentence for the *Tribune.* "'Guests of the Lowell-Drake wedding felt romantically moved to see the loving couple clasp each other tightly throughout the ceremony.' ''

If there had been bells beneath the bed, his laughter would have rocked them all. ''And of the kiss that caused the minister to clear his throat?''

''Umm . . .'' Her thoughts fled. He was far too near to be reminding her of kisses. She knew she must send him away, ought never to have allowed him in her room, much less on her bed.

''I knew it,'' he said with triumph. ''You have no words to describe that part of the ceremony.''

Stung, she replied, ''Of course I do. 'The newly married Mr. and Mrs. Drake celebrated their vows with an enthusiastic kiss before accepting the good wishes of their guests.' ''

''Enthusiastic kiss,'' he repeated, his gaze fixed on her lips. ''I like the sound of that.''

She looked away. Breathing was becoming difficult, especially when every breath brought a faint scent of clean male skin. ''Mr. Drake, we have an agreement!''

''Such a pretty parrot,'' he murmured. ''Is that all you can say?'' His fingers traveled up her throat to her chin. His thumb traced the outline of her lips. She clamped them together against tantalizing sensations.

He chuckled. ''You surprise me, sweet. I expected to be bitten.''

''Get off my bed! Please.''

''Surely I deserve a kiss for ridding you of the bells.'' He didn't give her time to answer before lowering his mouth to hers. His lips were as warm as she remembered, their pressure as insistent and as irresistible.

She wondered who was waiting for him in town. Someone voluptuous, no doubt. Someone who enjoyed his kisses. Someone . . . She lost the thread of her thoughts as his warm mouth caressed the curve of her throat, then trailed sparks over the silken rise of her breasts.

Somehow, her fingers found their way into the soft thick hair at the back of his head. A bewitching lethargy came over her. She wanted him to keep kissing her, to keep stroking her bare skin in that tantalizing way.

From deep inside her head, an alarm began to sound. Kissing led to lovemaking, and lovemaking to babies, and babies to... "No!" she exclaimed, wrenching away. "I won't be trapped for life with a saloon keeper."

He looked as if she had slapped him, and then, briefly, as if he might slap her. She was appalled by her words, but certain of the awful need to say them.

Swinging off the bed, he grabbed his shoes and strode from the room, leaving the adjoining door wide open. Seconds later, she heard his footsteps rapidly descend through the tower to the street.

Toward that willing mistress, she thought, with envy she tried to ignore. Slipping to the carpet, she crossed the room, removed the key from his side of the door, closed and locked it. Her emotions rolled about like croquet balls.

Ridiculous! She couldn't be starting to care for the wretched man. That was not a part of her plan. One of the cowbells lay near her foot. She gave it a hefty kick, sending it clanging into the others.

On the stairs, Nick stopped abruptly at a savage clatter of cowbells. Then he smiled with dark satisfaction, pulled on his hat and headed into the night.

By the time he reached the wharf, he had walked off most of his frustration. Still, the lively saloon did not appeal to him. He didn't want drinks and music and laughter, particularly when his presence there on his wedding night would direct the laughter toward him. He wanted his soft, fragrant wife in his arms.

He walked a block farther, onto planked piers that held the railroad line, where he stood looking out over the dark bay. Waves washed in cold slaps against the pilings. Timbers and ropes on nearby ships creaked.

He tried to think of business problems, of the ruined streets and the present system of financing repairs. His thoughts kept spinning back to his wife.

"Marry for position, not love," a friend had once advised. "A man can always find love away from home."

On the other hand, Jon Brunswich was completely besotted with his pretty wife—witness all those cloying sentiments and flowers. Envy twisted. Turning abruptly, he strode toward his saloon, changed his mind at the thought of ribald humor and paced alone through the dark streets.

Chapter Eleven

Drake hadn't come home last night. Lyris heard it in the silence inside his room when she pressed her ear to his door. She imagined it in the faces of the servants when she came downstairs, after forcing herself to wait until a decent hour of the morning before summoning her maid to help her dress.

Mrs. Ramsey bustled forward, making a fine pretense of having seen nothing out of the ordinary. "Good morning, ma'am."

Lyris greeted her serenely. "Please have a breakfast tray sent to the garden room. Mr. Drake has had an urgent message from his place of business and will not be free to join me this morning."

She didn't miss a glimmer of relieved sympathy behind the woman's eyes. The rest of the staff would soon learn that their whispered concerns for their positions were misplaced.

The flood of sunlight into the glass-enclosed porch where she had chosen to breakfast failed to cheer her. She forced herself to chew and swallow, but the flaky pastries and crisp bacon seemed tasteless.

Her mind was too filled with the image of Nicholas held fast in the arms of a rosy blonde whose vivid charms matched a careless nature. Men appreciated blonde hair and plump arms—and careless natures—or so she understood.

Suppose he never returned? Giving up on breakfast, she walked restlessly into the parlor. Of course he would return. Nothing had changed between them. She was to be mistress of his elegant home and prepare his sister for society. Neither planned nor wanted anything more. It was absolutely ridiculous to feel cheated.

Besides, she had ample chores to keep her busy and should be thankful that entertaining Nicholas Drake was not among them. After an hour with Mrs. Ramsey, Lyris seated herself purposefully before Amelia's scrolled rosewood desk. For a moment, she toyed with a box of engraved thank-you notes, then rebelliously put them aside. Finding paper and pen, she began recreating the details of her exquisite garden wedding.

Nick woke in a foul mood in the quarters behind his office at the Golden Harbor. This was the first day of his marriage, the groom's day. Irony enough in that, considering that his bride wanted nothing to do with her groom. He had walked alone for hours, finally letting himself into the saloon well after his bartender locked up for the night. If people were surprised to see him this morning, they could damned well keep it to themselves.

As he pulled work pants and a sweater from a trunk, he tried to come to terms with the situation. Lyris's candor attracted him as much as her beauty, but he could not have her continuously flogging him with his background.

Slapping lather onto his night's growth of stubble, he muttered in frustration, "Blast it all, I am master of the house."

A cynical voice at the back of his head asked why, then, was he sleeping in a saloon?

Letting her deal with the curiosity of the staff, he answered bitterly. She was likely paying for her cutting words with embarrassment. He had no doubt she was capable of putting the servants' questions to rest, however.

He shaved with swift, firm strokes, thinking of his parents. His mother had never corrected her husband's rough behavior before their children. Nick doubted that she'd done so when they were alone. When his father drowned, his mother's life had ended.

Nick didn't expect Lyris to fall so dizzily in love that she couldn't face life without him. But he did want respect. He slammed a towel onto the stand, determined to settle the matter once and for all.

When he reached home, he located his bride in the parlor, bent intently over her desk. For a moment he remained unnoticed in the doorway, held despite himself by the way light from a nearby window fell over her, adding a blush of rose to her cheek. She had pulled her hair into a cluster of curls at the crown of her head. As she leaned forward, loose tendrils played across her cheek, obscuring, then revealing her delicate profile.

Catching himself with a sharp reminder of his purpose, he forced a neutral tone. "Good morning, madam."

She looked up with a start of relief and welcome, which changed at once to a frown. "Is it? *I* have not been out."

He hid a smile at the rebuke and wondered again if she had had a devil of a time convincing the servants that all was in order. Casually, he strolled across the room.

Her stiff posture suggested armor, and her level tone threw down a gauntlet. "We will begin again, Mr. Drake, with neither apology nor recrimination. And we will both remember our agreement."

He met her fierce gaze for a long moment, then nodded, holding his own conditions in reserve. Apparently satisfied, she sat even straighter. "Now, another matter. There are keys to all the interior doors of this house except for one that closes off a section of the attic. That one has been locked since I was a child."

He shrugged. "It can't be important."

"It is to me. I've wondered for years what may lie behind that door!"

This was hardly the conversation he had expected to hold. Impatient with it, he said, "You'll find the key when you've had time to search."

"The competent Mrs. Ramsey has already searched," Lyris countered. "The key is missing."

The locked attic was curiously important to her. Nick watched his bride's expressive features reveal her childhood curiosity and tried to suppress resentment. She had been denied access to one room. He had been denied the entire house.

Still, it wasn't fair to blame her. "Do you suppose a mad aunt is trapped up there?"

"If so," Lyris said, "she has certainly expired by now." She leaned back to look at him. "I don't care for mysteries within my own home. I want you to break through that door."

Nick leaned closer to her, one elbow braced against the high secretary. "There are many things I don't care for in my home."

Wariness shadowed her eyes. Casually, he picked up a paper covered with graceful pen strokes. A glance showed it to be an account of their wedding. The path opened through which he might assert himself. "Now that we're married, you won't be writing for the newspaper."

She shot to her feet, snatching at the page while he held it from her. "Not write! What are you saying?"

"Do your married friends draw wages in the common workplace?"

"This is different."

"Different, Lyris? I understood our agreement was to elevate my position, not lower yours."

"You lowered mine by marrying me!" Her eyes widened as if the words had burst out, and too late, she wished them back.

"I don't believe you are naturally cruel," Nick said quietly. "Can you be afraid of discovering that I'm not the clod you paint me as—for fear of melting into my arms?"

"That will never happen!" Lyris grasped the edge of the desk to keep from snatching at the work that had taken all morning to complete.

Drake was dressed more casually than she had ever seen him and the clothing added to his usual air of danger. The close-fitting trousers emphasized muscles gained by hard, physical labor. In his heavy fisherman's sweater, he could pass for one of the workmen on the docks. And she had married him!

Yet Nicholas had worn his formal wear as if born to fine clothes. She appealed to the need in him to be accepted among gentlemen. "If mention of our wedding does not appear in the paper, we will slide even lower in society."

Nick considered. He had seen barmaids listen avidly while one of their number, more schooled than the rest, read details of society weddings. No doubt ladies in the grand homes consumed those stories as eagerly.

"All right. I'll take this to Brunswich and explain that it will be your last piece for him."

"*You* will take it!" Lyris exclaimed. "I see. As I am now your chattel, you have every right to my story and to the payment it earns."

If all his possessions were as difficult to control, he would be cursed with poverty. Mildly, Nick said, "I have no interest in your pin money."

"Exactly. Pen money. Competently earned."

"You have a quick way with words." He wanted to touch her, to lift her hair and kiss the heated skin of her throat. A pulse throbbed beneath the open lace of her collar. He longed to taste her there and feel her breathless response. He buried temptation beneath an inflexible tone. "You may well make a career as a journalist when we have divorced. Until then, you will fulfill the responsibilities of an obedient wife."

She drew in a breath to argue, but he cut her off. "You will support me in public and refrain from insulting me in private. As you yourself have pointed out, servants soon discover all that goes on in a home.''

Lyris twisted the ring on her third finger, a gesture that was quickly becoming a habit. "Very well, Mr. Drake. And you will play the role of an obliging husband. You may begin by opening that locked room."

She was remarkably set on that attic door. "Have you tried peering through the keyhole?" he asked.

Pride gave way to a rush of eager curiosity. "It's as dark as coal inside. Let us go at once."

Amusement nearly forced a smile. He held it back. "Curb your impatience, madam. The door has been locked for years. It will wait awhile longer."

Lyris bit off an argument that might cause him to leave the room locked forever. "Very well, but I had thought you to be more curious."

"And I thought you to be more adult." He paused, recognizing a second opportunity to declare authority. Her hope of his becoming an "obliging husband" had not struck him well. "For the strength of your developing character, sweet wife, we'll leave the question of the attic until I decide it's time."

"When *you* decide!" She reached toward him.

He stepped back. "I suggest you spend the intervening days in learning to check your usual headlong manner."

"You are too hard."

"Be careful, Lyris. The room may contain the remains of a difficult first wife."

He was joking. Wasn't he? She knew so little about him. For all she knew, the words might hold a warning.

"As for the door between our bedchambers," he added tersely, "you can stop worrying. I mean to have my things moved to a room across the house."

"The servants . . ." she began.

"Hang the servants." He folded her carefully written account of their wedding and placed it in a pocket. "Tell them

I want some distance from my younger sister, who will arrive any day.''

Lyris felt her temper rise. She certainly didn't want him in
the next bedchamber, but his decision to remove himself
rankled. She possessed both keys. Did he think she meant
to harass him? ''That's very considerate, Mr. Drake. I'll no
longer be disturbed when you leave the house for your
plump mistress at the saloon.''

''My what?''

She tossed her head, her eyes filling with fire. One of Jon
Brunswich's folk warnings flashed through Nick's mind:
kiss your wife when she's angry or she will be kissing another man before the year is out.

The devil she would. With a long step forward, he caught
her into his arms and pressed his mouth over her startled
lips. She felt soft and supple, as if he could mold her to suit
him once the fight went out of her.

And as he deepened the kiss, he learned it was true. Her
lips yielded beneath his. Her breasts and hips seemed to melt
into him. She wasn't armored with stays beneath her thin tea
gown. Her sweet body fit warmly against him, stirring a
rush of passion.

He couldn't get enough of kissing her, and kissing her was
not enough. Abruptly, he remembered that when her head
was clear, she considered his kisses degrading.

With an effort, he drew back. Lyris looked dazed, but her
eyes soon came into focus. As he expected, she gathered
herself as if shuttering doors and windows against a storm
that had taken her by surprise. She defended her response
by muttering, ''I see why she welcomes you.''

''There is no mistress.'' Her glint of satisfaction made him
add quickly, ''But if there should be, madam, she would not
be your concern.''

That statement brought the fire back to her eyes. Did she
expect him to remain celibate? ''As for the newspaper,'' he
said, ''I do not expect to see your name in further issues.''

Outrage flared in her face. "Journalism is my future. I need to hone my skills."

"It's not your immediate future. Give me your word."

He watched her struggle before accepting the inevitable. Lowering mutinous eyes, she said, "You will not see my name on any more stories."

"Then we understand each other."

"We understand each other very well."

Lyris managed to swallow biting words while her obstinate husband strode from the room. Drake was utterly unreasonable. After only a few hours of marriage, he had become as demanding as Papa or Edwin Chambers, men who had crushed their wives' spirits.

That wouldn't happen to her. She rubbed her hand across her lips, trying to rid herself of his kiss. She could scarcely wait to become independent of the wretch.

Chapter Twelve

"Drake is a beast," Reba exclaimed, while Evelyn shifted closer and lowered her voice as if the red-breasted robin plucking at the lawn nearby might repeat her words. "But Lyris, do you *dare* oppose your husband?"

The three of them perched on iron lawn chairs beneath head-high azaleas in a sunny corner of Lyris's garden. While all but ignoring a tray of tea cakes and fresh fruit, they devoured Nicholas Drake's black character. Five days had passed since he'd slammed his foot squarely over his wife's writing career.

That Lyris vowed to continue despite her husband's edict both excited and terrified her friends. Since journalism meant more to her than the marriage, Lyris not only had no qualms about what she was doing, she felt driven to continue.

Serenely, she poured the tea. "Mr. Drake practically ordered me to select a nom de plume." Well, she excused herself silently, he had said that he didn't want to see her name on any more stories. "Come now, both of you. Help me think of one."

Evelyn selected a grape from a silver dish. "You might sign your pieces as The Blushing Bride."

"She might as well use her name," Reba exclaimed, while Lyris said sharply, "I never blush!"

"Never?" Evelyn asked archly. "Mr. Drake must be less inventive than one would expect."

To Lyris's dismay, she immediately proved her lie with a furious blush. Severely, she said, "The idea is to conceal my identity, not offer hints. I'm thinking of something such as Without Suffrage or Under His Thumb."

Choking, Reba exclaimed, "You're writing social news, not political pieces. Be serious, Lyris. You need a pseudonym at once for a story on the Thompsons' musical evening on Sunday."

Startled, Lyris said, "I haven't heard of it." Richard Thompson's parents often staged musical evenings. She had always been invited in the past. "No doubt they feel it's too early in our marriage to intrude."

A shadow crossed Reba's face, while Evelyn looked as if she were uncharacteristically holding her tongue. Sensing a slight to her husband, one she had been trying to deny, Lyris asked, "You don't agree?"

Reba answered carefully, "I believe your husband and the younger Mr. Thompson have crossed swords. But never mind. I promise to give strict attention to the details of the evening and will tell you everything."

"So will I," Evelyn said promptly.

Lyris clapped her hands, the social rebuff losing its sting by providing a partial solution to her problem. "Perfect! If the first story under my pseudonym describes an event I haven't attended, Drake can't possibly accuse me of writing it."

Her friends glowed with relief. Thoughtfully, Reba said, "We must think of a name that identifies the author as on the inside of social doings, while not giving you away."

"I have it," Evelyn exclaimed. "The Crone in the Corner."

Moaning, Lyris covered her face with her hands.

"Would you read stories penned by such a creature?" Reba asked with scorn. She paused. "How about the crone's opposite, the Seattle Debutante?"

"That would conceal Lyris," Evelyn said. "She hasn't been a debutante for years and years."

Lyris agreed cheerfully. "And am thankful for it." She repeated the name, her lips quirking with amusement. "Seattle Debutante. I like it. It is so unlike me, it can't help but succeed."

"So long as Drake doesn't guess," Reba warned darkly.

Lyris grinned, feeling as if a cloud had lifted. "You judge him too harshly. Why, he never beats me twice in one day." At their horrified gasps, she exclaimed, "There, you see! You are ready to believe it, both of you. The logic in that sentence is that he has never beaten me at all and would not. Drake may be stubborn, but he is never cruel."

"He doesn't yet know you plan to continue writing for the newspaper." Evelyn plucked another grape from the dish and tossed it playfully at Lyris.

Lyris pitched it back, unintentionally bouncing it off her friend's white silk bosom.

With a shriek, Evelyn grasped an entire cluster of grapes and advanced on Lyris, who sprang laughing to her feet to take shelter behind Reba.

Nick paused at the entrance to the garden, smiling at the sight of his wife and her friends frolicking like schoolgirls. She must have overcome her disappointment to lark about like this.

He was finding marriage more satisfying than he had thought possible, although his wife kept him verbally at arm's length by refusing to use his given name. Still, it was good to come home after a day's work to Lyris's bright, quick nature. Her intelligence pleased him. She kept herself well versed in local and even world events, devouring news reports and asking remarkably perceptive questions.

It surprised him that she cared to use her sharp wit to write empty pieces about society, although in reviewing her past stories, he saw her clever touch. It made him wonder how she would handle an important issue, such as the deplorable condition of the downtown streets.

Was it wrong of him to halt her journalistic career? He shrugged the question aside. She was laughing with her friends as if she hadn't a care, no doubt relieved that the need to produce copy for Brunswich had been taken from her.

His father's advice on trolling for salmon came to mind. If you hauled in all the line at once, it would snap and the fish would escape. It was necessary to play your quarry, giving slack until the salmon thought itself free. When it forgot to struggle was the time to reel it closer.

The fight could last for hours, with the fish losing more strength with each battle. The fisherman was equally taxed, but that only deepened his satisfaction at the inevitable moment of triumph.

When he ordered his wife to stop writing, he had reeled the line tight. He allowed slack by indulging her questions about Seattle affairs. That he enjoyed her lively interest made it easy to oblige. The unsettling part came in wondering at times just which of them had swallowed the hook.

The game in the garden came to an abrupt end as the ladies spotted him. Nick strode forward, grasping for a wry comment to hide his pleasure in their frolic. "Where is the nursemaid, that you girls are allowed to spoil each other's frocks with a waste of good fruit?"

Their blushes matched the breast of the robin that flew up at his approach. Within minutes, he was alone with his wife.

"I shouldn't have told them that you beat me," she said.

"That I what!"

Her eyes sparkled. "How else could I explain why I have given up my writing career?"

Nick told himself it was time once again to reel in the slack.

Hours later, over dinner, he wondered if she had made a similar decision. Between correcting her staff on proper methods of serving the various courses, she cheerfully corrected him on the use of cutlery, making him feel like a lout off the docks.

With a scowl at his salad fork, which he had mistaken for one meant for the trout, Nick said, "Your Mr. Thompson is set on avoiding his share in the cost of improving the street."

"He is not *my* Mr. Thompson," Lyris protested.

Nick shrugged. "During the ball where we agreed to marry, he seemed quite taken with you."

"He is *taken* with Reba. I had long since lost his interest by commenting on his mustache."

Nick couldn't resist a grin. He wondered how she had offended the mustache Thompson so prized. "At any rate, the fellow flatly refuses to go along with other businessmen on accepting an assessment."

"Why should he?" Lyris asked crisply. "The sin tax pays it all." She tilted her head. "Mr. Drake, I'm afraid you are using your fruit knife to butter your bread."

He slapped the offending silver onto the table, holding his patience with an effort. "Thompson is claiming full advantage of the Yesler ruling of nine years ago."

"And what is that?" Lyris remembered her father roundly cursing one of the city's major property holders some years back. When she asked why, he'd simply said it wouldn't do to clutter her pretty head with matters of commerce.

Fortunately, her husband was willing to answer. "The fellow gained five-hundred-fold in property value when his street was regraded, but refused to pay his share."

"And the court agreed?" As interested as she was in the inner workings of the city, Lyris found herself more interested in the inner workings of her husband's mind. Did tradesmen naturally discuss business matters over the dinner table? Possibly Nicholas took her interest to mean she was accustomed to such talk. She wouldn't be the one to tell him otherwise.

He emphasized his answer with a stab of the bread knife. "The act that created the territory didn't authorize the legislature to incorporate cities. The supreme court ruled that, legally, Seattle doesn't exist. Therefore, it can't level assessments or taxes."

"Why does the Golden Harbor buy a license from a nonexistent city?"

"The police exist," Nick answered. "So does public opinion. If I refuse to pay, the Golden Harbor will go out of business. And as long as the so-called sin tax pays, Thompson refuses."

"I think you should run for a seat on the town council and see about correcting the situation." As he glanced up in surprise at her unexpected confidence in him, she added gently, "You are slicing the roast duck with the bread knife."

Nick hurled the implement aside. "Hell's teeth, woman, leave off. What is the sense in surrounding each plate with a barricade of cutlery?"

"If you expect to be welcome in the better homes, you must know which silver to use."

"I know enough to watch my host." He scattered all but a few utensils from around his plate. "In my own home, I prefer to use common sense."

Lyris lifted her shoulders in an expressive shrug. "Shall I instruct the servants to remove your wineglasses? Surely, a water goblet is sufficient."

"Be careful," he warned. "I may change my mind about opening that room in the attic after dinner tonight."

"Tonight!" Her face lit with excitement. Nick leaned back in satisfaction. He had skillfully reeled her in. She was on the verge of leaping straight into the boat.

Heat stirred inside him as he pictured her creamy skin glowing through the sheer material of her gown on their wedding night. He imagined peeling the lace away, inch by slow inch, while pressing kisses over her bared throat and breasts.

Candlelight flamed in her eyes as she leaned forward, her lips parted with excitement. She had never looked more delectable. Eagerly, she asked, "Will you chop down the door?"

Nick choked on his wine. "You are an aggressive little wench." He looked for the serving maid. "First, let us finish our meal."

Fearing that an argument would make Nicholas put off the opening even longer, Lyris directed the maid to serve the baked raspberry pudding. She held back her impatience by admiring her handsome husband. He had removed his tie and opened his collar above his green satin waistcoat, thus acquiring an air of indolence unseemly for the dinner table, but so devastatingly attractive she hadn't corrected him.

There were times when she caught herself regretting that the marriage was not to be taken seriously. She reminded herself of the joys ahead, when she would be free to manage her own life. Then she would write serious pieces. Perhaps she would travel. As she dreamed of prizes won and adventures taken, it was almost possible to forget that the cost of that future was an end to Nicholas's company.

At last he set his cup aside. With a careless smile, he drew a set of thin blades from a pocket of his waistcoat. "Did I ever mention that my grandfather Drake is a locksmith?"

How little she knew of his background. "Tell me now."

Nick was pleased by her interest, but personal information could become ammunition that her sharp mind might one day turn against him. So he balanced the tip of the blades against one palm, saying only, "I used to watch him at work. If he and my father had not prized honesty, I might have become a thief."

"Not you," she said, with a conviction that startled him.

"For that remark, my sweet, you have won access to the attic. Shall we go?"

Snatching a candle in a glass holder from the buffet, Lyris led the way. When they reached the attic, memories engulfed her. She knew every table and trunk. The big case with leather corners, for example, held a collection of hoopskirts that had once enchanted her. She remembered shaping a tent of dimity and steel and pretending to be a desert princess.

Fortunately, the exaggerated bustle that sprang so outlandishly into fashion in recent years was now joining the hoops and crinolines in women's attics. Drake grunted with satisfaction and she spun about. "Do you have it?"

He placed his hand on the knob. "Ask nicely."

As a child, it had been her habit to test that knob every time she came to this attic. She had imagined all manner of secrets hidden beyond. Now she felt that if she had to wait even one moment more, she would explode.

"Don't tease me," she exclaimed, grabbing his hand in an effort to hurry him. The contact was electric. She jerked her hand back and buried it in a fold of her skirt.

Nick smiled at his wife, tempted to hold her off even longer. Candlelight danced in her lively eyes and cast satiny glints in the thick swirls of her hair. Her breasts lifted beneath her shirtwaist, betraying her impatience and tempting him into forgetting all about the attic.

She had reclaimed her hand so swiftly he knew she had felt the same jolt that had shot through him. He longed to hold her, to feel that vibrant sensation spark throughout his body, and hers. There was probably nothing beyond the door but cast-off furniture. He would be sorry to see her disappointed, and wanted to prolong this moment of high anticipation.

Of course, there would be a lesson in the attic's mundane contents. Lyris had far too vivid an imagination. Disappointment might teach her to restrain it. As he let the pause draw itself out, exasperation edged her voice. "Will you open the blasted door!"

He laughed at her language and was tempted to demand a kiss. From the look in her eyes, she would deliver a punch. The moment had come. With a flourish, he turned the knob.

Holding her candle high, she rushed into the room, then stopped in surprise. "Why, it's all toys."

Ice coated Nick's stomach. Old longings sank sharp talons into his memory. Holding at bay the knowledge of what must lie ahead, he followed her into a crowded space with a vaulted roof and stale air. Beneath the musty smell of a room long enclosed lay a faint, haunting scent of spring violets.

His stunned glance took in a rocking horse near the door. A large dollhouse stood beside it. Beyond loomed a puppet theater the size of a lady's wardrobe. Years of dust grayed the velvet drapes. The room felt hushed and secret. Lyris was like a butterfly moving in delight from one discovery to the next. He felt as if he had entered his mother's grave.

As Lyris lit a set of candles discovered on a chest, a profusion of dolls came into focus, all with china heads and ruffled skirts. The room boasted a window, after all, a tall narrow one set into the slope of the roof, but so tightly shuttered that no light came through. A sleigh bed stood beside it, with an infant's wheeled wicker carriage turned upside down on the spread.

Why was the carriage here? By the time the Chambers had moved to Seattle, their daughter had been married for years and had a son of her own.

A ripple of music dragged his attention to Lyris, who had discovered a small clavier. Each note struck him like a glass splinter. His grandparents had kept every toy and piece of furniture their daughter ever possessed. Even her baby carriage.

He choked on a flood of emotion and hid it with a cough. Pretending to brush at dust motes, he stepped over boxes and dolls and shoved open the shutters to let in fresh air. As he groped for composure, Lyris came toward him towing a dusty wooden elephant on wheels. Wonder filled her voice. "You said they had a child. How did you know?"

He was not ready to trust his voice or to let her into his heart. As he turned away, his glance fell over a delicate wicker chair with a tufted satin cushion. Fresh pain jarred through him, making his teeth ache and his nerves become raw.

He could almost believe in ghosts, so clearly did he see Ivy Chambers seated here as a girl before she fell in love with Ethan Drake, before her comfortable world was torn from her and her parents turned their backs.

"She died," Lyris said softly. "She must have." Distracted by a box of paper dolls dressed in ribbons and lace, she didn't see his reaction, but continued wistfully, "Do you suppose she was lost to consumption? So many are. I wonder how old she was."

He wanted to silence her, to back out of the room and slam down the lock. But if he relocked the room, he would have to explain. That would bring pity. His pride held him back.

Sighing, Lyris closed the lid on the paper dolls. "Her death must have broken their hearts. They put all her things in here, then discarded the key."

She was drawing all the wrong conclusions, but Nick couldn't correct her. He clamped down on his rage, while bitterness left a metallic coat on his tongue. The devil take the old lady, he thought viciously. Most likely, her husband was already in Satan's bitter clutches.

The two of them had locked Ivy's things in, while they locked their daughter out. Her children as well. They pampered a patrician neighbor as their godchild. Pain from that old rejection took new strength from the sight of his mother's lost childhood.

He heard again Amelia Chambers's disgust when she found him in her garden. *How dare you speak to me?* As his soul rebelled, he fought against blaming Lyris. None of it was her fault. But she was mistaken in thinking their hearts were broken. That rotten pair didn't have hearts. It was their vanity his mother had damaged, and they'd never forgiven her.

"There aren't any pictures of her," Lyris murmured. "Not even in here." Her voice lifted suddenly. "Oh, look! Here is a name carved into a table by a young hand. *Ivy.* How pretty." Her eyes filled with moisture as she turned to him.

It incensed Nick that she was oblivious to his torrent of feelings, even though he struggled to conceal them. Lyris placed one hand on his arm, still turned inwardly to the tragedy she was mistakenly putting together. "Amelia and Edwin must have suffered so deeply, they tried to forget her very existence. Yet they couldn't bring themselves to dispose of her things."

Edwin knew their value, Nick thought acidly. Turning away from Lyris, he set the baby carriage on its wheels. It bounced lightly, although the springs had not seen oil in decades. Edwin and Amelia had spent lavishly on their daughter while she pleased them.

He had hoped a mundane storeroom would curb Lyris's vivid imagination. Instead, her fancy had taken new life. He burned to tell her she sounded like a foolish kitchen maid, that her iron-willed godparents were not saints, but demons. She was inscribing them with her own tender sentiments and it seared him to hear her.

To correct her would be to reveal himself. He had to remember that she meant to cast him off as readily as had his grandparents. All she wanted of him was that ill-made portrait and then a divorce.

He compressed his lips. It was crazy to feel that he still stood on the walk beyond the hedge, looking with longing toward the great house. It was his now. All of it. Even this locked room full of toys. As for the divorce, if he couldn't touch his grandmother's heart, how had he hoped to reach her goddaughter's?

It slowly occurred to Lyris that her husband had not said a word since opening the room. She had been too entranced to notice. Now he stood looking into a baby carriage as if it held his future.

She stilled a leap of her senses. If Nicholas Drake wished for a child, he would have to wait for a second marriage. She put out one hand and set the wooden horse rocking, wondering why she suddenly felt out of step with herself.

It occurred to her that his impoverished youth could not have allowed for toys such as these. Was he resentful of the mysterious Ivy's privileged childhood? Impulsively, she asked, "Were you happy as a child?"

For a moment, she thought he wouldn't answer. Then he said in a strained voice, "Happier than Fanny, I suppose." Selecting a volume bound in Moroccan leather, he hefted it briefly. "One of my strongest memories is of Fanny as a skinny six-year-old trying to balance a book like this on her head. Her playmates jeered at her for trying to walk like a highborn lady. When the book fell, Mother scolded her for scuffing the cover."

Swiftly, as if to excuse the mother he had obviously loved, he added, "The book was one of the few things she had brought from . . . brought to her marriage."

His cheeks were shadowed in the candlelight, the skin drawn tightly over the bones, leaving hollows beneath. When he raised his head, his intensity pierced her. "I didn't have much cash to spare, but as soon as I could, I sent an entire crate of books to Fanny."

Lyris placed one hand on his shoulder, deeply touched by the unexpected revelation. His muscles felt rigid, as if he was keeping his emotions under iron control. Gently, she said, "Now she will have all of this."

"Yes. She will." Satisfaction rang in his voice. "Fanny will have it, after all."

Even now, after discovering such tragedy, he resented Amelia. Lyris protested more sharply than she intended, "You sound as if you are taking from Amelia, rather than giving to your sister."

"Then you heard me right."

Loyalty to her godmother flared. "You are unnaturally cold."

She saw him draw in, as if preparing gladly for a fight. "Come, madam, the word you want is *common*."

Instinctively, Lyris snapped back, "The word I want is *unkind*. We've just seen the broken heart that Amelia has bravely concealed all these years. Yet you continue with your childish resentment of the wellborn."

"Try to curb your own childish trust," Nick said with venom. "You don't know a damned thing you're talking about."

For a moment, they glared at each other. Lyris felt helpless to stem the quarrel. They seemed to be arguing on two different levels. More than anger darkened her husband's face. Why had this collection of expensive toys and furniture caused such fury?

He glanced past her and his eyes became shuttered. Lyris saw that a maid had come timidly up the stairs. Shortly, she demanded, "What is it?"

"A telegram, ma'am. Just delivered." The girl blushed deeply when Nicholas stretched out his hand. After dropping the missive into it, she fled from the attic.

Lyris looked after her, then spun about at her husband's sudden curse. His eyes had become molten gold. "Why in blazes didn't they wire sooner?" He scowled as if Lyris were to blame. "My sister will arrive by train tonight. She may already be at the station."

Chapter Thirteen

Lyris started nervously as her husband rapped on the carriage roof. He shouted at the driver, "Can't you go any faster?"

She pulled her cape more closely about her. They had left at once for the station, without taking time to change into heavier clothing. One of the dolls from the attic lay blank eyed between them, as if puzzled to find itself in a carriage after years in a locked room.

She wondered if Fanny was bringing her favorite toys. Her clothing was probably inappropriate for her revised situation. Making a mental note to send for a seamstress, Lyris considered her friends' children and their current mode of dress.

"One train a day from Tacoma is damned stupid," Nicholas muttered, settling back. "Especially when it arrives at night."

Lyris murmured agreement, more concerned for Fanny than with the rivalry between rail barons that led to the present sorry state of transportation.

Nicholas tapped one fist nervously against his knee. "I can't think why in flaming hell we weren't notified sooner."

Lyris wondered if the child previously described as unruly had become even more so. She said only, "Someone may have canceled, making an earlier seat available."

Parting the side curtains, she saw they were rattling at a fast pace toward Railroad Avenue, built on piers over the bay. Fog rolled in from the sea, veiling the lampposts and muffling the sound of the horses. Through it came the wail of a train whistle.

As her husband stiffened, Lyris knotted her hands together, scarcely able to breathe. The train was already in the station. The poor child must think she was not being met. Nicholas swung from the carriage before it came to a complete stop. Lyris sprang after him. People hurried past, all looking thankful to have their journey ended.

The dark bulk of the steam engine pulsed nearby, exhaling hot grease and wood smoke. Billows of steam from the stack mingled with the fog. There was no sign of a confused young girl among the disembarking passengers. The only children in sight clung fiercely to their mother's skirts or were carried in their father's arms.

"Look in the station," Nicholas said crisply. "I'll check the cars. She may have fallen asleep."

As Lyris started away, he called after her. "She's eleven or twelve. Skinny. Brown hair. Eyes like mine."

Eyes like his? As she rushed toward the station door, Lyris mused that the boys now growing up in Seattle had better learn to guard their hearts.

Many couples met with kisses, but one pair made a spectacle of themselves. The young man's arms were beneath the girl's cape and he held her scandalously close. She made an effort to shield her face with her hood, but it slipped from her fingers. Raven curls swung against her shoulders.

The wanton intensity of the kiss was revealed to all who would see. Lyris clicked her tongue in disapproval, causing the young woman to turn her head.

Lyris had started past before her mind registered the gleam of amber eyes. A trick of the light, she told herself. She was looking for a child. Wrenching open the door, she cast a quick glance around the station. No forlorn little girl huddled on any of the wooden benches.

When she returned to the platform, she saw Nicholas step alone from the last railcar. She looked again at the romantic couple, this time noticing that the young man nuzzling the girl's tender throat wore the uniform of a train conductor.

Apprehension skittered down Lyris's spine. This girl was no twelve-year-old. The light from the station fell over a petulant mouth and, when she opened them, eyes very much like Nicholas Drake's. Stumbling over the memory of a room filled with ruffles and dolls, Lyris asked, "Fanny?"

The young conductor stepped backward, his face flushing with guilt. The girl stared at Lyris. "Who are you?"

"Your brother's wife."

"No, you're not."

Forcing a smile, Lyris said, "My name is Lyris."

The girl said firmly, "I don't know you. And my brother isn't married."

Obviously, he hadn't informed his grandparents. And he thought Fanny was eleven or twelve. This family needed a lesson in communication. "He is now," Lyris said. "And he's looking for you." She glanced toward the train, where Nicholas had stopped to talk with a station employee.

With a shriek, the girl dashed toward him, her loosened cloak billowing behind. "Nicky! I'm here!"

He staggered as she plummeted into him, then held her at arm's length and stared disbelievingly into her face. "Fan? How in blazes did you grow up so fast?"

She had grown up even faster than Nicholas guessed, Lyris told herself. There was no point in worrying him by mentioning that kiss. And now Fanny sparkled with the radiance of a young girl. "I had the chance for an earlier seat, so I took it. Gramma said you'd be upset. Are you?"

He shook his head, still looking bemused. "I'm thankful to see you safely arrived, but I was looking for a child, not a young woman."

Laughter rippled from her. "Nicky! You've been away too long. I'm fifteen."

His expression suggested a rapid mental rearrangement. Lyris was doing a great deal of that, herself. Suddenly remembering her, Nicholas reached out one hand and drew her closer. "Fanny, this is my wife, Lyris."

"Your wife!" Fanny set her fists on her hips as if to deny the fact. "Since when?"

People were watching with far too much interest. Lyris tugged at her husband's sleeve. "Fanny has had a long journey. Shall we continue this in the carriage?"

"Do you let her tell you what to do?" Fanny demanded. "I never thought you'd marry a nag."

Nicholas stiffened. "You're tired, but I expect you to apologize."

The girl made a mock curtsy. "Sorry, ma'am."

Lyris called on all her training to maintain a welcoming manner. With his brows drawn together, Nicholas clasped Fanny's arm and marched her toward his carriage. He must be thinking that he now had two unpredictable females on his hands. Lyris's brief amusement faded as she remembered she was to turn Fanny into a lady before the girl turned eighteen.

Nothing was the way Fanny had expected. She wondered when her stuck-up sister-in-law would tattle about catching her with the conductor. Once Nicky would have laughed. Not now, though. She knew from his hard grip on her arm that marriage had changed her brother.

Disappointment billowed up like steam from the engine. Nick was so much older, thirty-one now to her fifteen. He had always indulged her as if she were a kitten or a puppy. Of course, she hadn't seen him in years, but he sent money to buy her pretty things.

He worked hard. She knew that. It was why he didn't come to visit. That was all right. The harder he worked, the more freedom she expected to have. Gramma and Grampa practically chained her to the house. She was looking forward to staying with Nicky.

Now it was all changed, she told herself forlornly, thinking of the way his wife had clicked her tongue. That one would probably be worse than Gramma for setting down rules. Again Fanny wondered when her flirtation with the conductor would be trotted out for Nick's disapproval.

As her brother opened the door of a swank carriage, Fanny cast a quick glance at the woman he had married. She still couldn't believe he'd done that without telling the family. Maybe he didn't want them mingling with his fancy friends.

For the first time she wondered if he resented being stuck with her. Did he and his nasty wife sit up late talking about boarding schools and other ways to get her out of their lives?

Through burning eyes, she saw him take an elaborately dressed china doll from a seat in the carriage. A family was walking past, and without saying a word, he handed the doll to a little girl with braids. Regret stabbed Fanny. That doll had been meant for her.

As Nicholas placed Fanny's luggage in the back, Lyris settled in the carriage beside her sister-in-law. She offered a smile, but the girl turned away. Nicholas had said that her grandparents had despaired of coping with her. Lyris was beginning to understand why.

Still, Fanny must feel rejected, as if she'd been dumped on the brother whom she had not expected to find married. She had been genuinely glad to see him. Her rudeness surely stemmed from feeling unwanted. Sympathy surged through Lyris. Really, Nicholas should have warned Fanny that he was taking a wife. No doubt, he had hoped to avoid distressing his grandparents with the subsequent divorce.

Putting warmth into her voice, she said, "I hope we will become great friends, Fanny. There is a room prepared for you next to mine. It's set up at present for someone rather younger, but just today we discovered some furnishings in the attic that will do beautifully for you."

"So I'm to have castoffs," Fanny said as her brother climbed into the carriage.

"You're to have a decent tongue in your mouth," he answered curtly.

She turned on Lyris as if Nicholas's attitude were his wife's fault. "What do you mean, *your* room? Don't you sleep with Nicky?"

"Fanny!" he exclaimed. "If you can't mind your tongue, keep it silent."

"You've changed," Fanny cried. "I hope you didn't sacrifice your freedom to *her* just so you'd have someone to look out for me."

Lyris hoped the girl hadn't noticed her direct strike. Belatedly taking her brother's warning to heart, she curled into a forlorn knot in a corner of the carriage. She was showing the effects of her journey at last, her thick lashes drooping over her eyes.

Again, Lyris sympathized. Once the girl had the benefit of a night's rest, she might prove to be a more pleasant companion. She would surely be an interesting one. Nicholas rarely discussed his early years, but Fanny must know stories about his childhood.

Deciding to try again to make peace, she pressed the girl's arm, "We'll have some fabrics brought to the house tomorrow and a seamstress in to discuss fashion. Would you like that?"

Fanny pulled away. "You haven't seen the clothes I brought. How do you know they're wrong?"

The girl was even more sensitive to potential criticism than her brother. "You misunderstood me," Lyris said gently. "We want you to enjoy living in Seattle. Do you have any special interests, Fanny?"

The girl's slow smile added years to her age. "Yes," she said. "Men."

Her brother jerked forward as if kicked. "What in the devil do you mean by that?"

"Don't be stuffy," Fanny said. "I'm sure you kissed a lot of girls before you got tied to *her.* Why shouldn't I have my fun?"

It occurred to Lyris that Fanny had not yet called her by name. Apparently, that was a way of denying her authority. One more obstacle to be overcome.

The skin had pulled tightly over Nicholas's cheekbones. His voice was hard. "Listen, Fanny. While you live with me, you'll behave like a lady. That includes talking like one."

She tossed her head. "Gramma and Grampa didn't care. They said the sooner I found a boy I liked, the sooner I'd be out of their way."

Shocked, Lyris turned sharply to Nicholas. He looked as if he didn't believe the girl's charge. Was she a liar, as well as free with her favors?

Lyris couldn't hold back a sigh and Fanny turned smoldering eyes on her. "Your stuck-up wife can't wait to tell you about catching me kissing a conductor. As if I care. Why shouldn't I kiss him? He was smashing. Someday, when I get married, my husband will appreciate what I've learned."

Lyris caught her breath. The girl was pushing her brother much too far. What in heaven did she expect to gain by her outrageous behavior?

While Nick scolded again, Fanny picked at a loose thread in her wool skirt, refusing to listen. That seamstress would be told to work overtime. The bright colors and trims on the clothing in her trunks, which had looked so pretty at home, seemed garish now. She could see just by looking at Nick's wife that what she had chosen was all wrong.

She wondered how well Nicky lived. Both he and his wife looked like money. This carriage with its velvet cushions was the icing on the cake. It made her uncomfortable. If her brother was putting on airs, he would expect the same of her.

She almost wished she were back on the train. She'd had such great hopes then, all colored with memories of Nicky's rare visits, when he'd carried her about on his shoulders and bought her sweets and told her stories. Whenever Gramma or Grampa scolded, Nicky always laughed and said the years were making them stuffy. Soon he'd had them laughing, too.

Now he was the one who was stuffy. She felt as if the sunny world she'd expected was covered with clouds. Gramma said she talked too freely. Fanny knew she shouldn't have said some of those things to Nick and his perfect wife.

But if they thought she would just fade into the woodwork, they were wrong. She wasn't cut out to serve tea in china cups and chat with boring women. Grampa always said that if you wanted folks to know where you stood, you had to tell them.

Lulled by the rocking motion of the carriage, she curled into her corner. The inner fire of rebellion dimmed, but didn't go out. She wasn't sorry for anything she'd said. Nicky and Mrs. Perfect might as well know right now that she knew her own mind and wasn't about to be shaped into somebody's fancy idea of a debutante.

Chapter Fourteen

Nick stood outside his wife's bedchamber, steeling himself to disturb her. He ran a hand roughly through his hair, thinking that she couldn't be half as disturbed as he already was.

God, who would have expected Fanny to be nearly a grown woman? Not to mention unsettlingly pretty. And recklessly attracted to men. He groaned. How in hell was he to keep her under control? He was counting on Lyris for advice.

He stared down at the carpet, thinking of their return to the house. Fanny had dozed in the carriage, but had woken quickly enough when invited to step into her new home.

After a first wide-eyed moment, resistance replaced wonder. She didn't know the place had once belonged to their maternal grandparents. That wasn't what troubled her. It was the fact of his marriage. Clearly, this house and a new sister-in-law suggested restrictions Fanny was unwilling to accept.

The matter was better discussed out of her hearing. Raising one hand, he rapped impatiently on his wife's door. She didn't call out an invitation, but neither did she order him away. He stepped inside the room. Embers glowed behind the glass windows of the porcelain stove. The bed was turned back, but empty.

Feeling oddly let down, he picked a copy of Sir Arthur Conan Doyle's *A Study in Scarlet* from the dressing table, intrigued by his wife's taste in literature. She would likely need the cunning of Doyle's new sleuth to deal with Fanny.

Tossing the novel aside, he sank onto the bed and lowered his head into his hands. His temples pounded. He hadn't yet learned how to deal with Lyris. How in hell was he to manage them both?

After braiding her hair and slipping into her nightclothes, Lyris had decided to look in on Fanny. In her slumber, the girl looked younger than her fifteen years and far less defiant. She was at a crossroads, just out of childhood but not yet the young woman she thought herself to be. Gently, Lyris stroked a wayward strand of hair.

When offered a late supper, Fanny had taken little more than a few sips of hot chocolate. Her weary glance had scanned the mahogany-paneled dining room as if testing the limits of a prison. She possessed a quick intelligence, but her grandparents were either unable to hold her to rules of conduct or didn't care to try.

Lyris drew the comforter over the girl's shoulders. She would have to count on Fanny's bright mind. All the rules in the world wouldn't make a difference until she realized that her best interests lay in fitting into society.

There was irony in that, Lyris admitted as she checked the fire screen, then withdrew from the room. She was set on urging Fanny to accept the very restrictions that she herself had always resisted.

When she returned to her own room, she was startled to find her door ajar and even more surprised to see Nicholas sitting on her bed, elbows braced on his knees and his head in his hands.

Her first flash of resentment at finding him there dissolved into compassion. There was nothing of the barely leashed animal in him now and her treacherous heart softened. Instinctively, she raised a barrier. "Your sister shares your independent spirit, Mr. Drake."

He glanced toward the hall. "You've checked on her?"

"She's sleeping." He hadn't countered her comment about spirit. That and the troubled look in his eyes made Lyris speak more gently. "Fanny has had an exhausting journey, in her heart as well as over the rails."

Rising restlessly, he stared into the dying embers in the stove. "I'll have a talk with her in the morning. I promise she'll learn to keep a decent tongue."

Lyris clamped her arms about her body. The house was cooling quickly and the wind, thrashing branches against the outer wall and seeping in as drafts, made her shiver. So had the hard note in Nicholas's voice. "Try to understand," she urged. "What we heard tonight was surely a cry for love."

He shot her an incredulous look, then asked with impatience, "Why are you standing there shivering? Get into bed."

Intensely aware of her flannel robe and gown, Lyris wanted to order him away. Yet they needed to discuss Fanny in private. Nicholas had rolled up his sleeves and discarded his stiff collar so that his shirt folded open at his throat. It occurred to her that he was seductively dangerous in his concern for his sister. She made a conscious effort to guard her heart.

He looked at her, his scowl deepening. "Will you get under the bedcovers on your own or shall I put you there?"

Afraid he would suit action to words, Lyris ran across the carpet, leapt into bed and pulled the coverlet to her chin. Her husband looked at her with the astonishment he had first shown Fanny. "What is it, Lyris? Do you see me as some sort of ravaging beast?"

"It's late," she said. "And I . . . I'm tired."

"I could see that in the way you dragged yourself across the room."

Making her voice firm, she said, "Can we not discuss
your sister in the morning?" When he continued to look at
her, she added, "It is Fanny you wish to discuss?"

"Yes. Fanny." He turned to pace the room. "I can't believe our grandparents encouraged flirtations."

"Of course they didn't. They sent her to you because they
saw she needed a stronger influence."

"I don't understand," Nick exclaimed. "Fanny had better judgment as a toddler."

Lyris laughed softly. "Every girl tests her appeal, Mr.
Drake."

His dark look said he had as little patience with feminine
foolishness as with Lyris's continued formal use of his name.
Uncomfortably aware that she and Fanny were alike in using forms of address as a weapon, Lyris added gently, "Your
sister and I are at the opposite ends of availability. She is just
entering that marketable age, while I am happily on the
verge of leaving it."

"You're not available," he said, then disconcerted her
further by dropping onto the bed.

She skidded backward against the headboard. "You're
absolutely right. In a short three years, I will gladly thumb
my nose at those who scorn divorce."

"I see you can hardly wait for that day."

"Isn't this amazing?" she asked archly to hide distress.
"Twice in succession I agree with you."

"Luckily, I'm not thin-skinned," he said, sounding exactly that. Abruptly, he switched the subject. "Just what did
you see at the station tonight?"

Lyris hesitated. It would serve neither Fanny nor Nicholas to describe that wanton kiss in detail. "Your sister is
confused," she said gently. "We must be patient."

Nick thought unhappily that Fanny wasn't the only one
feeling confused. He had married Lyris partly to help his
sister. Somehow, things had become turned about. He
wanted the marriage to last. Fanny's rash behavior could

destroy any hope of that. Lyris had been damned quick to remind him the marriage was meant to be temporary.

Frowning, he clenched one fist on his knee. "Thanks to our mother, neither Fanny nor I fit comfortably into our lives."

"Then your mother served you better than you may realize," Lyris said. "I've often noticed that you carry yourself with the confidence of my father's associates."

"So you think there's hope for me?"

Wistfulness in the slant of his smile put Lyris on guard against her roiling senses. She found a flippant answer. "Certainly, Mr. Drake. If you will only learn the proper use of your forks."

"Lyris," he said, "will you please call me Nick? Your formal address scarcely suits our present situation."

"There is no situation," Lyris shot back, adding deliberately, "Mr. Drake."

"Isn't there?" He tumbled her onto her pillows. The teasing mood slipped away. As he leaned above her, looking down into her wide eyes, Nick longed to ask, "Is there hope for us?"

He held the words back. He knew what she would answer and didn't want to hear it. Her shoulders were delicate beneath his hands.

Her lips parted with husky warning. "Mr. Drake—"

He kissed her while his name, however formal, was still on her lips.

Lyris felt suspended. A part of her sounded alarms, yet her hands moved of their own will to circle his shoulders and tangle in the soft thickness of his hair. His mouth caressed her lips, exploring every contour, and she could not wish him away, much less insist on it. After the hostile behavior of his sister, it was seductively pleasant to feel wanted.

His fingers moved gently to unplait her hair. Her entire scalp came alive to his touch. When he had spread the silky waves outward on the pillow, he buried his face in their fragrance.

Lyris raised one hand in protest but he captured it and kissed the inner surface of her wrist. His lips felt heated against the fragile skin and a sigh rose through her. In the dreamlike state he was creating, she could not hook on to reality to pull herself free.

An unexpected bite of night air on her bare shoulders warned that he had slipped her gown lower. He stroked away the chill while her blood leapt to his touch. His lips moved over her cheek to a pulse beating wildly below her ear.

Easing the gown still lower, he brushed lingering kisses over the soft rise of her breasts. She slipped one hand beneath his collar and with the tip of her thumb, found a pulse in his throat that beat as wildly as her own.

He raised his head, his eyes dark with questions. She couldn't answer, couldn't think, wanted only to kiss him again. He read the yearning in her eyes and brought his mouth back to hers. She spread her fingers against the back of his head, drawing him closer.

He urged her lips apart. When their tongues brushed, her senses scattered like the burst of a Roman candle. She felt cool air and then the exciting warmth of his hand before she realized her breasts were fully bared. Somewhere deep in her mind, a part of her objected. That part faded before his tantalizing caress.

Her nipple hardened beneath his palm, and that was strange, she thought dazedly, since she was no longer cold at all. Then, with shock, she felt him suckle. She pressed against his shoulders. "Nicholas!"

He raised his head at once, the expressions crossing his face too swiftly for her to catalog, finally settling on ironic. "I knew you could say my name if you tried."

Lyris's senses swam. How could it be possible that she regretted the cessation of his shameless caress? She was even forced to admit she'd felt a certain pleasure in the hot, wet tug of his lips and tongue. And if that weren't dreadful enough, she had blurted out his given name, losing what little advantage the formal address had offered.

Lyris's start of surprise had wakened Nick to his senses. Alarm flickered in her eyes. He closed them by kissing the lids. She was like a fawn, her trust to be won gradually.

He longed to caress every delectable inch of her body, to awaken her for the first time to a lover's touch. Her startled resistance warned him to wait or hear again the damning words that had sent him stumbling away on their wedding night.

His hands shook despite his decision as he replaced the lace-trimmed flannel. To win her heart was a greater goal than seduction, and one he wanted even more.

"Don't say anything, sweetheart," he murmured. "We'll just hold each other. That's all." He stroked a feather-light touch over her throat and felt her shiver. "When we love each other," he added, "you'll find pleasure in it, I promise."

For a moment, Lyris tantalized herself with the forbidden. She was certainly finding pleasure in what he was doing now. The mental warnings she had managed to suppress returned in force. She turned to tell him he must leave, but he cradled her in his arms so tenderly that she decided a few more minutes could not matter.

His breath stirred tendrils of hair against her ear. "Tell me how you think of me."

Confused, she spread her fingers against his chest and toyed with the top button of his shirt. "I believe you are honest. And a man of honor." She swallowed. "I'm counting on that."

"I know you are." With an effort of will, he kept his voice light. "If you are tempted to unfasten my shirt, sweetheart, feel free to explore."

She pulled her hand away at once. "I wasn't thinking any such thing."

"Too bad." He settled her more comfortably. "Relax, love. Just let me hold you."

She surprised him by nestling closer. He was intensely conscious of her sweet warmth, but kept himself under strict control, holding to the image of a startled fawn who would someday come willingly into his arms.

Banked embers shifted in the stove. The wind continued to sweep tree branches against the outside wall. His thoughts lost focus, lulled by the faint scent of roses from his wife's warm skin. As her breathing deepened, he realized she was drifting into sleep.

Tenderness nearly overwhelmed him. Never before had a woman slept in his arms without first sharing the pleasures of her body, but there was no disappointment. To rush her would have been a mistake. That she trusted him enough to sleep told him more than had her reluctant compliments of the part he was winning in her heart. To his own surprise, he felt deeply satisfied.

Long minutes later, the quiet night was rent with a shriek from down the hall. Lyris jerked upright, hauling the coverlet with her. "What . . . ?"

"Fan!" Nick sprang from the bed, swung around the footboard and sprinted toward his sister's room.

Lyris felt like a kite whose string had been let go. She couldn't quite gather her senses. While she groped for her slippers, the terrified shrieks rose again and again.

She reached Fanny's room shortly after Nicholas. He knelt by the bed, holding his sister and stroking her hair. She sobbed in gulps that still held panic. "It's all right," he said. "She's just had a nightmare."

Lyris felt herself heat with a memory of all that had occurred between herself and Nicholas. Unable to meet his gaze, she crossed the room and sat on the sleigh bed. Gently, she rubbed the girl's trembling shoulders. "Fanny? Would you like me to stay with you tonight?"

"You don't have to."

"You've had a difficult and wearying day," Lyris told her. "There is little wonder your sleep is troubled."

The girl's thin shoulders lifted in a shrug that tore at Lyris's heart. Fanny was trying desperately to hide her need beneath adult pride, yet misery pulled down her mouth and glittered in her eyes.

"You will feel safer if you're not alone on this first night," Lyris said.

"I'm not a baby," Fanny said.

"Of course not." Lyris stroked damp hair from the girl's cheek. "But you're not yet familiar with your new home. Let's have no more argument."

"I guess I can't stop you," Fanny muttered, not quite hiding her relief.

Lyris felt intensely aware of Nicholas's steady gaze. Her heart contracted with alarm when she thought of their kisses. He had stopped the lovemaking, not she. Even now she ached to feel his arms about her. Heaven knew what might have occurred had they spent the entire night together.

"Kiss your brother, dear," she said firmly. "Then I'll lie down beside you." She spoke to Fanny, but her final words were for Nicholas—and for herself. "Tomorrow will look more sensible to us all."

Chapter Fifteen

In the morning, Lyris left Fanny still sleeping. After Jenny helped her into a muslin day dress and arranged her hair, she peered into the mirror. Faint blue shadows showed beneath her eyes. She had lain awake long after Fanny slept. Thankfully, there were no more nightmares. Lyris's mind was too filled with her own demons to deal again with Fanny's.

By allowing Nicholas into her bed, by letting him hold and caress her, she had nearly betrayed herself. That the experience had been sweet made it more dangerous. His words rang in her head: *When we love each other, you will find pleasure in it.* That might be true, despite Evelyn's hints to the contrary. It must not happen. She had to make that clear.

Every outrageous demand her husband had ever made marched through her head. There was the returned wedding gift. She hadn't even been allowed to open it. Worse was his order to end all contact with her godmother, for reasons he refused to discuss.

And there was the matter of the newspaper. She could hardly forget that! Her entire future depended on honing her skills. Yet Nicholas expected her to stop writing for publication because he thought it was unsuitable. How would he know? Was the proper occupation for a lady a matter of discussion on the waterfront? She very much doubted so!

In firm control of her senses, she asked Jenny to wait on the needs of the still-sleeping girl and walked downstairs to breakfast. Nicholas rose instantly. His expression brought to mind every tender—and absolutely unacceptable—moment of the night before.

She was going to have to speak to him about coming to the table without his jacket or shirt collar, she thought distractedly. His bare throat and half-dressed appearance were not suitable. Certainly not for her frame of mind. Still, she managed a cool nod to his warm, "Good morning."

His eyes became slightly shuttered. "I see you have succeeded in becoming 'more sensible,' as you advised last night."

Unwilling to fence with him, Lyris gave her attention to the sideboard. Potted sardines, ham pies and cold tongue did not tempt her. Nothing did. After selecting a few strawberries and a hot muffin, she took a seat near Nicholas.

There were things she had to say, but her well-planned words deserted her. All the soft touches and mute yearnings of the night shimmered between them. She twisted her ring, trying to think how to begin.

He seemed willing to wait. She told herself they were both uneasy. He was probably as eager as she to return their relationship to its proper footing. In a low voice, she began, "I realize I was remiss last night in allowing things to go on."

His brows slanted together. "Remiss?"

"The word means careless."

"I know what the word means!" he broke in.

She hadn't intended to insult him. She tried again. "Despite our differences, Mr. Drake, a strong attraction exists."

"Ah, you've noticed."

She lost her conciliatory tone. "If you would refrain from mocking me, we might decide how to go on."

He inclined his head. "You have my full attention."

He was still mocking her. She could see that, but said earnestly, "I've given the problem considerable thought and I believe I've found an explanation."

"You've realized that we're of opposite gender?" Hastily he wiped away a grin. "Sorry. Go on. Please."

"Forbidden fruit is the most desirable." She leaned forward to impress him with her reasoning. "As a girl, I much preferred apples from my neighbor's tree to those on our own."

"Stolen apples, sweetheart? You surprise me."

"Don't you see?" she persisted. "This is the same situation. We are sworn to a celibate marriage and the very fact tempts us to steal kisses." Her cheeks warmed at the words, but she kept her gaze on his.

An odd light came into his eyes. "The wharf rat lusts after a lady, while the lady is tempted by the primal qualities of a common man."

"I wouldn't have put it in quite that way."

"Sweetheart, you are a snob."

"What we must agree on," she snapped, "is to stay on guard against..." She faltered.

"Lust," he supplied.

She started to her feet and he caught her hand, stopping her. "Relax, Lyris. A few kisses won't make a baby."

"I know what causes babies." She glanced about, praying that none of the servants were within hearing.

"You do?" Speculation gleamed in Nicholas's eyes. "How is that?"

"Not from personal experience, I assure you." This conversation had gotten entirely out of hand. She wanted to rush toward safety. Whatever her unruly senses might feel on looking into his golden eyes... The moment stretched out. Coming to herself with a wrench, she tore her gaze away.

Retreating into practical matters, she said stiffly, "I mean to go over Fanny's clothing this morning and start a seamstress on whatever should be needed. Now, about furnishing her room."

He settled into his chair, physically withdrawing. "Do as you will. There's no need to trouble me with details. You have servants who can bring what is needed from the attic." He paused, his eyes darkening. "And to return what is not."

All those dolls, Lyris thought, with a sudden pang for the child's room he had ordered prepared for his sister. He must be feeling foolish for having so misjudged her age. Above all, Nicholas did not like to look foolish.

A maid appeared at Lyris's elbow, and with relief she accepted a cherub-and-rose-bedecked calling card on a silver tray. "Mama has stopped by. Is she in the parlor, Ruby? Please take in the chocolate service."

Her husband rose, and she added swiftly, "Mr. Drake, we must have this clear. In the future, we will conduct any private discussions in the library, not in my bedchamber."

He nodded briefly, his expression no longer readable. She locked her fingers together to resist furiously twisting her ring while he walked from the house.

Rebellion churned. Why should she be made to feel at fault? He was the one who had proposed this arrangement. He could just follow the plan he himself had promoted.

When she trusted herself to join her mother, she found her inspecting the new chintz curtains. "Lyris, darling, you've done wonders with this room."

Lyris sank onto a chair newly covered in gray striped silk and poured steaming chocolate from a Sevres pot, as if she had nothing more than curtains on her mind. Her mother continued to glance about. "Have you been deluged with callers?"

Lyris kept her smile steady. She had managed so far to keep Nicholas from recognizing the slight in her friends' failure to visit. "Only Evelyn and Reba. Everyone must believe we are still honeymooning."

Her mother's smile faded by degrees before she asked intently, "Darling, are you happy?"

"Why, Mama, how can you ask?" Quickly, Lyris changed the subject. "You will be interested to know that Nicholas's young sister has just been put into our care. Fanny arrived by train last night."

Her mother pursed her mouth. "So soon? Such a responsibility."

"I expect to enjoy her company," Lyris said, with a degree of heartiness she had last heard when Papa handed her over to Drake.

Her mother set her cup abruptly into its saucer. "There is no use in postponing my news. I have had a letter from Amelia. She knows your husband."

Chocolate splashed over the rim of Lyris's cup and onto her wrist. She hid her shock in the business of locating a napkin and cleaning the damage. "After all, he bought her home."

"Through a solicitor. Amelia's letter said she has just learned your husband's name and fears that she is to blame for his marrying you!"

The napkin fell unheeded into Lyris's lap. She looked at her mother in stunned disbelief while her mind flew back to the awful day when Nicholas had learned Amelia was her godmother.

She had offered to take down the portraits that upset him. He'd said they were to stay, that he wanted those two to watch him take possession. Later, he'd spoken triumphantly of having acquired both Amelia's home and her precious goddaughter.

How did he know Amelia? Why in the world would she believe the marriage had anything to do with her? Lyris refilled her cup, steadying herself with deliberate effort. "What else did Amelia write?"

Her mother's hands fluttered over a tray of small cakes without settling on any. "She is returning to Seattle. She means to contact you the moment she arrives."

Lyris dropped her cup into its saucer and watched without seeing as the beverage again sloshed over the rim. She longed to welcome her godmother into the home that had once been hers.

But Amelia must not visit. There was a great deal here that Lyris didn't understand. Deep in her heart, she wanted to hear the story first from Nicholas.

Fanny spoke defiantly from the doorway. "I'm down. I suppose I'm late."

As they turned together, Lyris heard her mother's dismayed "Oh, my." The girl's dress was far too old for her and out of fashion besides, with a severe bustle and a décolletage that on her small chest dipped disconcertingly low.

Lyris put a smile into her voice. "Come in, Fanny. I want you to meet my mother, Mrs. Lowell."

The girl looked as if ready to bolt and yet came forward with a defiant swagger. "Fanny, dear," Mama said, regaining genuine warmth, "how nice to meet you. Have you traveled far?"

"Far enough," Fanny said, her glance taking in both women's costumes.

"Let me assist you," Lyris murmured, producing a porcelain cameo and efficiently raising the neckline of the girl's dress. "Jenny should have taken more care."

To her relief, Fanny allowed her to rearrange her gown while she looked hungrily at the cake tray. "You scarcely ate a bite last night," Lyris said. "Won't you bring a breakfast tray in here with us? Let me just make sure the buffet is still set."

She counted on her mother to charm Fanny while she made sure of the foods on the sideboard. After making a few corrections, she instructed Ruby to assist Miss Drake in carrying her choices to the parlor. When she returned, she heard Fanny say woefully, "Lyris doesn't like me."

"Oh, my dear, you are mistaken," Mama exclaimed.

Lyris paused beyond the curtains. Her sister-in-law was perched on an embroidered stool at Mama's knee. Sadly, she said, "It's true. She even gave away my doll. I suppose I'm past dolls, but my brother had chosen it. I would like to have kept it on my bed."

Lyris clenched a fold of fabric in one hand. Fanny was trying to turn her own mother against her! Keeping the girl's loneliness in mind, she stepped into the room and asked calmly, "What doll was that, dear?"

Fanny had the grace to look abashed. "The one with gold curls."

"Golden curls," Lyris mused. "Assist my memory. Exactly when did I give away your doll?"

A bright flush stained Fanny's cheeks, but she kept to her story. "Last night. At the train."

Lyris's heart urged her to make this easier and yet, Fanny must understand that lies would not be tolerated. "Won't you tell us more?" she asked quietly. "What exactly occurred?"

The girl's flush deepened. Lyris's mother looked uncomfortably from one to the other, then started in surprise when Fanny hurled herself into her lap and buried her face in the folds of her skirt. "She hates me. Make her stop!"

"No one hates you, Fanny." Lyris clasped the girl's shoulders and raised her. "Your weariness last night has caused you to lose sight of the details. I believe memory will remind you that it was your brother who gave away the doll—from disappointment at your behavior."

Fanny scrubbed the back of one hand across her eyes, then stared unhappily at the carpet. Gently, Lyris prodded. "Do you remember now?"

The young fingers pleated a ruffle in her skirt before Fanny muttered with reluctance, "Maybe it was that way."

"Thank you, Fanny," Lyris said. "We'll say no more about this. Your breakfast is waiting. Take the second doorway on your left from the hall. Ruby will assist you."

She didn't relax until the girl left the room with stiff spine and high chin.

"You say that you entered this arrangement willingly," her mother murmured. "Forgive me, dear. But I wonder if you didn't take a little too much champagne during the mayor's ball."

In his office at the Golden Harbor, Nick rubbed aching muscles in the back of his neck. He had spent most of the day engrossed in record keeping—a dreary enough task when he would rather be active; a difficult one when his wife's green eyes kept peering through the blurring figures in his ledger.

However, when he concentrated long enough to tally a line, the results were gratifying. His investments in the shipping industry were paying handsomely, even more than the saloon or his rental properties.

If only his home life ran as well. Stretching, he rose and walked over to the window. The sun was lower in the sky than he expected. He pulled out his watch and saw that he had left Lyris and Fanny together for an entire day. Slamming the ledgers closed, he grabbed his hat. "Sam! Did you make that purchase?"

"Sure did, boss." Sam appeared in the open doorway, carrying a wicker basket tied with a wide ribbon bow.

"What color?"

Crinkles deepened around Sam's eyes. "Cinnamon, like you said."

Nick hefted the basket. "There isn't much weight to it."

"A lady don't need much weight, boss," Sam said slyly. "Not when she's got a lot of sass."

"Smart fellow." Nick clapped him on the shoulder and, with the basket on one arm, set out to pour oil over whatever troubled waters he might find at home.

Chapter Sixteen

Fanny wished Mrs. Lowell had stayed longer. The lady didn't keep her nose in the air the way her daughter did. Sure, Nick's wife pretended to be friendly, but it was easy to see she didn't mean it.

Her mother, though, really was nice. She had stayed while the seamstress measured Fanny from top to bottom and talked over designs for new clothes. A good thing, too. You could tell Mrs. Lowell knew fashion. Fanny hadn't argued with her the way she had with Nick's wife.

But the older woman stayed only until lunch. Then fabric samples arrived and it was Mrs. Perfect who picked out materials for the new dresses. Whenever Fanny liked something, *she* turned up her nose. Fanny wished with all her heart that Mrs. Lowell would come again.

Or that Nick would come home. With an exaggerated sigh, she flopped into the deep cushions of an overstuffed chair. Her new sister-in-law had dragged her all through the house, telling her how each room was used. She probably wanted to make it clear just how far above Fanny all this was, as if she didn't already know.

Deciding it was time to speak up for herself, she looked around the big room they were in—the drawing room, according to Mrs. Perfect. "This sure is ugly. Nicky must hate it. If I was his wife, I'd make it prettier in here."

Of course, his wife was too high-minded to say anything right back. She hadn't even called Fanny a liar about that doll, had just made it clear that she was one. Now, as if sugar wouldn't melt in her mouth, she said, "That's exactly what I am doing. I haven't touched this room yet. What would you suggest?"

As if the new Mrs. Drake cared what she thought, "First, I'd get rid of that mean-looking lady. Who is she, your gramma?"

"As a matter of fact, she is my godmother." Nick's wife stood below the portrait, her hands curled at her sides. "This portrait was made by the artist John Singer Sergeant when Mrs. Chambers visited London a few years ago. Notice how the background causes your eye to focus on the figure."

Fanny grimaced. Why should she care about some old picture? Even if she did, she wouldn't say so. Moving into a swanky house didn't mean she belonged there. She had seen that almost at once. What would happen when Nicky realized the same thing?

A lost feeling assailed her, making her sink lower in the chair. Grampa and Gramma Drake didn't want her back with them. If Nick sent her away, she wouldn't have anywhere to go. Arguing with his wife could mean a fast trip to nowhere, but she felt dumpy next to her. Lyris...what kind of name was that? Real girls were named Mary or Agnes or Fanny.

Gladness rushed through her as Nick strolled into the room, looking big and handsome, and bringing fresh outside air into the stuffy house. Fanny ran to kiss him before his wife could, but that woman didn't make a move. Maybe the upper class kept their kisses private, but it seemed strange to Fanny. She felt sorry for Nick and protective of him.

He only glanced at Lyris before giving Fanny a big smile. "There's a surprise for you in the hall."

"A surprise?" Fanny slipped a glance toward Nick's wife to see how she liked it that he'd brought a surprise for his sister and not for her. Of course, she was too well-bred to let anything show on her face. Poor Nicky.

He tugged one of her curls. "Don't you want it?"

"What is it?" Without waiting for an answer, she flew into the hall. She saw the basket at once on the floor beside a table. Dropping to her knees, she pulled the hinged top open and peered in. "Oh, Nicky!" Her scream made a fluffy orange kitten cower into a corner.

Gently, she lifted the kitten into her arms. It snuggled against her and she rubbed one cheek against its fur. Her eyes blurred and she had to swallow hard. Nicky still cared about making her happy. Maybe it wouldn't be so bad living here.

As Nicholas smiled at his sister's shriek of pleasure, Lyris said in a guarded tone, "Tell me it isn't a pony."

"Not even a dog." He crossed to the fireplace and leaned near her. "No gray hairs? Your day can't have been as difficult as I expected."

Lyris moved a vase of flowers on the mantel, consciously avoiding his gaze. "Whatever you've brought, it pleases Fanny far more than the prospect of a dozen new dresses."

"It's only a kitten."

"A kitten!" He had seen his sister's loneliness, after all. "Nicholas, that was very thoughtful."

She had used his name without thinking and watched with dismay as his expression changed, becoming more intimate. His tone gave an added meaning to his words. "Maybe it will keep her from requiring your company in bed."

She was about to retort that he should not expect it, either, when Fanny came in, cradling her new pet.

"Well, imp," Nicholas said, straightening. "Have you chosen a name?"

Fanny's eyes glowed as the kitten rubbed its head against her chin. "You name her, Nicky."

Lyris saw his glance return to her, as if to invite a suggestion. Fanny stiffened noticeably. The girl's jealousy could become a problem. Lyris stroked the kitten's soft fur. "Why don't you wait until the right name comes to you?"

The kitten rubbed against her hand, purring so loudly they could all hear it. Fanny sank to the floor, removing her pet from Lyris's touch, then giggled as it batted her curls.

Her brother watched with a bemused smile and Lyris thought that an artist might at that moment capture them as a family. It made her wonder at the real lives behind the apparently contented family groupings portrayed in galleries. That thought reminded her unpleasantly of *The Naked Huntress*.

He was far too near, and had completely misread her expression. Turning, she gazed up at the painting of Amelia. How much simpler life had been when she'd played carelessly in her godmother's attic and halls.

Nicholas surprised her by saying, "Tell me about her."

Her mother's warning sprang to mind: *"Amelia knows your husband."* She chose her words carefully. "Amelia is always kind. Edwin sometimes was not."

"I can't imagine any man being unkind to you."

"A rare compliment!"

"There are ways other than words to compliment a woman." His low-voiced reminder brought their lovemaking vividly to mind.

Thankful that Fanny was occupied with her kitten, Lyris forced her unsteady attention to the painting. "As a child, I came here often. If the day was cold or rainy, we would curl up in a chair before a fire in the parlor, or in Amelia's room upstairs. She had a wonderful way with fairy tales. I positively shivered when she read of giants and ghosts."

Alight with the memory, she turned. His dark expression made her reach out to touch his sleeve. "Have I said something to upset you?"

He shook his head. "Go on. What of sunnier days?"

After a pause, she continued uncertainly. "Oh, hoops in the garden. Or we painted. We often took her carriage to the waterfront. She liked to watch the fishing boats in the bay."

Memory flooded her. "If they were in the harbor, we read each of their names. If they were out, she would gaze toward the sound as if she wished to be with them."

Nicholas laughed harshly. "That's as likely as your fairy tales."

"How would you know?" Lyris asked. His jaw tightened and he turned away. Urgently, she said, "Life with Edwin was difficult. She must have yearned to be free."

"Lyris," he said in a flat tone, "you were living a lie."

"What on earth do you mean by that?"

For a moment he seemed about to answer, then he shrugged and turned away.

Fanny looked up, her expression far too penetrating. "You don't like that portrait, either, do you, Nicky? Even if it is a John Singer Sergeant."

That Fanny remembered the name of the artist, even in sarcasm, was as startling to Lyris as was Nicholas's strange comment. As she puzzled over his words, she realized she had painted a carefree childhood, one that must have been in sharp contrast to his and Fanny's upbringing. There had been difficult times in her own. Maybe she should have spoken of that, but she wanted him to know that Amelia was loving and kind.

She had only raised greater resentment. Now, standing at a window with his hands braced against the frame, much as on their first day in this house, he closed her out.

His jibe earlier burst into her mind—that she was a lady tempted by the primal qualities of a commoner. It couldn't be true. Before Nicholas, she had never in her life been drawn to a man not of her class.

Except once. An old memory slipped into her mind and she saw herself at thirteen, peering with a girlfriend through Gram's hedge. A burly young gardener had rolled up his

NO RISK, NO OBLIGATION TO BUY...NOW OR EVER!

CASINO JUBILEE
"Scratch'n Match" Game

Here's how to play:

1. Peel off label from front cover. Place it in space provided at right. With a coin, carefully scratch off the silver box. This makes you eligible to receive two or more free books, and possibly other gifts, depending upon what is revealed beneath the scratch-off area.

2. You'll receive brand-new Harlequin Historical™ novels. When you return this card, we'll rush you the books and gifts you qualify for, ABSOLUTELY FREE!

3. If we don't hear from you, every month we'll send you 4 additional novels to read and enjoy before they are available in bookstores. You can return them and owe nothing, but if you decide to keep them, you'll pay only $3.19* per book, a saving of 80¢ each off the cover price. There is **no** extra charge for postage and handling. There are **no** hidden extras.

4. When you join the Harlequin Reader Service®, you'll get our subscribers-only newsletter, as well as additional free gifts from time to time, just for being a subscriber!

5. You must be completely satisfied. You may cancel at any time simply by sending us a note or a shipping statement marked "cancel" or by returning any shipment to us at our cost.

YOURS FREE!

This lovely heart-shaped box is richly detailed with cut-glass decorations, perfect for holding a precious memento or keepsake—and it's yours absolutely free when you accept our no-risk offer.

CASINO JUBILEE
"Scratch'n Match" Game

SCRATCH HERE

PLACE LABEL HERE

?

CHECK CLAIM CHART BELOW FOR YOUR FREE GIFTS!

YES! I have placed my label from the front cover in the space provided above and scratched off the silver box. Please send me all the gifts for which I qualify. I understand I am under no obligation to purchase any books, as explained on the opposite page.

(U-H-H-08/92) 247 CIH AGLE

Name _____

Address _____ Apt. _____

City _____ State _____ Zip _____

CASINO JUBILEE CLAIM CHART	
🍒🍒🍒	WORTH 4 FREE BOOKS, FREE HEART-SHAPED CURIO BOX PLUS MYSTERY BONUS GIFT
🍒🔔🍒	WORTH 3 FREE BOOKS PLUS MYSTERY GIFT
🔔🔔🍒	WORTH 2 FREE BOOKS CLAIM N° 1528

shirtsleeves, and the two of them had stared with innocent lust at his sweat-slick muscles.

For months afterward, either could send the other into a fit of giggles, completely mystifying their parents, simply by whispering the word *sweat*. Youthful curiosity, she assured herself. If that gardener were here today, he would bore her with interests entirely different from her own. Moreover, her often-acidic tongue would send him rushing for the door.

She was never quite sure what Nicholas might say or do, and even less sure what he might be thinking. And there was his puzzling reaction to any mention of Amelia. It wasn't the man she wanted, merely her curiosity satisfied.

Pleased to have the matter settled, and completely ignoring her startling physical response to his lightest touch, she turned to his sister. "I believe you have an eye for art, Fanny. Would you enjoy visiting a gallery?"

"Yes," Nicholas said for her, while Fanny's eyes widened. "I want her exposed to culture until it drips from her. Begin a tour of galleries tomorrow."

Fanny clutched the kitten closer. "My new dresses won't be ready that soon. *She* says my clothes are all wrong."

"You have a good cloak. Wear that and you'll do all right."

"It might be too warm."

"You are not to argue," he said in a voice neither was likely to challenge. "Not with Lyris. Not with me. Is that clear?"

Fanny lowered her eyes. "Yes."

He walked over and rumpled her curls. "You needn't look condemned, imp. You'll enjoy the experience."

Inwardly, Lyris sighed. With luck, the galleries would have few other visitors tomorrow to observe the girl's unpredictable behavior.

Lyris's favorite gallery was housed in one of the city's earliest homes. She decided to begin there. Fanny clutched her wool cloak about her, casting an occasional glance at Lyris's fashionable walking suit.

The displays gradually caused her to relax. Lyris saw she had guessed correctly at Fanny's interest in art. The girl became enthralled by the collection. The morning passed so swiftly that Lyris felt guilty for her doubts.

As she considered continuing the tour rather than returning home for lunch, she heard Evelyn call out, "Lyris! How nice!"

After greeting her with a hug, Lyris introduced Fanny. Evelyn studied the girl curiously. "How charming! Although it is bit early in your marriage for a prolonged visit."

Lyris was dismayed to hear a patronizing note in Evelyn's voice and braced herself for a sassy retort from Fanny. When the girl simply returned a polite greeting, she was equally dismayed to feel disappointed.

The three of them strolled together along the gallery's north wing, Evelyn explaining that she had stolen an hour to restore herself from the hectic business of preparing a dinner party. "Oh?" Lyris asked, smiling. "And when is this strenuous endeavor to take place?"

To her astonishment, Evelyn blushed furiously. "I am so addle-tongued. Forgive me, Lyris."

Amusement faded. "You're forgiven, dear friend. But for what?"

With a rapid flutter of her lace fan, Evelyn said, "Lyris, you know I wouldn't upset you for the world."

"You are upsetting me," Lyris said. "Will you please stop agonizing and explain?" Evelyn's blush faded, but she gave all her attention to the complex business of closing her fan.

"Evelyn," Lyris said quietly. "Are you having a dinner party without inviting me?"

Placing one gloved hand on Lyris's elbow, Evelyn drew her aside. She glanced at Fanny, then leaned closer to murmur, "Of course, we would love to have you join us, *dearest* friend. But your husband . . . Well, he simply would not fit in."

The words sank through Lyris's consciousness, chilling her. Nicholas had married her hoping to be welcomed into society. Why hadn't she realized that in marrying a trades-man, she had closed doors for herself?

She had excused the lack of calling cards and invitations. She had even been grateful for their absence, feeling Nich-olas wasn't ready to enter society. Did that make her as shallow as Evelyn?

Forcing the unflattering question aside, she clamped her lips together. Whatever else might be true, she had not been prepared for an insult from one of her closest friends. "You will excuse us, won't you?" she asked coolly. "We wouldn't wish to detain you further from your chores."

She practically marched Fanny through the gallery. When they reached the walk, the girl squirmed free. "Have we been snubbed?"

Lyris gathered her dangerously slipping composure. "Yes, we have. By a great many people, apparently. We are not going to let them get away with it, however. Come along, Fanny. Your brother is about to host the most scintillating dinner party Seattle has yet seen."

"I suppose I'm too young to join your table."

"Oh, Fanny, I'm afraid you are." Lyris looked at her with honest dismay. "Will you mind terribly?"

To her astonishment, Fanny's eyes lit in relief. "Mind! I'm thankful to be spared. I'm not ready to face all the forks and knives Mama used to tell about. Anyway, Lyris, I'd only get into trouble. I'd be sure to say something Nicky would make me regret."

Her smile seemed genuine. Her eyes sparkled. And for the first time, she had called her sister-in-law by name. Amazed, Lyris saw that Evelyn's snub had at least momentarily bridged the gap between herself and Fanny.

Chapter Seventeen

Nick stood at a window of Richard Thompson's office staring glumly into the street. "It's only a matter of time until somebody breaks a leg out there."

He heard Thompson strike a match and smelled cigar smoke before the man answered lazily, "I'll speak to the council about raising the sin taxes. What do you say, Alex?"

Nick swung about, ready to argue, while Alex Shore helped himself to one of Thompson's cigars. The hotel keeper leaned back comfortably. "I think we'll have the streets in order faster if we assess ourselves as property owners."

He grinned at Nick. Both knew that most of the businessmen along the street had agreed to an assessment. But Thompson, who owned three buildings rented to small shopkeepers, was as stubborn as he was closefisted.

After blowing a smoke ring toward the ceiling, he said, "Let's not rush the matter, gentlemen. I suppose we'll have another chance to discuss it after the Ellises' dinner on Saturday?"

As Shore nodded, Nick realized they were speaking of Lyris's friend, Evelyn, and her husband, Brewster Ellis. Lyris hadn't mentioned a dinner party. In fact, there had been few visitors and no invitations since their marriage.

Evelyn Ellis was supposedly one of his wife's closest friends. Keeping anger from his face, he said coolly, "I'll count on you to carry the argument, Alex. My wife and I will not be available on Saturday."

The hotel keeper winked. "It's about time you take your pretty lady on holiday."

Thompson regarded him through a veil of smoke, his mustache tilting upward as if the lip beneath it curled. "As a matter of fact," Nick said, resisting an impulse to punch the smug look from Thompson's face, "my young sister has just joined us. We've made plans to take her to Mercer Island."

Whether the other two guessed the plan to be spur-of-the-moment didn't matter. Fanny and Lyris would enjoy a holiday. And by removing Lyris from Seattle, Nick hoped to keep her from learning of Evelyn's false friendship.

When he reached home, Lyris was at her desk in the parlor. Her spine was straight and her expression intense. Steam appeared to be rising from her nostrils, but that might have been an effect suggested by her set lips and racing pen.

Fanny sat nearby, playing with her kitten. With a cautious eye for his wife, Nick asked, "Have you chosen a name yet, imp?"

"Feisty," Fanny answered, then grinned. "After Lyris."

His wife turned, her eyes sparking dangerously. "We are planning a dinner party. Is there anyone in particular whom you would care to invite?"

So she had heard. Moved with a need to protect her, he curled one hand gently around the back of her neck. "Is your friend Evelyn to attend?"

"Oops," Fanny murmured.

Lyris looked startled. "Is news of her snub all over town?"

"No, sweetheart." He wanted to lift her into his arms and kiss her until she forgot about Evelyn and everyone else. He wanted to prove she hadn't made a disastrous mistake in marrying him. All he could do was try to reassure her that Seattle wasn't laughing behind her back.

"Two of the fellows offered to discuss street repairs after the Ellises' dinner. I told them we were planning to take Fanny on an outing to Mercer Island and would miss the affair."

"An outing?" Fanny asked, her eyes lighting.

"Would you like that, imp?"

"Are you serious?" Lyris asked. "You mean to make time for a trip?"

"Why not?" Nick stroked one fingertip over the petal-soft curve of her cheek, wondering if he would have time alone with her. "After all, we haven't yet enjoyed a honeymoon."

She drew away from his touch, leaning toward Fanny as if she hadn't heard him. "I've had an inspiration! We'll plan our dinner theme around the shore. We can bring back shells and stones, perhaps agate and jasper."

Eyes alight with enthusiasm, she whirled back to her desk. Fanny grinned. "See why I named my cat?"

Nick leaned close enough to breathe in his wife's sweet fragrance as he checked her list of names. "The Brunswichs," he said with approval. "And you *are* inviting the Ellises."

"Of course." She spoke with such conviction that he smiled. Lyris would hear the details of her friend's dinner and make certain that her own put Evelyn's in the shade.

"Reba Winters. Who will you invite for her?"

"Richard Thompson, I suppose. He's sweet on Reba, but she's beginning to tire of him. I can't think what took her so long."

"Yes, invite Thompson. Alex Shore, as well. We may as well have a go at street repairs along with Evelyn's vanity." He clasped her hand, thinking how fragile her bones felt. Yet she possessed a fierce inner strength he was just beginning to appreciate. "Have you an unattached friend to invite as a dinner partner for Alex?"

Lyris frowned thoughtfully at their clasped hands, but didn't pull free. "There is the younger Sinclair girl, Cynthia. She's frightfully curious. I believe she would accept."

He stroked one thumb along the inner side of her palm. "Curious... about your unfortunate marriage?"

"They all are, Nicholas. We should expect that." Lyris reclaimed her hand, looking stern. "Don't be surprised if our evening receives a mention in the *Tribune*. Cynthia is clever. It may be she who writes as the Seattle Debutante."

"I doubt it," Nick answered. "The Sinclairs are a good family." As fire sparked in Lyris's eyes, he saw his mistake and added hastily, "Let Brunswich write his own story."

But the damage was done. This time, he was sure steam rose from his annoyed wife.

Although the season was early and the sky heavy with clouds, holiday seekers crowded the wharf on Lake Washington. Many hauled camping gear aboard a waiting steamer, where passengers thronged the covered deck. Lyris stood at the rail between Nicholas and Fanny while, with flags flying and a merry blast of its whistle, the vessel set out across the thirty-mile lake.

Mercer Island rose ahead, a long, tree-covered dome with white tents scattered along the shoreline. "Are we camping?" Fanny asked.

Her brother shook his head. "No, imp. You're a lady now. We'll stay at the lodge."

The girl's hair blew freely in the wind. Her cheeks glowed and her eyes shone. Lyris might have been encouraged except that Fanny's artless question had followed a thoughtful study of several young men with tents.

They were to spend three days on the island, surely time enough to gather the wild materials needed for the party. Before leaving for their holiday, Fanny had helped cut invitations in the shape of seashells, tint them with watercolors and carry them to the post.

The dining room was to resemble an underwater garden representing Lost Atlantis. Lyris had even designed uniforms with mermaid tails for her serving girls. Fanny was so eager to eclipse Evelyn that Lyris wondered with a tinge of guilt if she was encouraging unfortunate inclinations in the girl.

Near the island, men in canoes and rowboats raced the steamer. A dead tree leaning from shore held a half-dozen laughing young women in bathing costume, cheering them on. Anticipation coursed through Lyris. She felt light-hearted for the first time in too long a while.

The lavish three-story lodge loomed above the trees. Fanny ran ahead of them up a grand stairway to a suite of rooms on the third floor. There, Lyris's enthusiasm received a jolt. The wall decorations were handsome. The hearths and mantels were costly. The ceilings were freshly painted with cupids and flowers. But only two rooms opened off the narrow parlor, each containing a solitary bed.

She turned to Nicholas with outrage she couldn't express in front of Fanny. He grinned lazily. "I hope you won't try to take advantage of me."

"How can I?" Lyris answered. "I have no idea where you'll be sleeping." Carrying her traveling bag into one of the rooms, she tossed it possessively onto the bed.

Fanny was too impatient to unpack, and urged them to the lakeshore. She looked on the quest for party decorations as a scavenger hunt and proved to be remarkably sharp-eyed.

While Nicholas watched with amusement, Lyris joined his sister, lifting her skirts and stepping in stocking-covered feet into the cold wash of waves in search of bright stones. By late afternoon, they had gathered a fair collection of clam and mussel shells, as well as jasper and agate.

The lighthearted mood shifted at dinner, which, to Lyris's scandalized eyes, was served in a public dining room. She grew increasingly uneasy as the evening wore on. The bright smiles that Fanny offered young men at nearby tables were as unsettling as her own qualms about the coming night. It occurred to her that life must be far easier in lands where the sun never set.

Before anything could come of Fanny's bold glances, Lyris shepherded her sister-in-law to her room, no happier with the role of chaperon than was Fanny. Nicholas remained downstairs, engrossed in a conversation that Lyris hoped would continue late into the night.

She wore a high-necked flannel gown, tugging the sleeves over her wrists and wrapping the full skirt about her feet. There was no possibility of sleep. By the time Nicholas came upstairs, her nerves were so fine-tuned, she silently rebuked him for making her endure the suspense.

She had nearly convinced herself he would wrap up in a blanket in the small parlor, but he came into the bedroom without pausing. Lyris felt every nerve clench. If she argued with him, Fanny would hear.

The clouds had blown on. Moonlight flooded the room. One quick peek beneath her lashes told Lyris that her husband had stripped to his undershirt and drawers.

The bed sagged beneath his weight. She clutched the edge of the mattress to keep from rolling toward him. Her heart beat so loudly she was sure he must hear it.

"If you should fall into my arms," he said dryly, "I promise to catch you."

"Don't flatter yourself, Mr. Drake." Why had she responded? She meant to pretend to be asleep, although she could not be more wide-awake.

"You seem restless," he said. "Would a back rub help?"

The thought of his hands on her sent electric shivers across her skin and she said in almost a hiss, "A gentleman would spend the night in a chair."

He chuckled. "But then, I'm no gentleman."

She was intensely, uncomfortably aware of him. How could she not be when he sprawled casually over most of the bed, leaving her only a few inches along one side? If she trusted herself to touch him, she would give him a shove. But she didn't trust herself. And there was no guessing how he would react.

"You mean to *become* a gentleman," she reminded him.

His voice caressed her. "The kitten is well named."

Lyris sat upright. "Fanny sleeps badly in an unfamiliar bed. I will stay with her."

"She's asleep," he said, before Lyris could swing her feet to the floor. "I looked in."

Reluctantly, she lay down again, her back turned to her husband. It occurred to her that she might as well spend the night in a chair, herself. She wasn't likely to sleep.

A knowing chuckle in his voice made her nerves wind tighter. "Poor love, what a struggle you have to keep one Drake from chasing men and the other from chasing you."

She ground her fingernails into the mattress, refusing to answer and trying valiantly to appear sleepy. Tomorrow he must make other arrangements. She would not go through this again.

Amused by Lyris's discomfort, Nick told himself that if he wasn't allowed to kiss her, he might at least tease her. Stirred by the thought of kisses, he concentrated on simply enjoying her nearness. She edged even farther away from him.

"One good-night kiss?" he asked, playfully running a fingertip down her spine.

She recoiled so abruptly, she crashed onto the floor. He sat up with a start. "Are you all right?"

"No," she snapped, scrambling to her feet. "I'm going to sleep with Fanny."

"No, you're not." His tone stopped her at the door. "My sister is confused. I don't want her made even less secure. Come to bed, Lyris. Believe me, I won't touch you again."

She had bruised his pride as well as her anatomy. And he was right about Fanny. The girl had lost two homes. There might be no controlling her if she learned that her brother's marriage was only temporary.

Lyris inched beneath the sheets once again. Nicholas had turned his back, freeing a good share of the bed. She stretched out, taking care not to touch him, vitally aware he was near.

She thought she would not sleep, yet woke abruptly at dawn when her husband patted the blankets over her bottom. "Wake up, sleepyhead. The day awaits. We'll rent a canoe and paddle around the island to better pickings."

The room was scarcely light. She burrowed more deeply into her pillow. "I might have known you were an early riser." As Nicholas moved about, she ruthlessly suppressed images suggested by the sounds of male clothing being donned.

His toilet articles clattered. Razor strop. Brush. Shaving mug. "Must you be so noisy?" she grumbled.

"Must you waste the day?" he countered cheerfully.

The door opened and Fanny popped in. "It's beautiful out. Lyris, are you still in bed?" She glanced mischievously toward her brother, who stood at the washbasin shaving. "Did you know you were marrying a slugabed?"

"Out," Lyris said.

Fanny giggled. "I guess she wants to be alone with you." She whirled into the parlor, pulling the door closed.

"That's the last thing I want," Lyris said, mutinously swinging her feet to the floor and feeling for her slippers.

Nicholas startled her by dropping onto one knee and clasping his arms along her hips. "Is it, Lyris?"

She couldn't quite resist stroking his smooth, freshly shaved cheek. The bargain that had seemed so logical months ago at the mayor's ball was beginning to come apart.

"You promised a canoe trip," she said, wishing her voice sounded steadier. "Maybe Jon Brunswich will take a story on the expedition for the *Tribune*."

Nicholas rocked back on his heels, the momentary tenderness lost. "He might, if you were still writing for publication."

Lyris rued her impulsive tongue. She was never at her best in the morning. "Of course," she agreed, coming to her feet and whipping a robe around her nightdress. "I had momentarily forgotten your outrageous decree."

She sat at the dressing table and began to unbraid her hair. The back of her neck bristled as she waited for him to make the connection between his order to end her career and the appearance of her pseudonym in the newspaper.

To her surprise, he apologized. "I know you're unhappy, Lyris, but once we married, it was no longer suitable for you to work."

Arguments popped to her tongue. She swallowed them back. They were here for a holiday, not a fight. Besides, she had not given up journalism and had no intention of doing so. She had her future to consider, after all.

Fanny was delighted with the idea of a canoe trip. With a picnic basket from the hotel kitchen stashed in the bow, they arranged themselves on wooden seats. Nicholas's smooth strokes propelled the vessel away from the boathouse, parallel with the shore.

Both Lyris and Fanny wore summer white, with wide-brimmed hats to shade their skin. Fanny soon abandoned hers to the bottom of the canoe. Lyris didn't have the heart to insist that she wear it. A scattering of freckles would be the least of her problems in preparing Fanny for society.

When they rounded the island, Nicholas pulled the canoe onto a beach far from the crowds and waded with them along a wild stretch of shoreline, joining the search for agate and jasper. He was soon laughing with Fanny, lifting her high and threatening to toss her into the water, while she shrieked with happy excitement.

Lyris laughed with them, confused by her feelings. It was almost as if she belonged with them, as if the future held more carefree days like these, when she knew it could not.

After lunch, Fanny explored trees beyond the beach, returning intermittently with dry mosses to pile into the wicker picnic chest, which had become a cache for their finds. While Fanny foraged, Lyris plaited grass stems into wreaths. Nicholas sprawled nearby, watching her. "What will you do with your freedom?" he asked suddenly.

She concentrated on her work. "When we are divorced?"

"Have you made plans?"

Wondering what lay behind his serious gaze, she answered lightly. "Well, Mr. Drake, since you have promised to enrich me, I shall probably travel." Her lips twitched. "I will compose acerbic accounts of the people I meet and become known as a troublesome old lady with a wicked pen."

"You'll be lonely."

"Not at all."

She slanted a glance toward him as he straightened on one elbow. Devilment danced in his eyes. Before she could escape, he tumbled her into the grass. "I say you will." He brushed a tendril of hair from her cheek. "A woman without a man is a curiosity. You won't like that."

She answered stoutly. "I'll love every minute."

"You'll remember the night you fell off a bed to escape a man's arms and you'll wish for a second chance."

"You are hopelessly conceited."

"And you are a lovely liar." He leaned down to her, his lips brushing hers as gently as a sunbeam, then with deepening pressure. Water lapped rhythmically against the shore. Far out on the lake, boaters laughed and called to each other. Lyris slipped her arms about his shoulders. Her lips parted for his deeper kiss.

Dry moss dropped beside them, bits flying into their faces. Sounding petulant, Fanny asked, "Don't you two have a bedroom for that?"

As her eyes flew open, Lyris saw tolerant amusement on Nicholas's face. He helped her sit up before he answered his sister. "You're right, imp. We do."

Sending him a telling look, Lyris brushed moss from her face and hair, then collected her grass stems, along with her composure. "I've been weaving tiaras for the ladies, Fanny. Come sit beside me and I'll show you how."

Thanks to Fanny's jealousy, a dangerous moment had passed, but it was difficult to appreciate the fact. Lyris's heart raced at the thought of the night to come.

When the sun cast long shadows across the lake, they returned to the hotel. A large bonfire had blossomed on the beach, where merrymakers planned to roast clams over the coals. Nicholas's party was invited to join in. When everyone had eaten their fill, the fire was built up again.

Nicholas allowed his sister to remain with an older couple who were admiring her collection of agates, and walked to the lodge with Lyris. They sat together on wide stairs below the porch, watching the glow of the bonfire. Voices carried clearly through the night air as the revelers began a popular tune.

Lyris sighed happily. "It's a beautiful night."

Nicholas slipped one arm about her and she leaned against him. How pleasant it was to have him to herself for a few minutes. The thought brought an unsettling image of the bed upstairs and with it, a memory of kisses and caresses and thoughts of buttons and ribbons undone, of bare skin against bare skin.

She straightened abruptly. "Nicholas, we need to talk." But not about sleeping arrangements. Not yet. She was far too unsettled for that. "About Amelia."

His obvious resistance both saddened and puzzled her. "Amelia has written to Mama about our marriage," she added gently. "She said she knows you. How can that be?"

He was on his feet and at the bottom of the stairs almost before she knew he had moved. "Nicholas," she exclaimed. "Trust me enough to explain."

He stood silhouetted against the distant bonfire. Feeling chilled and alone, Lyris pleaded, "It isn't fair to dislike her so and refuse to tell me why."

He came back to the stairs and sank onto the step just below her. "Do you remember the garden party where I first tried to court you?"

"I insulted you because of Papa."

"A boy sneaked in off the street, but a waiter got hold of him. You rescued the lad." His voice deepened. "I knew then I was going to marry you."

She felt moved that her nearly forgotten impulse had so affected him. Of course, she had infuriated him immediately afterward by loudly scorning the courtship of a saloon keeper. "It seems ages ago. What caused you to think of it now?"

After a silence, during which he seemed to debate with himself, he said in a strained voice, "As a boy, I invaded a similar party. Amelia Chambers had me thrown into the street. I've never forgotten. I'll never forgive her."

"You were a child," Lyris exclaimed, instantly protective both of Nicholas and of her godmother. "I'm sorry you were hurt. But you misunderstood her. You must have."

"I understood," he corrected harshly. "You are a lady, my sweet. Your godmother is a coldhearted witch."

"Nicholas, you don't know her! If you did, you would see that you're wrong."

"You're to have nothing to do with her, Lyris. Do you understand?"

"No, I don't! In some ways, you are incredibly block-headed." She clenched her hands, longing to comfort Nicholas, needing to speak for Amelia. "A child's memory nourished through the years is not reason enough to treat her so harshly."

"There's more to it than that."

"Then tell me."

As tension stretched between them, she felt his need to confide along with a sense of his yielding. She reached out one hand to encourage him, but at that moment a couple strolled toward the stairs. She recognized the pair as those left in charge of Fanny.

Nicholas rose, asking, "Is my sister still on the beach?"

"She said she was going to join you, Mr. Drake," the woman said in surprise. "Isn't she here?"

Without answering, he strode toward the bonfire. Lyris tried to reassure the troubled couple. "I expect she is still showing her stones to the others. Her brother is rather protective."

They nodded and continued on into the hotel. Lyris felt driven to search for Fanny, but forced herself to wait on the porch in case the girl had the unlikely good sense to return. Nicholas had been about to confide in her—at last. While concerned for his sister, Lyris fought her resentment at the fact that Fanny's reckless behavior had stopped him.

An hour passed before he marched the sobbing girl to the hotel. He was white with anger, while Fanny cried tearfully that she had only been enjoying the young man's company and Nicholas had no right to embarrass her.

Lyris took the girl into her arms, trying to calm her while she urged her up the stairs. Once in their suite, Nicholas ordered Fanny into her room, where he held a tense, low-voiced conversation with her, punctuated by her indignant outbursts.

Lyris paced the small parlor, clenching her hands together and hoping that in his present state, Nicholas would not undo all the progress she felt they had made with Fanny.

When he came out at last, she turned to him, questioning with her eyes. He was in no mood to answer. "Go on to bed."

Placing a chair at the doorway of Fanny's room, he set himself as guard. His expression was remote, his mouth a hard, angry line. There seemed nothing Lyris could do but climb into her own bed alone. She slept very little.

During the morning steamer voyage home, Fanny sulked at the rail while her brother remained dour and uncommunicative. The moment when he had nearly shared his deeper thoughts might never have happened. To Lyris, the blissful day spent gathering treasures from the beach seemed only a dream.

She cast an unhappy glance at the wicker chest that she had purchased from the hotel. Its contents were all they had to show for those brief, happy hours. And now with Nicholas and his sister in such dark moods, she was having serious doubts about her dinner party.

Yet the invitations had gone out. They reached home to find a flurry of waiting messages: every guest had accepted.

Somewhat desperately, Lyris set about transforming the dining room into Lost Atlantis. Fortunately, the activity lightened Fanny's mood. Lyris could only hope that Nicholas's attitude would also improve. But she felt she was walking on eggshells. She hadn't yet found a way to warn him that her godmother meant to return to Seattle.

Chapter Eighteen

Fanny peered through the pantry door. Behind her, the kitchen bustled with cooks and serving maids. Mouthwatering smells mingled together—of spices and rich sauces and the toasty aroma of baking pastry. She scarcely noticed, far more caught up with the scene in the dining room. The dinner was a great success and Fanny savored her own contributions.

Lyris had been upset with her for talking with the houseboys while they strung ivy from the ceiling, but the results were spectacular. Tendrils swayed with every draft of air, like kelp moving in an ocean current. Fish cut from colored paper hung on strings, swimming through the seaweed forest.

Plucked heads of roses lay about, pretending to be sea anemone. Clustered among them were the gathered shells, agates and common beach stones. Some were piled at the base of plaster columns tinted an antique ivory to resemble ruins.

Other stones lay scattered along the dinner table, the prettiest in water-filled crystal trays to make them shine. Vines and roses twined about tall white candles.

"Pardon me, miss," said a voice behind her. Fanny stepped aside while Ruby maneuvered the fish tail of her mermaid costume as she carried a tureen of chowder to the table, then she peered in again.

Garnets and opals glittered at the ladies' ears and throats. The rich fabrics of their gowns matched their jewels. Lyris was prettiest. No one would guess that just hours ago, she'd been running around in a panic, pushing agates and shells into position and catching her hair on one of the fish, so that it had to be strung up again.

Now she smiled at her guests, looking as calm as a queen in the cool depths of Lost Atlantis. Fanny turned her attention to the men. They looked as striking as the ladies. Light glinted from jeweled shirt studs and fobs.

She wished she could hear the conversation. Everyone seemed to be having a good time, the women's lighter voices floating above the men's and often mixing with laughter. She wondered which name went with which guest. Evelyn Ellis, she knew, of course. That stuck-up lady flirted with Nick as if she had never snubbed him.

Fanny wondered if Lyris noticed. If she were Nick's wife, she would manage to spill something into Evelyn's lap. As she considered suggesting that to Ruby, a burst of masculine laughter caught her attention. The man laughing was almost as handsome as Nick, with a wonderful mustache and beautiful, expressive eyes.

He watched Ruby with an amused expression while she kicked her fish tail out of her way. When the serving maid returned to the kitchen, his gaze followed, but stopped at Fanny. She knew she should slip away, but neither Lyris nor Nicky were looking. She risked a smile. The man winked.

Fanny fled into the kitchen. Her heart felt as if it would jump right out of her chest. She wondered who he was and when she would meet him. There was no question in her mind that a meeting would take place.

Lyris allowed herself a glow of well-earned triumph. The table glittered as grandly as her guests, while the mystery of Lost Atlantis fairly swam about them. Evelyn's pout pleased her more than Reba's beam of congratulations.

Reba and Alex Shore were casting romantic sparks off each other. At the moment, both ignored their dinner partners while pretending to read each other's fortunes from the markings on their mussel-shell place cards.

That put Richard Thompson into a funk, but Lyris couldn't be sorry for him. He kept trying to insert his more recent triumphs in the amateur boxing ring into the conversation, a subject more suited to the gentlemen's after-dinner cigars and coffee. If he expected to impress Reba with the unsavory subject, he might as well save his breath.

Lyris only wished she had thought to put Reba and Alex together from the start. Cynthia Sinclair appeared to bore Alex nearly as much as Richard did Reba. At least she rounded out the table, Lyris told herself, and Cynthia would add an impressive name to the Seattle Debutante's account of the dinner.

She cast a careful glance toward her husband. With the editor and his wife present, there shouldn't be any mystery in how the details reached that anonymous reporter, but she hadn't yet forgotten the electric silence between herself and Nick when she'd mentioned the *Tribune* during their stay at the island.

Memories of the island woke too many conflicting feelings to be comfortable, particularly during a dinner party. Yet every glance at her decor brought back a visual image. She had to keep wrenching her mind from the memory of Nicholas wading with her after agates. She felt him catch her hand to steady her with a warm, sheltering grasp. She heard his rich laughter over one of Fanny's antics.

And she relived that poignant moment on the stairs when he had begun to explain his deep resentment of her godmother. What little he had said simply confused her more. Why stay angry for years over being rejected from a garden where he didn't belong? And somehow, Amelia knew him by name.

This was no time to worry about the question. Forcing her attention to her table, Lyris saw that her husband was about to use the wrong spoon for his chowder. She picked up her own, raising it meaningfully when she caught his eye.

Jon Brunswich brought up the work of a new author of current interest to the city's elite. Since Nicholas wasn't likely to be informed on the matter, Lyris saved him embarrassment by offering her own opinion. As she did so, she saw his lips thin.

Couldn't he see she was doing her best to protect him? He had been short with her since their return from the island. She knew he regretted offering that single rare glimpse into his past.

He could be extremely frustrating, as she had told him more than once. She turned her attention to Ruby, who was serving a tray of trout in pastry cases garnished with filberts. Evelyn's dull husband, Brewster, offered one of his pedantic comments. "Let us hope, Mrs. Drake, that these pretty sirens of yours are not serving the delectable nuts that will turn us all into Circe's swine."

"Why, Mr. Ellis," Lyris answered lightly. "You have guessed my surprise!"

She was gratified by laughter, but annoyed with Ellis. Little wonder Evelyn flirted, although it was certainly ironic that she should spend this evening in provocative conversation with a man whom she considered unworthy of an invitation to her own table.

Thoughtfully, Lyris considered her husband. Nicholas always gave the impression that he held a dangerous nature just under control. She couldn't blame women for being fascinated, but if her supposed friend Evelyn was entertaining romantic ideas, she had better think again.

Nicholas had begun to carve portions of braised ham. Richard Thompson offered a verbal jab. "You do that as well as if you were born to the task." He was obviously reacting to Reba's near-snub of his company and had drained his wineglass too often, besides. Still, Lyris bristled.

"No," Nicholas answered. "I was born to catch fish." He leveled a steady gaze at the other man before adding, "Some of us succeed in rising above our station." The words *While others descend* were implied.

Alex Shore laughed, while an ugly flush spread over Thompson's face. Lyris searched desperately for a change of subject. Shore forestalled her. "Nicholas, my friend, you should consider politics."

"Start with the town council," Jon suggested. "Seattle could use a man with your farsighted views."

"Gained by years on a trawler," Richard said peevishly. Since there were no vacant seats on the council at present and he intended to run again at the next election, he took the suggestion personally.

Evelyn smiled behind her hand, as if expecting flaring tempers to spoil the occasion. "Please, gentlemen," Lyris protested. "You are wearying the ladies."

Lightly, Reba said, "Our hostess is afraid the mysterious Seattle Debutante will report that her dinner party concerned itself more with politics than with its theme."

"Who is the creature behind that pen name?" Shore demanded. "Jon, you can tell us."

Lyris felt her heart stop. This was not the change of subject she wanted. She looked swiftly at her editor and was reassured. "The lady prefers anonymity," he said smoothly. "As I consider myself a gentleman, I must decline to betray her."

"He won't even tell me," his wife lamented.

Aware that both Reba and Evelyn were pretending an intense interest in their plates, Lyris made herself say carelessly, "Oh, come, Jon. Surely you can give us just a hint."

"A hint," he repeated, his gray eyes amused. "I can tell you the lady is quite beautiful, and as accomplished in social graces as she is adept with her pen." He paused as if about to say more, then shrugged. "Beyond that, please don't ask."

"Then let us guess," Evelyn exclaimed. She tapped Nicholas playfully on the arm. "Tell us, oh farseeing host. Have you no hint of whom it might be?"

Lyris wanted to kick her. Since Evelyn had flirted with Nicholas all evening, he took her challenge in the same light, regarding her with cool amusement. "I'm sure you have an idea, Mrs. Ellis. Why don't you tell us what you think?"

"Well," Evelyn murmured, while Lyris wondered if outdoing her friend's dinner had brought on a craving for revenge, "according to Jon, she is beautiful." She leaned toward the editor. "Would you say the Seattle Debutante is as beautiful as our hostess?"

Lyris fought back rage, but he answered equably, "The man who dares to compare women is the man likely to see his own head rolling in the street."

While the others laughed, Lyris saw Nicholas reach for the butter dish with his dinner knife in hand. Grasping her own butter knife, she tapped it meaningfully against her bread plate. She succeeded in drawing every gaze. Meekly, she lowered the knife.

As if at a tennis match, every head turned back toward Nicholas. Lyris cringed, but was not spared his reaction. "Thank you, my sweet. Would you like to carve my serving of ham into properly bite-size portions?"

His wife's furious blush gave Nick a twinge of regret, but she had brought it on herself. Did she think the others were blind? In trying to correct him, she merely pointed out his lack of social graces. His pride finally rebelled. Now, for once, Lyris appeared to have nothing to say, while their friends looked greatly entertained.

For the most part, the evening had gone well. Evelyn Ellis was a pest, but harmless. Too bad Reba Winters had put Thompson in the sulks. He wasn't likely to engage in any useful discussion after dinner.

Libby Brunswich broke an awkward silence. "I have missed seeing your stories in the *Tribune*, Lyris. When will you again take up your pen?"

Nick answered for her. "My wife doesn't work."

"Oh, but surely you will allow her to indulge so special a talent," Libby exclaimed. "It isn't as though she sat behind a typewriter in the office, after all."

Lyris's challenging glance toward him was obvious to everyone. Nick felt his temper rise. Apparently, Libby believed with the others that Lyris had married below her station and might as well do as she pleased.

"When my wife's name appears in social sections of the *Tribune*," he said with finality, "it will be as the subject of a story, not as the author."

Libby looked ready to continue the argument, but her husband nudged her. Lyris had remained silent, while obviously annoyed. Her two close friends were equally silent, although each glanced at her as if expecting a response.

Cynthia Sinclair exclaimed brightly, "Oh, good, here is dessert. My favorite! Raspberry-and-currant tart!"

Everyone marveled with an excess of enthusiasm while Ruby settled the tart on the table. A second maid hired for the dinner carried in a tray of lemon creams. Again, the guests raved in excess, putting uncomfortable discussion to rest.

As she peered from the pantry door, Fanny told herself it was a foolish custom for the ladies to retire to the parlor just so the men could enjoy their cigars. Lyris had planned games to entertain the ladies, but it was dumb to bore each other with games when they could enjoy the far more interesting company of the men.

She hovered just inside the pantry door, longing to peer in again though she knew she had already pressed her luck. Behind her, the maids thankfully peeled off their fish costumes. In the dining room, voices rose suddenly. Fanny cracked open the door. Nick and the smashing-looking man with the mustache were arguing, while the other two tried to calm them. It had something to do with a council seat. Fanny couldn't quite make it out.

Nick looked as angry as he had when he'd caught her on the beach that night. She backed into the pantry. Her admirer would probably storm right out of the house—if Nick didn't throw him out!

With impulsive decision, she ran up the kitchen stairs to her room, caught up her cloak, then rushed down to the back door and outside to the carriages.

She didn't have long to wait. He came from the house, crushing his hat onto his head while taking long, angry strides. Fanny stepped into a square of light near a window.

He stopped abruptly. "Well. Hello."

With her heart beating like Indian drums, she said, "You're leaving early."

"A well-timed departure." He stepped closer. "Who are you, pet? Not part of the staff."

He was angry with Nick. Would that make him angry with her, too, if she told him who she was? Unwilling to risk losing him so quickly, she said, "I'm visiting. My name is Fanny."

"Fanny," he repeated, making her name sound dizzyingly musical. "And I'm Richard." Taking her elbow, he moved her into the shadow of a carriage.

His touch made her feel warm all over. She longed to lean closer, but didn't want him to think she was fast. "Now, Fanny," he said, again thrilling her in the way he said her name, "tell me about yourself. How long are you visiting?"

"I don't know." She hesitated. "A few weeks."

"Then we will have time to get acquainted." He tilted her chin upward, his touch exciting against her skin.

She barely breathed. "I'd like that."

He seemed to consider. "I wonder what activity a pretty young girl would enjoy? I have it! Do you roller skate, Fanny?"

"I could learn."

"I will enjoy teaching you." His words seemed to promise more than skating. Her heart pounded so hard she felt dizzy.

"We must make an adventure of our friendship, Fanny," he said, stroking her cheek in a way that made her shiver with anticipation.

"What do you mean?" she whispered.

"I mean, my pet, that we will surmount stodgy disapproval by meeting in secret. You're trembling," he added, with such concern that she melted inside. "Does the prospect frighten you?"

She wasn't trembling because she was frightened. With a secret smile, she said, "It seems to me that our adventure has already begun."

"Ah, you are clever as well as pretty." His hand moved to the back of her neck and slowly urged her closer. A door banged and she started nervously.

One of the maids came out. Richard made a shield of his body until the girl went inside. "That's part of the adventure," he said, his voice low. "The risk of discovery. Does it make your blood run faster, Fanny? It does mine."

He was so near that she felt the heat of his body. All she could think to answer was, "Yes."

"Yes," he repeated, making it sound like a promise. "We will meet on Tuesday, pet. My carriage will be around the corner at eight o'clock, waiting to carry my pretty lady to the thrills of the roller rink."

Lyris usually had dinner served around eight. Fanny thought rapidly. She would pretend to be sick and would ask for a bowl of soup to be sent to her room at six. It would be easy to slip out at eight. She whispered, "I'll be there."

He bent to her then, pressing his mouth warmly over hers. His mustache felt soft against her face. She wanted to wrap her arms around him, but too quickly he raised his head, then brushed his fingers against her cheek.

"Sweet," he murmured. "But you'll be missed, pet. Go inside now. Remember, Tuesday. Eight o'clock."

She wished he would kiss her again, but he sauntered to his carriage. "Good night, Richard," she called quietly. Happiness soared through her as she slipped into the kitchen. He liked her. He really did. On Tuesday, he would be free to tell her so.

Chapter Nineteen

Sunlight drenched the kitchen on Tuesday afternoon as Lyris prepared to help Fanny wash her hair. They were both in chemise and drawers and had banished all males from the house. Ordinarily, Jenny would help, but Lyris was making an effort to get on better terms with Nicholas's sister.

Dousing each other's heads with warm water over a basin in the sink put them both in high spirits. With her own wet locks wound up in a towel, Lyris massaged soap into Fanny's dark curls. "You have lovely hair, Fanny. Shall we try a new style?"

Fanny pressed a towel over her eyes. "Let's put it up. Can we? To see how it would look?"

Smiling, Lyris swirled the soapy tresses into an upswept pouf. "There, Miss Drake. Prepare to outshine the debutantes."

Fanny snatched up a hand mirror. Her eyes were wide, her breathing excited as Lyris teased tendrils to frame her face. Fanny was strikingly pretty with her hair up, Lyris mused, even when the dark tresses were held by soap and water.

Her eyes looked especially bright. Realizing that the girl had seemed flushed all morning, Lyris touched her temple. "You're rather warm. Are you feeling well?"

"I might be catching a cold," Fanny said promptly. "I'll go to bed early and maybe I can head it off."

"Yes, do that. And enough of this. You are only fifteen, after all." Lyris washed out the soap along with the adult styling. "I'll have cook prepare a light dinner on a tray."

"Early," Fanny suggested. "So I can go right to sleep."

Nick stood transfixed in the kitchen doorway. Lyris and Fanny looked as if cast in a stage production of domestic harmony. He had heard them laughing as he came through the dining room. Now they talked quietly, the murmur of their voices sounding as pleasant as the hum of bees in a summer garden. His throat tightened against a surge of longing. He wanted a marriage, a real marriage, not a business arrangement.

As he watched, Lyris rose on her toes to rub a large towel vigorously over Fanny's hair. The fluid play of muscles in her shapely hips and bare legs sparked a rush of desire. Then she threw back her head, laughing at some comment from Fanny. Sunlight turned her profile into a vibrant life-filled cameo.

Nick felt shaken. He wanted to stay, but not to reveal the impact she had on him. Silently, he turned away. Lyris craved a pen for company, while he longed to make her truly his wife.

In the parlor, he tried to distract himself with his newspaper. The Seattle Debutante, whoever she might be, had written an account of their dinner party. Jon must have described it in detail. Or the Sinclair girl was the author, after all. A bitter pill for Lyris.

Tossing the paper aside, Nick shoved a hand through his hair. For at least the hundredth time, he wondered how to reach his wife's heart, without loss of pride. Her body responded to his touch, yet her mind stayed stubbornly her own. She was determined to have her divorce. Increasingly, she was all he could think of.

The accounts awaited his attention at the Golden Harbor, but he'd pushed away the books after making many mistakes. It was useless to stay. Admit it, he chided himself. You came home because you wanted to see her.

Restless, he ranged through the house to the dining room, where he again stared up at the portrait of Amelia Chambers. He waited for the familiar fires to stir in his guts, fires that could drive out even the constant longing he felt for his wife.

The first sight of the painting had nearly driven him wild. Lyris must still wonder what had hit him that day. Now the taste of ashes in his mouth didn't seem as bitter. "I've won," he said softly to the painting. "I have your grand house. And I have your precious goddaughter."

The hell of it was that he didn't have her, not yet.

Dinner was served promptly at eight. Lyris gazed down the table at her husband. He wasn't happy about dressing for dinner, but she had convinced him that they must both provide an example for Fanny. Tonight he looked particularly handsome, if somewhat remote.

"We've received an invitation from Evelyn," Lyris told him. "She added regrets at our missing her last affair, as if it were by our choice and not hers!"

He frowned, uninterested in the Brewers. "Why isn't Fanny at the table?"

"She isn't feeling well. I'm sure it's no more than a summer cold, but she retired early."

"I haven't seen signs of a cold."

"For heaven's sake, Nicholas," Lyris exclaimed. "Can't the girl run a low fever without you questioning her motives?" His sardonic expression served as an answer. Lyris toyed with her goblet. "She might try harder to earn your trust if you occasionally showed some."

"We trusted her at the lake. Have you forgotten the result?"

Lyris turned the goblet in her fingers. "I don't believe Fanny is naturally promiscuous. She simply yearns to be loved."

"That's understandable," he said in a low voice, and Lyris felt a surge of satisfaction that he agreed with her, after all.

When they withdrew into the parlor, she took up a piece of embroidery. Needlework was the least of her skills, but she couldn't bear to keep her hands idle. Neither could she concentrate on a book while in the same room with Nicholas.

Her glance kept lingering over the thick waves of his hair and the shadows his eyelashes made against his skin as he studied his newspaper. What an expressive mouth he had. She could always gauge his mood by the curve of his lips.

It occurred to her that he had been staring at the same page for quite a long while. He looked up and she lowered her eyes to her embroidery.

"Lyris," he said, but stopped at a tap on the door.

Sam stepped inside, looking troubled. "Can I talk to you, boss?"

Lyris wished the man would learn a more elegant speech. The thought slipped shortly after her husband followed him into the hall. Nicholas's angry roar startled her into dropping her needle. As she searched the chair cushions, he charged into the room. "Get your cloak and come with me."

Apprehension caught at her throat. "Nicholas, what is wrong?"

Color had drained from his face except for an angry flush over his cheekbones. He ignored her question and she gestured toward her velvet house shoes. "I must change."

"You won't be leaving the carriage." He swung toward the door. "But if I'm alone with her, I swear I'll wring her neck."

"Who?" Had Amelia contacted him? Distraught, Lyris rushed for her cloak. The carriage was already rolling into place when she reached the drive. While Nicholas gave sharp orders to the driver, Lyris scrambled inside.

Her husband climbed in after her, then pounded one fist against his knee. "Sam took his girl roller skating tonight. He was startled to recognize one of the couples at the rink."

"Roller skating?" Amelia didn't skate. Confused, Lyris struggled with her thoughts. Dread moved through her. What she suspected could not possibly be true. "Not..." She gulped and cleared her throat. "Not Fanny?"

He glared ahead. Answer enough. Lyris moaned. How could she? How *could* she? Drawing into her corner, she wished with all her heart that she could turn the clock back to Fanny's request for a tray in her room.

"How in hell did she meet Thompson?" Nicholas demanded. "You run a lax household, madam. Or did you know about it?"

Thompson! For a dreadful moment, she feared she would be ill. Her husband's accusation about her housekeeping went past her. If Thompson was courting Fanny right under her nose, she *was* lax. She could only say in a dismal voice, "I didn't know."

It seemed an eternity that they raced through the rough streets, yet they arrived too soon. Nicholas's anger had not in the least subsided. Lyris dreaded the coming encounter. "I should go with you. Fanny—"

He cut her off. "She wants her hide tanned and I don't need you for that. Stay here."

He sprang from the carriage and strode toward the rink. Lyris held the door ajar, listening to the carefree lilt of music and the sound of wheels circling the wood floor. Would Nicholas barge among the skaters, oblivious to pileups? A scene of mass carnage rose into mind, with her husband at the center.

Thompson was trained as a boxer, while Nicholas was toughened by life on the wharves. Suppose they fought? They were already at odds. Fear ground through her. Fanny could not have made a worse choice.

A movement at one side of the building caught Lyris's eye. She peered into the darkness. With a start of relief, she recognized Thompson. A glimmer from the streetlight betrayed him. She recognized his mustache, and the nervous way he stroked it as he glanced about.

The man was a cad, but she didn't want him to confront Nicholas before her husband's first rush of anger had cooled. At the same time, she was tempted to fly at him herself. He had been a guest in her home. This was her thanks.

On impulse, she stepped from the carriage and called out, "Mr. Thompson! I believe my husband is looking for you."

He jerked a hand toward his mouth as if to silence her, then jerkily doffed his hat. She had to credit his nerve when he strode into the light, ambling rather swiftly toward his carriage. "Afraid I can't wait. My regrets."

"He won't be long."

"That's what worries me." After a word to his driver, he jumped into the carriage and pulled away.

With a faint smile, Lyris sank back onto the seat. He was a cad and a coward, but he wasn't stupid. He would stay clear of Nicholas for a few days. He might even agree to the street assessment. If this particular cloud should prove to be silver lined, perhaps Fanny could be forgiven.

The door to the rink burst open. Nicholas appeared in the lighted rectangle, shoving his sobbing sister ahead. When he handed Fanny into the carriage, the girl collapsed into Lyris's arms.

"Steady," Lyris soothed.

Fanny clutched her frantically, pressing her wet face into Lyris's shoulder. Her body heaved with sobs. "He's hateful! Hateful! How can you stand him?"

Nicholas climbed in and slammed the door. As they traveled toward home, he snapped to Lyris, "You're supposed to be keeping an eye on her. Isn't that what this marriage is all about? It's sure as hell not about the pleasures of the marriage bed."

Lyris had been stroking Fanny's hair, unhappily aware that the girl had pinned her curls on top, in rough imitation of their playful styling with the shampoo. At her husband's furious words, her hand stilled. "It's about promises," she said quietly. "Including one you have yet to keep."

"And one you're failing at miserably."

She hoped Fanny was too immersed in her own despair to attempt to make sense of the discussion. The girl's sobs annoyed her brother. "Sit up," he said sharply. "Lyris is too lenient. That's going to stop."

Fanny cried harder. Her hands clenched in Lyris's cape. "Nicholas, please," Lyris protested. "She's distraught. Let us settle this tomorrow when we are all more calm."

His reply belonged on the waterfront. With a gasp, Lyris clamped her hands over Fanny's ears.

"She's heard worse than that," Nicholas muttered, but with apology. He leaned forward, bracing his forearms across his knees, his body rigid with disappointment in his sister and, Lyris feared, in his wife.

Mrs. Ramsey stepped into the hall when they entered the house. Lyris shook her head and the housekeeper tactfully withdrew. Defiantly, Fanny announced, "I'm going to bed."

"The devil you are," her brother shot back. "Wash your face. Then come into the library."

"Why don't you just take a knife and cut out my heart?" Fanny cried dramatically. "Then I'll be out of your way."

Lyris felt a twinge of pity. But she had given the girl her friendship and had seen it thrown into her face. She led her sister-in-law firmly into the kitchen.

"I suppose you'll let him send me away to school or somewhere," Fanny exclaimed.

"If so, you will have driven him to it." Lyris dipped warm water from the reservoir at the back of the stove and wrung out a facecloth.

Fanny began crying again. "I want to go to bed. If you were my friend, you'd let me."

Lyris thought it would be best to postpone a discussion of tonight's affair, but she wasn't going to suggest that to

Nicholas. "When you have something unpleasant to face, it's best to get it over with at once," she said. "Come along, Fanny. I don't advise keeping your brother waiting."

Nicholas stood by the library fire, hands clasped behind his back, and dourly surveyed them. "Sit. Both of you."

A protest sprang to Lyris's lips. Biting it back, she sank onto a chair.

Fanny dropped onto a low cushioned stool. "Are you going to send me away? *She* says so."

With regret, Lyris heard herself renamed *she*. Worse, the girl was attempting to manipulate them both.

Nicholas's glance at Lyris was as black as the one he leveled at his sister. "I want to know exactly how this happened."

"He asked me and I went," Fanny said promptly. "We were just skating. What's wrong with that?"

Lyris closed her eyes, thinking that the answer to Fanny's question could keep them there all night.

"Lyris," Nicholas said coldly. "By dinnertime tomorrow, I expect Fanny to be prepared to tell me exactly what is wrong with that."

Lyris nodded, but he wasn't through. "'Trust her,' I believe you said, making me feel like a savage for doubting that she was sick."

Unhappily, Lyris said, "You obviously know her best."

"Thank you." He swung toward Fanny. "Now, miss, tell me how you managed to meet the one man in Seattle whom I most despise."

"It was at *your* party."

Lyris looked at her sharply. "How was that possible?"

Fanny appealed to her brother. "How could I know you didn't like him? You invited him. Or did *she* do that?"

Nicholas's brows drew together. "Thompson didn't leave the table. After arguing over the blamed election, he stormed out."

With a defiant toss of her head, Fanny said, "I waited for him outside."

"Oh, Fanny!" Lyris caught her breath in disbelief. She had been willing to see Thompson as a seducer, but not Fanny as shamelessly chasing after him.

Nicholas strode to the window. His jaw looked rigid. Muscles stood out in his throat. Lyris tried to think of a way to assure him that this wouldn't happen again. Nothing came to mind.

Defiantly, Fanny burst out, "*She* doesn't do as you say. Why get mad at me?"

He glared at his sister. "Lyris has been naive enough to trust you. That's all."

"She's still writing for the newspaper. Doesn't that count?"

As her husband turned slowly, Lyris jerked to her feet. Long steps took Nicholas to the desk. He ripped through the newspaper until he found the column.

Smugly, Fanny said, "She's the Seattle Debutante. Everybody knows that."

"No," Lyris said in horror. Her husband's face had darkened. He would think all of Seattle was laughing behind his back. Sickened, she knew she could not have infuriated him more had she made him a cuckold.

When he raised his head, the pupils of his eyes were so enlarged the gold scarcely showed. "Is this true?"

"Not entirely," Lyris said. "Very few know." Fanny must have seen her writing the story. She could have shaken the girl for throwing this at him. Fanny was as sly as she was foolish. And she had succeeded in diverting the sword from over her own head.

"We had a bargain." His cold voice opened a gulf impossible to cross. "Since you haven't bothered to keep your word, madam, I see no reason to keep mine."

He thrust open a side door, not bothering with a hat. Lyris ran after him. "Nicholas, no! You can't mean to show the canvas!"

The door slammed on her words. She wrenched it open. He turned halfway down the walk. "If you have any sense," he said, "you'll stop right there."

Shaking, she clung to the door. He wouldn't exhibit that portrait. He only meant to frighten her.

Behind her, Fanny asked curiously, "What's he got over you? How did he get you to marry him?" She backed away when Lyris swung around. "All right, don't tell me. But I'll find out. I always do."

"You will go to your room. Right this minute." Lyris hauled on a rope to signal Mrs. Ramsey. "I'm sending Ruby upstairs. From now on, she'll sleep by your door."

Chapter Twenty

Nick propped his elbows against the desk in his office and leaned his head into his hands. He had done the unfashionable thing by falling in love with his wife. He didn't intend to compound the error by telling her so. She would either laugh in his face or cry out in horror.

During the two weeks since Fanny's escapade with Thompson, Lyris had thrown herself and the entire staff into preparing the house for summer. She had taken down winter curtains and hung white dimity, and had put everyone's wool clothing away with camphor. And that was just the start. It was as if by keeping the house in a turmoil, she could more readily avoid him.

He never knew what he might return to. It could be having the floors in disarray, because she'd had the carpets taken up. It could be finding all the cupboards and closets turned out. One day recently he'd come home to find her having the kitchen whitewashed, which meant a cold dinner that night.

At any rate, meals had become so constrained that most of the food returned to the kitchen untasted. Now, apparently, Lyris had an unhappy cook on her hands, as well.

He would rather have her lash him with her wit than continue this way. They had had it out over the matter of the newspaper, with Lyris insisting she had promised only that her name would not appear. She also reminded him of their plan to divorce. She needed to write, she said, to prepare for a career later.

He felt that she'd made a fool of him, that while he publicly stated that his wife didn't work, her friends had known that she worked behind his back. But he heard more than her plans for a journalistic future in her vehement insistence. He understood that by escaping into the world created by her pen, she was just able to endure her marriage.

So he had agreed. She could write, as long as her identity was kept secret. And she was to let Jon and her friends know that he was not fooled. At least she had his sister on a short rein. Just last night, Fanny had complained loudly about being sent to her room after dinner, shouting that she might as well be in prison.

Where was the happy domestic scene he had happened upon in the sun-drenched kitchen? Lyris was angry that he blamed her for his sister's deceit, but blast it all, she knew what the girl was. Lyris had her own tender heart to blame.

He didn't want her heart to harden, particularly against him. It was her kindness that had first attracted him to her. He wanted her love, not her obedience. He wanted to make love with her in the full meaning of the word, to join their hearts and minds as well as their bodies. Uttering a low groan, he massaged his aching temples.

A rap at the door brought him upright as Alex Shore sauntered in. The hotel keeper's eyes held an unusual twinkle. Helping himself to a cigar from a case on Nick's desk, he leaned back in a chair. "I've just had an interesting visit with our mutual friend, Mr. Thompson."

Nick felt his fists clench. "If that bastard is spreading stories..."

"It's good news," Alex broke in. "He's willing to share in the cost of repairs."

Nick forced himself to relax. Lyris had suggested something of the sort. However, he wanted a guarantee that his sister's name would never pass Thompson's lips. "How did you run him down? I've tried for weeks."

"Richard doesn't appear eager to talk with you. Asked me to carry the word." Alex lit the cigar, sucked deeply and released a pungent cloud. "I thought his nervousness stemmed from the argument at your home that night. Is there something more?"

"There is. But it's between the two of us." Nick opened a cupboard near his chair. "So the street will see repairs. That's worth celebrating. You'll join me in a brandy?"

"Anytime." Alex allowed the question of a feud between Nick and Thompson to be diverted. "By the way," he said as Nick poured from a crystal decanter, "an interesting guest checked in after the train from Tacoma last night."

"Oh?" Nick passed a glass across the desk, then settled back with his own.

Alex raised a toast. "To a street we can be proud of." After drinking, he added, "The guest I mentioned is the lady who once owned your house."

Nick choked, sputtering brandy. Alex jumped to his feet and pounded him on the back. Between coughs, Nick asked, "Are you talking about Amelia Chambers?"

"That's right. Seems she's sorry now that she sold. Says she's moving back to Seattle."

For a moment, Nick couldn't move. Then he slammed down his glass and leapt to his feet, shouting for Sam. "Get my carriage!"

Alex called after him, "What the devil's got into you?"

Nick sprinted down the hall without taking time to explain. If the Chambers woman talked to his wife, God knew what she'd say. And Lyris was upset already. Cursing, he ran for the street.

Lyris was delighted to discover that Fanny took an interest in gardening. She was actually humming as she helped gather the roots of dandelions growing in the side yard. It was the first time since the affair of the skating rink that Lyris had seen the girl happy.

The two of them had established an uncertain relationship. Fanny resented the close eye Lyris kept on her, but they were united in trying to avoid further displeasing Nicholas.

On the morning after her shameful conduct with Thompson, Fanny had pouted through a lecture on rules of behavior: While a well-bred young lady might use her fan to subtly indicate interest in a man, she did not chase after him. She must never be in his company unchaperoned. Above all, she must not permit improper advances and never a kiss.

"How boring," Fanny muttered. When she later parroted the rules to her brother, it was clear she hadn't taken them much to mind.

Now, however, she looked up with laughing eyes. "Are you really going to make Nicky drink a tonic from these roots? I'd like to see that!"

Lyris smiled. "I expect you will be too concerned with choking down your own to take much pleasure in your brother's distaste."

Looking horrified, Fanny began poking the roots back into the soil. Lyris tapped her playfully with a trowel. "You'll only be out here longer. I mean to fill this basket."

In truth, she didn't have much confidence in her ability to force a tonic on Nicholas. She would probably have to resort to her mother's method of steeping tansy leaves in rum if she hoped to get healthful herbs into him at all.

"Be sure to gather the young leaves, Fanny. We'll have cook add them to a salad."

As Fanny wrinkled her nose, Lyris heard two carriages pull into the drive, one fast behind the other. What in the world was going on? She hurried through the side yard, then stopped short. Her godmother had just stepped from a public carriage in front.

Amelia was a tall woman who carried herself with dignity. She was dressed now in her favorite lavender silk, a jet-beaded reticule dangling stylishly from one arm. Even the waves of white hair beneath the sharp-beaked little birds on her hat showed a faint tint of lavender.

She looked as if she had just returned home from the shops, but this was no longer her home, and while Lyris longed to run into her arms, Nicholas was striding from his own carriage.

"Oh, dear Heaven," Lyris whispered, so torn by welcome and dread that she was unable to move.

Her godmother waved gaily, then heard Nicholas's approach and turned toward him. His hard voice shook Lyris to her soul. "You are not welcome here."

Lyris sprang forward. "Amelia! Of course, you are."

Amelia reached out her arms, but Nicholas stepped between them, blocking Lyris with his shoulder. The older woman spoke quietly. "I had hoped we could begin again, Nicholas."

"Didn't you hear me?" he snapped. "Get out of here."

Lyris tried to move past him, but he turned her toward the door, his hands strong at her waist. "Go in the house."

Amelia exclaimed, "You are a great deal like your father."

His father? How could Amelia know his father? More confused then before, Lyris fought to free herself.

Nicholas's voice rasped, "Old woman, I won't hesitate to throw you off my property."

Angry tears sprang to Lyris's eyes. She wrenched at his hands. "I won't let you do this!"

"You don't have a choice." Scooping her into his arms, he strode past his startled sister to a side door and dumped Lyris into the hall. Amelia's anguished cry followed them. "Oh, my poor Lyris. What have you gotten yourself into?"

Scrambling erect, Lyris lurched for the door. Nicholas stopped her, his eyes stormy. "Stay here."

"I will not!" She slammed an elbow into his stomach and, when he doubled over, leapt for the door.

He caught her by one arm, throwing Lyris off balance. Her head smacked against the wall. She gasped, reeling. "Nicholas! Stop this! What is the matter with you?"

Reaching out blindly, he pulled her into his arms. His cupped hand cradled her head. "Oh, God, Lyris. I never meant to hurt you."

She pressed the momentary advantage. "Either tell me now why I can't see her, or accept the fact that I will."

He stiffened, then stepped back. Their eyes battled. "See her and you will also see your portrait on public display."

"You are so proud of your word," Lyris exclaimed. "I expect you to keep it. Amelia had nothing to do with our bargain. You only threw her in later."

They both started when the door banged open. Fanny burst in. "That lady left. Who was she? What's going on?"

Nick fought for composure. They were standing in a narrow hallway off the kitchen. God knew how much the staff had heard. Worse, Lyris might never forgive him for hurting her.

He couldn't keep her away from Amelia, not with the two of them in the same town. It was all he could do to keep Fanny away from Thompson, and he needed Lyris's help for that. Feeling beaten, he said, "Come into the parlor, both of you."

As they started forward, he thought ironically that it was the first order he had given that they'd obeyed without argument.

In the parlor, he knelt and stoked up the fire. It was still cool in the house, although outdoors it was warm on this first day of June. He realized he was avoiding an explanation, just as Fanny had tried to escape telling her own uncomfortable story.

Lyris perched on the edge of her favorite chair with a demand for answers in her expression. Fanny knelt nearby, her eyes wide with curiosity. After crossing the room, Nick dropped heavily into his own chair.

He looked at his wife, wishing he could appeal to her loyalty. But her loyalty was for Amelia and she did not appear at all forgiving.

Sick at heart, he leaned forward and rested his arms on his knees, then stared morosely at his loosely linked hands. How could he put into words the most hurtful experience of his life?

If he didn't tell her, Amelia would. Who knew what she might say? Bitterness coated his voice. "Fanny, tell Lyris our mother's given name."

She looked from her brother to Lyris, as if more confused than before. "Ivy. Mama's name was Ivy."

A muscle flickered in Nick's jaw. He turned to his wife. "Does that name mean anything to you?"

Where had she heard it before? Lyris's mind leapt to the table in the attic, carved in a child's hand: Ivy. The answer came so swiftly, she wondered if she had been preparing for this through the past weeks. "Dear God," she whispered.

Fanny said impatiently, "Will one of you please tell me what is going on?"

Lyris continued to look at Nicholas. When he was only a child, Amelia had ordered him thrown from her garden! Her own grandson! Disbelief followed horror. None of this could be true! Amelia had always been loving and kind. She could not have rejected her own daughter and grandchildren.

Again, Lyris pictured the locked attic. Nicholas had not spoken for long minutes after entering that storage room. He must have been stunned by the discovery. Why, even Ivy's baby carriage was there. He had stared into it, so transfixed that Lyris feared he longed for children of his own.

She had been blind. How could she have missed seeing his torment? Yet he had kept his thoughts hidden. Or almost hidden. When she'd spoken of the apparent tragedy in Edwin and Amelia's lives, he had answered with anger. *You don't know a damned thing you're talking about.*

He was right. She hadn't known. He hadn't trusted her enough to tell her. Now she felt betrayed. "I just don't understand."

"Ivy married beneath her station," Nick said savagely. "She had to elope to do it."

Lyris felt numb. "I didn't know. I never heard of Ivy."

"Nor of her children."

"No." Tears filled her eyes and she reached out to wrap one arm around Fanny, aware of the girl's confusion but too confused herself to help. "You said Amelia had a daughter. And we found all those things locked in the attic...."

In a small voice, Fanny said, "Are you saying that lady was our gramma?"

"Yes," Lyris said. "But Fanny, there has been some sort of terrible mistake."

Nicholas answered harshly. "There's been a mistake, all right, but your miserable *godmother* made it. I'll never forgive her for the pain she caused my mother."

Aching for Nicholas even as her heart resisted, Lyris said urgently, "Why wouldn't you tell me?"

He looked away. "We haven't exactly pledged our hearts and lives to each other."

No, the marriage was to end with Fanny's launch into society, an event that seemed less likely all the time. Lyris put that problem aside for the greater one. She thought of the night at the beach when he had revealed a raw childhood memory. Later, she'd believed he regretted telling her even that.

He hadn't wanted her pity. He had it now, wanted or not. "During that garden party years ago, did you know who she was?"

He nodded, his eyes bleak. "I used to stand outside this house, thinking how grand it looked and dreaming of the marvelous toys my mother described."

"Those dolls and things in the attic," Fanny exclaimed. "They belonged to Mama!" Jumping to her feet, she said, "I need to look at them again."

Lyris watched her run from the room, thankful that Fanny seemed more excited than disturbed. But then, she hadn't lived with the bitterness that drove her brother. "I just can't believe this. I *know* Amelia. She couldn't close her heart like that. When she ordered you out of her garden, she couldn't have known who you were.''

"Lyris, she knew. I'll never forget the disgust in her face when I called her 'grandmother.' '' His voice shook. "I've devoted every minute of my life from that time on to proving how badly she misjudged me.''

Lyris looked at him through a shimmer of tears. "It isn't a victory if it hurts.''

"I'm sorry it hurts you. But I hope it hurts her like the devil. For the rest of her days.''

Couldn't he see that it hurt him, as well? Lyris longed to comfort him, but he had reminded her that their marriage was not a pledge of hearts. She was as much a part of his vengeance as the wealth he had acquired. "Did you plan to use me from the first?''

"No. I chose you because you were kind to a child.''

The urchin who had trespassed at a lawn party. Compassion twisted her heart. It was easy to follow what had happened from there. He'd overheard her tell Papa that she would never so lower herself as to accept the courtship of a common tradesman.

She had rejected him in the same way his grandmother had, without even being aware of it. And he'd retaliated with that odious portrait. Sadly, she said, "You are a vindictive man, Nicholas.''

"You still won't accept the truth.''

She did see the truth, at least as he presented it. He believed that Amelia had substituted a child of higher status for grandchildren who were not acceptable in her eyes. But it wasn't possible to reconcile her kindhearted godmother with the monstrous creature he described.

As she frowned past her tightly knotted hands, Lyris noticed a calling card on the floor where Fanny had leapt to her feet. Carefully, she moved her foot so that her long skirt concealed the familiar tea-rose design.

Her swift glance had noted the name of a hotel penned beneath her godmother's engraved signature. Amelia must have meant to leave the card if she wasn't admitted to the house, then must have taken the opportunity to give it to Fanny.

And yet, she hadn't identified herself to her granddaughter. Why not? Lyris knew she would have to hear Amelia's side of all this. She wanted to go to Nicholas, to comfort him. But if she moved, she would reveal Amelia's card.

So she remained in her chair, hoping her expression conveyed sympathy, while vowing to take her carriage to her godmother's hotel at the first opportunity.

Chapter Twenty-One

Nick started awake from a nightmare, sweating and shocked. As his pulse slowed, he thought of that first night, when Fanny's dreams were disturbed. Lyris had slept with her to calm her. He could imagine his wife's response if he asked her to come to him.

Instead he lay awake staring into the dark, unwilling to surrender again to nightmares and longing for the woman who had, however unintentionally, promised to cherish him until parted by death.

Seeing Amelia again had shaken him deeply. The woman *still* had power over him. Despite his wealth. Despite his marriage. Despite the fact that he'd acquired her home and most of her possessions.

But not her goddaughter. Behind the compassion in Lyris's lovely eyes lay lifelong loyalty to her godmother. Even when the truth was laid out for her, she defended the old woman. He stood at one pole, Amelia Chambers at the other. Lyris would have to choose, and he knew what her choice would be.

Lyris woke, thinking she had heard a cry from Fanny, then realized a loose shutter creaked in the wind. Even so, she slipped into her robe and walked down the hall. The girl lay fast asleep.

They had practically had to pry her from the attic. Then she had emerged clutching a worn teddy bear with a missing eye. It was as if she had suddenly recovered a childhood lost in her rush to grow up.

If only her brother could share that sense of a mother magically recovered. He had nourished old pain until it was destroying him. While her heart ached with compassion, Lyris believed that his memory of Amelia's garden party had been distorted by his youth and by the passing years.

If Edwin had hurled him into the street, she would believe it easily. She had always been somewhat fearful of Edwin. But Nicholas mentioned only Amelia. Sighing, Lyris returned to bed, determined to learn the full truth from her godmother in the morning.

When at last Lyris set out on foot toward the wharf, the hour was well past midday. Instead of leaving early for his office at the Golden Harbor as was his usual habit, Nicholas had lingered over breakfast. His eyes were haunted, the skin dark beneath them. She doubted that he'd slept any more than had she.

His grim expression told her he was guarding against Amelia's return. He must know he couldn't keep the two of them apart forever. He was only postponing the inevitable. The fact must have finally occurred to him. Even so, before leaving for town, he gave direct orders. "That woman is not to set foot in my house."

Lyris reached out for him. "Won't you just talk with her?"

"I tried that, years ago."

As she watched him stalk to the carriage, Lyris felt torn with conflicting loyalties. Amelia had chosen a hotel near the Golden Harbor. Although Lyris couldn't imagine her dignified godmother stepping inside a saloon, she hoped Amelia did not intend to confront her grandson there.

She waited only until his carriage was out of sight before setting out herself, on foot. When she reached the business

district, moving carefully over worn planks, she kept a sharp
lookout for her husband or his man, Sam, who had carried
the tale of Fanny's escapade. Holding her skirts higher, she
hurried into the hotel.

She nearly collided with Amelia, who was on her way out.
They clutched each other in startled delight. "Come
quickly," Amelia exclaimed with a wary glance at the door.
"We'll have tea sent to my room. Dearest Lyris, I have a
thousand and one questions."

"Then ask for a double pot," Lyris said. "I have at least
a thousand and two."

At last they were seated at a pretty wicker table in a sunny
bedroom on the hotel's second floor. A pot of fuchsias
echoed the floral design on the walls. The setting flattered
Amelia's fragile beauty, yet the cheerful look of it was so
contrary to her own mood, Lyris was tempted to draw the
drapes.

Amelia regarded her fondly. "I knew you would come to
me."

"There was never any question." Lyris watched her pour
tea into delicate china cups. "Do you really mean to move
back here?"

In the same moment, Amelia asked, "Are you at all
happy?"

They both stopped and smiled ruefully, then Amelia said,
"I know you were taught not to interrupt your elders, so I
will insist that you answer my question first."

Lyris had meant to broach the subject delicately, but after the scene yesterday, it was ludicrous to pretend it wasn't
on both their minds. She answered with as much truth as she
could give. "I am satisfied with the arrangement I've
made."

Her godmother pursed her lips. "The arrangement?"

Partly to protect him, but mostly because she could not
hold it back, Lyris blurted, "I was stunned to learn of your
relationship to my husband. And to Fanny. Amelia, why
didn't you introduce yourself to Fanny?"

Amelia set her cup sharply in its saucer. "That was Fanny? I thought she was a girl you had hired to help in the garden."

"She and Nicholas greatly resemble each other."

"Lyris, I was so distressed I scarcely looked at the child. I understood that Fanny was living in San Francisco with her paternal grandparents. I have been trying to gather the courage to make a visit there."

"Fanny was sent into her brother's care." Lyris hesitated. "She has a somewhat frivolous nature. To be honest, she is the reason he married."

"I don't understand," Amelia said, shaking her head. "You have always been set against marriage. Why in the world did you accept Nicholas Drake?"

"I long to invite you to dinner," Lyris exclaimed, sidestepping the question. "I want you to know both your grandchildren and for them to love you as I do."

Still shaking her head, Amelia sipped her tea. Lyris leaned forward. "It distresses me to ask this, dear Amelia, but I must have an answer. Nicholas revealed a painful incident between the two of you when he was a child."

The older woman touched her lips with a linen napkin. Lines deepened in her face. The sprightliness Lyris had always ascribed to her faded so that she looked every day of her age. "That would be the interruption of my garden party."

Even to nod was painful. Lyris realized she had been hoping that event had taken place only in the nightmares of a troubled young boy.

"I was terrified," Amelia said. "You remember how cruel my husband could be. Ivy loved Ethan Drake deeply, or she would never have dared defy Edwin."

With a trembling hand, she returned her cup to its saucer, the tiny clatter of china seeming to startle her. "Edwin became obsessive about the marriage. Ivy and her husband moved to Seattle when Nicky was eight years old, hoping to

get away from him. He moved the headquarters of his shipping business to follow our daughter here.''

''But I thought he never contacted her.''

''Never.'' Amelia pursed her lips. ''When we moved from
San Francisco, Edwin brought along everything Ivy had ever
used—even her baby carriage—and locked them in the attic.''

''I don't understand. Why in the world would he do such
a thing?''

''He believed she would come to her senses and leave that
man. She would then be permitted to come home, you see.
He refused to recognize the marriage. Whenever a young
bachelor made his mark, Edwin would say, 'There's a fellow for Ivy.' ''

She shuddered and Lyris clasped one of her hands, distressed to learn how fragile the bones had become. Amelia's voice quavered. ''You can't imagine how it was. I knew
Ivy would never leave her husband and yet Edwin went on
and on. It was I who finally forbade mention of her name
and I who 'lost' the key to the attic, blaming a housekeeper
who had left in a rage because of Edwin.''

She brushed unsteady fingertips across her eyes. ''To the
day he died, he expected Ivy to come home. He nearly drove
me to the edge of sanity. You were like sunlight in that
house, Lyris. I dread to think what my life would have been
without you. Each time the door closed behind you, winter
returned.''

Throat aching, Lyris stroked her godmother's hand. ''I
told Nicholas he was wrong, that you are loving and kind.''

''Ah, but not to him.'' Amelia gazed into the past. ''Edwin broke my heart when he closed our door to Ivy and even
to her children. I sent gifts without his knowledge, but never
found the courage to openly risk his anger. He would have
cast me out as surely as he cut off his daughter. And I had
no family, no funds of my own, absolutely nowhere to go.''

Nicholas hadn't mentioned gifts. Lyris felt a ray of hope.
If she could convince him that at least part of his memory

was mistaken, she might have a chance to overcome his bitterness. "Tell me about the gifts," she said softly. "How were they received?"

For a moment, Amelia's eyes flashed. "Exactly the same as the set of gold inlaid photograph albums I sent to your wedding." The flicker of anger gentled into sorrow. "They were returned, all of them. After a period of years, I realized it wasn't worth risking my husband's fury only to see my gifts thrown back at me."

Lyris looked at her in dismay. "Was Ivy as resentful as Edwin? She must have had her father's nature."

"Not Ivy. We managed to meet, although rarely and in secret. Meeting was as difficult for her as for me. You see, her husband was as proud as Edwin. Rather like Nicholas, I'm afraid. He insisted that she reject her family as severely as they had rejected him."

Her voice broke and she pressed her fists to her mouth. "Oh, please, don't," Lyris whispered, then wondered if Amelia had ever been allowed to express her grief.

"They had that other grandmother," Amelia said brokenly. "She loved them. She held them. She baked for them and treasured their small gifts. As I could never do."

Lyris slipped from her chair to take the older woman in her arms, holding her as she would comfort a child. Nicholas was thirty-one years old. For at least that many years, Amelia had lived with a broken heart.

At last Amelia drew away, controlling her sobs as she groped in her reticule for a lace handkerchief. When she dried her eyes, she reached a trembling hand toward her teacup. Lyris still had unanswered questions, but she couldn't bear to upset her godmother even more.

A sip of tea seemed to restore her, however. Looking slightly abashed, she said, "You must forgive me, dear. I honestly did not come here to cry on your shoulder."

Lyris exclaimed, "You've held it in for much too long."

"Oh, I shed an ocean of bitter tears, Lyris." Amelia's tone strengthened. "That is in the past. Drink your tea, dear. I promise not to collapse off my chair."

With a faint smile that admitted exactly that fear, Lyris returned to her seat. Amelia said staunchly, "You are wondering about that interrupted party."

"If it is too painful . . ." Lyris began.

"Since you have taken it upon yourself to live with the man, you should know the source of his bitterness." Amelia clasped Lyris's right hand with both of her own. "It happened so quickly. I don't excuse myself, but I vow I meant to protect the boy."

"From Edwin?"

"My husband was only a few feet away. Fortunately, he was engrossed in conversation. He would not have recognized Nicky, of course. He didn't know that I occasionally saw the child, although always from a distance. I was amazed that Nicky knew me."

She paused, with so lost an expression that Lyris tightened her clasp on her hand. "The child burst suddenly from the shrubbery. He called, 'Grandmother, I'm Nick.' I thought my heart would stop."

Lyris remembered his bleak expression when he'd answered that his grandmother knew who he was that day; that he had told her. The pain inside her grew greater, as did a need to right the situation, though she didn't know how. She loved Amelia. And she loved her husband. The recognition shocked her. How long had that been true?

Caught in her own pain, Amelia continued. "I was so frightened that Edwin might have heard. Lyris, you know he was a hard man. But you don't know how cruel he could be. He had actually hit servants upon occasion, and discharged them for the least misstep. He would not have hesitated to strike Nicholas."

"Oh, no," Lyris protested.

"For the boy's own good, you see," Amelia said grimly. "To teach him not to set himself above his class. It would have made perfect sense to Edwin."

Lyris shook her head, wanting to offer comfort but unable to find the words.

"And there was his pride," Amelia continued. "Our garden brimmed with people of status that day. For the boy to be heard calling Edwin 'grandfather' would have been a disgrace. A boy of common blood. And then it would all have come out. Ivy's betrayal. And the fact that Edwin had disowned his only child. It would have shamed him. He would have made deadly certain that Nicky never attempted to contact us again."

Lyris felt Amelia's terror on that day, even this much later, in the retelling. "A servant marched the child back to the street," Amelia said painfully. "I have lived ever since with the memory of anguish in that little boy's face."

"He has to hear this."

"It's too late." Amelia clasped her hands in her lap and gazed at them sadly. "I had hoped... but I saw yesterday that I have no place in his life." She hesitated, then raised her head with a wistful expression. "Do you think Fanny would meet with me?"

"Yes, but not right away." Lyris twisted her wedding ring, thinking. Fanny would be curious and probably charmed, but there had been too many hidden meetings. "Nicholas is adamantly against any contact, you know, and Fanny is already in trouble with him."

"Trouble?" Amelia asked anxiously.

Lyris smiled, her spirits lifting for the first time in long minutes. "You will like Fanny, I promise. She's as high-spirited as I was as a child and as determined to test every rule."

As she reached for a tea cake, Lyris felt a rise of hope. There would be a happy ending, after all. There must be. "I am determined to see the three of you reconciled."

"You are so young," Amelia mused. "I remember when I faced life with just such optimism, but with time, my dear, we learn that some things can't be changed. It's clear that Nicholas is as stubborn in his pride as was Edwin, and for that matter, his own father."

Nonetheless, Lyris set herself the task of moving the seemingly immovable stone in Nicholas's heart. "He can be loving, even playful. I want you to know that. When Fanny was unhappy, he bought her a kitten. I am certain I can bring him around."

With a gentle smile, Amelia asked, "You are basing your hope on a kitten?"

"I'm basing it on an inner side he rarely shows but cannot fully suppress." Lyris returned Amelia's smile with a staunch one of her own.

The certainty that she could influence Nicholas remained solid, despite her godmother's doubts. Lyris left the hotel room an hour later with high anticipation.

That attitude faltered when she stepped into the hotel lobby and met her husband's startled gaze, from where he stood at the desk talking with Alex Shore.

Chapter Twenty-Two

Lyris felt her heart drop to her stomach. Her husband must have guessed instantly her purpose in being here. She had no choice but to smile gaily and cross the lobby. "Nicholas! I didn't expect to see you."

The warning in his eyes boded ill for the future. "I'm sure you didn't, my sweet." After a pause during which her heart thudded uncomfortably, he added, "I assume you have been visiting the interesting Mrs. Chambers?"

He would never air their disagreement in public. Lyris seized the opportunity. "I have! Nicholas, I must tell you how mistaken you've been."

He cut her off. "Calm yourself, madam. I shouldn't have to tell you to behave like a lady."

She began again. "Amelia isn't what you—"

He spoke to Alex, a warning to Lyris shading his voice. "My wife has a tender nature, but scarcely a thought for her own welfare."

She knew exactly where the risk to her welfare lay. It splintered the air between them as he turned back to her, his voice dangerously pleasant. "Did you walk all this way, sweetheart? You should have asked for the carriage."

And have him forbid her to leave the house? "You are too obliging, Mr. Drake. I didn't wish to inconvenience you."

"But you have, my sweet. For now I'll have to see you safely home."

It wasn't inconvenience that upset him. It was her meeting with Amelia, and she did not want to be alone with him while he was angry about that. "Please don't bother."

Grinning, Alex broke in. "Come, my friends. Don't be quarreling in public. Let me offer a private room upstairs."

Nicholas answered stiffly, "As far as that goes, I have a private office across the street." With a nod for Alex, he escorted Lyris smartly from the hotel.

She protested in a low voice as he marched her toward the saloon. "There is no need for you to be so angry, if you would only listen."

He escorted her the length of the public room while bar patrons watched curiously. Lyris's pride suffered while her stomach resisted the unsavory stench of spilled liquor and unwashed men. With a nervous lurch of her senses, she remembered that Nicholas had sprung from just such a rough background.

He closed the two of them into his office, his eyes colder than she had ever seen them. His voice chilled her more. "I've been easy because your high spirits amused me. That was a mistake. You've betrayed me at every turn—with the newspaper, with Fanny, now with this."

"If so," Lyris protested, "it's because you have been unreasonable."

His brows drew together. "We need to refresh your memory, sweet wife. Sit there."

Warily, she perched on a heavy, slat-backed captain's chair behind his desk. He unlocked a drawer and drew out a key she recognized as the one to the wardrobe.

Her glance flew to the letter opener. He saw it and picked up the blade, then with a wicked glint in his eyes, placed it on a corner of the desk. "We'll leave it there, just out of your reach."

Uneasily, she asked, "What do you mean?"

He unbuckled his leather belt and whipped it free. Lyris lurched to her feet. He thrust her back onto the chair, slung the belt around her waist and pulled the ends through the chair slats. In shocked disbelief, she wrenched at the belt. "Have you lost your mind?"

He secured the buckle, then leaned against the desk, watching with satisfaction as she groped futilely through the slats. "When I have your word that you will never again contact that woman, I'll free you, Lyris. How long you remain like a trussed calf is up to you." He crossed to the wardrobe and inserted the key. "This may speed your decision."

Her skin became chilled when he set *The Naked Huntress* against the opposite wall. She had nearly convinced herself the portrait couldn't be as obscene as she remembered. It was.

With a hiss of breath, she lunged against the belt. "You bastard!"

He leaned one arm across the top of the frame. "I wonder where a lady learned such language."

"Set me free!"

"Do I have your promise? You will never again contact your godmother?"

Lyris thought of Amelia's heartbroken sobs. Never see her again? How could she promise that? Through a sheen of angry tears, she glared at her wretched husband. "She loves you. She has always loved you. It was Edwin who—"

"Hold your tongue! Her name is never to cross your lips. Swear it."

"But you're wrong!"

He thrust the portrait forward. "Our bargain was that you would have this when we divorce—not that it would remain hidden. Shall we begin a private showing with Sam?"

No more than an hour ago she had believed she loved him! She had even thought he loved her. Now, there was no telling what he might be capable of doing. And yet she whispered, "You would never do that."

"Can you imagine the flight of gossip?" he mused. "Sam to his adored Rosy. Rosy to her mistress, and from Evelyn... My mind falters, sweetheart. After Evelyn, where?"

"You would not!" Lyris's voice vibrated. She clamped her lips together to keep them from trembling.

Nicholas set the portrait against the wall. "Give me your word and put an end to this."

"Never!"

He straightened. "The devil take your mulish heart! Do you think I'm joking?"

She cringed as he wrenched open the door into the hall. "I'll leave this ajar," he said. "Call me when you're ready to agree. If your luck holds, no one will wander in."

As his steps receded into the hall, her imagination filled the doorway with jeering men whose gossip would inevitably reach the ears of her friends. She strained so desperately for the letter opener that she nearly cut herself in half.

If she could just move the chair, she might reach the blade and saw through the beastly belt. The chair was heavy and she was awkwardly positioned. Her skirts got in the way and when she did succeed in raising one chair leg, it banged down on the fabric, wrenching her painfully sideways.

Gulping, she dragged at the navy blue faille. Her mind spun. She forced herself to calm down, to think. She had believed that reconciling Nicholas with his grandmother would be merely a matter of clearing up misconceptions. She had been naive. If she hoped to resolve this, she would have to see through his eyes.

The terrible experience in Amelia's garden had dramatically proved his grandparents' scorn, not only toward Nicholas, but for everyone he loved. In begging him to forgive Amelia, she was asking him to change the direction of his life. If he gave up the anger that had driven him to acquire wealth and property and even to marry, he would be without purpose. Or so it must seem.

If he learned to forgive, it would not be she who taught him. Change in him would have to come through Amelia. For the life of her, Lyris couldn't see how that would happen.

With the palm of one hand, she scrubbed at tears, then, feeling severely galled, raised her voice and called clearly, "Nicholas! You win. Set me free."

Nick heard her from the post he had taken just beyond the door. He told himself he should feel triumphant. Instead, by forcing her to back down, he felt as if he had lost. Damn it, he was in the right. Lyris was far too headstrong. Her own father couldn't control her.

Even so, victory tasted bitter, especially when he walked into his office and saw tears shimmering in her eyes. Her expression damned him. Steadily, she said, "You have my word that while we are married, I will not speak of or see Amelia."

The brave words faltered. Her throat worked as she swallowed, but she kept her gaze level. Feeling diminished by her injured spirit, Nick walked behind the chair and unfastened the belt buckle.

No sooner was she free than Lyris leapt forward, snatched the letter opener and lunged for the painting. Nick dived after her, stumbled over the falling chair, but caught a fistful of her skirt. As she drove the point of her blade into the canvas, he dragged her backward.

He held her pinned against him, arms at her sides. Even in this, he felt intensely conscious of her body and of the sweet fragrance of her hair. Her aim had been desperate. The slash in the canvas marred the goddess's shoulder, but not her provocative and familiar face.

His stubborn wife raised one foot and kicked back at him, hampered by her skirts. He slid his hand down the delicate length of her arm and relieved her of the letter opener before she could think to turn it on him.

"Calm down while I put the portrait away," he warned. "If you force me to leave it in full view while I take you home, anyone might see it."

"Isn't that what you want?"

He suppressed a crazy desire to kiss her. His final warning had taken the fight out of her. Cautiously, he let her go.

She remained beside the desk, her shoulders slumped, while he locked the portrait inside the wardrobe. "Take heart," he said. "Our union will end soon enough."

"It wouldn't be soon enough if it ended yesterday," she said rebelliously, and against all good sense, Nick took pleasure from her unquenched spirit.

For the next three days, Lyris continued to drive herself, preparing the house for summer. It wasn't that she enjoyed the work. She had to keep busy, or go wild with her thoughts.

Her husband had also banned Fanny from mentioning Amelia Chambers. During a tumultuous interview in their drawing room, he'd told his sister that blood was all she had in common with the woman and that if Amelia could drain her patrician share from them both, she would do so gladly.

Fanny reacted by withdrawing. The sunny personality Lyris had glimpsed in the garden soon disappeared entirely.

When the housekeeper complained that Fanny was interrupting the boys at their chores in the yard, Nicholas confined the girl to her room. She slipped out and somehow got into the locked liquor cabinet. They found her in the conservatory, sprawled among the plants, drunk on stolen wine.

After kneeling to check on his sister, Nicholas turned on Lyris. "You're as slipshod with your keys as with your supervision."

Stung, Lyris protested, "Fanny's careless upbringing has provided her with a number of distressing habits. I'm not surprised they include picking locks."

He caught her into a crushing embrace, his stormy kiss bent on dominating her will. Lyris's treacherous body betrayed her and she hotly returned the kiss. The aroma of fresh earth and crushed greenery rose from an overturned pot nearby, adding a primitive air to the dimly lit room.

His mouth moved over her throat, her ear, her lips, her eyelids. He held her so tightly that even through their clothing she felt the intensity of his desire. That erotic pressure seared her and she jerked back briefly, but then with a moan melted into his arms.

He thrust her away. Her momentary doubt had apparently given him strength. In an uneven voice, he said, "No, Lyris. Not now."

She reached for him. "Nicholas..."

He stepped back as if her touch might scorch him. "I won't misuse you. Even if you have temporarily forgotten what your haughty comment on Fanny's 'careless upbringing' just revealed. You still despise us."

She turned away, shamed by desire. She had always thought Nicholas dangerous, but never more so than now. She had forgotten that danger also smoldered within herself.

Brutally, he said, "You're here as a companion for my sister. If Fanny is difficult, it's because she recognizes your low opinion of her."

Lyris's head jerked up. "That's unfair. You drove her to this. When she asked about her grandmother, you made her feel even more unloved."

The forbidden words hung between them. In despair, Lyris exclaimed, "How can I never mention Amelia when she is at the heart of all this?"

He bent to gather his sister into his arms. "I'll take her upstairs. Send for her maid." Doubly scorned, Lyris yanked the bell rope.

After assuring herself that Fanny was in no danger from her foolish behavior, Lyris retired unhappily to her own room. Sleep evaded her. She tossed and turned uncomfortably, while trying to sort out her life.

She and Nicholas had entered marriage with good intentions, but it wasn't working. They were alarmingly drawn to each other, while their separate worlds simply did not blend. She would have to make him see that, but no longer dared be alone with him at home. She must once again invade his office.

In the morning, she found her cook in a state. Nicholas had refused breakfast, leaving for the Golden Harbor without taking time for so much as a cup of coffee. Lyris spent the better part of an hour assuring the woman that her meals were appreciated.

Only by promising to administer a good dose of spring tonic to every member of the household was she able to talk the cook out of giving notice. That promise would be another one difficult to keep.

Nick stared at his ledgers while the figures jumped around. He couldn't concentrate on goods ordered and received while his thoughts kept returning to his wife. When the door opened, he looked up, welcoming a distraction.

Lyris stood there. Startled, he rose to his feet. "What in blazes are you doing down here?"

She braced both gloved hands against his desk. "We have to face the truth, Nicholas. We've made a mistake. Our marriage is hurting Fanny, not helping her."

He longed to touch her, to remove her hat and take the pins from her hair so it would spread like raven's wings through his hands. He forced his thoughts to his sister. "What has she done now?"

Lyris's sea green eyes fixed on his face. Her voice remained steady, revealing none of the longing that he sensed in her. "As far as I know, she's still sleeping off the results of last night's escapade. Nicholas, can't you see that your own resentment of society inflames Fanny's rebellion?"

How easily she turned the truth around. Resenting the turbulent feelings she caused in him, he said shortly, "No, I can't."

"If she had really been twelve or thirteen, as you first told me, I might have been able to reach her," Lyris insisted. "It's too late. Fanny is not going to change, no matter how many rules we force her to learn."

He came around the desk to stand closer, grateful to feel unwanted tenderness shift to hostility. "You're a snob,

Lyris, so certain Fanny can't rise above her birth that you won't give her a chance."

"Snob!" Lyris exclaimed. "I joined the working world myself. Have you forgotten?"

Nick knew his laugh was humorless. Lyris believed she was without prejudice, yet nearly every word expressed it. With scorn, he said, "A rich girl's whim. Look where it got you."

"Into an impossible marriage," Lyris shot back. "The sooner ended, the better."

The sweetness of her fragrance cast a net, drawing him closer. The flash of her eyes heated his blood. He knew he could kiss her. He could make her angry body soften against his, kindling fresh desire in them both. Her physical awareness of him glowed in the vibrant depths of her eyes. He knew what he could do. And knew as well that she would despise him for it.

Abruptly putting the length of his office between them, he fixed his gaze on a steel engraving. "I mean to move into my rooms here at the saloon." He might have added that he no longer trusted himself with her, but she knew that.

Her indrawn breath told him as much. He continued coldly. "When Fanny has been launched into society—and not before—you will have your divorce." He turned to face her simmering frustration. "Two years, Lyris. Plus a few months. I have more confidence in you than you have in yourself."

She swung away and he hardened his voice. "You know the alternative. The canvas can be repaired. And hung in a public gallery."

"You are a—"

"I know what you think of me," he cut in sharply. "Set your inventive mind toward keeping your bargain."

Fanny waltzed into the saloon as if she had every right to be there. Any number of interesting men turned to look.

When she'd followed Lyris downtown, she hadn't expected such a bonus.

Nicky had something on Lyris, something that made her stay with him when they could scarcely say a pleasant word to each other. When Lyris had put on her hat and walking shoes and set off at a fast pace down the hill this morning, it was a fair guess she had decided to have it out.

She hadn't even noticed that Fanny followed, just steamed along like a ship under full sail. Fanny had been busy with thoughts of her own. That awful time when Nicky caught her at the skating rink had kept her from thinking about the things he and Lyris had said to each other.

But she hadn't forgotten. They'd argued about an agreement they'd made. It had something to do with a painting, but Lyris wouldn't talk about it and Fanny knew better than to ask Nick.

Now, though, she might have a chance to find out for herself. She looked about with eager interest. A handsome bartender came toward her, his eyes taking her in, his voice polite. "Are you looking for the hotel, miss?"

She gazed upward through her lashes. "I'm looking for my brother, Nicholas Drake."

"Your brother!" Interest glowed brighter in his eyes. "His wife is with him now. Shall I take you to them?"

"His wife isn't very happy with me," Fanny admitted. "Neither is he. I've come to make an apology." She smiled in a way that she knew would bring dimples. "I'd much prefer to wait for that."

"Mr. Drake won't like you sitting in a public room. You had better come with me."

With a shiver of pleasure, Fanny took the arm he offered and walked with him through the saloon to a hall at the back. He indicated a heavily carved panel. "That's your brother's office. He has living quarters close by, from when he stayed here at the saloon. I'll take you there to wait for him."

They both froze as the office door swung open. Lyris's angry voice came through. "I should have known better than to expect reason from you."

The bartender hauled Fanny into a supply room at one side. Light came dimly above the worn sill. "I don't think it would be a good idea to let her see you just now."

Fanny hid her giggles against his chest. "You may have just saved my life."

"Does that give me rights to it?"

"Fresh!"

He tilted her chin upward. "I don't get many complaints."

She expected him to kiss her, but they both heard Nick's footsteps. Her friend stiffened while they listened to her brother stride down the hall. A door slammed.

The bartender murmured in her ear, "It's lucky we didn't put you in his quarters, after all."

"What do you suggest we do?"

"Saucy, aren't you?"

With a soft laugh, she gave him back his own words. "I don't get many complaints."

She realized he was nervous, for all his flirting. It would be worth his job and maybe his neck if Nick caught them together in a dark storeroom. "Why don't we go to my brother's office? If he comes back, I'll say I was waiting for him."

Her escort cracked open the door and peered through. "You go on ahead. I'd better make sure he's not looking for me."

Fanny hurried up the hall, then smiled back at him before slipping inside and leaving the door ajar. Hoping Nick would stay away for a long time, she looked curiously about the office. It suited Nicky, she decided, from the heavy furniture to the engravings on the walls.

His voice, coming from just outside, shocked her. "Sam! Where in hell are the invoices for that last shipment of whiskey?"

His sharp tone told Fanny she would not be welcomed. She glanced about for a place to hide. A large wardrobe caught her eye. She tried the handle, then swiftly searched her reticule for one of Grampa Drake's lock picks.

Within seconds, she had the wardrobe open. She scrambled inside, crowding a large oil painting, just as Nick came into the office.

Fanny forgot about Nick. The portrait was of Lyris. She had barely glimpsed it before closing herself into the dark, but she was certain. That was Lyris. And practically naked.

Fanny longed to crack open the door and get another look, but she didn't dare. This was what her brother had over his wife. He must have threatened to hang the picture in his saloon. With a shiver, she thought what that would mean to a lady like her sister-in-law.

Lyris had a lot of spirit, but she wouldn't be able to hold up her head if this portrait was shown. With a surge of sympathy—after all, Lyris had tried to be kind—Fanny decided to take matters into her own hands.

The office door slammed. Cautiously, she peeked out from the wardrobe, then hurried to the desk and snatched up a letter opener. Grasping the blade, she studied the painting.

How could it ever have come about? Wondering at that and at a small slash in the figure's shoulder, Fanny began sawing the taut canvas from the frame.

When it was free, she laid it out on the floor, then rolled it tightly. Her heart pounded. If Nick caught her at this, she was going to be in big trouble. Still, she took time to relock the wardrobe before slipping the canvas under her cape.

She couldn't risk going back through the saloon. After a moment's thought, she opened the shutters and climbed through the window. That fresh bartender would wonder what had become of her. But he could stop worrying about losing his job.

Chapter Twenty-Three

Fanny felt very satisfied with herself when she slipped into the house through a side door, the rolled canvas beneath her cloak. A sharp question from Lyris nearly caused her to drop it. "Where have you been?"

Wait until Lyris saw the portrait. That ought to make up for a lot of small sins. She had her hands on her hips now, though, and was looking anything but pleased. "You know very well that a young lady does not go out alone."

Bristling, Fanny exclaimed, "You did. I saw you."

"I have been worried sick since I discovered you were missing," Lyris said furiously. "Where were you?"

Fanny knew Lyris was angry with Nick. There was no need to take it out on her. She clutched the painting. Maybe she wouldn't give it to Lyris, after all. "I went downtown."

"Downtown. Where?"

"To see Nick."

Her sister-in-law clenched both hands in her skirt. "In the first place, you have no business inside a saloon. And in the second place, I have just come from your brother's office. You were not there."

"I was, too, there," Fanny said indignantly. "And I saw you. You looked mad, so I hid with a bartender." Oops. That was not a smart thing to say.

"A bartender!" Lyris's voice shot up an octave. She took a step forward while Fanny braced herself. But she only said angrily, "Go to your room. I will speak with you when I am calmer."

"I'd rather stay there than talk to you," Fanny shouted and ran to the stairs. When she reached her room, she threw the canvas against a wall. Lyris didn't even know what had happened. She just automatically believed the worst. After all Fanny had done to get the painting for her.

Well, she wouldn't have it now. Fanny looked for a hiding place. The way Lyris had been driving the maids lately, they dusted even the tops of the wardrobes. Yesterday they had even hauled the mattresses outside to air.

Struck by inspiration, she yanked off the bedding and tugged her mattress aside. While it was airing, she had noticed a solid pine bottom on the sleigh bed.

Carefully, she unrolled the painting. Would Lyris care if it got scratched or cracked? Probably not, but Nick might. She took care to keep the canvas smooth while she replaced the mattress.

After straightening the bedclothing, she plumped her mother's old teddy bear on the pillows and surveyed her work with satisfaction. No one would guess the painting was in there. As far as she was concerned, Lyris could spend the rest of her straitlaced life wondering what had become of it.

Nick spent the night at the saloon, miserably out of sorts. In the morning, he snapped at his help until they began to avoid him. Fire bells in midafternoon made a welcome diversion. He walked out to see the cause.

Only blocks away, a plume of black smoke rose into the clear sky. Shouting men hurried from every direction. As he reached the site, a two-story frame building on Madison, a pair of horses pulled the Gould steam fire engine to a thundering stop beside a hydrant. The hose cart had already arrived and firemen rushed toward the burning structure.

Near Nick, someone commented, "Remember the fire in the Arlington? It only took two lines to control that one."

"What started this?" Nick asked.

A third man shouted over the uproar. "A cabinet shop in the basement. Some fool threw cold water on a burning glue pot. The whole damned stove exploded."

The street was filling with men, everyone shouting and talking at once. Heavy smoke billowed above the street. Fire bells rang as a second engine roared toward the wharf to draw from the bay.

A cheer went up as the first engine started to pump. Two streams of water shot onto the burning building, but minutes later, flames burst from windows of a neighboring store. Firemen pried up sidewalk planks and an inferno drove them back. A scream went up. "It's burning through the basements!"

A third building caught. Coughing, choking men rushed goods from nearby stores. The fire fighters worked furiously. The entire block appeared doomed. Still another hose was connected to a hydrant—and all the streams weakened. Everyone shouted at once.

"What the hell!"

"My horse can match that."

"There's supposed to be four million gallons in the reservoir!"

A rush of hot air mocked them with cinders and firebrands. Across the street, wild tongues of crimson lapped the wooden buildings. For the first time, Nick felt alarmed. Two- and three-story wood frame structures shouldered each other all through the business area. Canvas advertising banners stretched across plank sidewalks. If there was no water . . .

Before he completed the thought, flames shot to a nearby saloon. Fire roared up the walls. Whiskey barrels exploded with a blast that shook the street. The screaming crowd cringed under a rain of burning whiskey.

Nick raced to help a crew with a hose cart. Again a hydrant failed to deliver more than a trickle. Word came that the tide was out. The second engine couldn't draw water enough to help.

The fire spread rapidly north and south. With sweat running down his face, Nick raced for the Golden Harbor. Most of his customers had already joined the crowds in the street. Sam yelled from the back, "I've started loading what I can in your carriage. There's a ship at the dock that's promised to hold it."

Tearing into his office, Nick caught up stacks of record books. His horse danced nervously while he loaded them into the soot-streaked carriage. Heat shimmered in the air. What in hell had happened to those damned hydrants? Fire bells clanged wildly. Bells pealed from every church over low blasts from steamships in the harbor, crying all-out disaster.

Thank God his house was uphill, with plenty of greenery around it. Lyris and Fanny would be safe, but homes and businesses near the wharves were likely to go. One of his bartenders clambered onto the roof. Another hoisted a bucket of water. Coughing from the smoke-filled air, Nick sprinted over to help.

As Lyris stirred a pot of dandelion tonic on the kitchen range, Fanny's footsteps pounded through the hall. "There's smoke! Down by Nick's place!"

Flinging her spoon aside, Lyris dashed to the front porch. Black smoke furled upward from the city center, giving an odd orange cast to the sky. Explosions thudded through a bedlam of clanging bells. Horror clutched her.

"Is it Nicky's building?" Fanny cried.

Please, God, no. Shading her eyes, Lyris strained to locate the fire. "It's several, Fanny. And spreading. Look! There! And there! It's reached homes along Second Street."

She gripped the girl's shoulders. "Help Mrs. Ramsey. Have her cut off the gas line at once. And gather candles. People will need shelter and food. Tell her to do what she can."

Fanny's eyes seemed to fill her face. "What about you?"

"I'm going down there."

"To help Nick?"

"Yes." He wouldn't want her in the way, but how could she not go? Their angry words earlier warred against a choking need to get to him. Through that need came another. "Amelia! She's down there, too. I'm going after her."

With a gasp, Fanny exclaimed, "Will you bring her here?"

"Yes." She couldn't take time to worry about the consequences. The fire was clearly out of control. People crowded the streets, escaping uphill. She thrust her apron into the girl's hands and dashed through the gate.

Fanny's excited voice called after her, "I'll get a room ready for Gramma."

Holding her skirts high, Lyris raced toward town, the dual need to be with Nick and to help Amelia driving her on. The heat became terrible. She soon heard roaring flames, and her nose and throat began to hurt. Her eyes smarted.

She passed a woman blank eyed with shock. At another time, she would have offered help. Instead, she ran faster, terrified for Nicholas, desperate to reach her godmother. Ashes sprinkled her clothes. She panted, taking short breaths of hot, sooty air.

Panic leapt in the clanging, tolling bells. Shouts and screams were all but lost in the tremendous roar of the fire. She raced along a parallel street, hoping to get around the fire before it spread to Amelia's hotel—and from there to the Golden Harbor. She sobbed Nicholas's name, plunging on.

A man caught her roughly. She spun around, hope flaring, but he was a stranger, an older man with wild eyes. Urgently, he said, "Miss, turn back." She twisted free, and muttering to himself, the man continued uphill.

Tears and sweat ran down her face. When she rubbed her cheeks, her hands came away black. Coughing, she hurried ahead, feeling as if she pressed against the fire itself. Around her, people shouted, "The Opera House just went up."

That beautiful building! She gulped back sobs. Explosions rocked the air and she stumbled and grabbed at a fence. Beyond, a family dragged possessions onto their lawn. "Dynamite," the father yelled. "They're trying for a firebreak."

In the center of town, the air shimmered with heat. Above the roiling black smoke and orange flames, firebrands soared like hellish kites, flying up, falling back, then hurtling upward again, spreading the devastation. Gulping air into tortured lungs, she ran on.

Wagons and people crowded the streets, the horses white eyed with terror. Owners fought for control. Ahead of Lyris, a horse shied and reared. She lunged past, inches from its hooves.

Her ears rang from the incessant clamoring bells. In the business district, shopkeepers rushed from their stores with merchandise. Goods stacked in cross streets were beginning to char.

The city had become a flaming anthill, with panicky people darting in every direction. Men clambered along rooftops with buckets of water and soaked gunnysacks. A volley of gunfire stunned her until she realized flames had set off a hardware store's stock of cartridges.

It really was a battle, one the city was losing. Scarcely able to see through the smoke and her own burning eyes, she plunged across still another intersection. Her godmother's hotel was just ahead. How in the world would she find her?

She couldn't even see the Golden Harbor through the smoke. Her heart lurched with fear. Nicholas was sure to fight the fire to the last moment. Would he take dangerous chances? She thought that he would and her terror deepened.

What if she lost him before she ever really knew him? Her angry demand for a divorce tasted like ashes. She had to find him—to hold him and kiss him and tell him she didn't mean it. They couldn't end like this, with angry words between them.

As tears blurred her eyes, the wind shifted, parting the smoke. Suddenly, Amelia was there—a gray figure in the hellish scene ahead—tightly gripping a soot-blackened carpetbag with one hand and her parasol with the other.

Lyris screamed her name, but her voice was lost in the inferno. Amelia tramped sturdily toward the bay. There was no safety there. Lyris had heard shouts that the docks were burning. The ships had pulled into deeper water.

Her heart urged her to find Nick. Yet she knew he could take care of himself. Amelia could not. Somewhere a wall crashed in. Consumed with fear for them both, Lyris rushed toward her godmother. Pushing between carts and people, she shouted futilely, "Amelia!"

Sweat and tears stung her eyes. She scrubbed at them, fighting to keep her godmother in sight through the shifting smoke. Ahead, a man caught Amelia's arm, stopping her. Waving and shouting, he turned her away from the wharf. She saw Lyris then and with a cry lost in the fire storm, started toward her.

Briefly, they clung together. "Uphill," Lyris gasped, while Amelia coughed into a handkerchief. Her frantic glance found the Golden Harbor through roiling smoke. It wasn't burning. Not yet. Men clambered over the roof with buckets.

There was nothing she could do for Nick, she told herself again. But she left her heart behind as she hurried Amelia away. The uphill streets were mobbed with people clutching whatever they had managed to save. Lyris kept one arm about her godmother, who trembled and gasped for breath, but marched steadily uphill.

"There won't be a hotel left," she told Lyris wanly. "I will have to beg shelter from friends." She looked around at haggard faces. "If they haven't already filled every available space. These poor, burned-out souls."

"You're coming home with me. Fanny is preparing a room."

Light came into Amelia's blanched face. "At last, I am to meet her." The eager glow faded as quickly as it came.

"Lyris, I love my grandson dearly, but you know his feelings against me."

"It's a large house. We simply won't tell Nicholas you're there."

"Not tell him?" Amelia shook her head. "My dear, you are inviting another horrible scene. I cannot let you risk your marriage."

Regret lanced through Lyris. Marriage? There was no marriage. She was desperately afraid she would lose Nicholas to the devastation behind her before they learned whether a real marriage was possible. She couldn't explain any of that to his grandmother.

With finality in her voice, she said, "You are coming home with me. I need to know you are safe." If only she could know the same about Nick.

By the time they reached the house, the older woman was too bone weary to argue. Lyris turned her over to Fanny, who greeted them both with joyful hugs. While Fanny helped her grandmother up the stairs, Lyris set about bringing whatever order might be possible among the hungry, frightened people sheltering in her home.

A stable boy and one of the maids had gone to their own families. The rest of the staff were at sixes and sevens, rushing about while accomplishing little except further upsetting each other. Even the normally unruffled Mrs. Ramsey wore her cap askew.

Lyris put some of her visitors to work preparing and distributing sandwiches. The effort helped take their minds off their personal losses as well as ease the burden of the overworked servants. Staying busy held her own fear for Nicholas at an almost bearable level. By sundown, with the sky glowing in shades suited for Dante's *Inferno,* she had the household in fair shape.

Tents were scattered over the yard. Several refugees simply lay in the grass, staring up at the reddened sky. Nearly all the rooms in the lower floor held people wrapped in blankets.

Lyris stared toward town. Where was Nick? He hadn't come home last night. If he didn't come home tonight, it needn't mean he lay trapped beneath smoldering rubble. The memory of their kisses made her weak with longing. The thought of their arguments left her sick with despair.

She sank onto a front-porch stair and lowered her head onto her crossed arms. Fanny spoke softly, settling beside her. "You've worked so hard. Don't you want to go to bed?"

"Soon." Too tired to lift her head, she added, "Is your grandmother resting?"

"Yes." Fanny hesitated. "She seems nice. Do you think Nick will be mad?"

Silently, Lyris answered, *I don't care if he's furious. I just want him to come home*. Aloud, she said, "Not until he finds out."

Fanny giggled, then sobered. "I wonder where he is. You'd think he'd come by to see if we're all right." She paused. "Did the Golden Harbor burn?"

"It was in the fire's path."

Fanny groaned. "At least we still have a house to live in, even if it is crowded right now."

Her words were a murmur barely heard. Lyris felt weary in every bone, but couldn't bring herself to go upstairs. She had to stay here, to wait for Nick.

Much later, she woke to Fanny shrieking, "Nicky!" Lyris jerked upright. He was just coming up the walk, revealed in light spilling from the open front door. Fanny flew into his arms.

A clock in the entry gonged three times. Lyris realized she had been asleep for hours. Relief held her motionless, then she broke free and rushed like Fanny to fling her arms around Nick. He smelled of smoke. He felt wonderful.

He held them both close. "We kept thinking we could stop it." A ragged breath sent him into a spasm of coughing. Lyris watched helplessly while Fanny ran for water. When he could speak, it was with heavy resignation. "The whole center of town burned. People are camped in every yard and on every street corner."

"Come inside," Lyris urged.

Fanny warned, "People are all over the house."

They got him to the candlelit kitchen where the kitten wound, purring, around their feet, happily oblivious to disaster. "I can't remember the last time I ate," Nick admitted, while Lyris brought a plate she had kept aside for him.

The ends of his hair were scorched in places. Beneath smudges of soot, his skin looked red and angry. His beautiful eyes were reddened, as well. It was an effort to keep her voice light as he continued to gaze at her. "Eat. You know how upset cook gets when her food is refused."

Nick picked up his fork. "She must have been in her element tonight, with all these people to feed."

"I heard her humming," Fanny said. "Imagine that."

His chuckle touched Lyris's heart. "Were you able to save anything from the Golden Harbor?"

"Yes, thanks to Sam's quick thinking." Nick swallowed as if the effort pained him and set down the fork. "He claimed one of the areas the ship captains marked off on their decks."

Lyris brought him a cold glass of milk and he sipped gratefully. "Many were too late. They hauled salvaged goods to the docks, but the ships had to escape to deeper water."

"Before they could load?" Fanny asked, her eyes wide.

"It was bedlam," he said. "Whistles blasting. The captains shouting. And men determined to keep loading. I saw one fellow cart a pump organ up a ramp while the ship pulled out. He leapt back to the dock, but the organ fell into the bay."

Fanny gasped.

"And all the piled goods?" Lyris asked.

"Burned."

Despite her fascination, Fanny yawned hugely. "Go to bed, imp," her brother said gently. "You'll be needed tomorrow."

Impulsively, she kissed his cheek, then wrinkled her nose. "You taste like soot."

He scooped the kitten from around one ankle and handed it to her. "Go. Take this other nuisance with you."

Grinning, she plopped the kitten into its basket. When the door closed behind her, Nick added to Lyris, "You'd better get some sleep, too."

"I've been sleeping." She dampened a cloth in the basin. "Take off your coat."

He stood to pull off the filthy jacket. "It's only good for the trash heap."

"But you're all right," she said, her voice thick with emotion.

She saw something shift in his eyes. Then she was in his arms, the cloth falling unused to the table. Like Fanny, she tasted soot, but she didn't care. She clung to him, her arms tight around him, her fingers splayed against his back.

He kissed her deeply, hungrily. She kissed him back with equal passion. When he buried his face against her throat, she moaned. "You need to eat. To bathe." But she couldn't let him go.

"Bathe, at least." Ruefully, he freed himself. "Just don't go away."

"I won't." She whispered the promise. The look in his eyes smoked her blood. Taking the cloth in trembling fingers, she dampened it again, then gently cleansed his face. He closed his eyes, as if looking at her might undo his control.

"Take off your shirt."

He offered a lopsided smile. "You won't be embarrassed?"

"I look forward to the sight."

He reached for her, shook his head, then began unbuttoning his shirt. He pulled off shoes and socks, as well. She caught her breath to see how charred they were. Muscles rippled beneath his skin as he walked over to the sink and poured a dipperful of cold water over his head.

Lyris grasped a basin and dipped warm water from the reservoir in the range. Although stiff with ashes and scorched in places, his hair felt alive and vibrant beneath her fingers. She concentrated on soaping and washing, while frankly admiring the fluid movement of his muscles.

With a startled yelp, he groped for a towel. "That soap stings worse than the smoke. Be careful, will you?"

"Sorry." Briskly, she rinsed and dried his hair.

He pulled the towel away and dumped it on the edge of the sink. Taking her by the waist, he gazed soberly into her face. "What are you feeling? Tell me."

She knew what he wanted to hear. How could she betray herself? Yet it didn't feel like a betrayal, it felt like release. She raised her hands to his bare shoulders. "I love you."

Smoldering hope blazed in his eyes as he pulled her to him and kissed her fervently. She thought of walls falling, of ceilings crashing in, of barriers crumbling. Nick lifted her in his arms, pushed through the doorway and stepped carefully around people sleeping in the hall.

She saw him frown and circled her arms around his shoulders, her reassurance husky with promise. "I've kept them all downstairs." He nodded, his eyes telling her far more than words. Vibrant with anticipation, she tangled her fingers in his damp hair.

He carried her into his bedchamber and lowered her onto the big bed. Smoke-dulled moonlight tinged their skin when he stretched out beside her. His hand shook as he stroked the outline of her face. Voice low, he said, "The fire raging inside me is fiercer than any in town."

Flames licked her nerves, as well. Her skin shimmered at his slightest caress. She felt greedy to touch him, to make sure with all her senses that he was safe.

The luxury of stroking his bare skin and trailing her fingers through the curling hair on his chest made her light-headed. He still smelled of wood smoke, an outdoors, masculine smell.

He spoke against her lips, his breath heating hers. "You're wearing far too many clothes."

Shakily, she teased, "Shall I ring for Jenny?"

"I can manage."

In fact, he dealt so efficiently with laces and ribbons that she began to wonder where he had gained the experience. Then she forgot to wonder as his hands and lips blazed wildfire across her skin.

In a daze, she thought of Evelyn, who had called this part of her marriage a duty, and of Reba, who'd commented only that she had rather enjoyed giving her husband pleasure. Why hadn't they told her of this quickening and heat?

When he had stripped off her chemise, Nick pressed his face between her breasts as if trying to slow senses that raced as wildly as her own. She cradled his head between her hands and he turned to kiss each of her palms.

Abruptly, he pulled away and stripped off the rest of his clothing. Lyris felt her heart leap. Was this the end of her pleasure? Would the rest be as unpleasant as Evelyn had implied?

He sat on the bed, silhouetted in the moonlight, and drew loose the ribbons that held her drawers below her knees. She shivered as he reached for the ties at her waist.

Momentarily shy when he tugged the drawers down, she hesitated, then lifted her hips so he could pull the garment free. The brush of his fingers flooded her with startled pleasure. Again she thought of flames. Her blood sang in her veins.

He touched her in ways she had never imagined, until she scarcely knew her own mind. At first, she hesitated to touch him intimately, but he insisted that she explore his body. With that freedom came a blaze of joy. He was unharmed and returned to her, and she needed to reassure herself in every way that he was safe and whole.

With his lips just brushing hers, he said, low-voiced, "How I love you. More than you can possibly know." He positioned himself above her and she felt brief uncertainty through breathtaking anticipation.

She said with conviction, "I love you," then gasped. She hadn't expected a quick firebrand of pain, but it was over at once, with her husband joined to her in a way that filled her heart with joy.

He guided her and yet she seemed to know what pleased him and what would most please her. There was power in it—both the taking and relinquishing of power. There was a deep sense of belonging, of homecoming when she hadn't known she'd been away.

She knew again the fear of losing him and the exhilaration of his safe return, then abandoned herself to an ecstatic celebration of life that blazed thought and memory into a shimmering burst of golden heat.

She clutched him to her, taking him deeply, feeling as if he spilled the molten essence of his life into her. When he lay against her, his heart still echoing the hammering of her own, deep tenderness dissolved her entire being.

He moved to lie beside her, nestling her close, and she ran a wondering hand over his chest. The two of them had been adversaries for so long that she groped for words to express her feelings, and at last simply murmured, "I wish to be a dutiful wife. How soon may I perform this particular chore again?"

He shook with startled laughter, then cradled one of her breasts with his palm. His answer held tender amusement while his thumb brushed her nipple with promise. "Very soon, I think. But take warning, sweet wife. I'll expect you to devote a great deal more of your time to the task."

He suited action to his words, eventually raising her to astonishing flights of sensation. When at last they lay exhausted in a tangle of bedclothes, clasped in each other's arms, the first smoke-shrouded light of dawn showed through the bedroom window.

He stroked a sheen of perspiration from her temple. "When did you know you loved me?"

Sighing, she turned sleepily toward him. "When you didn't come home from the fire."

"So recently? I believe you've been lying to yourself." He kissed the tip of her nose. "I knew I loved you weeks ago, when I happened to see you and Fanny washing each other's hair."

"I wasn't aware of you."

"No. I couldn't let you see how much power you had gained over me."

"Had I?" She trailed her fingers through the soft hairs on his chest. "Strange. It feels the other way around."

He nestled her closer. "Sleep, sweetheart. Tomorrow—today—will be busy. The town council called a meeting for shortly before noon. I expect a good part of Seattle will attend."

She didn't want to think of his leaving her side, even for a minute. Feeling cherished, she drifted to sleep.

Chapter Twenty-Four

Lyris woke bright with joy, her husband still asleep beside her. The fire had intensified the natural wave in his hair. Her heart moved with tenderness at the sight of scorched tendrils at his temple.

Voices from the lawn drifted through the partly open window. She would have to get up soon and see to the household. Breakfast must be provided for any who wanted it. Half drowsing, one hand against Nicholas's warm back, she pictured the state of her pantry. How far would it stretch?

Her sleepy musing jolted to a stop. Amelia! Pleasure collapsed. She had completely forgotten Amelia. How in the world could she tell Nicholas that she had established his hated grandmother in his house?

It was easy to say they would not tell him of her, but far less simple to keep the secret. If he heard first from the servants, he would be more than furious. Lyris closed her eyes in despair.

In a low voice, Nick asked, "Regrets?"

Her eyes flew open. He was watching her warily and she answered at once, "Not about us." He leaned over to kiss her and she clasped her arms about him, pressing close, determined to make him love her so deeply that Amelia's presence in their home could not drive them apart.

With the clear reality of morning, she had begun to believe that much of the rapture of the night before had sprung from the drama of the fire and relief in her husband's safety. Surely, nerves and heart and mind could not fly together to such heights of sensation.

He soon proved they could. As she clung to him, dazed with love, he kissed her bare shoulder. "You were right about Castor's work, sweetheart. It is a lie. You're far more beautiful than the artist could imagine."

The painting! She hadn't given it a thought. Sitting upright, she exclaimed. "It's burned. Isn't it?"

"How quickly your vigor returns," he said with a grin. "I envy you."

"Don't tease me." She swung her feet to the floor, then paused. "You are teasing. The portrait was destroyed with the saloon. You no longer have a hold over me."

Lazily, he asked, "Do I need one?"

The impassioned look on his face sent even the painting from her mind. With fluid muscles, she melted into his lingering, loving kiss. Sensual humor glowed when at last he looked into her eyes. "Now that's a proper answer."

She raised up and braced her arms against his chest. "What of my question? Was the saloon destroyed?"

He ran one hand up her spine, making her shiver. "Our block was the last reached by the fire. Unless embers started up again, the building partially stands."

Lyris wriggled away from the distraction of his touch. "Which part?"

For the first time he looked unsure. "The rear."

His office! "We'll go there at once. As soon as I've spoken to cook about our refugees."

"Lyris," he warned, "we'll go when I decide."

If the office hadn't been destroyed, the wardrobe and the painting still existed. Desperately, she asked, "Would you have a looter take it?"

"The militia is on watch. However," he added, pushing back the covers, "be quick about your chores, love. I want to drive through the ruined area before the council meets at noon. We'll leave right away."

As he swung from the bed, her breath rushed out in relief. She could even forgive him for his domineering attitude—this time, anyway. After a swift, admiring glance at his naked body, she rushed to her own room.

The refugees were eager to return to whatever remained of their homes. In the kitchen, Fanny chattered to the cook while stirring a large bowl of batter. Her eyes shone when she turned to Lyris. "I'm making pancakes for the children and their mothers. Most of the men have gone."

"We'll send lunches with their families. Have one of the boys bring apples from storage." Lyris paused. "Fanny, I do appreciate your help."

"We all have to do what we can," the girl said primly, but her eyes glowed at the praise.

Remembering how little Nick had eaten last night, Lyris tried to curb impatience while she filled a plate for him. Fanny tugged at her sleeve, then rolled her eyes toward the ceiling. "Does he know about *her?*"

Lyris shook her head. "We're going to drive through the ruined area as soon as he's had breakfast. I'll find a way to tell him then. In the midst of such desolation, he can't object to giving shelter to his own grandmother."

"You don't know Nicky."

But she did. She knew him so well now, her heart ached at the prospect of losing him. A cowardly thought wriggled into her mind. Why not smuggle Amelia to her parents' home?

And give up an opportunity fate had dropped right into her lap? Lyris pulled her shoulders back. Inside, she must have known all along why she'd brought Amelia here. The fire had created an opportunity to unite Nicholas with his grandmother. She simply had to find the right way to tell him.

The thought raised her spirits through breakfast, through final instructions to Fanny and during the carriage ride downhill. But when she saw the battlefieldlike ruins, Lyris's hope faltered. Her husband had grown progressively grimmer.

The carriage jounced over littered streets where men with rifles stood guard. A pass was demanded before they were allowed into the burned area. There, block after block lay in ruin. Jagged walls loomed above heaps of rubble. Stone or brick shells stood empty. Where brisk business had been conducted just the day before at her father's bank, empty windows and doors gaped on desolation. An armed guard sat in a chair tipped against the locked vault, which loomed from the rubble. Other vaults were similarly guarded.

Black ribbons of warped steel curved over charred piers— all that remained of the rail line. Some streets were so choked with rubble, the carriage had to turn back. The acrid pungency of burned wood penetrated everywhere. Lyris pressed shaking fingers to her lips. "What will become of Seattle?"

"Don't count her out," Nick said tightly. "Seattle wasn't built by quitters."

Several men picked through the ruins of their shops. Some were already clearing out rubble. In one block, a merchant had raised a canopy over the shell of his store and was preparing to sell goods from crates. Another was setting up business from a wagon in front of his ruined shop.

Nick halted the carriage and stepped out to talk with three men at a corner. Lyris caught only a few words, enough to know they discussed improvements made possible by the devastation.

These men clearly respected Nick. Pride rose in Lyris. He was a fighter. He could become a driving force in the city's reconstruction. Satisfaction rang in his voice when he returned. "It's beginning already. Give us a few months and we'll raise a brighter city than before."

She wanted to hear what others thought of him. "What did they say?"

"What everyone will be saying shortly." He caught her hand, fired with ideas as the carriage rolled on. "The entire waterfront is gone. All those shacks. The haphazard construction of the docks. We have a chance to start over. This time we'll do it right!"

"We'll have newly planked streets," she said, catching his enthusiasm.

"We won't just plank them, sweetheart. We'll raise them. We'll get rid of those damned stinking sewers, along with a host of other ills."

Was this the time to tell him of Amelia, while he was flushed with challenge? As she gathered her thoughts in a search for the right words, she saw him glance out the window and stiffen. They were approaching the remains of the Golden Harbor.

As Nick had told her, the fire had burned out here. Scorched buildings stood across the street. From the saloon south, ruined walls rose from a haze of rubble. At the Golden Harbor, a good three-quarters of the office area remained, a charred guardian overlooking the acrid rubble of the rest.

Lyris ached for the pain she saw in Nick's hooded eyes. His grand view of a greater Seattle couldn't keep him from grieving for his ruined saloon. She glanced out again and her heart froze. The wardrobe lay on its side near the charred desk.

"Wait here." Swinging from the carriage, Nick picked his way through ashes and fallen stone. The wardrobe door was wedged in place. He kicked it loose. Castor's frame tumbled out. Curled bits of ragged canvas wove a mocking trim around the inner edge.

After a stunned glance toward Lyris, Nick hurled the frame to the ground. Ashes swirled upward. Lyris felt dazed. Then doubts rushed in, swirling like the ashes. They had argued before the fire, argued furiously. Nick had moved to the saloon to be away from her. When fire threatened, had he cut the canvas hastily from its frame? He must have. And put it . . . where?

She tried to tell herself she was wrong, that Nicholas would not do such a thing. Yet doubts rushed back. Months ago, she had suspected him of plotting with Castor to produce the miserable portrait. They had never had that out. And since then, she had badly raked his pride.

And yet she loved him. She felt for him. She would not believe he could mock her this way. Then who had the painting? A looter? Better that than Nicholas, after all they had shared.

Reason scoffed at her tender feelings. Had she forgotten his lifelong bitterness toward his own grandmother? He'd made it clear more than once that she seared his pride as harshly as had Amelia.

Would his vengeance never be complete? Her heart twisted with pain. She had believed he loved her. She could not think that he merely mocked her, that all along, he knew they wouldn't find the portrait here.

Her need to believe in him warred with rational thought until her torn emotions seemed one with the stench of wet, charred wood. For hours last night she had waited, cramped with fear. And when he'd come home at last, joy drove out everything but the need to blend her life with his in delirious celebration. Could it have been lies? All of it? Even that he loved her? Her stomach rebelled and she willed it under control, while all the loving words they had exchanged returned to sear her memory. She felt heartsick to think he could do such a thing.

The Golden Harbor in ruins had hit Nick harder than he expected, even while he swore to rebuild and build better. The portrait had never entered his mind in the frantic hours of carrying account books and stock to safety. This morning, when he did think of it, he expected to find it in ashes. It stunned him to see the wardrobe relatively intact, and then to find the frame with the canvas slashed from it.

The painting must have been stolen during the fire, before the militia went on guard against looters. His fists clenched. Any man who displayed or even mentioned that picture was going to regret it. But he felt sick. After winning her love at last, he had failed his wife. Reluctantly, he opened the carriage door. "Sweetheart ..."

Her hands were curled, her body tensed to spring. Her voice shook as she broke in. "Did you offer the painting this morning, knowing that it was gone?"

He looked at her in disbelief. He understood her shock, but that she immediately believed the worst of him threw them back to the start of their relationship. He couldn't keep resentment from his voice. "Exactly what are you saying?"

The color had drained from her cheeks. Her eyes were haunted and yet her chin took on that too-familiar haughty lift. "Did you wait down here for the ashes to cool? Or did you remove the canvas when you saw the fire approach the saloon?"

Despite her words, pain etched her eyes. She looked as if she hoped he would say she was mistaken, that he would offer an explanation she could believe. He had none. And with raking helplessness came a painful renewal of angry pride. How easy it was for her to accuse him.

He climbed into the carriage, looking straight ahead, refusing to dignify her accusation with an answer. She retired to the far side. His pride felt as ravaged as the saloon. For a few brief hours, he had believed in a loving marriage. He'd been a fool.

However she felt about him physically, to Lyris he was still scum from the wrong end of town. He could see that in the proud lift of her chin and the tight, angry line of her mouth.

"No wonder you're so fond of your godmother," he rasped. "You're two of a kind." Leaning through the window, he shouted to the driver. "Take us back."

When the carriage lurched forward, he surveyed his now angrily silent wife. "Only a cur would do as you're accusing. So that's how you think of me. After all we shared last night.''

When she answered, her voice was thick with tears. "I wish last night had never happened."

Her tears scalded him, but so did her words, and he answered with equal bitterness, "At the moment, so do I."

"I could be with child." She spoke to herself, with horror at the apparently unspeakable idea of bearing his child.

He said harshly, "So soon?"

"It does happen." She pressed her fists against her stomach as if to reject his seed. "Women who find themselves so quickly facing motherhood must be thankful that, for a time, they may be excused from their husband's bed."

Derisive laughter shook him. "I may have had a common upbringing, *sweetheart*, but I know when a woman goes wild with ecstasy in my arms."

Lyris was stunned into silence. Wild in his arms! Even if it was true—and there was no comfort in thinking of that— he was a boor to speak of it. "I suppose you boast to your cronies of your romantic skills."

His curse shocked her. "That you can even suggest so is more insulting than your belief that I hid the blasted picture."

She knew she had pushed him too far, but exclaimed, "How do I know what you may or may not do? You are miserably vindictive when it suits you."

Even through anger and raw pride, Nick tried to understand what she was feeling. He made himself speak quietly. "Part of your contempt for me is because of your godmother." He glanced at her set expression. "I did look for her during the fire. Alex said she had already left the hotel."

"My godmother," Lyris repeated, her tone scathing. "You can't bring yourself to say 'grandmother,' can you?"

"She's no grandmother to me."

"She loves you," Lyris said. "And you can't have tried hard to help her. By the time I located Amelia, the street was thick with smoke."

Nick narrowed his eyes. "Are you saying you came into town during the fire? You might have been killed!"

"So might Amelia, despite your supposed effort to help! She was confused and walking toward the burning wharf." Lyris turned on the seat, fired with defiance. "I brought her home, Mr. Drake. Your *grandmother* is now established in your house."

Nick couldn't speak at all. Betrayal twisted his guts. He had been through every emotion possible in the last twenty-four hours and had had precious little sleep. Only an iron need to keep Lyris from seeing his pain kept him from groaning aloud.

The carriage pulled under their porte cochere. He wrenched open the door. "Get the woman out of my house."

Lyris sprang after him. "Your grandmother has nowhere to go."

"I'll tell you where she can go." He stopped himself, shaking with the effort it cost. "I'll leave the carriage. Jack will drive her all the way to Tacoma if need be. She's to go east, back to her sister-in-law. This time, she can damned well stay there."

"She can damned well stay *here*," Lyris shouted and ran into the house.

She had flatly defied him! Forget the staff and their blasted gossip. This had to be settled. "Lyris," he called after her. "I want her out of here by the time I return from the council meeting."

There was no answer. He couldn't leave it there and stalked into the house, slamming the door so hard it bounced open again. "The devil take you, woman. I expect to be heard."

As he glared down the empty hall, wondering if he would have to search every room, Ruby peered through a doorway. He snapped at her, "Where is my wife?"

The girl looked too frightened to find her tongue. She managed to peel one hand away from her apron and point to the drawing room, then fled toward the back of the house.

He stormed into the drawing room, expecting to see his grandmother. Lyris stood alone beneath Amelia's portrait. Through clenched teeth, Nick said, "You are living dangerously, madam." Reaching past her, he tore the portrait from above the mantel and hurled it into the fire. Ashes flew out. A live ember landed on the polished floor. He kicked it back.

Lyris gasped as if she were watching a madman. She grabbed for the painting while flames licked the frame. "No! Nicholas! What are you doing?"

Nick trapped her by the arms while flames licked the canvas, his grip merciless against her desperate struggles. She sobbed as the canvas began to burn and he thrust her aside. "I want that witch out of here. See that she's on a train heading east by the time I come back."

Lyris dashed after him to the porch. "Nicholas!" she cried. "Tell her yourself!" He didn't look around. Long angry strides carried him toward town.

Lyris rubbed her arms where his grip still burned. Her heart ached for the portrait, for Amelia—and for Nicholas. She knew he was devastated by his losses. And she had unwisely insulted him. If he didn't have the painting, she had injured him deeply. But if he didn't have it, she couldn't bear to think who might.

Instead of leading gently into a discussion of Amelia, she had presented him abruptly with his unwanted grandmother. Why had she waited to tell him? Why hadn't she told him of Amelia after their lovemaking, when he'd seemed ready to grant her anything that would increase her happiness?

The question brought those rapturous hours in his arms flooding back—vivid memories of kisses, touches, whispers and vibrant, life-affirming love.

Lyris clung to the doorframe, anguished with loss. Yet defiance sparked. Perhaps the meeting would put Nicholas into a kinder frame of mind. Eventually, he must talk with Amelia—for when he came home, his grandmother would still be here.

Chapter Twenty-Five

Amelia spoke from the hall behind Lyris. "That man is as muleheaded as his father and possibly as arrogant as Edwin."

Lyris turned with a quick defense springing to her tongue. Her godmother's eyes twinkled. "Nevertheless, the fact that you seem to love him gives me hope."

"Is it apparent?" Lyris let her shoulders droop. "I do love him, even though he absolutely infuriates me." She walked over to Amelia and clasped one of her hands. "Dear Amelia, you should know that Nicholas searched for you during the fire. You had already left the hotel."

Yearning bloomed in Amelia's face. "Did he truly?"

"Yes, he did," Lyris said firmly. "You must keep that in mind, since I suppose you heard all that he shouted just now."

"My dear, I suspect he was heard aboard ships in the bay."

Amelia's expression had taken on the plucky resolution Lyris remembered from the days when she and Gram had conspired like a pair of schoolgirls. "You're plotting," Lyris said.

Her godmother urged her toward the parlor. "Perhaps, just a little."

* * *

When Nick walked into the armory on Union Street, he felt bleaker than the ruins. He had been in control of his life almost since he could walk. Why couldn't he control his wife?

Glumly, he edged through a crowd numbering into the hundreds. Spotting Jon Brunswich, he shouldered a space for himself nearby. "Half of Seattle must be here."

The editor looked up from his notebook. "Feel the optimism, Nick! These people aren't defeated. Nor should they be. Cables are arriving from all over the country, pledging aid."

At the head of the room, the mayor and members of the town council clustered together. Even the territorial governor was present. Sounding puzzled, Jon added, "You're the only man in the room who looks discouraged. That's not like you, Nicholas, my friend."

"Oh, I'll build again. And better. Like everyone else." Nick spoke automatically. His heart wasn't in it.

Jon continued to study him. "I haven't asked about your family. Are the women safe?"

"God, yes!"

"Domestic problem, is it?" With a relieved grin, Jon clapped his shoulder. "Don't let it bother you. These little squalls blow over."

Nick doubted that Jon and Libby had ever argued as furiously as he and Lyris. Deep in his heart, he knew that when he returned home, his grandmother would still be there.

Not only that, his wife's opinion of him was so low he'd have to dig a hole to get any lower. What in hell could have happened to that portrait? "Jon," he asked cautiously, "have you heard anything about looting?"

The editor frowned. "There's no question some of that occurred during the excitement of the fire. What have you lost?"

"A portrait disappeared from a locked cabinet in my office." Nick glanced at his friend. "You know that Lyris once posed for Samuel Castor. If the picture is shown, she'll be humiliated.''

Jon pursed his lips. "You may hear from someone bent on lining his pockets at your expense.''

"Blackmail?'' Sourly, Nick surveyed the crowd for a knowing glance or a sly smile. The meeting had been called to order. The mayor announced pledges for aid, including ten thousand dollars from Tacoma and another ten thousand from San Francisco.

A man rose from the audience. "We collected over five hundred dollars for victims of the Johnstown flood of last week. That money's still here. Shall we use it or send it on?''

Lyris's father thundered, "Send it to Johnstown." The entire audience concurred.

"There's our Seattle spirit at work," Jon said with approval.

Nick nodded. The city would rebuild and ultimately benefit from the fire. He was far less sure of rebuilding his marriage. When a planning committee began to form, he decided to join. The work might keep his mind off his wife.

He saw Richard Thompson join the relief committee. That would give the fellow a hand in distributing all those donations. Nick felt a flicker of apprehension, then told himself he was judging Thompson as unfairly as Lyris had judged *him*. As unfairly as he judged his grandmother, she would say. With a silent curse, he broke the circle of his thoughts and concentrated on plans for a bright new Seattle.

Spencer Lowell joined the planning committee, along with many of the city's leading citizens. A mood of high optimism led to rapid agreement on every question. Merchants would be allowed to operate from tents until they could rebuild. Wooden structures would be prohibited forever in the burned district.

Streets in the lower end of town were to be raised as well as widened, some as much as thirty feet above their present level. Lowell, with other bankers, promised to help without taking a profit.

The heady sense of accomplishment stayed with Nick until he reached home and remembered the problems left there. Had Lyris defied him? Might as well ask if ducks could fly. Shoving open the door, he demanded of a startled servant, "Where is my wife?"

The girl regarded him with an almost flirtatious fascination. Had he lost control of all the women in his house? "Did you hear me? Speak up!"

Dimpling, she directed him into the parlor. He swept past lace hangings in the doorway and stopped cold. Reba and Evelyn were taking tea with Lyris and her godmother. They all looked at him expectantly.

How much did the other two know? They were Lyris's closest friends, but he didn't believe she would air intimate problems any more than he would.

She obviously relied on her visitors to keep him from throwing out her godmother. He greeted them coldly, pointedly ignored the older woman and gave Lyris the full force of a look that should tell her exactly what she could expect when they were alone.

Amelia spoke gently. "Nicholas, dear, would you mind bringing my shawl from the chair beside you?"

If he refused, she would win the other women's sympathy. His name would be blackened even more. With stiff resentment, he picked up the length of cashmere, crossed the carpet and dropped it over her shoulders.

Lyris engaged her friends in vibrant conversation, apparently to distract their curiosity. At the same time, Amelia spoke, her voice so soft that he had to bend close to hear. "I find your sister charming, Nicholas. I look forward to introducing her into society." She paused, then added, "That is a process I can promote far more easily than your wife could."

If he had a weak spot, it was Fanny, despite her unruly behavior. Forced to listen to a voice grown surprisingly fragile, he dropped to one knee. Lyris's satisfied glance made him feel even grimmer. She had planned well and it nettled him to fall into line.

"For his own reasons," Amelia said quietly, "my husband continued to enlarge this house throughout his life. There is room enough that I could stay well out of your sight, if that is your wish."

Darkly, he said, "You know full well what I want."

"Yes, Nicholas, I do. You wish to see your sister accepted into polite society."

He glared at the whorls of design in the carpet, while Evelyn recounted a humorous description of her cook's frantic efforts to feed a horde of refugees. Again he wondered how much Lyris had told her friends.

A muscle flickered in his jaw. He straightened, about to rise. Swiftly, Amelia said, "Let us have this in the open, Nicholas. I once rejected you. It is within your power to reject me. But your wife believes you to be a reasonable man. By now, you must realize that Fanny's entrance into society depends a great deal on her background."

His voice grated. "Wealth creates its own background."

"Fanny will have both," Amelia countered. "Allow me to stay and I will take pleasure in introducing her as my natural granddaughter. She will also inherit my entire fortune, a fact that will be made generally known."

Nick looked at Lyris, wondering if she knew about that. If she expected to inherit from her godmother, she would be disappointed by Amelia's plans—and more dependent on him.

It was a small and petty satisfaction, but it allowed him to say tightly, "Agreed. Just see that you stay out of my way. As far as I'm concerned, there is no kinship between us."

He expected to see triumph in her face, not sorrow. Her mouth drew down and her eyes became sad. Against his will, he remembered Lyris insisting, "She loves you."

Lyris was naive. The woman was using them all, God knew why. Maybe there was no fortune. Maybe she needed free board. Yet as long as she kept her word, his sister's place in society was assured. She would keep it, he vowed as he got to his feet. He would damned well make sure of that.

Lyris heard her husband's harsh agreement with mixed feelings of relief and despair. Amelia's plan was working. She would be allowed to stay, but at what cost to them all?

As Nicholas crisply excused himself to her friends, she saw a chill behind his eyes. He was withdrawing from her as well as from his grandmother. The house would likely become as cheerless as when Edwin had been master.

Reba and Evelyn turned together to Amelia. They had learned with amazement that Nicholas was her grandson. They had also learned that because of Edwin, bad feelings existed, but they didn't know why.

"He has agreed that I may stay," Amelia told them quietly. "You must help us prepare Fanny for society."

Evelyn clapped her hands. "Literature. Music. I know just the tutor. What fun!"

Fun? Lyris wondered. She was having trouble simply keeping the girl under control, much less teaching her manners or dance steps or any of the hundreds of things she must learn. Still, with the four of them working together, there might be a chance to make a lady of Fanny, after all.

In the following weeks, those sessions provided the only lively hours for Lyris. During them, her natural high spirits sparkled. Fanny became as lighthearted as the others while she struggled to learn things they had known all their lives and still remain her own unique self.

Evenings were different. When Nicholas returned at night, a wintry feeling clamped down on the household. Lyris was almost thankful that he worked long hours rebuilding the Golden Harbor and long evenings with the town council.

A meeting only three days after that first optimistic gathering in the armory had ended badly. Property owners absolutely refused to give up land in order to widen the streets. After arguing late into the night, the group rejected, item by item, everything that had been approved three days before.

Almost three weeks later, the council rammed through an ordinance to widen all north-south running streets, adding a fine of three hundred dollars a day for any obstruction left at the original line.

Most property owners had begun construction with little concern for the proposed regrading. Within two weeks of the fire, a hundred and thirty-eight new structures were underway, all at their original levels.

"We may never know why water wasn't available at the hydrants," Nicholas said one night in answer to a question from Fanny.

"What do you think?" she persisted.

Fanny was the only one who could still win a smile from him. The rare sight closed Lyris out even more. She could scarcely believe he had ever teased her, much less given her rapturous hours in his bed.

"Everyone has a theory on the failure of the hydrants," he answered his sister. "I go along with the fellow who says the Almighty got tired of our sewers."

Fanny giggled, and for at least a few minutes, Lyris could pretend that good feelings were the rule at her dinner table.

Shortly after his grandmother joined the household, Nick decided to move back into the master bedroom. He didn't want Amelia speculating on his reasons for sleeping in a room across the house. The same pride that kept him from admitting his marriage was a sham made him pace his bedchamber while longing to kick open the adjoining door.

Lyris rarely spoke to him. He couldn't remember the last time her eyes had held a sparkle. He felt raw inside, and knew he grieved for her lost animation.

As he dressed for another cheerless dinner, a light knock came at the hall door. Expecting a maid, he was startled to admit his wife. Lyris wore a close-fitting tea gown of ivory that made jewels of her hair and eyes. His composure faltered. He nearly reached for her, but caught himself.

There was no indication in her voice or manner that she felt anything but disdain. "Forgive me for interrupting, but I wish to speak in private."

His stomach knotted. She was with child. She must be. The possibility had horrified her in the carriage, weeks ago. Silently, he motioned her into the room.

The hours when they had celebrated life in his bed rushed vividly to his mind. She'd said then that she loved him. Love meant trust. She had never trusted him, so the words were a lie. But now she was carrying his child. His heart ached with a need to end the bitterness.

She closed the door and stood against it. "This will just take a moment. I felt you should know you have no need for concern. Our reckless behavior did not start a child."

He had dreaded hearing that he was to become a father. Now he felt a sickening rush of loss. He didn't understand his own reaction. Did he want a child? Her child? God, yes. But not with hostility between them.

She must have felt vast relief on learning she was safe. He turned away to keep her from seeing his pain. Roughly, he said, "It's good of you to tell me."

Lyris fought a desire to fling her arms around him, to kiss him until he admitted that he cared for her. She chided herself. It would be mortifying to throw herself at him, only to be rejected.

The exhilarating night in his arms was like a chapter in a novel, a story that had so engrossed her that she'd lived for a brief time in another's life. That story had ended. The book was closed. She was left with the cold disappointment of her real life.

For days, she had wavered between hope and fear of a child. When she learned there would not be one, she closed herself in her room, struggling for hours with anguished disappointment.

Amelia didn't know this marriage was to end with Fanny's debut, but that part of the bargain was increasingly more certain to Lyris. Nick had become a stranger on the day she humiliated him by bringing his grandmother into the house.

Lyris could see no way to reach the man she loved. He was gallant enough to keep his relief to himself, but his silence wounded her. Quietly, she opened the door and slipped into the hall.

Chapter Twenty-Six

As Lyris sat at her desk, sketching ideas for a dinner party, she became aware of a familiar scent of violets. Her entire body tightened. With gentle reproof, Amelia murmured, "Lyris, darling, you can't mean to costume your serving girls?"

"As Miss Liberties," Lyris said, trying to maintain a serene manner despite her godmother's habitual fussing. During her six months in residence, Amelia had gradually forgotten which of them was mistress and which was a guest. "With Washington newly become a state," Lyris explained, "the costumes will be perfect."

"But, *dear* Lyris, statehood was declared an entire month ago. Christmas garlands would be far more fitting. All these red streamers, paper bursts and spangles simply do not work."

"Everyone uses Christmas decor in December." Lyris returned to her designs, nerves braced. As she expected, Amelia became conciliatory.

"You know I wouldn't interfere for the world, dear. But I fear you are forgetting the purpose of your dinner. This is not an entertainment for friends."

"No, it's for business," Lyris retorted. "The gentlemen may talk late into the night over Seattle's problems, but not while at my table. The decor will remind them of their manners." With an effort, she softened her tone. "Blazing desserts will complete the theme. Have you a favorite, Amelia?"

"Blazing desserts may ignite blazing tempers," Amelia warned.

Lyris struggled with her own temper. The success of this dinner meant more than pacifying warring businessmen. She hoped to ease the battle between herself and her husband.

The respect Nicholas believed he didn't receive at home, he readily found away from it. As Lyris had anticipated months before, his hard work and farsighted ideas were earning the high status he had attempted to gain through marriage.

People often spoke of their admiration for him. Frequent dinner invitations proved it. Far from being embarrassed by her marriage to a tradesman, Lyris had grown proud. Yet the gulf between them was too wide to cross.

He would not speak of Amelia, would not see her, would not even allow her into the rooms he used while home. Despite her own problems with Amelia, Lyris ached when she saw the pain Nicholas caused her godmother.

With Seattle's rebuilding heavily underway, problems fell as persistently as the winter rains. There was constant bickering over debris dumped from private property onto streets or from streets onto private property. The matter of condemning land to widen streets was still raising tempers and threats of lawsuits. Statehood brought other clashes.

When Nick had asked her to plan a dinner where he could gather opposing forces in a pleasant social setting, Lyris had readily agreed. She intended to create so scintillating an evening that he would remember why he'd once loved her.

On the day of the party, Amelia looked critically around the dining room while Lyris helped a servant center a large paper eagle over bunting-draped walls. "My word, Nicholas must be planning to run for public office."

Lyris pretended not to hear. She had created a wall mural of Seattle, set out white china on red cloth and even placed a model train in the centerpiece to represent the city's hopes of attracting the Great Northern Railroad. The effect pleased her.

"It appears to me," her godmother said, "that in decorating to prevent business talk at your table, you have done everything imaginable to provoke it."

To Lyris's considerable dismay, her godmother proved to be right. The women among her guests were as eager as their husbands to discuss the city's future. Conversation sizzled as to whether city water should be publicly or privately owned. Then there was the matter of rivalry between Olympia and Vancouver for the state capital.

"Why place our capital on the Oregon border?" one man thundered, while Lyris wondered if her guests would suffer indigestion and blame it on her food.

Troubled, she gazed down the length of the table to watch her husband argue heatedly over dealings with the railroad. Richard Thompson started to disagree. Nicholas cut him off.

Lyris longed to intervene, but if she had learned anything from this marriage, it was never to correct Nicholas in public. Two men near her exchanged meaningful glances. An earlier exchange between them when they were unaware of her presence suddenly became clear. "Drake won't get far trying to drive everyone as hard as he drives himself," one had said.

The other had answered in a sly tone, "If our host weren't possessed of a lovely wife, I'd say he needed to marry."

She hid her dismay in busying herself with the next course. *Did* Nicholas drive himself and others because of unhappiness in his marriage? She resented the implication as well as the men who made it and turned decisively to her nearest neighbor. "Tell me, is it true that a teamster backed his wagon into your second-story window?"

Another answered for him. "It's true, all right. Emmett nearly toppled off the street in his rage."

Laughter led to a discussion of the raised streets, which passed many of the rebuilt structures at their second- and even third-story level. Emmett defended himself stoutly. "That won't happen again. I'm having planks put across to that window. I'll make a door of it. Just as my neighbors have done to either side."

"I'm farther uptown," another mused. "The elevation isn't so great, but I'll admit I'm tired of climbing up and down a ladder to reach the street. It's not helping business, either."

"Still," Emmett mused, "a wagon through a window is nothing compared to your mishap, Nick."

Lyris wheeled to face him. "Mishap?"

Her husband tried to turn the subject, but others were eager to fill her in. Yesterday, an entire wall had fallen, narrowly missing him. As Lyris sat dazed with horror, Richard Thompson said cheerfully, "Are you sure it was an accident? There are those who feel pressured by your ideas."

Nick wished the subject hadn't come up. He knew he had enemies and counted Thompson among them. He was certain the man was profiting from his position on the relief committee, and had quietly begun an investigation. In suggesting that the falling wall and other accidents were deliberate, Thompson might be delivering a warning.

As he glanced down the table, trying to judge the other men's thoughts, Nick was distracted by his wife's stunned expression. She was lovelier than ever this evening, wearing her grandmother's sapphires with a velvet gown of the same deep blue. Candlelight glowed in eyes that had grown wide over news of the fallen wall.

When she looked at him that way, he couldn't put his thoughts anywhere else. Too often, he found himself gazing for long minutes at the delicate lines of her profile and the porcelain perfection of her skin. He could lose startling amounts of time just in watching the graceful movements of her hand as she worked on a story for the *Tribune*. Her fingers were remarkably fragile. Each supple flex of her wrist fascinated him.

When she frowned or smiled, the play of expressions held him spellbound. If she knew he collected every story she wrote, she would probably arch those expressive brows, purse her luscious lips and drive him wild with derision while he longed for kisses.

There was some satisfaction in hearing from Fanny that Lyris was increasingly at odds with her godmother. He had considered allowing Amelia to join them at dinner, but rules once made were difficult to unmake.

It still rankled that Lyris and her godmother had tricked him into the arrangement in the first place. If Amelia countermanded many more direct orders to a servant, however, his wife might well be the one to order her from the house.

That was an appealing thought. Not only would he be avenged at last, but Lyris would see that he had been right all along. Of course, there was still the problem of the missing portrait, a subject they never discussed. Wondering if she thought of it as often as he did, Nick forced his attention to his guests.

Fanny peered through the serving door, wishing Lyris had let her join the party, even if it was for business. Richard Thompson was here and more handsome than she remembered. She pushed the door a little wider, remembering how soft his mustache was. How exciting his mouth had felt on hers.

He hadn't come to visit her, but after Nick's fury that night at the skating rink, she wasn't surprised. Nick had called her a child and Richard even worse. She had been afraid they would fight, but while Nick was scolding her, Richard had disappeared.

She wasn't a child now. She was sixteen and had pinned up her hair so she looked even older. She longed for him to notice. Then he looked directly at her, his eyes sparkling as if he knew she would be there behind the door. When she shaped a kiss with her lips, he winked. Unfortunately, Nick happened to look at Richard just then. Fanny ducked into the pantry.

Nick hid a rush of annoyance. Anything he might say to Thompson must be said in private. But he caught Lyris's glance and nodded sharply toward the kitchen. With a murmur to her dinner partners, she excused herself from the table.

Lyris reached the kitchen too late to catch Fanny. Softly, Ruby said, ''She went to her granny's rooms, ma'am.''

Lyris decided not to follow. When she found the opportunity, she would advise Nicholas to see Thompson to his carriage to prevent any clandestine meeting. After lighting the plum pudding, ostensibly her reason for leaving the table, she returned to the dining room.

The hour was long past midnight before the last guests departed. Lyris turned to her husband, daring to hope she had succeeded in putting him into a more accepting frame of mind. ''I believe the evening was a success.''

''*You* were a success.''

He looked at her with appreciation she had not seen in months. Anticipation made her breathless. ''I wanted to please you.''

''Did you?'' A faint smile turned his mouth upward at one corner. ''You please me more often than you know.''

''Nicholas,'' she murmured, swaying toward him, but Fanny called from the stairway. ''I want you both to see that I'm safely inside and not running after the gentlemen.''

Nick swung around. ''One particular gentleman will not be calling here. I made certain he understood.''

After a look of outrage, the girl burst into tears and ran up the stairs. Lyris said in dismay, ''Perhaps you are too harsh.''

His expression closed. ''Go on to bed. I'll close the house.''

Feeling as discouraged as Fanny, Lyris walked up to her room. For long minutes, she stood gazing at the adjoining door, then turned the key she had kept in the lock for six months.

She pulled the door ajar and hurriedly slipped into the whisper-sheer nightdress given to her on her wedding day. Her heart raced. For months she had fiercely suppressed any memory of lovemaking. Now every detail swept into her heart and mind until she became flushed with longing.

Downstairs, Nick put the last of the fire screens in place, trying unsuccessfully to get his wife out of his mind. He could let his pride crumble, he told himself. He could go to her, plead that he loved her, argue that he had not hidden her portrait, although he took full responsibility for its loss. He could agree to listen to Amelia's lies and allow her at his table—all if Lyris would only open her arms.

He could also fly, if he jumped off the roof.

He didn't trust himself to go upstairs, not while his mind churned with thoughts of her lovely body writhing with pleasure beneath him, a memory still vivid—little wonder, since it reoccurred nightly in his dreams. If he went upstairs now, he would likely kick open the door between their rooms.

And then what? Insist on the matrimonial rights he had promised to forgo? Drive her forever from him by forcing her to accommodate him? With a muffled curse, he strode into the hall for his hat, then left the house for the less complicated pleasures of the Skid Road.

The street roared with life, as if the fire had never happened. Loggers and mill workers bumped shoulders while crowding in and out of bars and gambling houses or competing for the favor of bar girls. Holly and mistletoe wound incongruously in windows where cardboard angels leaned against liquor displays.

He stepped around a fistfight, ducking a flying whiskey bottle. The contents splashed his coat. Eager to release his tension, he swung about, fists clenched. A woman's soft voice cooed at his shoulder. "Looking for company, handsome?"

She was small and pretty, if somewhat worn. The red in her hair owed more to henna than to nature. In the street-light, she looked to be in her twenties, but he suspected that honest sunlight would add at least ten more years.

Still, for a price, she would free him from the demons that had driven him into the night. "I have a place just down the street," she urged him. "Decorated all pretty for the holi-days. Why don't you come with me?"

He felt absolutely no desire for her. Shaking his head, he turned at random into the nearest saloon, shouldered his way to the bar and ordered whiskey. A poker game caught his attention and he wandered over to watch, then joined in. For several more whiskeys and a few more hours, the game held him.

As he raked in a winning pot, a big unshaved logger who had been losing heavily staggered to his feet. "Hold on, pretty boy. You pulled that last ace out of your sleeve."

Nick rose with dangerous purpose. "I didn't hear you rightly, fellow. Maybe you'd like to repeat that."

"You heard me. I said you're a cheater and a bastard be-sides."

With a rush of exhilaration, Nick slammed his fist into the logger's jaw. He ducked a return punch, swung his fist up-ward and again felt it connect with skin and bone.

Cursing, the logger stumbled back, braced against a ta-ble, then charged ahead like a battering ram, shoving Nick into the table. Men jumped aside while cards and coins clattered to the floor. Glass shattered.

A fist crunched below Nick's eye. He grunted. A second punch smashed into his jaw. He fell heavily onto the table, then rolled while a third blow crashed with splintering force near his head.

Pulling one leg upward, he slammed his foot into the logger's midsection, driving him back. He swung to the floor and crouched, fists ready. Hamlike hands grabbed him by collar and belt. A heavy voice grated, "Take it into the street, mister."

The bouncer topped him by nearly a hundred pounds. Nick crashed into the unpaved street with a force that made his head spin. Humiliated and angry, he struggled to his feet, ready to charge back into the saloon.

A woman's hand brushed at his coat. As she smiled at him, her large breasts swelled encouragingly from the low cut of her dress. "Never mind all that, sweetie. Let Sadie show you how to forget."

Forget, he thought, still dazed. That's what he needed, why he was here. When Sadie slipped her arm through his, trapping him against the soft weight of her breast, he let her guide him to a narrow crib newly built over the tide flat.

Chapter Twenty-Seven

Nick slumped on a sagging mattress while Sadie cleansed his face with a cloth wrung out in cold water. She had shaken his coat and draped it over a chair, near a small tree bowed under the weight of oyster shells with Christmas scenes glued into them. "There now," she said cheerfully. "A bit bruised and scraped, but you won't scare the ladies."

She wrapped one plump arm around his shoulders and played the fingers of her free hand down the front of his shirt. A wave of cheap perfume did nothing to dispel the rank smell of the bay at low tide. "Now, let's get on with that forgettin' I promised."

Nick's head spun from the whiskey and the fight, but he realized he didn't want to be where he was, smelling sweat and stale bedding and being petted by a woman whose kisses stemmed from an interest in his pocket. Six months had slipped by since that one night with his wife, but to blur the memory with the body of a slattern was unthinkable.

Getting unsteadily to his feet, he groped for his pocketbook. "Thanks, Sadie, but I find I don't want to forget, after all."

She snatched up the money. "Tell your lady for me how lucky she is."

With a harsh laugh, he left the crib. Dawn already brightened the sky. He entered his home through the tower and climbed wearily to his room. There, he hurled his coat to the floor and sank onto the bed to remove his shoes.

The door was open into Lyris's room. He stared at it without comprehension, then spun around to inspect his bed. She wasn't there. Cautiously, he crossed the carpet to look into her chamber.

She lay asleep, the comforter loose about her waist. Her face was turned toward him, her lips parted, thick lashes resting against her creamy skin. One arm was flung above her head, her graceful fingers tangled in the dark waves of her hair.

He recognized the sheer nightgown of their wedding night. The warm glow of her skin through the lace made his throat ache with regret. She was exquisite. He loved her. God, how he loved her—and had lost her to a night on the Skid Road.

He pictured her waiting expectantly for a lover who never arrived. To wake her now at dawn, smelling of stale whiskey and cheap perfume, was unthinkable.

What could he say? That he'd been delayed by a whore? That would spark a tender scene. Sick at heart, he quietly closed the door and collapsed across his bed into the oblivion of long-postponed sleep.

Lyris woke late in the morning. The adjoining door was closed. She looked at it with painful humiliation. She could not have more openly offered herself if she had crept naked into his bed.

He had declined. Eyes stinging with angry tears, she rang for Jenny to help her dress. Her first impulse was to shield herself in heavy clothing. Her second was the opposite. "Never mind the corset," she told her maid. "I intend to spend the day relaxing in the comfort of a tea dress."

She chose an apricot silk cut Empire-fashion. Web-sheer sleeves, caught at the wrists by satin bands, left her arms sensually visible. Her unconfined breasts pressed gently against the bodice. She meant for Nicholas to see what he had rejected. If he should be tempted by her now, he would receive a cold response.

That closed door was a physical slap. It occurred to her that Nick must have felt something like this on the day when she first rejected his courtship. That was different. They hadn't known each other then. They hadn't enjoyed a night of lyrical lovemaking or taken an interest in each other's lives.

She hurried down the stairs, determined to have this out, but Mrs. Ramsey called her aside. "Ruby is waiting in the kitchen for your displeasure, ma'am."

"Ruby?" Lyris asked with impatience. "What has she done?"

With thinning lips, Mrs. Ramsey offered a folded paper. "I'm afraid, ma'am, that she passed this on to Miss Fanny. The young lady has left the house."

Lyris's spirits plummeted even lower as she snapped open the note. A florid script invited Fanny to a meeting in the "romantic space created where forgotten sidewalks are roofed with the new." The address given was near Thompson's office, the signature an elaborately scrawled letter *R*.

Sick with dread, she asked, "Where is my husband?"

"At his breakfast, ma'am." The housekeeper paused, then added stolidly, "And in a black mood, I'm sorry to say. He's ordered his carriage around and is about to leave. I thought it best to give that message to you."

Even Mrs. Ramsey avoided Nicholas in a rage. His mood couldn't be any blacker than her own, Lyris thought darkly as she swept into the dining room. What was between herself and her husband must be set aside for now in concern for Fanny.

He stood as she approached. She saw an apology for the closed door in his cautious manner. Rather late now, she told him silently.

A bruise on his cheekbone caught her glance. A result of that falling wall? She should have noticed earlier, but if that failure had caused him to reject her, he was remarkably thin-skinned. Stiffly, she offered the note. "This was just handed to me. I'm told Fanny is not in the house."

Nick scanned the message, an angry flush rising in his face. Turning on one heel, he strode into the hall. Lyris ran after him. There was no time to change into a street dress. Snatching a cloak, she dashed outside and clambered into the already moving carriage.

Nick hauled her in beside him as the driver brought the startled horses to a halt. "Are you trying to get yourself killed?"

Breathless, she said, "I'm going with you."

"Dressed like that?"

"You may need someone to hold Fanny while you thrash Thompson and there isn't time to change." She clutched her bundled cloak. "I have cover enough."

For a moment, their expressions battled, then, draping the garment loosely about her, he shouted to the driver, "Go on!"

The ride downtown was made in smoldering silence. Lyris felt Nick glance at her. When she looked at him, he turned away. She forced her mind to Fanny. If the meeting were innocent—dare she hope so?—Nick might let Thompson off with a warning.

Ice settled in her stomach. Fanny was foolish, but not stupid. Yet she was smitten with Thompson, a man far too old for her and with a grudge against her brother.

The carriage came to a stop where hammering and shouting racketed on every side. The busy scream of mill whistles echoed the urgent blasts of ships' horns in the bay. Nick swung to the street. "Wait here."

Lyris scrambled after him. "Fanny will need me."

"To do what? Coddle her? You're too blamed lenient."

"And you're too harsh. You know Fanny is starved for love." His mouth tightened. Would they always argue? Lyris touched his sleeve. "Please, there isn't time for this. We must find her."

They stood on a planked street beside the second-story windows of a block of rebuilt office buildings. In many places, planks or bricked walks were laid from the new street across to the walls. Where gaps remained, stairs led to first-floor doorways that had become basements. Nick started down the nearest set. Lyris followed.

When they reached the cobblestones laid after the fire, they walked along a dimly lit tunnel between the blank wall of the new street and the brick faces of buildings. At first they encountered merchants and customers, but after turning a corner, they moved alone on a deserted walk.

The slope became steeper. Nick reached for Lyris's arm. "Watch your step. There's loose rubble along here."

For a moment, Fanny was forgotten while they looked into each other's eyes. Lyris became intensely aware of Nicholas's touch. He had not allowed her this close in months. She let her eyes ask the question that tore at her heart.

Rough-voiced, he answered. "When I went up last night, you were asleep."

"Do you mean it took well over an hour to close up the house?"

Inwardly, Nick winced. The thought of Lyris waiting while anticipation faded made him burn with guilt. He had probably made matters worse by closing that damned door.

"Sweetheart," he said uncomfortably, "the truth is, I, uh, walked down to the Skid Road for drinking and cards."

Comprehension dawned on her face. She fixed her gaze on his battered cheekbone. "A friendly game."

Better she think him a fool than a rat. "A long one." He pushed the whore to the back of his mind for fear Lyris would see the woman in his eyes. "I reached home at dawn, stinking of whiskey. I'm not proud of it. Believe me, you would not have cared to have me wake you then."

Lyris knew him well enough to see that he held something back. A woman? Someone who'd left him too well satisfied for interest in his wife? Pride was a cold companion, but she couldn't help asking, "Is there anything else you would like to have off your conscience?"

Nick inwardly flinched again. She had guessed the whole of it. He saw it in the flash of her eyes, but damned if he would admit that when opportunity offered, desire had fled.

Lyris had ruined him for other women, but he wasn't going to tell her so. To let her know the power she held over him would be to put himself completely into her hands. Roughly, he reminded her of Fanny. "We're wasting time."

She followed, trying to swallow the painful certainty that Nick had turned from her to someone else. She should despise him, yet she yearned for his touch.

He paused to assist her over loose rocks and masonry. Again, their eyes held before he continued on. A few steps farther, a heavy piece of lumber blocked the way. He lifted her across, pausing, his arms tightening about her, then abruptly set her on the far side.

This time, he kept one arm protectively about her waist. Lyris leaned into him, unwilling to humor hurt feelings. Beneath worry for Fanny, she felt dizzy with longing.

A nearly featureless gray stone block of buildings broken only by an occasional windowless door stretched ahead. Wagon wheels ground along the planked street above, part of a distant world.

The sharp scent of new lumber freshened a chill wind sweeping through a gap in the overhead walk. "Nicholas," Lyris said to break the silence. "When we find them..."

A furry animal darted across the hem of her cloak. With a shriek, she flung herself into Nick's arms, all but climbing up his body.

He held her close. "A cat, Lyris! It was only a cat."

"Are you sure?" She peered around him, heart pounding.

"I'm sure." His voice softened. She looked into his smoky expression and lost all thought of the cat. With desperate need, she crushed her lips to his.

When he returned the kiss, joy blazed through her. She learned again the shape and taste of his mouth. As she pressed against him, he slipped his arms beneath her cloak.

Her skin woke at the electric touch of his hands. When he cradled the soft weight of her breasts through the sheer fabric of her tea gown, she felt his breathing change. She longed to melt into him, to become part of his heart and skin and bones.

Sliding her hand upward, she tumbled his hat carelessly into the street and tangled her fingers in his hair. With a tortured groan, he pulled her through a narrow doorway into an abandoned basement.

Mindless sensations careened through her as he stroked the sensitive inner surface of her lips with his tongue. She dared to return the caress and felt heat surge deep within her.

His taste was achingly familiar. For months she had dreamed of it, longed for it. Now she couldn't get enough. Her hands moved desperately through his thick, unruly hair, holding him while she drank his kisses.

She fit herself even more intimately against him, trembling to discover he was vitally aroused. Excitement coursed along her nerves. She wanted to keep kissing him, to forget everything else, even where they were.

Nearby, someone giggled. The sound was shatteringly familiar. They both froze. After an agonized moment, Nick raised his head. In a strained voice, he said to Fanny, "Come here."

She stood in the street just outside the doorway, ready to run. Before she could escape, he caught her arm, whirled her inside and against a wall. Fanny's eyes widened. "Nicky!"

He shoved her toward Lyris. "Take her home. We'll have this out later. After I've talked to Thompson." Snatching his hat from the walk, he strode deeper into the tunnel of the underground street. Unhappily, Lyris wondered if he was headed for some fallen woman who would be glad to finish what she had started.

Rather than being chastened, Fanny sparkled with curiosity. "For two people who don't much like each other, that was some kiss."

For all her flirtations, Fanny was still innocent. Lyris was sure of that. Yet Nick must be humiliated and certain that his sister understood why.

Fanny needed love, but Lyris was far from capable of such a tender emotion at that moment. Grasping the girl's arm, she marched her back the way they had come, toward the waiting carriage. "Your brother is not the only one who is furious with you, miss. I advise you to keep your thoughts to yourself."

Chapter Twenty-Eight

Fanny sat on her sleigh bed, propped against pillows with the kitten in her lap, waiting for her brother. Lyris was so angry she hadn't said a word during the ride to the house. She and Nick were always getting mad, Fanny told herself dolefully.

Richard was the only one who really liked her. He had been waiting when she came down from the street. There were people around, so he hadn't kissed her, but she could see that he'd wanted to.

He'd hurried her along the covered sidewalk, away from people and farther downhill until the only light filtered from gaps in the street above. After a while, he linked their hands. "Only a little farther, pretty Fanny."

He glanced around, then tilted her head and kissed her. When she put her hand on his chest, she felt his heart beating. It excited her and she wanted to go on kissing, but he pulled back, then started talking about Nick. "Your brother is giving me a hard time, pet. Does he listen to you?"

"Not much," she said. "Mostly, he makes me listen to him."

"But you're close to him," Richard said, putting his arm around her and hugging her to his side.

"The only one he's close to is Lyris," Fanny answered, hoping for sympathy. "You should see him look at her, as if she was sugar when all his life was sour."

"Ah, yes." An odd note came into Richard's voice. "The lovely Lyris."

Jealousy sheared through Fanny. "Lovely! She's mean!"

Richard agreed with a hug that reassured her. "Your sister-in-law has a sharp tongue. I don't envy your brother."

"Why are we talking about them?" Fanny demanded.

Richard put both arms around her then. His body felt good against hers. He was tall and strong and she liked leaning against him. She liked it even better when he kissed her. She cuddled close, loving the warm, firm pressure of his mouth.

But he stopped kissing her and pressed his cheek against her hair. "I could become fond of you, pet. I'm afraid your brother wouldn't like that."

"He doesn't own me."

"But you are his responsibility. He wouldn't like to see any harm come to you." She didn't understand his expression. For a moment, he looked sorry about something. Then he straightened. "We'll walk a little farther, pet."

They'd stepped into a basement. She saw that it had once been the first floor of an office building. Richard led her up a set of stairs to a new first floor that opened onto the street, then grinned broadly. "My office, pet. What do you think of it?"

Women sat at typewriters near clerks studying ledgers. Richard asked her to wait on a chair while he talked with two other men. She felt uncomfortable because they kept glancing at her as if she didn't have any right to be there.

Then to her horror, Fanny saw Lyris's father come in from the street. One of the clerks greeted him. At any moment, he would look over and recognize her. Slipping off the chair, she edged along the wall down the stairs to the basement. She meant to wait for Richard there, but voices outside made her curious.

What a surprise to see her brother and Lyris. At first, she'd been frightened. Ruby must have told. They must have come after her. But then they started kissing! When they moved into the building, Fanny slipped behind the stairway.

She hadn't meant to giggle. It had just popped out, and now she was in trouble. That wasn't all. Richard must think she had run away from him. She had to go back and tell him why.

Lyris sat impatiently at her desk, unable to work, wondering where Nick was and when he would come home. He was sure to blame her for allowing Fanny to slip from the house. Rightly so. She should be able to keep one young woman in sight.

What had happened between them was not to be thought of, much less discussed. Yet those wanton, irresponsible kisses had inflamed her until she could think of little else. Such passion in a public place was unthinkable. She should be embarrassed and ashamed. Instead, a fierce longing to melt again into his arms, to feel the full force of his ardor, drove all thought of propriety from her mind.

Her thoughts were so absorbed that she jumped at the housekeeper's voice. "Excuse me, ma'am. Mr. Drake would like you to join him in the library." Nervously smoothing her skirt, Lyris hurried down the hall.

Nicholas turned from the window, his remote expression raising a barrier between them. "Sit down, Lyris."

She wanted to go to him, to put her arms around him and ease the pained look from his face. His expression forbade her. Reluctantly, she perched on the edge of a chair. "Did you talk with Richard?"

He shook his head. In a voice as pained as his expression, he added, "It's more urgent to settle the matter between us. I hope you'll accept an apology."

Apology meant regret. She refused to regret their passion. Lyris leaned toward him, aching with a need to reach past his formidable pride. "That isn't necessary."

"Isn't it, Lyris?" His eyes were brooding. "I'm well aware that no patrician blue blood would maul his wife on a public street."

"I believe I leapt into your arms," Lyris exclaimed. The closed bedroom came to mind. He had tried hard to resist her. If anyone was at fault for those kisses, it was she.

Stiffly, she added, "I know I forced you into that embrace. But, Nicholas..." Springing to her feet, she went to him. "I'm only sorry we were interrupted."

She saw his skin darken and knew his humiliation went even deeper than she'd thought. Still, she wasn't prepared for his crisp words. "Nothing like that will happen again. I've begun a petition for divorce."

Dizziness swept her. She braced one hand against the window ledge. Mistletoe berries fell loose from a garland beneath her fingers and skittered along the floor. "Nick, I don't want—"

"Think of it as an early Christmas gift," he said grimly. "You were right from the beginning. There's no need to prolong this."

"But Fanny..."

"She'll never become a social butterfly and wouldn't be happy if she could."

"She is making progress," Lyris argued. "She's learned a great deal. It's just that she's impetuous."

He slammed one hand flat on the desk. "She needs a husband. I mean to see that Thompson makes an honest offer."

"She is barely sixteen!"

"Her mother's age when she eloped."

Lyris was near enough to touch him and yet felt as if they were separated by a distance too vast to cross. "Your mother may have been mature at that age. Your sister is not. She doesn't want Richard. It's the adventure that lures her. Can't you see that?"

"What I see is a girl who will find herself in serious trouble if she isn't put into a boarding school or a marriage, and frankly, I don't think a school could handle her."

"Nicholas," Lyris pleaded, "don't force Richard to marry her."

"Why not?" Nick's eyes narrowed. "Do you have your own plans for him?"

Outrage sharpened her voice. "You can ask that, when you know how I feel about you?"

His silence said he was prepared to destroy what both of them most wanted. Lyris swept around the desk, yanked open a drawer and pulled out a folder she had discovered earlier in a search for writing paper. "Why have you clipped my stories?"

He reached toward the file, then stopped, his eyes stormy. "I keep them, dear wife, as a reminder that you have never taken me seriously. Do you think I enjoy knowing that you're slumming with this marriage? You've always thought of me as your inferior, my direct orders to be ignored as you choose."

"That may have been true in the beginning," Lyris said fiercely. "I didn't know you then. As it turns out, I didn't know myself, either."

With a sound of disgust, he wheeled around to face out the window. Lyris dropped the file and walked to him. "Nicholas, I have learned to respect you, as my friends have."

His voice grated. "We're too different. In the beginning, I thought... It doesn't matter what I thought. We don't belong together. The marriage was a miserable mistake."

"You've decided that?" With angry despair, she clutched his arm. "Tell me, how do you justify that decision with the intense feelings we arouse in each other?"

She had hoped to touch his heart, but he answered coldly. "Where is your high mind, sweetheart? Surely you mean to commit your life to something grander than carnal appetite."

She knew he was brutal to discourage her. Yet she had never been more sure of her need for him, or less confident of her ability to win. "I love you," she said steadily. "I believe you love me."

His eyes darkened, but the emotional barrier held. "You're prepared to put sentimentality above reason? I'm not. I don't want to live with a woman who, at the least provocation, throws the facts of my birth in my face."

Tears flooded her eyes. She couldn't call back words thrown out in the past. But she had changed. He must see that. She reached out, but he strode to the door. There, he turned for a last hard comment. "If you *should* forget that common birth, madam, you have your blessed godmother to remind you!"

Lyris collapsed onto a chair, shaking with sobs while the front door slammed. She felt as if it slammed on her heart. Divorce. The word drummed in her head. He had already petitioned. He couldn't wait to get her out of his life.

Spirited resistance rose through the tears. He could leave her, but he couldn't make her leave him. She didn't think he would easily give up this house. As long as they both were in it, there must be a way to prove to him that he was making a terrible mistake.

Nicholas didn't come home for dinner. Lyris considered waiting in his bed, but her pride wouldn't allow that. She was desperate, but not so desperate that she could face having him physically reject her.

She lay awake plotting. For six months they had seen little of each other, just an hour or two at dinner and more rarely, an evening in the parlor. That was the problem. From now on, she was going to be wherever he was, whether he liked it or not.

In the morning, she asked Jenny to help her into her favorite walking suit. After warning Ruby to keep a careful eye on Fanny, she ordered the carriage. Her husband had apparently spent the night at the Golden Harbor. Very well, she would seek him there.

She stood at a hall mirror, adjusting a feathered plume on her hat and making plans. The saloon was partially rebuilt and open for business. She would go there and tease him into seeing what a humorless brute he had become.

She would begin with his hat. After removing her feathers and satin, she would place his derby on her head. "This is the hat you wear when you walk out on me," she would say. "I need to feel its magic."

He might at least smile. He might think again before walking off. He might be willing to talk.

As she stepped toward the door, she heard someone crying. Puzzled, she swept a glance up the grand staircase. Ruby huddled in the space beneath, her face cradled in her arms, her entire body shaking. Lyris hurried to her. "Ruby? Whatever is wrong?"

"Oh, ma'am." The girl's voice quavered. She raised her head, tears streaming down her frightened face. "Oh, ma'am, she's gone again. Mr. Drake'll beat me. I know he will."

"Gone?" Lyris braced herself against the bannister as the girl's meaning sank in. "Fanny?"

With a trembling hand, the maid held out a note. Sniffling, she added, "She left this on her bed."

Fanny's penmanship was improving, Lyris noticed with dazed abstraction while wanting to deny the carefree words. "I have to tell Richard why I disappeared yesterday. I'll be back before Nick gets home, so don't worry."

All the brave plans to win Nicholas splintered around Lyris's feet. He wouldn't blame Ruby for losing Fanny. He would blame her. "Don't worry," Fanny had written. Lyris wanted to laugh, but was afraid of inviting hysteria.

"Oh, ma'am," Ruby said fearfully. "What will you do?"

Do? She had three possible courses of action. She could wait for Fanny to come back, hoping nothing untoward had taken place. That was unacceptable. She didn't trust

Thompson. Besides, when Nick found out, and he would find out, he would force Fanny into an unsuitable marriage.

It would be better to tell him immediately than to have him find out later. That was her second choice. The carriage was already waiting to take her to the Golden Harbor, but she had meant to sensually harass Nick, not deliver disturbing news. Already, he meant to divorce her. She tightened her hold on the bannister while the reminder sank in.

She had blamed Nick for losing the portrait while it was in his care. It was far worse to have lost Fanny while responsible for the girl. Nick would take this as further proof that she had no real interest in either of them. If she took him this note, she might as well petition for divorce herself.

That left the third choice. "Do, Ruby?" she said with decision. "There is only one thing to do. I am going after her."

Chapter Twenty-Nine

Again, Lyris descended stairs to the old street level. Her heart filled with longing when she reached the place where she and Nicholas had kissed until they both lost their senses. For a moment, she felt the strong muscles of his back beneath her hands and the urgent pressure of his mouth on hers. Then she forced her thoughts to Fanny.

Again, a basement door lay ajar. She knew now that this was Thompson's building. Fanny must have come down those stairs the day before. Preparing for an emotional scene, Lyris marched inside. A large male hand clamped around her mouth. Behind her, the door slammed shut.

For an instant, she was disoriented. Outrage followed. She punched one elbow backward into yielding flesh and heard a grunt. The hand eased. She sprang forward, but was caught and spun around.

Thompson glared at her, his face mottled above his mustache. "Nasty little minx, aren't you?"

Lyris clenched her hands in her skirt, preparing to kick. He guessed her intent and turned to shield himself as he rasped, "We're going upstairs. If you care for the girl, you won't give me any more trouble."

"You don't yet know the meaning of trouble," Lyris told him furiously.

Her glance fell on Fanny, who stood near a stairway, eyes bright with excitement. "He doesn't mean any harm," the girl said quickly. "He just wants you to reason with Nicky."

Thompson gave Lyris a shove. "Upstairs." With stiff dignity, she swept ahead. When they reached the second floor, he thrust her into a room holding only a table and a pair of straight-backed chairs. A narrow window at ceiling level let in gray daylight. "Make yourself comfortable. You're going to be here for a while."

Lyris looked hard at the girl, hoping to penetrate past her romantic haze. But Fanny gazed at Thompson with her heart in her eyes. "What is this all about?" Lyris demanded.

Thompson wrapped an arm about Fanny. "It's about many things, my dear. Money, for example. Your virtuous husband is threatening my access to funds that are not his concern."

"For your word *access*," Lyris said with contempt, "I suspect one might better substitute the word *theft*."

She was pleased to see him bristle, but his arm tightened about the girl. "It's also about love."

Derision dripped from Lyris. "Women of your own age must all have recognized your low nature, that you would stoop to deluding this child."

"I'm not a child!" Fanny exclaimed.

Thompson pulled at his mustache. "I was referring to your husband, dear Lyris, a man who has *deluded* himself into believing that a woman of your class could learn to love him. He'll come at a rush when Fanny delivers my note."

Still sounding annoyed, Fanny said, "Richard just wants to talk to Nick. You know how stubborn he can be. This is really all Nicky's fault."

"Fanny," Lyris said, "you and I are friends, aren't we? We've had some rough times, but some good ones, too."

"You aren't going to be harmed," Fanny said stubbornly. "You just have to wait here for Nick."

"That will be early this afternoon, I should think," Thompson added. "I know Drake is in the habit of taking lunch at home. Fanny will carry word of your whereabouts when he's had time to find you missing."

After that scene this morning, he would think she had left him. Ruby was too frightened to tell him the truth, although why she expected a beating was beyond understanding. Nicholas never abused servants. He was too close to them.

The thought shocked her. Was he right? Did she still instinctively devalue him? No, that wasn't true. She loved and respected him. Most of the men of her acquaintance scarcely realized their servants had lives of their own. Yet she had heard Nick ask about the cook's young daughters and Ruby's ailing mother. He cared about people, not position.

"That's right, Lyris," Thompson said. "Think it over. We'll let your temper cool for an hour or so."

As Fanny left the room, Lyris lunged forward. Thompson slapped her across the face. She stopped, stunned. He slammed and locked the door.

Left alone, she rubbed her burning cheek, trying to think. All her hope of winning Nick's love lay like ashes in her heart. If she had accepted him as an equal, she wouldn't have schemed to make him accept Amelia, or to change him, or to humor him into a better mood. She would have worked beside him, and helped him to restore the Golden Harbor.

She had even believed he'd conspired with Castor to paint her as if nude. Nick would never have done so. Nor would he have kept the painting after promising it to her. She had been too arrogant to believe in him.

Why had it taken Thompson to show her that? She sank dismally onto a chair, wondering if she had learned too late.

Time passed slowly, the light from the overhead window shifting while her thoughts ran in circles. Thompson wasn't stupid. He knew Nick would be *less* inclined to listen to him after this, not more.

If he was stealing money meant to help Seattle rebuild, he risked dishonor and ruin. Obviously, Nick had threatened to expose him. Horror sank through her. Thompson meant to lure Nick here, not to reason with him, but to silence him.

He may have meant to use Fanny as his lure, but on guessing that Lyris would follow, had taken her instead. He would never have dared slap her if he thought she would tell of it. What did he have planned? A boating accident, perhaps. He was clever enough to clear himself of any part in their disappearance.

She turned her wedding ring with angry despair. Nick had worked hard to build success. His vision and honesty had won the respect of every man of importance in Seattle. Now all was at risk.

She had to get out. Pulling a pin from her hat, she worked intently at the lock.

A shout from Fanny made her start. "Lyris! I'm going after Nicky now. I thought you'd want to know."

"Listen to me," Lyris screamed. "We are all in danger!" She pounded on the panel. "Fanny? Fanny! Listen to me!"

There was no answer. From the depth of the silence, she knew the girl had gone.

Fanny heard Lyris shouting as she ran down the hall toward the basement stairs, but after all, there was nothing to worry about. If Lyris was upset, it was her own fault.

All Richard wanted was to explain that he wasn't doing anything wrong. As always, her brother had jumped to conclusions. He always thought the worst of people, even of her.

Richard thought she was wonderful. He had told her so, but he'd seemed distracted and she guessed he was worried about Nick. To be honest, she was worried, too. Nick was going to be awfully mad before he calmed down enough to listen.

When she located the carriage waiting for Lyris and told the driver to take her home, Fanny decided it might be smart to learn exactly what Richard had put in his note. She broke the seal, then read the message twice with confused disbelief.

This wasn't what he'd said he had written—that Lyris would be his guest until Nick agreed to a meeting. This said that after Richard had his way with Lyris, she would be sacrificed if Nick didn't show up.

Had his way with her! For a moment, jealousy nearly made Fanny turn back. Suppose Richard was with Lyris right now? No. She didn't like him. If he tried to kiss her, Fanny was sure Lyris would make him wish he hadn't.

The rest of the note hit her suddenly. *Sacrifice Lyris.* Fanny fell back against the cushions, her mind spinning with thoughts she tried to deny. Richard's own note condemned him. Nick was right. And Richard meant to shut him up.

Her stomach twisted. She wanted to cry. She wanted to go back there and scream at him for using her. When they reached the house at last, she burst through the doorway and into Ruby.

"Oh, Miss," Ruby gasped, stumbling for balance. "Mrs. Drake is out looking for you."

"I know," Fanny exclaimed. "Is my brother home?"

"He's at lunch, miss."

Courage deserted her. She fled through the house, threw herself at her grandmother's side and buried her face in her lap. While gentle hands stroked her hair, she gasped out the story, barely able to get the words past frantic sobs.

Nick dipped into thick pea soup, then found he had no appetite. He stared at the soupspoon, which he could now recognize from its myriad cousins, and felt numb. Lyris must have returned to her father.

He had left her in tears, a memory that had haunted him all morning. Without her, the house felt lifeless.

What he felt was sentiment, he told himself ruthlessly. What good was love without respect? But God, the house was a shell without her. The light had gone out of it.

He realized he had been holding the soupspoon for several motionless minutes. With a muffled curse, he dropped it into the bowl and gulped down a swallow of wine.

To go after her would be to subject himself to a marriage that his wife considered socially degrading. The thought tormented him. If he accepted her love, he risked having his pride shredded. What was pride without love? It occurred to him that refusing her love was a form of cowardice.

The troubling thought was diverted when his sister tugged her grandmother into the room. They both knew Amelia was not allowed here when he was home. He lurched to his feet. This he could deal with.

Amelia forestalled him. "Lyris is in danger."

Panic in his sister's face sent fear splintering through Nick. "What's happened? Where is she?"

Fanny caught back a sob. "Richard has her. It's all my fault."

"What!" He lunged toward the door.

Amelia called after him. "Nick! Don't be a fool. He's using her to get to you."

"He'll get his wish." Ice coated Nick's stomach. All he could think of was to get Lyris back.

Fanny sobbed brokenly. "I'll never trust a man again. Please don't send me away. I'll do everything you tell me."

Her grief reached him and he caught her into a rough hug, while every impulse urged him to race after Lyris. "Tell me exactly what happened."

Amelia offered a folded paper. "You had better read this."

As he scanned Thompson's insolent message, rage burned a red haze before Nick's eyes. The thought of that slimy bastard's hands on Lyris made him crazy. His own hands clenched.

Dimly, he heard Fanny say, "He didn't kiss her or anything, just locked her in a room. He wrote that to make you mad."

Nick's voice cracked. "If he so much as touches her, I'll feed his guts to the gulls." Hurling the crumpled paper into the fire, he added, "I'm going down there."

"Think, Nicholas," Amelia warned. "She's safe while he's waiting for you. You won't help her by walking into his hands."

His heart urged him to rush after his wife. Reason told him to wait. Nick braced his hands against the doorframe. "What do you suggest?"

For him to ask advice was a victory for Amelia. But nothing mattered at this moment but to get Lyris to safety. He loved her so desperately, he was mad with it. Why, in God's name, couldn't he have told her so?

If Amelia felt any sense of victory, there was no sign of it in her voice. "Fanny knows the place. She will take you there along the old walks. I will create a diversion outside."

"A diversion? Are you putting yourself in danger, as well?" Why did he care? There wasn't time to wonder.

Fanny had been gone for a good thirty minutes, maybe more. Lyris thought furiously. She was no locksmith. She'd learned that in her effort to get the portrait. Now this door had foiled her as well.

Dropping the hat pin, she glowered at the chairs she had piled on the table. A climb to the window had only proved that it overlooked a gap between the building and the street. If she managed to squeeze through, she would drop a good twenty feet to the cobblestones.

Every minute she remained here was a minute closer to putting Nick in danger. She glared at the door. The panel was solid oak and so new its brass hinges gleamed.

Thoughtfully, she considered them. Each was about six inches high, the halves held together by a long pin. Dropping to her knees, she inspected the lower one.

The pin moved easily. Breath held, she slowly withdrew it. Rocking back on her heels, she looked up at the second.

Chapter Thirty

With her breath coming in fast, nervous gasps, Lyris recovered one of the chairs and shoved it against the door. Scrambling onto the seat, she reached for the hinge. The second pin lifted out as easily as the first. The hinges were unlocked.

Dropping to the floor, she held the knob to keep the door from falling, then pushed until the hinge plates parted and the panel edged open. She squeezed out into the hall. No one was in sight. She stood there briefly, unsure whether to flee through the basement or to go on to the business offices.

Thompson might already have Nick trapped there. She ran silently along the hall. The floor was unusually quiet. No one worked over ledger or typewriter. Thompson must have called a holiday. Her heart chilled.

Voices came from the front. Quaking, she peered past a center partition into a large outer room with windows onto the street. Thompson talked with two men, while slapping a weighted sap against one palm.

One of the men let out a harsh laugh. "Drake won't be the first man found dead below a whore's shack on the bay."

Lyris pressed a fist against her mouth to keep from crying out. Her mind filled with an image of her husband sprawled in the mud while the tide licked at his body.

She nearly retched. What did Thompson have in mind for her? And for Fanny? Something equally revolting, no doubt. She forced herself to listen as he spoke. "Be ready, boys. The lovesick fool should be along at any minute."

Nick did love her. And she loved him. It could not end this way. Despair woke angry resolve. She would save Nick and her marriage. She glanced about for a weapon.

A sudden commotion in the street brought shouts from the men. "What the bloody hell?"

Thompson yelped. "What's the fool doing?"

Horses screamed. A weight crashed into the building. Glass shattered. Lurching forward, Lyris saw a carriage leaning at a wild angle across the gap in the street. The upper end teetered through the broken window. Men raced from every direction. Some fought the rearing horses. Others hauled on the carriage.

What a fortunate time for someone to back off the edge, Lyris thought, astonished. Thompson wouldn't dare attack Nick with all that going on. She may have made a sound of relief. Thompson spun around. There was no hope of getting to the outer door. She fled through the hall.

She heard him close behind her as she raced down the stairs and ran mindlessly, searching for a place to hide. As she flew toward the lower door, Nick wrenched it open. With a startled glance, he pulled her through.

"Look out," she gasped. "He has a sap."

Fanny tugged her aside as Thompson hurtled after her. "Nicky can take him. We have to stay out of the way."

The two men slammed together. The sap spun harmlessly from Thompson's hand. Savage punches moved them both along the narrow walk. Dirt rattled from overhead. Lyris tore her shocked gaze from the men to carriage wheels above. There, men shouted. Closer by, Nick and Thompson grunted as fists smashed into skin and bone. Lyris winced with every blow.

Thompson was a trained boxer, while Nick had grown up on the brawling waterfront. They appeared evenly matched. She couldn't simply watch. She had vowed to fight for her marriage. Snatching up a piece of lumber, she stalked the two.

Fanny gasped, "Lyris! You can't!"

She wouldn't hesitate to use the lumber, not while remembering the fate Thompson had planned for them. She just didn't want to hit the wrong man. Holding the plank with both hands, she angled closer.

A blow from Thompson sent Nick stumbling backward and she jerked the lumber aside. He recovered and dived into the other man, driving Thompson against the raised street. Fanny screamed encouragement. Lyris jockeyed for a clear shot.

A solid punch sent Thompson reeling in her direction. Before she could move, his head struck the lumber in her hand, violently knocking it from her grasp. He crumpled to the walk. Nick stood over him, breathing heavily, but it was clear the other man was out.

Wiping blood from a corner of his mouth while Lyris rubbed her aching wrist, Nick managed to grin. "We make a good team, sweetheart."

She threw herself into his arms. Sobbing with relief, Fanny clutched them both. Nick kissed Lyris as if he would never stop. She kissed him as fervently. Fanny interrupted, sounding apologetic. "We ought to see if Gramma's all right."

All three looked upward. Overhead, the carriage grated as men hauled it onto the street. Dirt filtered down. Faintly, Lyris asked, "Amelia?"

Nick answered. "She promised a diversion. She didn't tell us she meant to drive off the edge of the street." As he started for the door into the building, Lyris cast a worried glance toward Thompson. Shortly, Nick said, "He's through."

"There are two others," she warned, following him up the stairs with Fanny close behind. The other two men were not a problem, however. Amelia had the situation in hand. Her rescuers were holding the pair for the law.

Fiercely, Lyris hugged her plucky godmother, then noticed a bruise reddening her temple. "You're hurt!"

Amelia's eyes shone. "On the contrary, dear. I have never felt better." She smiled at Nick as men headed downstairs for Thompson. "I believe we have finished here, Nicholas."

"Are you all right?" The concern in his eyes brought tears to Lyris. She had given up on ever seeing Nick look tenderly at his grandmother.

Amelia answered stoutly, "You had better ask if your carriage survived."

"It has," Fanny announced from the doorway. "Let's go home."

Nick nodded. "It is home, Amelia, for as long as you wish. I'd like to hear your story now, if you're still willing to tell it."

She waited until they returned to the house and were seated in a close circle near the fire in the parlor. While Fanny perched on a stool at Amelia's feet, Lyris sat on an arm of Nick's chair, resting one hand on his shoulder.

She longed to be alone with him. They had a great deal to discuss in private, but this was his grandmother's turn and she forced herself to wait.

After a strengthening sip of tea, Amelia spoke gravely. "Your grandfather was a hard man, Nicholas. He had some fine qualities, but he was absolutely unforgiving. Your mother would have been allowed to come home if she left her family. There was to be no contact with her otherwise."

"Left her family!" Fanny repeated indignantly. "He expected her to leave us?"

"You had your father's blood." Amelia shook her head in sorrow. "Of course, at the time of the garden party, there was only your brother, who already looked a great deal like his father."

She leaned toward him urgently. "I was terrified. Edwin might have had you beaten. In the instant that you called out 'grandmother,' I was consumed with the need to get you away, and in such a manner that you would never come back."

"You succeeded," he said, in a tone that still held resentment.

Amelia's eyes clouded. She fumbled for a handkerchief. "I have relived those few minutes a thousand times, choosing different words, searching for some way to shield you without causing pain."

Lyris stroked tense muscles at the back of Nick's neck. He seemed oblivious of her. His grandmother continued in a wavering voice. "I risked Edwin's wrath the very next day by going to your home, but your father had taken you out on his trawler."

Her shoulders shook and she dabbed at her eyes. "Ivy said it was best. She said your father would beat you himself if he knew you had gone to us. She said I should leave you alone, that it was better that way. For you and for her."

Sobbing, Amelia buried her face in her hands. Lyris ached to console her, but watched Nick as years of pain and anger began to crumble. As she held her breath, he rose and went to his grandmother. "We're together now." Wrapping his arms about her, he drew her close and kissed her temple. His eyes glittered and Lyris felt tears rise to her own.

Fanny lay across her grandmother's lap, her shoulders heaving with sobs. Amelia stroked the girl's hair. In a voice that was shaky but once again spirited, she said, "My word, look at the three of us."

"I am," Lyris said, smiling through tears. "It's wonderful."

Nick met her eyes, his own questioning. She knew her answer shone in her face.

Fanny suddenly raised her head. "I just remembered something." She looked from her brother to his wife, then shrugged. "I guess it will wait another day."

Again Nick's voice was husky, but with a different tone as he reached for Lyris's hand. "We have some matters to settle in private. Will the two of you excuse us?"

Once inside his bedroom, Nick held Lyris gently. His troubled expression reached her overflowing heart. Who would have believed that a day begun with threats of divorce would end with great tenderness?

Linking her arms about his neck, she said, "I can't tell you how thankful I am that you and Amelia have made peace."

His mouth crooked in a half smile. "She risked her neck to save someone who matters more to me than anyone else in the world."

"And who would that be?"

His kiss left no doubt. Sighing, Lyris leaned against him. "You do understand her now?"

"It isn't easy to give up a lifetime of hard feelings," he said slowly. "I'm afraid I may always react first and ask later where Amelia is concerned. But yes, love, I understand. She's welcome here—unless she makes life difficult for you."

Lyris thought of the run-ins with her godmother over household management. "We'll get along. It will be easier, I think, now that I feel I am truly your wife."

Framing her face with his hands, he leaned down to kiss her lips. Just before they touched, he paused. "Tell me. Why in hell do you blue bloods have separate chambers? A proper wife would share her husband's bed."

She felt suspended as she waited for his lips to caress hers, but said tartly, "A proper husband would not petition for divorce."

Lights danced in his eyes. "I wonder if any of your high-and-mighty friends would have stalked Thompson with a two-by-four."

"They would have, if married to you," Lyris answered, her last words cut off by the savage impatience of his kiss. Words were forgotten then, their attention caught by an urgent need to divest each other of clothing.

As her husband lifted her onto the turned-down sheets, it occurred to Lyris that he hadn't answered her question about the divorce. She opened her mouth to ask again, but was distracted by his lips and tongue.

She turned to flame beneath his hands, needing him closer, much closer. He was even more highly aroused than during their passionate kisses in the underground, yet he held back. She reached for him, impatient and greedy. When he entered her body, she embraced him with her legs and arms.

Even so, he held himself still. Sounding agonized, he managed to say, "We're taking a risk, sweetheart. If you want me to withdraw, say so quickly."

With a breathless gasp, she thrust against him. Her answer came urgently. "The only thing I want you to withdraw is that blamed divorce."

"What divorce?" He kissed her deeply, pressing her into the pillow while she clung to him, welcoming all he could give.

Later, when their heartbeats slowed and their breathing grew calmer, he nestled her into his arms and caressed the curve of her cheek. "You, my sweet, are a classy lady."

She laughed softly. "Classy? I believe you have invented a new word. That's all they are, you know—status, fashion, class—merely words, not important at all."

"They're not entirely unimportant, my love."

"Now *there* is a word of tremendous importance." She snuggled closer. "Love. A word to change the world. How dearly I love you."

His voice shook. "When I thought I might lose you, I nearly went crazy."

She touched his mouth with her fingertips, exploring the shape of his lips. "I was about to drive downtown to continue our argument when I learned that Fanny had left to meet Thompson." With a contented sigh, she added, "I was going to tell you that I would fight any divorce petition, however scandalous we might both become."

"My wife, my love, my life," he said, impressing the words against her lips and eyelids. When he raised his head, his eyes danced. "How could I let you go? We have an attic filled with baby furniture waiting to be used."

Lyris slid one hand boldly down his body. "Then we had best do all we can to meet the need."

"Gently!" he exclaimed. Cradling her face between his hands, he said again softly, "Gently, love," before kissing her with such tenderness, she felt her heart expand.

They woke in the morning at a knock on the door into the hall. Lyris nestled closer to her husband as he called, "What is it?"

Fanny answered. "I have something to show you."

Nick made sure they were both decently covered before answering, "All right, imp. Come in."

Mischief sparkled in the girl's eyes. "So it's happily ever after. I thought it would be. And here's an early Christmas present!" With a flourish, she unrolled *The Naked Huntress*.

Lyris sat up with a start, clutching the covers to her breasts. "Where did you find that?"

Nick nearly leapt from bed, but remembered in time that he was naked himself. "Explain, Fanny. Now."

She rerolled the canvas. "Remember the day just before the fire, Lyris? I told you I went to Nick's office. But I got scared when I heard him coming in, so I hid inside the wardrobe."

Grimly, Nick said, "The wardrobe was locked."

Fanny's dimples flashed. "Grampa Drake said I was a natural. How do you think I got into your wine that time?"

As Nick tensed, Lyris saw the subject changing. "Never mind the wine. What about the portrait?"

Fanny placed the rolled canvas on a chair. "I knew at once it could make a lot of trouble for you, so when it was safe, I cut it from its frame and took it along."

"And didn't tell me?"

"I would have, Lyris, but you scolded something awful just because I went downtown. So I put it under my mattress and it's been there since." She spread her hands and shrugged. "Until last night, I forgot all about it."

"If you knew the trouble you've caused..." Exhaling loudly, Nick lay back. "God, Lyris. Six months!"

She leaned on one elbow, holding back her hair while she smiled into his face. "Never mind. We're stronger for it."

"Gramma wants to talk to you," Fanny said, excitement lifting her voice.

"Later," Nick said, gazing at Lyris.

But Fanny couldn't hold back her news. "She's going to take me on a tour of Europe! When we come home, she says I'll be prepared to take my place in society."

Nick's eyes smoldered. "That may take a long time."

Lyris felt her body quicken with anticipation at the promise she saw in his eyes. Absently, she said to Fanny, "The house will seem empty without you."

Nick curved one hand around the nape of her neck, his fingers tantalizing beneath her hair. "We'll miss you, imp. How soon do you leave?"

"I think I'd better leave right now," Fanny said. She hastily backed from the room and closed the door.

As Lyris molded herself against her husband, early sunlight turned the air about them into a golden dazzle. Feeling as reborn as the phoenixlike city, she joyfully recommitted her life to the man she loved.

Arguments might lie ahead. There were sure to be fresh tests of will. Whatever came, they would meet it together, no longer fighting social barriers meant to separate.

As for *The Naked Huntress,* it would find a place among the outmoded hoops and bustles in the attic. If some distant granddaughter should ask about it, she and Nick would share a secret smile and reply that one should never take people for granted because of age or social status.

And then they would likely retire to the privacy of their bedchamber to prove the truth of it once again.

* * * * *

WELCOME TO

The quintessential small town, where everyone knows everybody else!

Finally, books that capture the pleasure of tuning in to your favorite TV show!

GREAT READING...GREAT SAVINGS...AND A FABULOUS FREE GIFT!

Each book set in Tyler is a self-contained love story; together, the twelve novels stitch the fabric of the community. The covers honor the old American tradition of quilting; each cover depicts a patch of the large Tyler quilt.

With Tyler you can receive a fabulous gift, ABSOLUTELY FREE, by collecting proofs-of-purchase found in each Tyler book. And use our special Tyler coupons to save on your next TYLER book purchase.

Join your friends at Tyler for the seventh book, ARROWPOINT by Suzanne Ellison, available in September.

Rumors fly about the death at the old lodge! What happens when Renata Meyer finds an ancient Indian sitting cross-legged on her lawn?

Take 4 bestselling love stories FREE

Plus get a FREE surprise gift!

HARLEQUIN *Temptation*

Rebels & Rogues

Dash vowed to protect gorgeous Claren—at any cost!

The Knight in Shining Armor
by JoAnn Ross
Temptation #409, September

All men are not created equal. Some are rough around the edges. Tough-minded but tenderhearted. Incredibly sexy. The tempting fulfillment of every woman's fantasy.

When it's time to fight for what they believe in, to win that special woman, our Rebels and Rogues are heroes at heart. Twelve Rebels and Rogues, one each month in 1992, only from Harlequin Temptation. Don't miss the upcoming books by our fabulous authors, including Ruth Jean Dale, Janice Kaiser and Kelly Street.

COMING NEXT MONTH

#139   BOSTON RENEGADE—June Lund Shiplett
After inheriting a ranch from her nefarious brother, spinster
Hanna Winters was threatened by outlaws searching for a missing
cache of stolen money. Yet the biggest threat of all came from
drifter Blake Morgan, who threw her well-ordered life into chaos.

#140   BODIE BRIDE—Isabel Whitfield
Spinster Margaret Warren believed she had everything she needed.
But when her father brought good-natured John Banning into their
home, Margaret was forced to recognize her loneliness—and her
undeniable attraction to the one man who infuriated her the most.

#141   KNIGHT DREAMS—Suzanne Barclay
Lord Ruarke Sommerville was drunk when he rescued French
noblewoman Gabrielle de Lauren from marauding soldiers and
impulsively wed her. Although the morning after brought
surprises, haste doesn't always mean waste—especially when the
courtship begins *after* the wedding.

#142   GYPSY BARON—Mary Daheim
Lady Katherine de Vere had always been loyal to king and country.
Nevertheless, when mysterious half-Gypsy Stefan Dvorak drew her
into a web of political intrigue, she began to doubt not only her
politics, but her heart, as well.

AVAILABLE NOW:

#135   THE RELUCTANT BRIDE
Barbara Bretton

#136   ROSE AMONG THORNS
Catherine Archer

#137   THE NAKED HUNTRESS
Shirley Parenteau

#138   THE DREAM
Kit Gardner